S.T. MCCREA
VISIONS

iUniverse

VISIONS

iUniverse books may be ordered through booksellers or by contacting:

iUniverse
1663 Liberty Drive
Bloomington, IN 47403
www.iuniverse.com
1-800-Authors (1-800-288-4677)

ISBN: 978-1-5320-5277-4 (sc)
ISBN: 978-1-5320-5279-8 (hc)
ISBN: 978-1-5320-5278-1 (e)

Library of Congress Control Number: 2018908548

Print information available on the last page.

iUniverse rev. date: 07/26/2018

To my daughter, Tracy. Thank you for your support,
even when you wondered if Visions would ever
be published. I did get there, eventually.

To Marcella Goulart, a life long friend, who forced
me to begin the self publishing process of VISIONS.
You are sorely missed. Via con dios, my sister.

A special thanks to the people of IUniverse
for their patience, understanding, and help in
making VISIONS a real, published book

PROLOGUE

The sun was an oven with no temperature control. On the Arizona mesas of the Navajo reservation, it baked with an ever-rising heat, not caring if the victim was rare or well done. After a time—and it didn't take long—it killed.

Samuel Hawk, retired Navajo detective, hunkered beside the body of the young girl, his sharp eyes missing nothing as he scanned the crime scene. Unfortunately, there was nothing to miss.

"What do you make of it?"

Samuel glanced up at the tribal policeman who'd spoken. Not long out of the academy, the young cop's bronzed and sweating face was slightly ashen right now. Most of his breakfast lay in the red rocks just beyond.

"There are no tracks, except those," Samuel replied, waving a hand at the single set of footprints that went nowhere. His eyes fell back to the body as he continued, "It took her time to die. How long did he give the parents?"

The cop's face twisted with disgust. "He called them at eight thirty Friday morning, about half an hour after the girl left the house. He must have caught her on the trail up to the school bus. Driver said she never got on. The parents tried to play his game, but by evening, they'd gotten nowhere. That's when they called us."

Samuel counted silently. "That makes her four days gone." He studied the body. "And about two days dead. Who found her?"

"Some kids, hiking back to the caves and pools. Saw the buzzards and followed them." The cop nodded his head toward the prints. "Can this bastard fly? How in the hell did he get in and out and leave only those?"

"He knows the Indian way to cover tracks." The old man rose, the smoothness of the movement belying his age. His deep-set eyes raked the body of the seven-year-old girl once more. Rippled sands of gold and red formed an almost obscene blanket beneath the thin body. Rocks of the same color surrounded the shallow basin. There was something to be said for vultures. Without them, she might never have been found.

"Is it the same man?" There was fear in the young man's voice as he spoke, but a deep burning anger filled his eyes. They all knew the story. In the last two years, the kidnapper had struck the Navajo reservation five times. There was no pattern. His timing, like his victims, appeared random.

But in the past, his victims had always come back alive.

Samuel nodded silently, studying the body. Why was this child killed? It made no sense. His gaze trailed to the harsh, cloudless sky. Six times now, the kidnapper's identity had eluded him—four times while he was an active detective and twice since he'd retired. The captain knew to call him. Samuel Hawk knew everything about the kidnapper—everything except who the bastard was.

"Do you want me to tell the parents?" The cop's question brought Samuel back to the present.

He stared at the young man a moment, suddenly feeling very old, and shook his head. The cop's face was still gray. Samuel knew that he would see worse than this if he stayed on the force. "Tell the captain to give me as much time as he can. It will take me at least an hour to get to the parents and tell them what we found. I should be back at the station by two. The FBI should be there by then. They'll want to see everything."

"He chose well," the cop said bitterly. "The girl's people were one of the few out this far to have a phone. I can't imagine anyone from the res doing this."

"He is not Indian."

"But . . ." Knowledge dawned in the officer's eyes. "He knows our songs, our ways."

"Evil has no skin color, and knowledge these days is easily obtained. This man is white. He is also a hunter and a soul scatterer, but this is his last victim. He is probably several states away by now."

"What makes you say that?"

"He has killed. He can do no worse than that."

"Hope the feds' profiler agrees. I hate having those . . ." The cop hesitated.

"Sons of bitches digging around here on the res," Samuel finished.

"We know you, Hawk. We trust you."

That said it all. Samuel Hawk laid the blanket he held gently across the small body and turned, his boots kicking up small clouds of red dust as he headed back to his pickup. The girl would need a singing. Once he told the parents what he had seen, they would agree.

At the ancient truck, he stopped and looked back, his vision filled with a darkness only he could see. Six children taken, their parents forced to play a mindless game. Five found alive—one dead.

"I also am a hunter. I will find you. I will kill you." His whisper carried softly across the still, hot desert air.

CHAPTER 1

He brought pain. In the pain was darkness—but in that darkness was the child. Sara had no choice but to let them both enter her mind. A boy's life was at stake, and the kidnapper knew Sara would do everything in her power to save the child. It was all part of his warped game.

"Don't be frightened," Sara whispered. Leaning against the cold window of her living room, she grabbed the heavy velvet drapes for balance and mentally plunged into the darkness, seeking that pinpoint of innocence that was a frightened child. Grasping his essence, she ignored the sickening drop in her stomach as she became the frightened little boy.

Coarse fibers burned tender flesh. There would be red marks on her arms tomorrow. Her nose twitched with the musty odor of damp hemp as she choked on the dust of long-gone grains. She swallowed hard, the metallic taste of fear coating her tongue. The bastard had thrown a burlap bag over the child's head—over her head.

She blinked hard, trying to see beyond the speckled lights that filled the open weave of the bag. She needed to see him, but it was no use. He always made sure the child never saw him. He would remain the faceless man.

"I'm with you. Don't be frightened," she crooned in her mind, struggling to keep the boy's essence with her.

She swayed and held her breath, her senses open. There was a click, then the squeak of a door opening. Vertigo swept over her as she felt herself tilted downward and dropped. Something soft cushioned the short fall.

Another creak. Another door opened, then slammed. Vibrations followed a grinding noise. Inertia threw her back. Muffled sounds of traffic, an occasional horn, the whoosh of tires on slush filled her ears.

"Let's play a game!"

The voice slammed into her head. Like shards of glass, the vision shattered; the child was gone.

"Damn." Sara stared out the window at leaden skies dotted with snow-filled clouds. Milford, Connecticut, was in for a storm, an early snow storm. It was strange, but it was coming. She could feel its coldness in her hands, which still gripped the heavy drapes so tightly her knuckles had turned bone white.

She straightened, flexed numb fingers, and closed her eyes again, reaching for the child who, in his terror, had touched her. Nothing. The boy was gone.

Max's whimper brought Sara back to the present. She glanced down. The big German shepherd leaned against her, bracing her with his body. Reaching a hand down, she gripped his rough fur as the dog guided her to the sofa. Sara grabbed her cell phone and punched in a code. Her husband, Detective John Allbrooke, picked up immediately.

"I was just going to call you. We're at the scene. Did you see anything? Have you linked with the boy? Did you see the bastard's face?" John's voice was breathy. He was walking—fast.

"Yes, we linked, but I didn't see anything. There's a bag over the child's head. I think it's burlap."

"How in the hell do you get out of Wilcox Park carrying a five-year-old with a burlap bag over his head?"

"He blends, John. He's a chameleon."

"Yeah, right."

She ignored the tinged sarcasm in her husband's voice. John dealt with logic and facts. Fifteen years on the police force had taught him that. "His bad leg," she said, "he's lurching."

"Sara, tell me something I don't know."

She bit back a retort. Her husband didn't—couldn't understand how she processed information.

"Is he still on foot, Sara?"

"No. He's in a vehicle."

"Shit! Any idea what kind? Where is he going?"

"'No' to the first question and 'don't know' to the second. Do you have the notes, John?"

"I'm waiting."

For the second time, the voice broke her connection with the real world. *"You bastard! You unspeakable bastard."* She hurled the mental curse at the unknown, faceless man.

"Sara, that's so un-teacher-like."

"Where are you taking him?"

"This one's easy. You'll hear the stories and have no worries. Find the gold and you'll find where he lies. Just follow the clues and no one dies."

"How much—"

The voice left.

"Sara. Are you still there?" John was shouting into the phone. "Yes."

"The notes were folded up in the boy's jacket. Bastard left it on a park bench. The word 'easy' is scribbled across the front of the paper. Mean anything?"

"Yes. What are the notes?" she asked.

"B, F, C, F, A, C. Should we know something about 'easy'?"

"Finding the boy won't be difficult," she threw out as she sat at the piano. "Sharps? Flats?"

3

"You spoke to him?"

"In my mind, as usual.

"No sharps or flats. You know better than that."

"Yes, well, I can always hope. It would make finding these songs a helluva lot easier." She played the notes as she spoke, then repeated the sequence using different times, different keys. "Nothing's coming."

"Concentrate, Sara."

"I am." She grabbed her hymnal, leafing through it, tearing the already worn pages in her rush. Songs flew by, numbers leaped out. Nothing.

"Link with the boy again."

"Damn it, John. Shut up and give me a moment."

Easy. The bastard had said it was easy. She should have it by now. She knew it, felt it. She ran the notes again. Something clicked. Maybe. Just maybe.

Her hand shook as she ran a finger down the titles, then stopped. She flipped to the hymn, played it. This was the one. She checked the number—fifteen. God, was the bastard only giving them fifteen minutes to find the child?

"It's 'How Firm a Foundation,' hymn fifteen. I can't make any sense of the words."

"Reconnect with the boy?"

"Give me five minutes and call back."

"Better make it two, Sara. It's starting to snow again."

Was this the child who would die? Was this the one she'd lose? Sara pushed the fear back, closed her eyes, and went into the blackness. Calling softly, she felt the boy open himself to her. With a quick breath, she once again became a frightened little boy.

Cold bit into her, burning her skin. The kidnapper held her so tightly she could barely breathe. She flared her nostrils, taking in the faint scent of salt water. The sea, the Sound. Long Island Sound. She could hear the waves. They were close.

Rough hands held her naked skin, then thrust her into something small, smooth. There was a banging, metallic sound, then complete darkness. Her body rolled as the prison moved. A sucking sound filled her ears.

He was gone. Frantically, Sara tried to reconnect with the child. Nothing. The kidnapper always struck close, but the Sound—that was too close. Fifteen. Only fifteen minutes to find the boy before he died?

Her hand tightened on the ancient Celtic cross she always wore. She melded once more into the darkness, trying to link with the kidnapper this time, struggling to see through his eyes. There was nothing, only a veil of evil. She swam back into the light. Child and madman were gone.

With a half sob, her gaze riveted to the hymnal. Parts of the third and fourth verses caught her eye.

When through the deep waters I call thee to go,
The rivers of woe shall not thee overflow.

When through fiery trials thy pathways shall lie . . .
Thy dross to consume and thy gold to refine.

Gershwin's "Rhapsody in Blue" filtered through the room. *John.* She grabbed the phone.

"He's in some kind of metal box." She fought to control the shivers that now shook her whole body. "There was grit and salt. He's near the Sound."

"Not good enough."

Her eyes focused on the hymn. Words popped out. "Deep waters," "overflow," "pathway," "gold." *"Find the gold,"* he'd said. *"It's easy."*

Gold. According to legend, Captain Kidd had buried gold on Charles Island. *Pathway.* Path! The tombolo—the narrow sandbar that linked the Silver Sands beach to the island during low tide. *Easy*—it made getting to the island easy. Oh God, she should have gotten it sooner.

"Charles Island, John. He's on Charles Island, on the tombolo."

"Are you sure?"

"Yes. He's half-buried in the sand. There's water seeping into the box. When does the tide come in?"

She heard John shout her question. A second later, his voice sent a deep chill down her spine. "It's coming in now. Charles Island, people. Move!"

All eyes were on the men. In the mustard haze of snow and half-light, they moved with a dreamlike quality, their motions slow, their words soft and slurred.

"We've got it!"

Everything swam sharply into focus.

Standing knee-deep in the cold, gray water, Detective John Allbrooke grabbed an edge of the metal chest they'd partially unearthed and bellowed for the rescue truck.

Men hoisted the box onto the beach. Minutes later the heavy lock was cut with bolt cutters and the slightly blue, limp body of the child was lifted from the watery casket. Paramedics swiftly wrapped the child in blankets, fixed an oxygen mask to his face, and started CPR.

This was the hardest part. John glanced around. It was quiet. The wind had died down. Even the sea was silent. Everyone watched, waited.

A cough, followed by a soft sob broke the silence. John closed his eyes in relief, listening to the ragged cheers. It took a few more minutes to load the boy into the ambulance. With lights and siren, the vehicle sped away from the scene.

"Now what?" a voice asked.

John, half his mind still on the child, the other half promising death to the elusive bastard who insisted on putting Milford's children in harm's way, looked up at the detective who'd spoken, Frank O'Brien. "I want this area and the area around Wilcox Park secured. And I want both places gone over with a fine-toothed comb."

"Why? We never find anything." Failure and defeat were strong in O'Brien's voice.

"I don't give a fuck!" John snapped. "Secure the damned areas and stay there until you're relieved." He glanced up as he spoke. The young detective was shivering. Rivulets of melted snow and ice ran down the lines in his face, making him look much older than he was. The detective was right. They never did find anything. So how could John expect them to find something in this weather?

"O'Brien." Reaching out a hand, John stopped him mid-turn. "I know it seems hopeless, but we can't overlook any chances to find this son of a bitch. Maybe he left something behind this time. Maybe this is the time good police work will find something."

"I know, John. It's just this damned weather." With a nod, the young detective plowed through the slush toward the crime scene, yelling orders as he went.

John could feel his men's frustration. How in the hell did someone manage to steal a child from a town park and bury a chest in the middle of a public area, all without a soul seeing anything? There was no explanation, except perhaps Sara's: *"He's a chameleon."* As a cop, John had difficulty buying that. There were always clues, always mistakes; you just had to find them.

"Take Sanders with you," he shouted at O'Brien's retreating back. "Question every morbid son of a bitch standing around. Somebody's got to have seen something."

Five kidnappings and no clues. Five children taken and their only savior was Sara. It was his wife's gift that found the children in time, not the police. And only he and the captain knew what she did. For God's sake, the bastard had a limp. That should stand out, help them find him. It hadn't. John called Sara, needing to make sure she was all right.

She answered on the fourth ring. "Is he okay?" Her voice was ragged.

John closed his eyes, feeling his wife's pain. At that moment, he wanted nothing more than to take her into his arms and whisk her away from a life that was becoming a nightmare, but he couldn't. He was a cop. There were things he had to do, things Sara understood. For that, he thanked God.

"I think he's going to be all right. How are you?"

"The usual headache from hell."

"Going to bed?"

"As soon as I can get upstairs. I spoke with the school secretary a few moments ago. Told them lunch made me sick and I wouldn't be in for the rest of the day."

"Good. It will take me a while to wrap things up here. I'll be home as soon as I can." John cut the connection and turned around, staring at the people still milling about. Opening his car door, he reached into the side pocket and pulled out a tattered sketchbook and pencil. For the next few minutes, he concentrated on recreating the scene. He never noticed the man who ducked and slid into the crowd.

James Joseph Campbell, JJ to his father, Joe to himself and his friends—of which there were few—pulled the hoody over his head, covering his carrot-red hair, and concentrated on two things: walking with as little a limp as possible and blending in with the crowd. Hunching a little made him seem shorter than his six foot plus, and he was approximately the same age as most of the yuppies milling around.

He should have left Milford an hour ago, as soon as the child was buried. He couldn't. As always, he waited, praying the police would find the child in time. And he always had a plan if the police or Sara failed. He would plunge in like a Good Samaritan, save the child, and be a hero. In his book, no child died. But his book wasn't his father's book.

Four blocks away, he got into the old Ford pickup, pumped the gas pedal a few times, and felt relief when the engine roared to life. He let it warm up, staring into the gathering darkness as he waited. With the weather closing in, his small home and studio in West Virginia were too far away. But the cabin in Pennsylvania, the Slane vacation cabin, was closer. He'd stay there, he abruptly decided. He couldn't explain it, but he felt safe there, as though he mattered, as though he had a future.

He was putting the truck in gear when his cell phone went off. Pain slammed into his head at the same time, and he knew instantly who was on the other end of the line. He answered, catching his father in the middle of a curse. The old man was mad, damned mad. Pain filled Joe's head as the voice filled his ears. When his father finally fell silent, Joe again explained why he had stayed—to make sure everything went according to plan. He couldn't tell his father the truth. That would mean his death, or worse. And his father would have no problem with the "worse."

Placated, the old man cut the connection. The pain gradually receded. Shaking, Joe reached into the glove compartment, pulled out a bottle of aspirin, and downed a handful, chewing the bitter pills thoughtfully. A few minutes later, he joined the traffic and turned west.

Just outside of Stroudsburg, Pennsylvania, Joe pulled into a truck stop. He was tired, drained. Talking to his father often did that. A hot coffee, some food, and a bit of a break would see him through to the cabin.

Though the truck stop was somewhat seedy, the young waitress was fresh and pretty in a quiet, comfortable way; not that full-blown, sex-goddess shit that Hollywood plastered across TV and theater screens. She was the kind of woman who would make some men take a second look and decide that a life change wasn't such a bad idea. And she was unhappy. Her eyes told him that.

Joe glanced at the other waitress, a more seasoned woman. In a few years, this pretty little thing would look just like her. Dreams would be gone, along with the shine in her eyes. Her voice, like her face, would take on an edge.

His eyes swung back to the girl. So young. So innocent. He

9

shifted, suddenly afraid for the girl. His father would have used her innocence, claiming her death would bring him power. It was bullshit—the whole Satan thing was bullshit.

Grabbing the coffee with both hands, he brought it to his lips. Sara had been slow today—too slow. The clues, the music, it was all so easy, and she'd almost missed it. Maybe she needed a break. He grimaced. His father wasn't going to give Sara any kind of a break. Sara Erin Slane Remington Allbrooke had a lot to pay for. And Joe's father was going to make sure that she and every living member of the Slane family paid the ultimate price.

He, James Joseph Campbell, was the instrument of that revenge.

"Would you like more coffee?"

Joe looked up at the young waitress and shook his head. Laying the ticket on the table with a "come hither" look, she sashayed away.

He wasn't even interested. Serafina had made sure of that.

Joe's grandmother had been right: When you find a good woman, you'll lust after no other. His father, on the other hand, would have taken the young waitress, screwed her, killed her, and bathed in her blood.

He pushed the half-eaten plate of eggs aside. He had lost his appetite. Throwing a twenty on the table, he left, giving the young girl one last glance. She was lucky. She would live tonight because he, not his father, had stopped in for a meal.

Joe stepped out into the cold wind. He'd made up his mind before he'd reached the Rover. It would be hours before he got home, but he needed to drive back to West Virginia. His home, his studio, that's where he needed to be. The Slane cabin might be safe, but it was too good for him. He belonged in his studio.

Hunched over, the man sat silently in the back of the restaurant and chuckled softly to himself, watching as the Rover left the parking lot. His stupid son never asked how he knew so much; he just accepted that somehow Malachi James Campbell knew everything. More than that, he actually thought that bitch found those children based on the notes Malachi gave Joe to leave behind. Stupid! It was Malachi's linking with Sara, his taunting, his vague clues, that led her to the kids.

His son could link with Sara; he had the power and the blood. But his dense son had never even thought of reaching Sara psychically. Malachi now knew what he could do, what he could achieve. He knew everything. He watched everything. He had been taught well, and he'd learned even better.

His eyes fell on the young woman his son had taken a passing interest in. Too bad that colored woman in the South had such a hold on Joe; the young waitress could have proved fun.

Well, if his son wasn't going to try, Malachi might as well. The youth, maybe even innocence, of the young woman should prove powerful, and Malachi was more than ready for fresh blood and power. He was also willing to gamble that Joe was driving back to West Virginia. That left the Slane cabin open, and Malachi knew where and how he could easily get rid of a body.

He flashed a couple of hundred-dollar bills as the waitress came closer, and he smiled as her eyes lit up. It was going to be a very interesting evening.

CHAPTER 2

Bits and pieces of yellow crime-scene tape waved forlornly in the wind. Sara stood on the wooden planked walk of Silver Sands State Park and looked out toward Charles Island.

Evening painted the world in a canvas of dark-shaded grays and blacks. Sky blended into waves; waves blended into sand. The island stood in dark silhouette, the tombolo gone, buried beneath the waters of the Sound. Sara took a deep, shaky breath and thanked God that a child wasn't buried with it.

Vestiges of the headache still clung to the inside of her skull. Sara pushed back thick, flame-colored curls and stared at the scene, her mind a maze of unanswered questions complicated by fears and wishes. She feared failure and she wished for the umpteenth time that the gift had passed her by. She was a schoolteacher and that was all she wanted to be.

She took a deep breath of air and sea. It smelled better out here than inside a metal box. God, she was tired, so damned tired; *bone tired* as her grandmother used to say. Even breathing was a chore.

The gift. The damned gift. Sara squelched rising anger. She never wanted, never asked for the gift, but it came with being a Slane, and Sara was a Slane.

Sara Erin Slane Remington Allbrooke. God that was a mouthful.

The females of the line all kept the name Slane as recognition of their heritage, and the first female of each generation inherited a psychic ability. Sara's ability was connecting with and finding lost or kidnapped children. Like generations of Slane women before her, she was expected to cope with and use her gift for the good of others, ignoring how it might tear her own life apart. The ignoring part was becoming harder.

But why in the hell was she linking with an adult? How was he able to link with her? Her gift had always been with children, only children. Yet, the kidnapper had easily invaded her mind, controlling, taunting her with words and clues, some useless, some helpful. It was a game to him, nothing more. But it was a dangerous game for the child. If Sara failed, the child died. And why couldn't she see his face? Even when she looked at him through the eyes of a child, there was nothing. Only darkness.

Of one thing, she was certain. He hated her. She could feel it. But why? What had she done to send this man down this god-awful road? For almost a year, she had been playing his cruel and mindless game. Five children taken, five children found. Was it the next one she would lose?

Failure. Sara shuddered as the thought ran across her mind. Failure meant death, and this one should have been easy. She had been slow, too damned slow.

Taking another deep breath, Sara cleared her thoughts and closed her eyes, opening her mind to everything around her, trying to pick up something, anything that would answer some of her questions. Like many times before, nothing came. Nothing was there. The kidnapper's face remained shrouded in darkness.

Hopelessly, she opened her eyes to the coming night. God, she wanted to quit; walk away and shut out the voices of helpless and frightened children. Maybe if she did, he would stop the game and disappear.

But what if he didn't stop? Could she ignore a child's cry, knowing that her lack of action could bring about that child's death?

Sara brought her mind back to the present. A few people, their clothing proclaiming them as die-hard joggers, milled about in the cold and snow, pausing to study the strands of tape. Then they were gone and she was alone—except for *him*. She froze.

The man stared at her from the end of the boarded walk. She had seen him before but never really noticed him. Tonight she felt his presence—and his strangeness.

His clothes were clean, the jeans worn, his cowboy boots marked and stained. The heavy sheepskin coat and western hat, pulled low, were from another part of the country, as were the long gray braids that fluttered in the wind.

She had seen him before. Three times before, she realized as she glanced around. They were alone, surrounded only by sand, sea, and night.

He continued to stare at her. In the darkness of his eyes, she felt the cold, tasted the salt of the Sound waters as they rose around her. *Is this the faceless man?*

Anger overrode fear and caution. She strode down the planks to the sand, stopping in front him. "I've seen you before, at other crime scenes."

If her abruptness surprised him, he didn't show it. Thin lips curled into the barest hint of a smile. "Yes."

"Who are you? What are you doing here?"

He held out his right hand. "My name is—"

Sara stepped back, suddenly afraid his hands might grab her, hold her beneath the cold waters. Only the need to know why he was here kept her from running.

"—Samuel Hawk." Slowly, as if sensing her fear, the man lowered his hand. "It's not because I have a macabre interest in all of this." He waved a hand toward Charles Island. "I am not from here, as you might have already guessed; but years ago, our reservation was hit by a man who took our children, placed them in harm's way, and used our songs as part of a game of clues to find them. We found all our children before they died—except for one.

The sixth child, he killed. From what I have read, your kidnapper is doing much the same thing."

"He's not *my* kidnapper," Sara retorted.

"I did not mean to imply that." He hesitated, as if searching for words. "A few months ago, I saw a New York newspaper dated from many years ago. There was a story about a psychic who worked with the police, finding lost or kidnapped children. There was a picture of you."

Sara took a deep breath, letting it out slowly. "I used to live in New York. For a while, I worked with the police. I am—was—a psychic."

"Yet, you do not work with the Milford police?"

Sara lowered her eyes. "No."

"Your work in New York was good," Samuel stated softly. Are you thinking of quitting?" He continued before she could answer. "To quit is not good. You cannot turn a gift like yours on and off like a water faucet. There will be repercussions."

"How do you know?" she demanded, bristling.

An ancient smile crossed his face. "Because there always are."

"Who are you?" She was growing angry, but she realized the fear was gone. His lined face and dark eyes were filled with compassion and something else she couldn't define.

The Indian shook his head. "As I told you, my name is Samuel Hawk, and I've said too much this evening. I have also annoyed and frightened you. I am sorry." He stepped forward.

Sara stood her ground.

For a few moments, he studied her; then he smiled slowly as though he had just discovered something. "You are tired. You should go home and rest—there is nothing here. And I had best be getting home too." With a quick nod, Samuel turned, walking swiftly down the narrow strip of beach.

Sara watched him slide quietly into the darkness, moving like a hunter.

"Honey."

She whirled at the voice. John was coming down the planked

walk. A wave of warmth swept over her. John Allbrooke wasn't a large man—he was barely five foot eleven—but he covered the ground he walked on, eluding confidence and determination. Sometimes the determination was frustrating.

"You look like shit, darling."

"Thank you, Mr. Allbrooke. You always were a charmer." Sara sobered. "Who was the boy?"

"Teddy Hansen. His mom was taking him to the doctor's today. He attends St. Mary's."

"That's a fifth hit for the school."

"Sara, I looked over the song. You were slow. It was easy."

She bristled. "It helps when you already know the destination. Don't you think I know I was slow? I've been beating myself up for it. I don't need you doing it too."

He dragged her to him, bringing her head to rest on his shoulder. "I know. It's just . . . it's part of my job to keep my people on their toes."

"I'm not your 'people,' John. I'm your wife." She looked up into gentle, brown eyes. "Please tell me someone saw something."

"I know you're my wife. You're also part of a team, a silent part so to speak. One woman has come forward. Said she thought she saw a man digging on the tombolo."

She felt a thread of excitement run through her. "That's something, isn't it?"

"Myra's our resident nutcase. Last spring, she came into the precinct about ten times, claiming she was being abducted nightly by aliens. She asked us to put a cop in front of her house to stop it."

Sara leaned into her husband's heavy coat, feeling his strength. Hope gave way to despair and despair to uncontrollable laughter. It took several minutes for her to catch her breath. "Well, at least she wasn't seeing the face of Jesus in the old elm tree on Holly."

John tightened his arms around her as she leaned deeper into the embrace. "No, she wasn't. The strange thing is, she might have actually seen something. Unfortunately, she's got cataracts so bad I'm not sure how accurate her descriptions will be."

"So we're back to square one."

"Well, maybe one and a half."

"And you still have a wife who sees everything, even talks to the bastard who does this," she waved a hand toward the crime tape, "but can't see his face."

He tipped her head back. "You know I still ask myself why the most beautiful woman in the world, the one I fell for, had to be a psycho."

"Psychic, darling, the word's psychic." It was their private joke and she loved him for it.

He chuckled as his brown eyes darkened, and Sara knew in an instant where he had gone, because she was already there. "John Allbrooke, how can you think about sex at a time like this?"

"Because we deal with life and death on an almost daily basis, or so the shrink says. I like to think it's because I have an extremely sexy wife." He planted a quick kiss on her nose, held her tightly against him for one more minute, then dropped his arms and stepped back, all business. "Did you park close?"

"Yes. And I brought Max."

"A lot of good he'll do."

"That's not fair. I think he'd defend me . . . under the right circumstances."

"Then why isn't he with you right now?"

"John, you know he's afraid of the water."

"According to police records, that was one of the most worthless dogs to ever try out for the force, and I have the feeling that's exactly why you love him so much."

"And you feel exactly the same way about him," Sara retorted.

With a short laugh and an arm around her shoulders, he guided her down to the parking lot. "There's nothing more you can do here, and you still look like shit. Go home. Get some rest. I've got some things to clear up."

"Will it take long?"

"Shouldn't. Keep the coffee hot."

He gave her another quick kiss and pushed her gently into the car. She watched as he walked away, limping slightly. He did that when he was tired and cold. It meant his knee was bothering him. She smiled to herself. He had a body that was beginning to bulk up, a knee that sometimes gave him fits, and a hairline that had receded noticeably; yet to her, he was still the sexiest man she had ever known.

Slipping the car into gear, she headed for the road and home. Would she ever see the kidnapper's face? It was a question that went through her mind a hundred times a day. She wished she knew the answer.

The precinct was only slightly warmer than outside. Deciding to leave his coat on, John headed to the captain's office. The door was open. He stuck his head in. "Got a moment?"

Captain Lyle Parker looked up. "I was wondering when you'd get back. Come on in—and shut the door behind you."

Throwing a sketchbook on the captain's desk, John sat without waiting for an invitation. Captain Parker, looking every bit of his sixty-odd years, stared at the book. "Anything interesting in that?"

"One man doesn't fit. I've already taken the sketch down to Luke Johnson. He said he'd run it through some sort of program he's working on."

"You ever regret becoming a cop, John? You were a damned good sketch artist."

"I never felt like I was doing enough by just sketching the bad guys. I wanted to catch them. Besides, with computer technology these days, sketch artists are almost obsolete."

"Heard our resident nutcase may have seen the kidnapper?"

John eased his leg out. "I had her working with Luke earlier. Didn't get much we could use, but I think she might have seen something. Captain, I want to go to the Hartford prison. I want to visit Duncan."

"Why?"

"Because Sara is a first grade, special ed teacher. She hasn't made the kind of enemies that I have. William Duncan Jr. could be one of those enemies." John leaned forward. "You didn't see that two-year-old boy, Lyle. Billy Duncan didn't hold your hand and look up at you through two black eyes that asked 'why?' That child spent almost three months in the hospital with casts on his arms and leg. He also had broken ribs and a broken nose. That was a beating, Lyle, a severe beating on that child."

"I know, John. I also know you shouldn't have even been there. The cops didn't need a detective that night. They were handling things."

"But I was there," John shot back. The call had come over his radio as he was driving home. He recognized the address and the name. Four times in as many months, complaints had come from the apartment complex where William lived with his wife Rachael and their son Billy. Four times, they had found William Duncan's wife beaten beyond recognition, and four times, she'd refused to press charges, even from her hospital bed.

That night John had had enough. He checked the road, and seeing he was clear, twisted the wheel, turning the car back the way he'd come. Whatever it took this night, William Duncan Jr. was going to jail.

Minutes later, he walked into a crime scene, sickened to see that Duncan had used his fists not only on his wife but also on his two-year-old son.

Lyle's voice dragged John back to the present. "And you and Sara spent the next three months visiting that child in the hospital, then kept him at your home an additional four months until social services found a permanent foster home. John, you have no proof that William Duncan Jr. is part of this. And that fancy-priced lawyer his father retains is sure to yell harassment."

"Hell, Lyle, we haven't got any proof on anyone. Not one damned thing. The only thing left is to start recalling some of the possible candidates and re-question them."

"Duncan wasn't one of the original persons of interest."

John took a deep breath and leaned back. "No, he wasn't. Call it a gut feeling. Bottom line, Duncan's family has the power and the money, and knows the kind of people that could do this sort of thing."

"Are we talking about Duncan Jr. or Sr.?"

"Both. But I'll start with prison and Jr."

Taking a sip of coffee, Lyle Parker leaned back. "How is Sara?"

"Holding it together—just."

"Think she's going to quit on us?"

"No, I don't. But she should." John shook his head. "There's a part of me that wants her to stop and a part of me that's absolutely terrified she will. We can't find those children, not in the time allowed, not like Sara does. But no, she won't quit. She's lost weight, she looks like shit, she's tired, but she won't let a child die needlessly."

"I can't imagine what she does or what she goes through, John. I'm thankful enough she helps us with the music. I just don't want anyone else around here, or anywhere, to know about her 'abilities.'"

"I agree. Sara couldn't face another New York."

"What does your gut tell you about her brother, Caleb Remington? Could he be behind this? He's got the money." As he spoke, Lyle casually opened one of his desk drawers and pulled out a file. He slid it across the desk. "And according to this, he's got the know-how."

"Sara says no. She swears Caleb could never do anything like this." John opened the file and read in silence for a few minutes, then looked up. "Shit. Is this verified?"

The captain nodded.

"Black ops—hell, Lyle, there isn't anything he couldn't do."

"Still want to interview Duncan?"

John hesitated, then nodded. "Like I said, call it a gut feeling, a hunch. I want to at least question the son of a bitch."

"Do you believe Sara about Caleb?"

John shrugged. "I don't know. I know she has a soft spot for her brother; though truth be told, she really doesn't know him. Hell, she was taken away when he was six years old and raised by her grandmother. They never really had a childhood together."

The room fell quiet, each man lost in his own thoughts. It was the captain who eventually broke the silence. "Something else came up this afternoon."

"What?"

"It seems Milford's politicians have found yet another reason and way to make our lives miserable. They want the FBI to take a bigger lead in this investigation—seems we're not moving fast enough."

John groaned.

The lit end of the cigarette pierced the darkness. John stood on the porch, watching the big German shepherd play in the snow and wishing for the hundredth time that the animal was more protective. After filing a shit-ton of paperwork, he had come home late to a pot of hot coffee, a wife already asleep, and a dog needing to go out.

Taking a last drag, he snuffed out the light and field-stripped the butt. *Damn!* He was lying to himself. The paperwork hadn't taken that long; the talk with the captain had.

The police had nothing. They knew it, and so did the people. And the people were getting damned tired of kidnapped children. Working with the FBI was shit, and if the people or the FBI ever discovered that the captain and John were using a psychic and that that psychic was John's wife . . . Well, as the captain put it, shit flows downhill. John felt reasonably sure he was going to be at the bottom of that hill.

His thoughts turned to Sara. He hadn't exaggerated anything to the captain. Honestly, he was scared as hell. She had lost weight. Even the bags under her eyes had bags. What kind of man let—even pushed—his wife to continue doing something that was destroying

21

her? It made him a lousy husband, and that put a very bad taste in his mouth. He had promised to love and take care of her. This sure as hell wasn't taking care of her.

John's attention homed in on the snow-covered lawns of their neighborhood. It was quiet—too quiet. Reaching inside his coat, he touched the butt of his Browning. A vulnerable feeling settled in his gut. He moved back into the shadows. It didn't pay to go against your gut; such feelings could keep you alive.

The night remained silent, the snow muffling even Max's playful runs. "Come on, boy. Let's go in."

Obediently, the big dog followed. Once inside, John made sure the door was locked. He hadn't had that fish-bowl feeling in a long time, not since he was a rookie detective and a stakeout went bad. He'd lost his first partner that night in a double-cross, and his limp . . . Well, a shotgun could play havoc with a kneecap.

John turned for the stairs. The only good thing to come out of this night was that the captain had given him permission to visit William Duncan Jr.

CHAPTER 3

Caleb Remington was dancing with the devil, and he knew it.

He stared across the boardroom table through eyes that were pure Slane—though unlike his sister Sara's, his eyes were moss green with a hint of silver. Hers were emerald with a touch of gold.

Moving carefully, so as not to touch the bottom folder, he slid the top one across the table. It stopped in the center as eager hands reached for it, passing it down to the older man who sat at the other end.

The man's eyes left Caleb only long enough to peruse the contents with an air of indifference. His look returned to Caleb. A slight smile crossed his craggy face.

"I'll have my lawyers look this over. We'll have a counter by next Tuesday." William Duncan Sr.'s gravelly voice still held the soft burr of Scotland. Gray hair streaked with white might have said he was old, but his eyes did not. They were still sharp, seeing things that Caleb preferred they didn't.

"No counters, no negotiations. That's my final and only offer, Duncan."

"So that's how you negotiate?"

"In this instance, yes. Remember, you came to me."

"Your father wouldn't call that good business," Duncan chided carefully.

"My father wouldn't have let you in the door. He was a social snob."

"You have a lot to learn, Remington."

Caleb leaned forward, his cultured voice dangerously soft. "So do you."

The big man rose with a smile, his entourage moving with him. Beneath the Savile Row suit and immaculate manicure, Caleb saw the Glasgow dockworker, still fighting to make coin. William Duncan was not a man to underestimate.

"My attorneys will be talking to yours next week." The burr was thicker, the threat unmistakable.

"Good afternoon, Duncan." Caleb nodded toward the door.

William Duncan and his people filed out.

Caleb leaned back, eyes closed, his hand beside the remaining folder. Slane eyes also saw much, sometimes more than he wanted them to see.

He could feel Duncan's folder, its power and its evil. The man's plans for a merger were a thinly veiled, subtle—and in some paragraphs, not so subtle—attempt to take over Caleb's company. Beneath the flowery legalese the man would assume control, making Caleb Remington nothing more than a puppet. As CEO and owner, Caleb wasn't about to let that happen. He might have inherited Remington's from his father, but he had worked hard over the years, expanding and solidifying the company. Their stock had risen steadily over the last five years, and most saw Remington's as a solid investment.

William Duncan Sr. had come to America in the early fifties, before Caleb was even born. According to background checks, the man had worked on his uncle's fishing boat, sailing out of New Bedford. Within a year, he'd owned the boat. Within three, he'd owned a fleet.

Like Caleb's father had done, Duncan diversified. During the next decades, the man put his fingers into as many pies as he could—salvage, electronics, real estate. His Hampton property alone was worth millions.

When Silicon Valley collapsed, Duncan resituated himself in Chapel Hill, North Carolina. He might have lost one fortune but he was well on his way to making several more.

Today, the net worth of his company was close to that of Caleb's. The merger would benefit both companies in some areas; in others, it would be mixing oil and water.

So why was Duncan at Caleb's front door?

A cautious man by nature, Caleb had checked and cross-checked every arm of the Remington empire. Nothing was soft. Nothing was ripe for any kind of takeover. Yet Duncan wanted it, wanted it all, and felt he could get it. How?

Caleb rose, feeling the air of dirt and something worse still in the room. Taking the folder he'd brought into the meeting, he slipped it over Duncan's proposal. It needed to be burned, and he alone would have to see to it. At his secretary's desk, he stopped. "Irene, please have the boardroom cleared, thoroughly cleaned, and sanitized—now. It stinks."

He remained by her desk, his mind still working. William Duncan had a dark side, one that Caleb neither liked nor wanted any involvement with. According to rumors, the man was the Scots-Irish answer to the Mafia, and more. He owned judges, lawyers, courts—anyone who could keep the seamier side of his life flowing smoothly and silently.

"Anything else, Caleb?"

He glanced down at Irene. "Yes get hold of Richardson Peterson. Tell him I need to see him early next week, if possible."

Caleb stepped back into his office. If William Duncan had any secrets, Peterson was the man to find them. Caleb and Peterson were ex-army; more than that, they were comrades-in-arms. Together they had carried out more than one black ops mission. Rich would always have Caleb's back.

He turned to the window and Boston harbor, his green eyes

dark. This was only the beginning of the dance, and it was one he hadn't asked for.

Samuel Hawk looked out over the green lawn of his daughter and son-in-law's New Haven condo. The green was enticing, but he missed the reds and golds of the Arizona cliff country, the sound of the eagle, the solitude of the mesas. In short, he missed the reservation.

He leaned back in his chair, thinking. His life had taken a strange turn four years before. A few weeks after his retirement, Leon Many-trees, a Hopi elder and friend, had turned up at Samuel's door. Leon had wasted no time on niceties. Hopi elders had reported seeing the Blue Star—something Samuel already knew, as he had seen it himself one night. Its sighting meant that the countdown to the "end of days" had begun.

Hopi stories told of a savior, a man or woman—or according to some legends, two men and one woman—who would save the Hopi. To that end, the elders had begun a search to find the ones who would save the Indian people. Though Samuel was Navajo, with his investigative background, Leon was sure he would be an asset to the search.

A week later Samuel found himself driving to South Dakota to check out a supposed psychic, a man who could foretell the future. He was a fraud. Samuel was crossing the border back into Arizona when Leon called; he was needed in New Mexico. There was a woman there, a healer, whom Samuel needed to check out.

For the next two years, he crisscrossed the United States, checking out stories, rumors, newspaper articles. Most people he met were frauds; some were real. But none were the savior the Hopi sought.

After demanding a vacation and having the idea rejected, Samuel piled into his old truck and drove to New Haven to see his eldest daughter. Rose had married a white man, a doctor, but

Samuel was now forgiving of this. In another three months, she would present him with a grandson.

When an article on Sara was discovered, Samuel was in the right place at the right time, at least according to Leon, and vacation or not, Leon had no qualms with asking him to research Sara Slane.

Samuel glanced down at the copy of an eight-year-old news clipping. A younger, more vulnerable Sara Erin Slane Remington Allbrooke, then known as just Sara Slane, stared back. The grainy newspaper photograph didn't hide the horror, sadness, and frustration in the woman's eyes.

According to the article, Sara sometimes worked with the New York City police, helping them find missing children. On this day, the police alerted her that a newly divorced and desperate father had possibly kidnapped his son earlier that morning. Sara linked with the child, but something went wrong during the rescue attempt. Before SWAT teams could reach the four-year-old boy, his father had shot him and then turned the gun on himself. Further articles indicated that after the murders, Sara stopped working with the police.

Samuel turned to the other, more recent clippings. Five Milford children taken, and a good, caring detective named John Allbrooke had found each child through good police work. It appeared his wife had helped him identify the songs.

Samuel looked up and stared at the green grass. It didn't feel right. Sara had to be doing more, helping the police in ways they couldn't know about. He was willing to bet everything he owned that she, not her brilliant detective husband, was finding those children.

More important to Samuel right now, though, were the similarities to the reservation kidnappings. It had to be the same man.

"Father." A soft, feminine voice brought him back to the present. Rose held out a cordless phone. "Call for you."

He took the phone, knowing immediately who it was. "Hello, Leon."

"So, you've met Sara. What do you think?"

"Who told you?"

"Your daughter, three minutes ago. Is she the one?"

"Leon, I can't really say I've met her. We spoke for barely thirty seconds. She was too frightened to even shake my hand."

"Why should that matter? She's not an empath—or is she?"

Samuel raised his eyes to the ceiling and gave an exaggerated sigh, one he knew Leon would hear plainly. "I really don't know anything about her yet, except what I've read."

"Rumor has it you asked for the police files on the kidnapping cases up there. Why'd you have them sent to the reservation and not straight to you? New Haven's practically on top of Milford."

Samuel squelched the second sigh. "I've never known a Hopi as impatient as you, Leon. I thought you people were long on waiting and short on everything else."

Leon snorted at the slight. "You're not the only one out in the field right now. We need everything—all the information on this Sara Slane Allbrooke, pronto."

"So you've reminded me, several times. In answer to your last question, it was easier to·have Chinle PD request a copy of the files from Milford, police station to police station. Chinle had no problems forwarding the information to me, but Milford might have. Means I didn't have to jump through a lot of the white man's hoops. As for the other questions, I still don't know. I don't know if she's the one. I do know she's getting tired. She may have even stopped using the gift. I have a strong feeling that she hasn't quit but wants to. According to what I've read in the newspaper, she helps her husband name some of the songs based on the notes left behind. There is no mention of her helping as a psychic."

"Then she's not the one."

Samuel heard the sorrow in Leon's voice. "How can you come up with something like that when I've just told you we barely had any time to talk?"

"Because the one we want will savor his or her power and use it to save us."

"I hope that's an inclusive 'us' and not just the Hopi."

"You know what I mean, Samuel."

"Yes, I do. I also know I don't have enough proof yet, either way."

"So what are you waiting for?"

For an instant, Samuel thought of throwing the phone down and stomping on it. But that would have been childish. Instead, he took a deep breath. "Leon, it will take time to gain her trust, and I'll need that to ascertain if she's the one we are looking for. Why are you pushing so hard?"

"Things are moving faster than we thought or planned. There have been other signs besides the Blue Star. The elders say we may not have that much time."

"We're not Mayan; 2012 has come and gone and the world didn't end. According to the Hopi stories, we still have a couple of years, whether it's 2018 or 2021, or whatever date the elders are now using. We need to be thorough. Besides, you know things always happen five minutes shy of too late."

"We may be in that five-minute time frame right now."

Silently, Samuel pondered this statement. "I'm going to visit the Milford police station and request that I consult on these kidnapping cases."

"Why?"

"For one, it will get me closer to her husband, and through him, maybe to Sara. I've the feeling they are using her in some way to find the kidnap victims. And two, I think this is the same person who hit the reservation a few years back."

"This isn't a Navajo vendetta, Samuel. It's a search for the person or persons who could save us all. Keep your eyes on the mission."

"I'm very well aware of my—our mission, but killing two birds with one stone is never a bad thing. Especially when one of the birds kills children."

"Samuel—"

"Leon, he didn't hit your people; he hit mine, six times. This is an evil we need to rid ourselves of, and now. Otherwise, the Hopi could be the next target."

"I understand." It was several minutes before Leon continued. "What does your gut tell you? Could she be the one?"

"If she's not a partner in these crimes, it's very possible she's the one we are looking for."

"I'll call back in a week."

"Leon, let me call you." Samuel was speaking to a dead line. He laid the phone down, staring at the grainy newspaper photograph. Unconsciously, he reached into his back pocket for his wallet. The picture was old, faded, but the face of his son still stared back. He put the picture on the newspaper photograph and watched in awe as they merged.

Sara was the light, Sam the darkness. They were so opposite, they complemented each other. Sara's strengths would be Sam's weaknesses and Sam's strengths would be Sara's weaknesses. It would be a strong match, a good match.

The old man shook his head and placed the photograph back in his wallet. Where had those thoughts come from? From what he had learned, Sara was happily married, and in time, his son would take a clan woman. Sam would never marry a white woman, even one with beautiful red hair and emerald-green eyes.

Samuel shook his head again. He must be getting old. And yet . . .

CHAPTER 4

Milford police patrolled the halls, schoolyards, and parking lot of St. Mary's Elementary School daily. They had been doing so since school began that fall. Their hope was that, one day, the kidnapper would slip up and they'd nail the bastard.

Sara didn't hold out much hope, but there was comfort in seeing them. With a quick wave toward a patrol car, she stepped inside the building and took a deep breath. Books, wet wool, the plop of rubber boots covered with snow and mud—the smells and sounds crowded her senses. She felt the tension in her bones relax. She was home. This was the only place in the world she wanted to be. Teaching was her life. Halfway down the corridor, a voice stopped her.

"Sara."

She turned.

Anne Stockton, St. Mary's principal, stood beside the door to the administration office. "I need to speak with you."

"My class—"

"I sent Beth to cover."

Tension seeped back into Sara's bones. Ignoring the knots forming in her stomach, she followed the tall, spare figure into the office.

"You look tired," Anne said, not unkindly, as she firmly closed the office door.

"I am." Sara sat without waiting to be asked, looked up into cement-gray eyes, and stiffened. Soft gray hair surrounded a kindly face. Normally, Anne reminded Sara of someone's grandmother. But when Anne's eyes went that cold gray, something was wrong, very wrong. "What did Billy do?"

Ignoring the question, Anne put her desk between them before speaking. "The schoolboard called a special, closed-door meeting last night. I've been ordered to give you a verbal reprimand and a written warning."

"For what?"

"For your continued absences."

"You're letting them reprimand me for absences?" The cold knot in her stomach vanished as hot anger took its place.

"Yes."

"You know why I'm gone, Anne. I thought that at some point in time you might even tell the schoolboard what I was doing." She struggled to keep her voice low and even.

"I've thought about it. But, in view of what's been happening, it would probably cost me my job. And I warned you that I would not put my job in jeopardy."

Anne hesitated, her voice dropping. "During the meeting last night, someone brought up the kidnappings and the fact that only St. Mary's students have been taken. They are concerned, very concerned. If they knew you were involved, if they knew you were helping the police, they would probably demand your resignation now. I'm afraid that you may be putting our students in danger. I don't know, Sara, maybe it's time you made a decision on whether you're a teacher or someone who works with the police." Anne's voice faded as she sat down heavily, her sudden silence speaking volumes.

"So you will let them get me on absences," Sara finished.

"He's only taken St. Mary's students."

"You want me to tell John that I'm not going to help him

anymore? You know what I go through with this kidnapper. You know what my linking to a child creates—I become the child. You want me to ignore that?"

"You might have to, to keep your job here."

A deep, thick silence fell across the room.

"They are very close to termination, Sara."

"What did Billy do yesterday?"

The woman hesitated, licking her lips. "You promised the children a treat after lunch. When they didn't get it, Billy became violent. He attacked the substitute."

"I don't believe that." Sara's voice was cold steel.

"I had to call Billy's mother."

"Billy Duncan misbehaves. He's even pushed the limits of my patience, but never once has he shown any tendencies toward violence. And the treat was a chapter from their book if they completed the morning assignments quietly, which they did."

"The substitute didn't know that, Sara. Your special-education students thrive on continuity and constancy. When you're not here to provide it, they are thrown off, especially when they haven't been warned you'll be gone."

"You know I can't exactly predict when this bastard's going to strike."

"The first thing Rachael Duncan asked was why you weren't with her son. Her comments were along the lines of 'you're either a teacher or you're not.'"

"And the fact that I helped save a child yesterday means nothing to you?"

"We're a school. We need teachers who are here."

"I am a teacher, a damned good one. And I'm only absent when it's necessary." Sara rose and turned for the door. Her hand was on the knob when she stopped. "Rachael Duncan is an idiot. But I'll consider myself warned. I'm assuming I'll find the usual note in my mailbox this afternoon?"

"Yes."

Sara hesitated for a moment longer, then turned back to the

older woman. "I have a gift, Anne. I never asked for it. I never wanted it. I have a job I trained for and love, but you're telling me to make a choice. All right, I'll shut the gift down. I'll stop playing the bastard's game. I'll tell John I can't help him anymore. Let the police handle things."

"Can you do that? Can you tell John you won't help find a kidnapped child?"

"That's exactly what you just asked me to do. You want me to quit helping the police, and I'm going to do that. It saves your job and mine."

"You'd do it for a job?"

"No. But maybe you're right. Maybe I am the danger. Maybe if I stop, he will."

"Sara, I—"

Sara jerked the door open, slamming it soundly behind her.

Fourteen pairs of eyes swiveled, silently watching Sara's every move. The fifteenth student stared straight ahead, his face half-hidden by a mop of bright red hair.

Throughout the morning, Sara made a point to stand in front of Billy. He ignored her. She directed questions to him. He remained silent. By lunchtime, she had to concede that she had failed to reach Billy Duncan.

At the first bell, the room became a cauldron of activity, although the usual giggles, clumps, and thumps were absent. Even the whispers were guarded. After several minutes of quiet chaos, the class sat, hands folded.

"You may go."

With no pushing or laughter, the children filed out. A sullen Billy brought up the rear.

As the class door shut, Sara leaned back in her chair. The morning had been an abysmal failure. Drumming a pencil on the desk, she stared absently at the pile of papers. She was behind on her grading, but her mind wandered, recalling that fateful night three years before when she first met Billy. All too well, she remembered the phone call and words that no cop's wife ever wants to hear once, much less twice in a lifetime.

John's been shot, Sara.

Sara could still hear the sound of her boots tapping hard along the cold hospital corridor. The nurse was friendly, understanding. John would be all right. It was just a shoulder wound this time. Nothing critical had been hit. When it came to the boy, though, they were more guarded.

William Duncan III, also known as Billy, had had a rough beginning. His mother had been on drugs when he was born. Consequently, his development was slow. When he finally started to walk, his father began using him as a punching bag. That night, it had gotten so bad that a neighbor called the police.

John caught the call on the way home and for some reason turned around. According to his story, he'd faced a hopped-up druggie with a gun, a woman so high she couldn't even remember her own name, and a child almost dead from a beating.

"See to the child," John begged Sara from his hospital bed. "I'll be fine. Make sure Billy's going to be all right."

When Sara walked into Billy's room, her heart fell in tatters at the sight of the bruised and broken child who laid so still, his body wrapped in bandages and casts.

She spent that night at the hospital with the two of them. In the days that followed, she often sat with Billy, talking nonsense to the child, hoping he understood that she was there because she cared. When John was released, they spent evenings at the hospital with the boy.

Two months later, Billy came home with them. He stayed for almost four months, until a permanent foster home was found.

It was a fiasco. Despite everything she and John tried to do, the boy fell through the cracks of an overworked, underpaid, non-caring, and sometimes crooked social services system.

During that time, Rachael entered a rehab program. It took her a year to dry up, get her GED, and find a job. It took her another year to convince the courts that she could be a competent mother.

Unfortunately, competent didn't mean caring. Sara figured her dog, Max, had more maternal instincts than Rachael Duncan.

Her thoughts slipped back to the present. This morning her students had been frightened. Of her? No. Of Billy? Several times, she'd caught them staring at him, as though waiting for something to happen.

The pencil fell from her fingers. That's what the students were doing—waiting. But for what? An explosion? Billy's anger? It had to be about Billy. The pieces suddenly fell into place. They were all waiting for Billy to explode again. He was mad at her, and when Billy got real mad, he threw a fit.

Sara rose and grabbed her coat. Billy was holding things in, which meant the most likely place for him to finally explode would be the lunchroom or the playground.

She needed to be there. She needed to be close enough to help the boy channel his anger. She could only pray that he listened and connected with her before becoming destructive or self-destructive.

"I didn't know you had playground duty."

Sara turned as Kelly Archer walked over. "I don't. After yesterday, I thought it might be best to keep an eye on Billy." She kept her voice low as she glanced over at the redheaded boy who stood alone by the fence, morosely studying something in the snow.

"If it's any consolation, Billy's only given me trouble once. He pushed Jimmy Anderson down. But to be honest with you, Jimmy probably deserved it. He can be a bully. Rachael likes to blow things up, Sara. She loves being the center of attention. And if it takes a child to make her that center, so be it."

"Anne said he was violent."

"That's not exactly how I would describe yesterday. He was loud . . . but not as loud as Rachael was. You could hear her ranting and raving all the way to my classroom."

"The kids were so quiet this morning you could have heard the proverbial pin drop."

Kelly frowned. "I think that's because of Rachael. They could be afraid she's going to make you leave. They like you. They don't want you to leave; it upsets their routine. And I'm sure they see Billy as the cause."

"So what do I do?"

"I don't know, but you're a good enough teacher to think of something. Did Anne speak to you about absences this morning?"

"How did you know?"

"Small school, small town, thin walls." Kelly shrugged. "We all got hit. It's a cover, so they can't be accused of picking on just one teacher."

"You think so?"

"Look, don't let the bastards get you down. The dust will settle and they'll find something or someone else to pick on. Besides, we're all taking bets that you're pregnant. That's why you're gone so much . . . right?"

Kelly looked so hopeful, Sara had to laugh. "For now, I'm taking the Fifth." Whatever else she was going to say was cut off by the bell.

Kelly grimaced as the children came running toward the school to line up. "Hopefully the little darlings have worked off some of their energy. Hang in there, Sara. Everything will be fine, and I want to be the first one you tell when you do get pregnant."

Sara watched as the children walked in, her mind racing as she tried to sort out what she was going to say. She wanted to tell them the real reason she was gone so much. She knew the children would understand, accept the unbelievable, and do so without judgment. But it was too much of a risk.

Billy was the last one in. As she watched the little boy stumble in, her breath caught in her throat. God, what if he remembered?

Once, during the four months Billy spent with them, a lost child had linked with her. She was putting a plate of eggs in front of the boy when the world dissolved. Sara became a little girl, rambling down an overgrown path, past barns, through mud and briers.

Sara's eyes suddenly focused on the real world. Max was at her side and she was sitting at the table, a terrified Billy standing in front of her with a growing wet spot on his pants. He stared at the scratches on her arms that seemed to have magically appeared.

She tried to comfort him, but the words wouldn't come. With trembling hands, she punched in John's number. She had barely finished what sounded to her ears like a totally incoherent sentence when the phone went dead. Twenty minutes later, John burst through the door.

"Are you okay?" He glanced at her as he laid his sketchpad on the table. Digging fingers into Max's fur, Sara nodded.

Turning to Billy, John gently picked up the frightened child and carried him upstairs.

Sara remained seated, replaying the journey the lost girl had taken. When John returned, Billy was in dry clothes and some of the fear was gone from his eyes.

Sitting down, John grabbed the sketchpad and pencil. "I'm ready when you are."

Haltingly at first, then more firmly, she described what she had seen. When John showed her his two sketches, it seemed as though her husband had photographed the child's journey.

Nodding, Sara leaned back in the chair, letting some of the tension out in a sigh. "She's about five years old, blond hair, blue eyes. I think her name is Jenny and I don't think she walked that far, but she's far enough away from home that nothing looks familiar."

"Get some rest, Sara. I'll take Billy with me."

Sara waited until she heard the car leave, then grabbed Max's ruff and let the dog lead her up the stairs to their bedroom.

Twenty minutes later, John called. An AMBER Alert had been issued for a five-year-old girl with blond hair and blue eyes. Her name was Jenny Brian.

An excited Billy and a relieved husband returned home several hours later. The girl had been found asleep under an old oak tree—exactly as John had drawn.

Unfortunately, the day didn't end there. Sara was serving supper when the first cramp hit her. John never even asked what was happening. He swept her into his arms, yelled for Billy to bring Max, and got everyone into the car.

Half an hour later, at the hospital emergency room, the baby she'd been carrying passed from her body with a minimum of fuss. A few hours later, they returned home.

John held her tight that night, their tears mingling.

"It seems my gift comes with a termination clause." She repeated the final phrase until the pills took over and she drifted off to sleep. It was the second baby they had lost, each one gone after Sara linked with a child.

Would Billy remember the incident? Would he—could he put two and two together?

The little red-haired boy finally sat down.

Walking to the front of her desk, Sara leaned against it, a closed storybook in her hand. Each child watched her. Only Billy looked away.

"Aren't you going to read to us, Mrs. Allbrooke?"

"No, not yet, Amy. I need to talk to you about yesterday. You need to understand why I wasn't here."

Robert, her one-day Rhodes Scholar, spoke up, "You were sick. We know that."

"Yes, and like you all stay home when you are sick, I do too."

"I'm not always sick when I stay home," Jesse Rodriguez said, her voice quavering.

Sara laughed. Trust Jesse to lighten the mood. "I am ill, Jesse. If I could be here, I would. But sometimes I can't." She glanced at Billy. His eyes were on her, but she couldn't read what he was thinking. "If you really needed me, I would be here, even if I was sick."

"That's a lie," Billy said, his voice whipping across the room. "I needed you yesterday and you weren't here." His accusing eyes burned into Sara.

"You didn't need me, Billy. You wanted me. And I should have been here; I am your teacher. But none of you died or was in danger because I was gone. You were all just fine."

The silence was deafening. She stared at Billy, half expecting an outburst or argument.

"My mom says you're helping the police find those kids that were kidnapped," Amy stated.

"No, my mom says she's pregnant." Jesse turned to Sara. "Are you going to have a baby, Mrs. Allbrooke?"

Sara laughed. "Not yet, Jesse. I will tell you all when I am." Still looking at Billy, she held her breath. A small light flickered deep in his dark brown eyes. Billy wasn't reacting—he was acting, thinking, trying to relate.

"If I could," she continued, still staring at Billy, "I would never be away from school. But sometimes," she hesitated, "sometimes, I just can't be here." It sounded lame, even to her ears, but Billy seemed to be buying it. "Remember, I miss all of you, as much as you miss me."

His head came up. He looked at her, not past her. She turned around and picked up the book. "Now, let's read some more about Chandler and Harley in *The Adventures of Lily the Lightning Bug*."

John grabbed his thermos from the seat, slammed the car door shut, and followed his own tracks to the large side porch. Precinct coffee was beyond terrible, and he just happened to know that Sara had brewed an extra pot of her special blend that morning. And if he remembered correctly, she had poured it into the thermos on the counter. With any luck, there was some left. He stopped at the porch stairs and studied the little house.

The weathered cedar, straight lines, and rectangular shape were out of place among the large rambling white Cape Cods and Nantucket's that lined the street. But its forlorn quality had appealed to Sara. John liked the not-quite-fitting-in part. Beyond that, they both enjoyed being able to see the Sound at the bottom of the block.

The front yard and home had undergone numerous renovations in the four years they'd lived there. They had widened doors, raised doorframes, and knocked out walls to open up spaces. Sara even had plans for an add-on. John was extremely glad she was going to call in a contractor for that.

The only part of the house Sara never touched was the large backyard. It was her "bit of wild," a place of overgrown bushes, brambles, and wildflowers.

John's hand was on the doorknob when something registered. Turning, he studied the expanse of yard and the wide tree-lined street. Neighborhood children had had a grand time in the snow that morning. Everything from snow wheels to snow angels dotted the landscape.

Only their yard was free of the artistic endeavors. His footsteps and Max's play area in the side yard were the only marks in the pristine snow.

John walked back to the steps and slowly turned in a circle. Something was off. Not quite right. He studied the yard clinically.

Footprints . . . by the bushes that edged the driveway. He stepped off the porch and walked carefully to the drive. Someone had watched the house that morning, using the bushes to conceal their presence.

Squatting, he studied the prints. It was a man, a large man. Was the kidnapper stalking Sara now?

Cursing eloquently but softly, John pulled out his cell phone and punched in a number. For God's sake, this was Elm Street in Milford, Connecticut, USA—the kind of place where people raised families, sat on the Green, watched concerts, and walked along the Sound or through the parks. This wasn't the kind of place that grew men who became serial kidnappers and stalked first grade schoolteachers.

Still shaking his head, he spoke to a disembodied voice. Someone else needed to see this.

CHAPTER 5

The magazine sailed toward the opening door. Instinctively, John caught it, shut the door with his foot, and stared at his wife, his eyebrows almost reaching his receding hairline.

"Bad day?"

"You could say that!" Sara deftly caught the return throw.

"And you're taking it out on this innocent magazine."

"I wouldn't use the word 'innocent.' It's trite. According to this batch of 'experts,' if a child can't read, write, or function as a small adult by preschool, they're so far behind as to be virtually unteachable. Parents expect babies to come into this world potty-trained, with a dictionary in one hand and a computer manual in the other." She tossed the magazine into the fire, watching the pages curl into blackness.

"You've known that for a long time." John threw his coat onto the chair and leaned over her, bracing his hands on the back of the sofa. He looked down into her emerald-green eyes, which were dark with worry. "So what's really pissing you off?"

"I keep replaying that damned conversation I had with Anne a few days ago. It sticks."

"You mean stinks, don't you?"

"Same thing." Uncurling her legs, Sara nudged him back and rose. "I'll get dinner started."

"Whoa." He stopped her, his large hands firm on her small shoulders. "We talked about this. Bottom line, you still have a job. So what's really bothering you?"

"Your sister called today, and so did Tammy's mom."

John's dark brown eyes gentled. When he spoke, his voice was soft, full of understanding. "What did Cora want?"

"She wanted to let me know that they are thinking of putting Tammy back in the sanitarium. According to Cora she's become very agitated, almost belligerent at times."

"I know she was your best friend when you were kids, but it might be for the best. Honey, Tammy's not been right since the kidnapping twenty years ago. You saved her life, you found her, but whatever happened to her those three days she was missing . . . well, her mind is gone and I don't think it's ever coming back. She still can't even really talk. Her conversations are the same three words repeated over and over again."

"I know. But I thought, with the new meds and stuff . . . I thought she was getting better."

John brushed a light kiss on her cheek before pulling her into his arms. She leaned into his strength, savoring the calm.

"What did my sister want?"

"To warn me."

"About what?"

"She says I won't be allowed into the public school system if St. Mary's lets me go."

"What?"

"Regardless of whether I quit or am fired, there are no teaching jobs for me here. Evidently, Milford has let the St. Mary's schoolboard know that I am neither wanted nor needed in Milford's public schools."

"It's not Milford. Some people are beginning to gossip about the possibility that you may be working with the police. The fact that you were a psychic who sometimes worked with the New York

City police has gotten out. It's just some loudmouths and gossips. Every small town has them."

"Maybe so, John, but they're the only ones talking right now."

He rested his chin on top of her head. "We'll get through this, honey. Everything will be okay. We'll find the bastard, I promise."

Sara blinked away tears. "I need to start supper."

He held her tighter. "What else is bothering you?"

"Billy attacked a substitute the day I was gone."

"He what?"

"He attacked a substitute."

"You didn't tell me that."

"I still don't believe it. At least the school didn't demand any disciplinary action. I promised to read them another chapter in their book after lunch if they worked hard that morning. They did. The substitute didn't know that, and Billy pitched a fit."

"You mean he attacked her." John's voice was soft.

"I don't think there was a physical attack. The substitute used the word 'attack' but wouldn't elaborate."

"And the school called Rachael."

"Yes."

"I'm assuming she came in like an avenging angel."

"With demands and questions. More demands than questions."

"That explains a lot."

"Do you think Rachael has something to do with my . . . unpopularity?"

"I wouldn't be surprised if she's got everything to do with it. Rachael loves to be the victim. Yeah. I could see her calling 'friends' and trying to get you blackballed."

Sara nestled into the solid embrace of the man she loved more than life itself. "I want to quit."

"Your job?"

"No. The case."

Joe Campbell was tired. He'd just driven from Arkansas to New Orleans and was now only halfway back to his home in West Virginia. But the long drive was worth it for more reasons than one. His latest carving now graced an old hotel in Crystal Springs, Arkansas, and he'd made enough money for Serafina and his father.

He hadn't planned the trip to New Orleans, but when the scent of Serafina's perfume had filled his truck's cab after leaving the truck stop the night the boy was found on the tombolo, he'd become frightened that something might be wrong. Going to New Orleans might be dangerous, but he felt it was necessary.

Joe flipped the wheel. The motel was somewhat secluded, looked cheap, and was the only one he'd seen in the last sixty miles. The need to rest, he knew, was an excuse. He wanted one more day with his dreams—his dreams of things that could never be.

Fifteen minutes later, he threw the battered duffle bag onto the floor. Based on the smell of Lysol, which couldn't quite overpower the stench of humidity and mold, the room seemed fairly clean. The carpet was stained but vacuumed, the bathroom without cockroaches . . . at least none that he could see. It was the best he deserved.

Stretching out on the cheap plaid bedspread, he eased his leg out. He limped thanks to the Navy. Hit by a falling pallet while loading supplies aboard a ship, a young ensign had gone overboard. Without thinking, Joe had dived off the ship, grabbing the unconscious shipmate. He held onto the young man, but waves and falling supplies slammed him into the ship's side, permanently damaging his knee.

His father imitated that limp when he kidnapped a child—which was rare. He said it would appear as though only one person was perpetrating the crimes. The words "like father, like son" ran through Joe's mind. Picking up the envelope of snapshots, he held tightly in his hand a dream, and silently prayed for the strength to let it go.

He should call his father. He knew the old man would be pissed by his absence, but once Joe told him about the sale, made some excuses about spending time in the art shops of Crystal Springs, and gave him the money, he knew his father would be content, at least for a time.

For now, he wanted to savor his time with Serafina. He opened the package and spilled the photographs across the bed.

Rolling over, Joe glanced at the clock. He had slept almost two hours. Photographs littered the bed, except for the one he still clutched. Seven years and a child later, Serafina was still beautiful. He ran strong, artistic fingers over the print. She hadn't seen him get this shot, but then, she never did. He made certain of that.

He'd left her the day he realized he loved her and she loved him; he wasn't good enough for her and he never would be. Then his father had slithered back into his life and he'd returned to West Virginia. After a few months, he knew he should never go back to Serafina.

For over a year, he'd stayed away, knowing in his mind it was the right decision. Then Katrina hit. He could still feel the terror, the anguish of not being there to protect Serafina. It took every ounce of self-control to remain in West Virginia. He held onto the fact that her house was in the French Quarter, a block from Jackson Square—that old part of New Orleans that her founding fathers had built over two hundred years before because they knew it could survive even the worst hurricane.

When the storm was finally over, Joe joined a FEMA crew going to New Orleans. Serafina was all right. She was helping clean up when he caught this shot. A colorful scarf was wrapped around her long dark hair and her blouse was soaked with sweat and covered in dirt. Yet, she still managed to look beautiful, even regal.

He had taken the photo, and then, like a man possessed, walked across the sea of devastation to stand beside her. She looked up, not surprised, and for several moments, they just stared at each other. When she fell into his arms, he knew he could never leave her. She would always be a part of his life, a very large part.

In the midst of the devastation, they loved. For two wonderful weeks, they loved. He left then, with a promise to return, and seven months later, he made it back to New Orleans. It was a beautiful, cool evening. He watched from across the street as Serafina locked her shop and turned toward home.

He froze at her profile. Serafina was pregnant, very pregnant. He fled down an alley before she could see him, spending the night alone in a seedy motel somewhere between New Orleans and Alabama.

He never doubted that the child was his. He could endanger his own life; even ask her to share that danger, but an innocent child, his child . . . never. He wrote to her, telling her it was over, but she remained in his life—at least in his own way.

He saw the birth announcement in the New Orleans paper and rejoiced quietly by himself. They had a son. The next morning, he was on the road to New Orleans. It was almost three days before he caught a glimpse of her and the child. She never saw him.

From then on, he drove to New Orleans as often as possible, seeing her always from a distance. He was never sure if she guessed who sent the money. It was random—as much as he could, whenever he could. He mailed the wadded-up bills from almost every state in the country. The return address was as fictitious as the names he used.

Putting the photos away, Joe pulled out the Blackberry. For a few moments, he simply stared at the phone. At times, it seemed as though his father was nothing more than a figment of his imagination. He saw the old man less and less these days.

Taking a deep breath, he typed in a number once more. It was time to leave dreams behind, dreams that could never be. Time to get back to reality—the reality others had made for him, the reality he wanted to change, but couldn't.

The money would help, at least until the coven—or whatever the hell the old man called it—began bringing in funds. His heart fell into his stomach. He knew his father was already planning the next kidnapping and would expect Joe to do it.

He counted the rings. On the seventh, a deep voice answered. He froze.

"You want to *what*, Sara?"

"I want to quit. And before you say anything, it's not because I'm afraid of losing my job. I'm tired. Tired and scared. I'm not thinking clearly anymore. I'm making mistakes, serious mistakes. And when I make mistakes, someone could die. I want to stop before that happens."

"Did you ever think that not playing *ensures* someone dies?"

"Yes," Sara fired back. "I think about it all the time." She hesitated, softening her voice. "I've got a feeling it's the game that's important to him. If I stop playing his stupid game, maybe he will too."

"That's a helluva gamble."

"I know, John." She looked up, green eyes filling with tears. "Believe me, I know."

Dinner that night was quiet, strained. Bed was stranger still. They lay side by side like two strangers, not talking, not touching.

Eventually Sara's even breathing filled the room. John rolled over onto his side, bracing his head with his arm, and studied his wife in the dim light.

She gave a half whimper, half sob, and stirred.

Reaching out, he ran his hand gently along her cheek and whispered her name. "Sara. Sara, no matter what you do, what happens, I love you. I don't want you to go through this, but I don't know what else to do. You're . . ." He fell silent.

Another half-sob shook her. He pulled her to him, pressing his lips against her cheek. She automatically curled her body into his, but it was not pleasure she sought; it was safety. He crooned softly, pulling her closer, willing her to relax her body into his.

John was no psychiatrist, but it didn't take one to know what was going on. Even safe beside him in her deepest sleep, Sara relived the brutality and fear of each kidnapping.

God, he was an asshole! He'd called himself one many times in the past few weeks. What kind of a husband was he? Why couldn't he have supported her decision to stop? Hell, he wanted her to quit.

Yet, when she told him, he had blown up. He didn't know what annoyed him most—the fact that he had just bragged to the captain that she would never stop, or the fact that they still didn't have a single lead. Either way, nothing felt right.

He had the next day off. In fact, he was home the whole weekend. Maybe they could talk. Maybe . . .

He had taught Sara the danger of playing the "maybe" or "what if" game. Now he was doing it. He'd think of something in the morning. At least he hoped he would.

He buried his face in her thick hair. Even in the darkness he saw its fire. He knew her strength, but it was her fragility he felt. He wasn't a large man, but he was solid, even stocky. At five foot two, Sara was small but strong—now, the weight loss made her seem even smaller, frailer. He chuckled softly into her hair. Sara, frail? He'd take a hard punch for that thought.

Closing his eyes, he held on, knowing that at that moment, he was her anchor. He was all she had.

CHAPTER 6

"Coffee?"

Sara looked up from the papers she was grading. John looked almost contrite as he held out the cup. "That's called bribery," she stated flatly.

"I know."

"It's illegal."

"I know that too."

"Then why are you doing it?"

"Do you want the damned coffee or not?"

She took the cup and cocked an eyebrow. "I'm still thinking of quitting."

"I know. And we need to talk some more. Last night didn't . . . it didn't—"

"Feel right. I know, John." She took a sip of the hot liquid before continuing. "Anne asked me the same question you did. Could I refuse to help a child that was calling for help? I honestly don't know the answer to that question."

"I'm a cop, hon; worse than that, I'm a detective. We need to consider all possibilities."

"I know . . . but—"

The Trans-Siberian Orchestra filled the air. John grabbed his phone, his voice tense as he spoke. "Allbrooke here."

Sara rose, reaching out to touch him, then dropped her arm. When John spoke like that, it usually meant one thing: another kidnapping. Closing her eyes, she searched for the child. Nothing.

"Are you all right, Sara?" John's voice, softer now, broke her concentration.

She looked up. He slipped the cell phone into his shirt pocket, one arm still tight around her. She realized he was the only thing holding her up.

"Who was it?" she asked.

"I thought you were going to stop."

John was the only man she knew who could frown and smile at the same time.

She took a deep breath and stepped back. "I am."

"There's no kidnapping." He pulled her back into his arms, bent his head down, and took her lips into a deep, thorough kiss.

She finally made it up for air. "You have to go in, then?"

"Later, yes. But first, would you look again at some pictures I've sketched?"

"Have I seen them before?"

"Yes."

"Why do you want me to go through them again?"

"I don't know. It's just a feeling. Maybe, because time has passed, you might see something different. Maybe it will jog something, something you didn't notice the first time. Maybe we missed something you can find."

"Okay."

He returned a few moments later with a tattered sketchbook. It was one of many. When a book was full, he bought another. In less than a week, it would look as worn as its predecessor.

Sara opened to the first series of sketches. John was a consummate illustrator. He could, with a few pencil strokes, recreate a moment of time in detail. She ran her fingers lightly over the sketch, almost feeling the harshness of the spring wind. It was March. Milford had been experiencing an unusually wet and early spring. Rivers were running higher than normal.

The metal cage had been wedged beneath a bridge, half hidden by flowing water. They'd had only sixty minutes to find the child before the river crested.

Her hand brushed across the faces John had drawn, then found the child's features. They'd saved six-year-old Danny MacBain, a St. Mary's student, but the boy would still go to his grave with the memories of that day.

She turned each page slowly. A chill touched her arms as she relived each horror. At the sketches of Charles Island she stopped, pointing to one of the figures. "Why is it you've never sketched him before?"

"It's the first time I've seen him."

"It's the third time for me."

"What?"

"I spoke to him at Charles Island. His name is Samuel Hawk."

"Why didn't you tell me this sooner?"

She shrugged. "I never thought about it."

"You're right. His name is Sam Hawk. The son of a bitch has a record. He almost killed a man." John hesitated. "At least, that's what Johnson just called to tell me. We think it's him."

"What do you mean, you 'think'?"

"According to the rap sheet, Sam Hawk is thirty-six years old."

"Then it can't be the same man. The man I saw, the man you drew, is in his fifties—easily."

"Could be a relative. What else are you keeping from me?"

Sara looked up. Her eyes had gone that deep, don't-push-it green.

"Did he say anything other than his name?" John persisted.

"No."

"If you see him again, don't—and I stress the word *don't*—engage him in any kind of conversation. In fact, don't even let him get close to you. Call me, call the station, call a cop—call anyone, immediately." He rose.

"John, he's—"

"He may be stalking you."

"What makes you say that?"

The Tran-Siberian Orchestra saved him from having to answer. "Yeah."

He nodded and clicked off. "They need me at the station. We'll continue this discussion later."

"No, we won't. It's over. I'm not one of your 'men,' John Allbrooke. I didn't tell you about the meeting," she hesitated, licking her lips, "because I don't feel that he has anything to do with the kidnappings, other than perhaps being a macabre voyeur, which he denied. He's strange, different. He made me nervous. I think that's because he was out of place. I'm not used to seeing a cowboy, much less an American Indian, in Milford. The more I ran the meeting across my mind, the more I was convinced he's not part of all this. I still feel that way."

He waved his hand. "We'll—"

"We'll do nothing." She rose and left the room before he could say anything else.

Caleb liked working on Saturdays, at least sometimes. It was quiet, peaceful; more than that, he got a lot done. A lot of thinking, if nothing else.

He pushed back and propped his feet on the boardroom table, listening to the quiet tapping of Irene's fingers on the computer keys. She came in some weekends. It meant her husband was fishing, and the house, although they had downsized several years before, was still too big with no children or grandchildren about.

The large boardroom had been cleaned, even down to the windows that overlooked Boston Harbor. Light filled the room now. The rich brown leather of the executive chairs placed around the large table shined, and the dark walnut table glowed. It was, once again, a pleasant room to be in.

The boardroom phone buzzed. "Mr. Remington, there's an Abigail Duncan here to see you."

"Who the hell is Ab—" he stopped as the vision of a dark-haired woman swam through his mind. Abigail, William Duncan Sr.'s only daughter. She was a lawyer in the firm that represented her father's business interests. They didn't travel in the same social circles, but Caleb had caught sight of her at a gala one evening. She stood out.

"What does she want, Irene?"

"She's got the counter offer. Said she was in the vicinity and decided not to wait until Monday."

He heard the dryness of disbelief in his secretary's voice and silently agreed with her take. During the past week, he'd had the strangest feeling he was being tailed, watched, whatever the current term was for someone else keeping an eye on your whereabouts and business.

"Send her in."

He lowered his feet and prepared to meet with a cold, pretty, professional woman.

Abigail Duncan was anything but. She walked into the room with composure and an apology. "I'm sorry to . . ."

Caleb rose. The woman wasn't pretty; she was beautiful. How could he have forgotten that? But then, he had noticed her that evening amongst all the other young debutantes and rich divorce's looking for the next wallet. That said something.

She stood out now, her pearl-colored Chanel slacks and jacket making a tasteful statement. Instead of a blouse, she wore a cream cashmere sweater, and over the ensemble, a white cashmere coat.

Long dark hair framed a strong patrician face. Eyes the color of a Scottish loch smiled. She was a soft, gentle, elegant version of Catherine Zeta-Jones, and she was holding something out for him.

"Mr. Remington?"

"Yes." He dragged his mind back to the present.

"I said I was sorry. I took a chance you might be here today. My father wanted you to have this counter as soon as possible."

He reached out for the folder. The fantasy cracked. Cold snaked up his arm as he took the papers. He dropped them onto the table with a small wince. This time he'd have to clean the damned boardroom himself.

"Thank you, Ms.—Mrs. . . ."

"Please, just call me Abbey. My father doesn't run an extremely formal office. I'm not used to being called Ms. anything."

"Won't you sit down? I could arrange for some tea." He glanced outside. It was a blustery day. The early September storm had barely left the east coast when another one hit, then another. The storms weren't large, but they kept things cold and slushy. Even now, the wind and clouds all pointed to more snow.

"No, thank you. I really have to go. We're having a family luncheon this afternoon." She hesitated. "Would you like to join us? You could see the Duncan's from the inside."

The fantasy finally shattered. Behind Abigail's dark blue eyes, he glimpsed calculation.

"No, thank you. I have other plans."

"Then, again, allow me to apologize for disturbing you and thank you for seeing me."

Before he could answer, she was out the door. Only the heavy scent of her perfume remained behind.

Caleb stared down at the folder he'd dropped. He didn't need to read the counter to know it wasn't for them. The old bastard had ignored his "no counter" statement. Caleb was sure that this offer would sweeten the pot in some areas—but whatever it said, it would still put far too much power into the hands of William Duncan Sr.

He stared at the folder, his mind spinning. He had already planned to spend Thanksgiving in the Remington summer home in Milford, but the need to be there earlier was growing. Caleb could feel it. He knew, without doubts, that the police would once more call him in for questioning about the kidnappings.

Striding out of the office, he stopped at Irene's desk. "Have

Charles throw my suitcase into the Rover and bring it around. If you need me, I'll be in Milford."

In his office he grabbed his coat, briefcase, and a silk handkerchief out of his desk. Returning to the boardroom, he used the handkerchief to protect his hand as he carefully slid the folder into the briefcase. He would dispose of it once he reached Milford.

Stopping again at Irene's desk, he stared pointedly at his secretary. "You need to go home. I have a feeling bad weather is going to settle in soon."

"That's not all that's going on, is it?"

He shook his head.

"Is your sister all right?"

"I think so, but I need to be in Milford, and soon. I'll be back after the holidays. Lock up the Boardroom. I'll deal with it when I return. Until then, no one is to enter or use the room."

The woman nodded. "Have a safe trip, Caleb."

Caleb strode to the elevators. Irene's years with the company made her as much a friend as an employee. She only dropped formalities when they were alone or when she was concerned. He grimaced. If it was concern, she might have good reasons.

CHAPTER 7

Joe gazed over the West Virginia valley at the small house on the far hill, now devoid of smoke from the chimney, and life. "Did you kill the man?" he asked.

The figure in the shadows ignored Joe's question. Mesmerized, Joe watched his old man's fingers fly, and as if by magic, the rifle came together. Still silent, James Malachi Campbell, known as Malachi to most people, checked the stopwatch. Joe knew, by the way he laid the rifle down, that the time was good.

"Yeah, I killed him." His father's voice was a harsh whisper.

"Why? He was harmless."

"He was unnecessary. More than that, he was here." Cold, dead eyes turned to Joe. "This is my valley, my land. I say who comes here, who lives here. His presence could have been dangerous to our plans. He had to go, and I took care of it."

Joe couldn't control the sharp intake of his breath.

Malachi's lips curved up into a half-smile, half-growl. "Don't worry. I made it look like an accident. And after talking to the sheriff, I'm sure that's what will be on the death certificate."

Joe stepped back. He was at the door of the cabin when his father's voice stopped him. "I need to leave the mountain, see some folks, make sure everything's ready for the December solstice. How are the cabins out in the meadow coming?"

"You mean the shacks?"

"Yeah, JJ, the shacks you are supposed to be making livable. Will they be ready by December?"

Joe hated being called JJ—and his father knew it—but he kept his voice even. It wouldn't pay to make his father angry. No one knew the depth of Malachi's cruelty and evil, not even Joe. "They'll be livable, but they are nothing fancy—not like what these men are used to."

Malachi uttered a short laugh, or what passed for a laugh. "My coven needs a bit of bringing down. They need to find out what is really important. We will see that the next solstice is more to their tastes once they give us the money to make things more . . . comfortable."

"Is it all worth it? Are you even sure everyone will be able to get back into these mountains in December?"

His father's face darkened, his voice dangerously low when he spoke. "Is it worth it, you ask? Hell, yes. The old Slane woman fucked with me. She threw away my life, my chances, and did the same thing to you. As for getting back into these mountains for the solstice, heavy snows won't hit us until the New Year."

"And you know this for certain?"

"Yeah. I know this for certain. We should be celebrating the solstice on December twenty-first, but the pussies will be too wrapped up in the holiday season. December thirteenth is at least close, and the weather will be no problem."

"You took care of the old Ms. Slane and her husband a few years ago. Weren't their deaths enough?"

"No." He glanced up at Joe. "It's not over. Their seeds still live. They still owe me, owe you. Wiping those seeds from the face of the earth will finish things, balance the scales a bit more, and give us a powerful beginning. People will discover that you are the bastard son and the only inheritor. We'll own the Remington empire."

"Are you sure about that? Do you have a copy of Remington's will? He might leave everything to his secretary."

Malachi's fist slammed down hard on the table. "Do you take me for an idiot? I know people, I've got people. The will is going to be in our favor."

"I carry her seed too, or have you forgotten that?" Joe persisted. "Are you going to kill me and declare everything yours?"

"As long as you do what I say, JJ, and please me, you'll live and have everything you ever wanted. Besides, you're important to my claim. After all, you will be the only living relative."

Joe turned and walked out into the crisp, cold air. No, he'd never have everything. He'd never have Serafina. Joe could hear his father laughing as he walked across the yard to his studio. It wasn't a comforting sound.

Sixty paces from the cabin Joe entered his studio, closing the door soundly behind him. He stood for a moment, breathing in the mixture of pine and sawdust, then took a sip of the hot coffee he still held. For a moment, he could almost imagine he smelled chicory. It went through him, cleansing his heart and lungs, clearing his mind.

Throwing a log into the stove, he welcomed the warmth as he turned to the half-finished carving. It would bring at least five thousand dollars. Thanks to some skillful lying in conversation with his father, the old man thought it was worth about five hundred. The extra money would go to Serafina.

Joe stroked the side of the piece. The wood was satin smooth, except for a small "JC" carved deep. Joseph Campbell, artist. His grandmother, seeing his bent toward carving, had added the name Joseph in honor of a more famous carpenter and woodworker. He liked the name. It fit him, and it was definitely better than the James he shared with his father. It was bad enough he was his father's "get," as backwoods people called him, referring to a man's children.

No—as an artist, the world would not call him "little Jimmy" or "James Malachi's get." He was Joseph Campbell and his grandmother swore he was blessed, the evil driven away. How wrong she was.

With a soft sigh, Joe grabbed an adze and dug deep into the rough side of the virgin wood. He had no doubt that his father would succeed. He just wondered how many more would die.

John turned in the direction of the skid and caught his breath in relief when the wheels gripped the road. The day was as gray as his mood. The trip to Hartford had been punctuated with fender benders and drivers afraid to go over forty on Connecticut's snowy highways. It didn't help his temper.

He pulled into the Hartford Correctional Center parking lot. There were some more names to the prison, but he could never remember them. God, he hated coming to this gray block-and-stone building, with its high fences and tight security. But then, it was a maximum-security prison. In his fifteen-year career, he'd only visited the place twice. This was the third time, and it was three times too many.

John's request had caused a bit of an uproar. After all, he was the police officer that William Duncan Jr. had shot, and John's reasoning for seeing the man was shaky at best. In the end, though, he was granted the interview.

At the office he showed his credentials, turned in his guns—all of them—and after going through a series of locked doors, ended up in a room with a table and two chairs.

He wanted to face the man—no phones, no separate rooms. He wanted to see his face, watch as Duncan answered each question.

John leaned back in the metal chair and stared at the walls. William Duncan Sr. had tried desperately to get his son transferred to a Massachusetts correctional facility, something closer to Boston, something more genteel, white collar.

But luck was on John's side. The Milford judge was having none of it. The son remained in Connecticut, and the facility . . . well, it wasn't a white-collar prison.

John heard William long before he saw him. The sound of dragging footsteps and metal echoed down the hall. He looked up as the door opened.

William Duncan Jr. still looked like a weasel—a black-haired, blue-eyed weasel, but the kind of weasel certain women would find attractive. The addition of a few million dollars didn't hurt.

His dark blue eyes actually focused on John. Evidently, the man wasn't able to get the quantities of drugs he was used to in here. John wondered about the quality, wondered if the man was smart enough to be careful whom he bought from and what he bought. But then, he was a weasel—of course he'd be careful.

William leaned over. "I'd shake your hand but . . ." He held up the cuffs.

The guard remained at the door, looking unimpressed. So was John.

"Sit."

"Ah, you mean there's no gun you're going to slip into my hand and aim at yourself this time? You know, I'm not a lousy shot. I could have killed you."

"You were too high to hit any mark other than the sky. I was just accidently in the way."

"Bullshit! I could have killed you. If I had, I probably wouldn't be here today. My old man would've gotten me off."

"Massachusetts doesn't like cop killers any more than Connecticut does. Ever think you might not be *here* at all had you killed me?"

The man smiled. John could see that the years of money made him feel invincible. And it appeared the money was still working its magic.

John wondered briefly how the funds were being smuggled in. How much was William Sr. paying to make sure his boy didn't end up someone's bitch, or worse? He threw the folder on the table and pushed it to William.

"Did you bring me some light reading?"

"Look at the damned clippings."

William opened the folder, spread the clippings across the table, and studied each one. He looked up. "You into child porn or something?"

John felt his jaw tighten. Out of the corner of his eye, he saw the guard slowly turn away. "Those are children who have been kidnapped. Know anything about who would be doing something like this?"

The man shrugged.

John lay down another article. "You know anything about the woman in this picture?"

"Nice babe. Looks like she's got a great ass."

"You might want to be careful. She's my wife."

"So what do you want?"

"You know anything about this?"

William laughed. It wasn't a pleasant sound. "Yeah. I fly out through the bars when it's about time to knock off some kid and I plan this big thing. Make them suffer, make her suffer. I'd like to see that. Tell me, you ever give it to her in the—"

He never got a chance to finish the sentence. John rose halfway, grabbed William by the shirt, pulled him up, and slammed him down into the chair, hard. "Look, you little mother fucker, if I find out you or your father are in any way a part of this, there won't be a hole deep enough for you to hide in. I will find you. In the meantime, what if I make sure it gets around that you give it to kids. You beat them until they're almost dead and then you screw them. Can your father's money protect you when that's discovered?"

William went white—and silent.

John sat back and glanced up at the guard. The man was still looking the other way.

"There have been five kidnappings. With my wife's knowledge of music, we've found each child before he or she died. Do you know anything about this? Do you know anyone who would do this?"

"Hey. You need to ask my old man. I never traveled in those circles."

"Really? You just beat up kids until they're almost dead?"

"I didn't know what I was doing!"

"You mean your son's screams couldn't cut through the fog of drugs."

William raised his head, not answering.

"I take it you're not going to say anything."

The man leaned forward and smiled. "Let's just say your interrogation tactics stink. Besides, I'm not afraid of you."

"You were afraid of me in the courtroom."

William Duncan Jr. sat back, staring silently into space.

It was over. John knew it. And he still didn't know a damned thing. He rose. "If I get even a hint that you're keeping something from me, I'll be back."

He was at the door when William spoke. "You never offered me a deal. What's in it for me?"

John turned. "Your life."

"Is that a threat?" William looked up at the guard. "You heard him. He threatened me. He physically abused me."

The large man glanced at John, then looked down at William. "I didn't hear or see a thing."

"It's being recorded."

The guard scratched his ear. "I'll have to check our machines. Sometimes those tapes just give out. Other times they don't work at all."

CHAPTER 8

Sara tightened the heavy shawl about her shoulders, feeling the sharp edge of the Thanksgiving evening. Glancing up from the front porch, she saw the bedroom light switch off. John's sister, Judy, must have finally gotten four-year-old Allen to sleep.

She'd left Joshua, the Caine's ten-year-old, mesmerized by an old Star Wars movie. Six-year-old Amanda had given up trying to keep a paper pilgrim's hat on a less-than-cooperative Max. In the end she had curled up on the couch and fallen asleep, the big dog at her side. John and Tom were still engrossed in an animated discussion in the dining room, probably about politics, as Tom was a Connecticut state senator.

Thanksgiving had been fun, filled with laughter, noise, good food, and family. John's sister and brother-in-law were great people and their children were wonderful. Nonetheless, the sudden silence was enjoyable.

Sara shivered. It wasn't the cold.

"Perfect night for a game, isn't it, Sara?" The guttural voice cut through her mind, leaving nausea in its wake.

"Damn you and your games to hell!" Her silent voice whipped through the cosmos.

"What? Don't you want to play?"

"Sara."

She whirled around, almost falling into John's arms. "He's going to strike again."

Holding her tight with one arm, he dug his cell phone out and flipped it open.

She leaned against him, listening to the solid thump of his heart and the familiar noise from the police station. He closed the phone. "Nothing yet. Do you have any sense of where, when?"

"No."

"It's cold out here. Let's go in."

Sara shivered, despite the warmth of the shawl and John's arm. It had touched her, a darkness descending on Milford, and it had nothing to do with the coming night.

Sara waved as Judy and Tom pulled away, then let the curtain drop. She didn't want to see the snow that was already piling up.

John seemed to read her thoughts. "They'll be fine. You just wanted them to stay so you could play with the kids and talk about babies."

"Partially." She had wanted them to stay. She wanted to tell them they weren't safe. But all that was stupid, and thinking such things was just giving power to evil. She smiled up at her husband. "For now, Mr. Allbrooke, you have a choice. Finish cleaning the kitchen or take Max out."

With a half laugh, he pushed her toward the kitchen, grabbed his coat—making sure the hidden pack of cigarettes was still there—and stepped into a world of black and white.

John took a deep drag, keeping his back to the house even though he knew it was useless. Sara would smell the smoke the instant he went inside. She wouldn't comment. She'd just give him that look. Sometimes it was worse than words.

He had wanted Tom to stay too—had tried to talk him into it.

Not because of the weather or the wine after dinner, but because of a feeling. Something had changed. The night didn't feel right. It didn't feel friendly.

He watched Max. The dog didn't seem to know anything was amiss. In the movies, the dog always knew. Not Max. Sara said he had ADD; John thought he was just dumb. Whatever—he was easily entertained. Snow, leaves, it was all something to play with.

John snubbed out the cigarette, field-stripped it, and gave a sharp whistle. Max came at once and sat in front of him, per his training. John lifted the shepherd's head with large, gentle hands and stared into his liquid brown eyes. "One day, pal, she's going to need you. Understand? And you'd damned well better be there."

John dropped his hands and looked around. Shit, he was talking to a dog. What in the hell was going on?

Sara wiped down the stove, keeping her mind open, waiting for the child. Nothing.

"Thought you were going to quit," John said, reading her body language, knowing her too well.

She kept working, feeling John's bulk behind her. "Habit. And I am. Definitely. Just watch." She dried her hands, turned to a grinning husband, and sniffed audibly.

"Yes. I had a cigarette. I love my sister, I love those kids, and Tom's like a brother to me . . . but God, the quiet is so nice. Please. Tell me when we have kids, it won't be that noisy."

She arched an eyebrow.

Snuggling beside John, Sara listened to his even snoring and waited.

"Help me."

She flung an arm out, hitting her husband with a solid thunk. He was awake instantly.

"What's wrong?"

Bitter cold. Rubber wrapped her naked body. She smelled plastic as she was tossed around. Darkness surrounded her.

Vaguely, she was aware of strong arms holding her. She pushed into the strength of John's body. But there was no warmth, no protection.

"Cold."

"Where are you, Sara?"

"Dark. I smell rubber."

"Can you move?"

"No. Wrapped in something."

John moved then, tucking a quilt around her and pulling her closer. He was grounding her as he spoke softly. "Stay with me, babe. You need to tell me more." Then he was talking to someone else. But there wasn't anyone else in the room.

The tapping, the small hammer in her head, increased its tempo. The edges of her vision swam, disintegrating. "I think he's in a car. In the trunk of a car." Her words were thick, hard to get out.

"Do you know where he's heading?"

"No."

"Can you connect with the kidnapper?"

She forced glued eyelids open to stare at her husband. He was making that request more often, but she understood his logic. The child couldn't know where he was going. The kidnapper would.

"I'll try." She closed her eyes. An essence like black oil touched her.

"Where are you taking him?"

"Play the game. I left a song."

There was a difference in the feeling. It was still black, still oily, but different. She struggled to open a visual link with the kidnapper, to see through his eyes, but the child drew her back to the darkness. He was frightened.

"We need to find the hymn," she whispered through gritted teeth. Tension hummed through her body.

"I'm going to the station." John put a phone in her hand. "Wait for my call, and don't get out of bed."

A cold draft told her he was gone. A whimper told her Max was close.

She went back in. She couldn't quit. The child's pull was too strong. She might be able to tell a parent she wouldn't help, but she couldn't tell a child. The boy's need was urgent and painful.

The roads were still clear but Tom Caine didn't trust the shiny, wet asphalt. This was Connecticut. Black ice was a major part of winter and something you rarely saw until it was too late.

"Maybe we should have stayed in Milford." Judy's voice was tight.

"It's not as bad as it looks, hon."

"Damn!" She touched his arm. "I forgot—we ran out of milk this morning. Is it too late to stop and get some?"

"No." He swung off I-95, drove a few blocks, and pulled into a small, almost empty parking lot. Leaving the engine running, he stepped into the half mush, half ice, and made his way into the convenience store.

It took him several minutes to locate the milk, a minute to choose the right size and kind, and ten minutes to get past the talkative cashier, a young girl who recognized the senator. Finally, he slid into the car and handed his wife the bag.

"Where's Joshua?" she asked.

Blankly, he looked up. "What?"

"He followed you into the store. I forgot we needed orange juice."

"We probably just missed each other. I'll get him." Tom Caine stepped back into the night.

The cashier was still leaning against the counter, popping gum and reading a celebrity magazine. She jerked up, smiling, when Tom pushed through the doors.

"Did you see a ten-year-old dark-haired boy come in?" he asked without preamble.

She shook her head.

His stomach fluttered as he turned down the main aisle and called Joshua's name. There was no answer. He was at the end of the aisle when the cashier shouted for him to check the restrooms. He gave a quick sigh and thanked her. Of course—he was being stupid. Joshua always had to use the restroom in a convenience store.

Tom opened the men's door and flipped on the lights. Nothing. Just to be sure, he checked the women's restroom. It too was empty. His voice rose as he paced the few aisles, calling for his son. All was quiet. There was no, "Here I am, Dad." Walking back to the front, he saw the cashier standing with a phone in her hand. His stomach fell.

"I think we should call the police, Senator Caine." She handed him the cell.

Numbly, he dialed 911. The unthinkable had happened. His son was missing.

Sara made her way down the stairs, keeping her mind open. She couldn't do as John requested and stay in bed. She would need the piano when he called back. And John would call.

Cell phone tight in her hand, she slumped onto the bench right as Gershwin's "Rhapsody in Blue" filtered through the room. She punched a button. "John."

"It's Joshua," he replied, his voice dangerously soft. "They stopped at a convenience store on the way home. Josh went in a few minutes after Tom and disappeared."

"Oh God. Have they found the song?"

"Are you playing the game?"

"I have to, John. It's your nephew. That's why the link was so strong. What are the notes?"

"E, F, E, D, D, E, E, D."

She picked them out as John spoke, varying the time. Nothing came. Changing keys, she tried again. Still nothing. "Damn."

"Take it easy, Sara. Don't get rattled, now. Concentrate."

"I am. It's not well known."

"What difference does that make?"

"Do you realize just how many hymns are out there? I can't talk and work. Call me back in a few minutes." She cut the connection.

She played the notes over and over, each time louder, each time faster. She ran through different keys, major then minor—nothing.

Her hands shook. She forced them back onto the ivory keys and began to run through the chords again. With two flats, the tune rang a bell.

She hummed the tune, words springing to mind.

Over life's tempestuous sea;
Unknown waves before me roll . . .

What was the name of the damned song? "Jesus, Savior, Pilot Me." The title sprang into her mind. She grabbed her hymnal, turning to the back. It wasn't that well known. It wouldn't be in the front.

Hymn 144. One hundred forty-four minutes. Over two hours. He'd never done that before. Was he changing the game? Sara punched in John's number. He picked up instantly.

"It's 'Jesus, Savior, Pilot Me.' Hymn one forty-four."

"Does that mean we have a hundred and forty-four minutes to find him?"

"That just went through my mind. I don't know. It's too much time. I have the feeling he's changing the game." As she spoke, she reread the lyrics. "Nothing stands out."

"Can you link with Joshua?"

She ignored the question. It was there for her to see. It had to be. She reread the first stanza.

Over life's tempestuous sea;
Unknown waves before me roll,
Hiding rock and treacherous shoal.

She glanced at the next verses.

As a mother stills her child,
Thou canst hush the ocean wild.

The first two lines popped out. "He's in the sea."

"Not good enough, Sara. Link. Now."

"John, stop playing detective."

"I can't," his voice softened. "I am a detective. And I need you to do exactly what I say. Try to link with Joshua. If he's in the sea, he's probably not blindfolded. He may see something."

She closed her eyes, calling his name. *"Joshua."*

"Cold. Can't breathe."

Her lungs constricted with pain. She could barely talk. "Where are you?"

"My name."

"Joshua."

"My name."

She cut the link before the cold rendered her incapable of speaking, and found herself listening to John's breathing.

"What did you get?"

"He's cold. He kept repeating 'my name.' Why didn't the bastard take Allen? He's never taken a child this old."

"Opportunity. Joshua was in the wrong place at the wrong time."

"He doesn't work that way. You know that, John. He plans everything carefully, like a hunter."

"None of that's important right now. We need something more. Can you link with the kidnapper again? See if he'll throw out more clues. Did he say it would be easy?"

"No. He hasn't really said anything." Her voice sounded distant, even to her. She punched the end-call button on the phone.

Closing her eyes, she called out. *"Where are you? Where have you taken Joshua?"*

"I'm busy, Sara. It's such a powerful thing, this holding of life and death."

"Bastard."

"You need to find another name to call me."

"That's not a problem."

"Listen to the boy." He cut the connection.

My name. The phrase ran through her mind again. She glanced down at the final stanza.

> *When at last I near the shore,*
> *And fearful breakers roar*
> *'Twixt me and the peaceful rest . . .*

The last lines felt important.

Staggering to the bookcase, Sara ran her hand along the line of books. At the Atlas, her hand tingled. Pulling the book out, she returned to the piano bench and bent over the map of Connecticut. Slowly, ever so slowly, her finger followed the coastline—then stopped, twitched. She stared down at the name and punched in John's number.

"It's the Thimble Islands. Joshua Point. That's why he kept saying 'my name.'"

"Christ, are you sure?"

She closed her eyes, briefly seeing through Joshua's. There was darkness, trees, water. She recognized it.

"I'm positive. You need to hurry. He's chained to something." Water—bitterly cold salt water gurgled in her throat. She couldn't breathe. She couldn't talk.

She looked out on high waves driven by the wind. They pushed against her, scraping, battering her, slamming her against the rocks. The chains held her while the water tried to free her. Her flesh was being torn from her body.

She dropped the phone, gulping air, the taste of salt choking her. *"You bas—"*

"You were too slow, Sara. This is the one you may lose."

She closed her eyes, looking for Joshua again. The thread of life was weak. *"Help is coming. Hold on. The bad man is gone,"* she chanted to the boy.

"No, he's not . . . he's here. He's still here! I can't breathe."

Blue fire flashed through her head. She felt herself slide off the bench, felt the thick rug cushion her body. The velvet black of nothingness welcomed her.

The song echoed throughout the room. With a moan, Sara turned her head, trying to ignore the pain. The faint light from the fireplace flared like a beacon, burning through her eyelids.

It was the phone.

Blindly, she felt around the rug. It had been on her lap. She found it. Squinting against the glare, she pushed the talk button.

"Have you got him?"

"I don't know. The state patrollers and cops out of New Haven are on it. Are you okay? You went out on me." His radio squawked in the background. "Hold on."

A few minutes later, John's voice was back. "They've found him. I'll call you when I get there."

She stayed on the floor, now warmed by Max's furry body. She focused on breathing through the pain of the headache. *Is there more than one eternity in a night?*

Her phone broke the silence. It would be, she knew, the last time. "Is he alive?"

"Barely. It doesn't look good, Sara."

She couldn't think of anything to say. Numbly, she hit the disconnect button and slipped into a dreamless, sterile void.

CHAPTER 9

Joe swung the old truck carefully around the bend, ignoring the pain in his head and the shaking of his hands. He could still hear his father taunting Sara. Somehow the old man always knew exactly what was going on when Joe took a child.

He had also guessed that Sara would be too tired to give them a good game. But the game wasn't really important tonight. Regardless of how Sara played it, Joshua Caine was supposed to die. Joe realized that now. The boy's kinship to Sara sealed his fate. Joshua's death was one more cog in the wheel that would crush Sara. That was his father's ultimate goal—destroy Sara Allbrooke.

Joe's hands tightened on the steering wheel. He had come close to killing tonight, urged on by his father's psychic voice. For the second time in his life, he had almost killed another child.

He could still feel the boy's pulse weakening beneath his fingers, hear the pounding of his own heart and his father's words. Then, everything had changed. Beneath his hands Joshua's face began to glow, the features melting, flowing, reforming into a new being, a new face.

Joe dropped hands that had gone numb and stumbled back into the water. The scent of Serafina was strong in the storm. He felt the strength of her hands as she stroked him, the satin of her flesh as she pressed hard against his body. Her voice was soft, a gentle whisper in his mind.

"You cannot do this thing."

He stared down at the boy struggling to survive, and his son's face stared back. It was his own son he was trying to kill.

Forcing oxygen into his lungs, he fought to clear his mind. When the voices were quiet, when his heart had stopped hammering, he knew what he must do. He couldn't kill the boy, but he couldn't let him live. His father might demand retribution—a life for a life. It could put his own son in danger.

Lifting his head to the black skies, the wail of a wounded animal tore from his throat.

Silence. For an instant, even the seas were calm. He opened his heart to the night and let darkness slip into his soul. Old knowledge seeped through his cold skin and ran singing through his blood. He had an answer. *Scatter his soul.* It was the only way to save Joshua Caine.

Staggering forward, he reached for the boy. His soul was young, and he was strong. He was frightened.

Joe's fingers tightened then loosened around the boy's throat, his mind focused. He fought the winds that pushed the seas and threatened to tear him from his goal. He fought the gentle voice that cried, and the dark voice that demanded complete death.

He took the boy to the edge of death, then let him have a short breath of life. He repeated this time and time again until he felt it. The soul was leaving, scattering into the winds. What was left would be a mindless shell of the boy called Joshua.

Joe appealed to the gods his father worshiped, then gave a final push, unprepared for the blinding light and pain that cut through his own mind.

It took long minutes for Joe's eyes to focus. He looked down at the still body, the open, vacant eyes. It was done. Joshua Caine was as though dead, his soul scattered to the universe. This was the only way Joe could save his body.

But someone could save his soul. They could gather the soul

strands and put them back. This mindless idiot could once again become a normal, functioning boy. Joe knew it, because once, a gifted man had gathered the strands of Joe's soul and put them back into his body. He'd gone from a catatonic state to a normal boy.

Turning, Joe weakly climbed the slimy rocks and teetered through the driving rain toward the trees. The police would find nothing, no tracks, no evidence; only the shell of a child floating, still alive, in the roiling waters of the sea.

Hidden by trees, he waited, knowing that if help didn't come soon, he would have to loosen the chains and drag the body onto the rocks. They had to find Joshua alive.

Lights broke through the night; sirens rose above the howl of the storm. Minutes later, men swarmed over the point. Joe waited until they lifted the still form, then melted into the night. The storm and the chaos would cover his escape.

He made it to the old truck without attracting any attention. With lights out, he started the engine and slowly moved into the storm.

At the road, he turned, joining a flow of traffic heading north. Then he turned west, traveling for over an hour before turning south toward West Virginia. It was best to avoid the large cities. He just hoped he could make it home. He was exhausted.

Flipping the truck's heater up, he clamped his jaw shut, trying to control the clinking of his teeth. He couldn't seem to get warm. Adrenaline—that's what was causing the shaking, that was all. But he knew better. He was terrified of what he had done and afraid of what his father would say when he found out the boy still lived. But who was he kidding? His father already knew what had happened.

Joe pressed down on the gas pedal. He needed to find somewhere to hide, at least for a while. He needed to give the old man time to realize he hadn't failed.

Had he failed? Would the boy live? Had he truly managed to scatter the boy's soul? Where did the dark thoughts, the power, the knowledge come from? It was evil. Only pure evil could do what he had just done. He had never tried to do anything like this.

His mind stopped. That wasn't exactly true; once before, he had touched someone, a young girl. It was an accident, but he remembered the darkness descending on him, and then her soul scattered like the dying leaves from a tree, and he looked into eyes that were blank. Like Joshua, the mind was there, but not the soul. Would the old man understand?

A half sob tore from Joe's throat. The pain. He shook his head, working hard to keep the truck straight on the icy road. Sara's probes sometimes caused pain, but not like this—and he could still hear Serafina's admonition, still see the face of his son. At least he could honestly tell her he hadn't killed the child.

He pulled off the road, killing the engine and lights once the truck stopped. Reaching into the glove compartment, he pulled out a bottle of aspirin, popped six into his mouth, and chewed the bitter tablets, letting his mind rest, calming his thoughts.

He could drive to New Orleans. It was a long way, but he could see his boy, make sure he was all right. Joe nixed the idea almost as soon as it came. That would make the old man really mad, and it could put his son in even greater danger.

He pulled back onto the road. There was a motel close. He'd stay the night, listen to the radio, and hope to find out how Joshua Caine was. Then he would return home and explain it all to his father.

He took a deep breath. The pain was receding but something still bothered him, something beyond what he'd done. Sara. Her energy had been different, cautious. In his mind, he replayed each scene, each thought from her, then smiled. So that's what was going on. Sara wasn't tired. His father had been wrong. Did Malachi know? Of course he knew. He knew everything . . . but maybe, just maybe, he didn't know this.

Joe stared at the road, praying to see the lights of the motel soon. There was a blackness to the dark, a blackness that seemed to roll over him, coating him like dirty oil. What difference did it all make? The bottom line was that nothing mattered anymore.

He was evil, like his father said. He didn't have a choice in his life. He never really had.

Sara stood alone on the rocks of Joshua Point, ignoring the cold winds that stung her face. Water slapped harshly against the shore like obscene applause for an evil that had once again won. Closing her eyes, she went as deep as she could, digging her fingers into Max's fur. He was her shield, her grounder, her touch with reality.

She went deep, deeper than she ever had, and found nothing, not even a whisper of the kidnapper. The only thing she felt was loss. A part of Joshua's soul was gone.

She reached upward, seeking to find anything that was her nephew. Bitter loneliness and betrayal met her. Like children everywhere, he'd expected the adults in his life to protect him. They had failed. She had failed.

Max quivered beneath her hand. She opened her eyes and took a deep breath, knowing full well who stood behind her.

"Hello, John."

He slipped his arms around her waist, pulling her back against him. "So much for resting. I figured you'd be here. Get anything?"

"Yes. Failure."

He nuzzled her ear, his voice gentle. "You didn't fail, Sara. Joshua's alive."

"Really?"

John remained silent.

"I know your people are still combing the area, but I need a few moments alone here. Can you arrange that?"

"Only if you promise me it'll be just a few minutes. You need rest."

She nodded.

Lips softly touched the top of her head; then he was gone.

She stared at the leaden skies and the murky waters of the

Sound. Opening her soul, she dove into the loneliness of the cold winds and colder seas.

Sara had no idea how long she had been standing there when she felt Max tense beneath her hand. Someone was coming, and it wasn't her husband.

She straightened up, throwing her weight onto the balls of her feet, ready to move quickly if need be. Silence met her senses. Dropping her hand from the dog's fur, she whirled to face the trespasser.

Samuel Hawk stood not more than five feet away, the collar of his heavy sheepskin coat pulled up, a cowboy hat jammed tight onto his head.

For a brief second, Sara again felt waters rising around her, tasted the bitterness of salt. Glancing down at Max, she was surprised to see his tongue lolling out as though he were meeting an old friend.

She looked up, hating the quiver in her voice. "What are you doing here?"

"I heard about the boy on the news this morning. I needed to see where it happened." He looked around. "I've been here for quite a while."

"Why?"

He shrugged.

"Is Sam Hawk related to you?"

"He is my son. And no, neither of us is involved in any of this. Nor, as I told you before, am I a voyeur." He looked beyond her. "My son hasn't spoken to me in over five years. He went to prison for beating a man who was beating a horse. While he was there, his wife died in labor. So did his baby son. He blames me."

His eyes fell back on her. "How is the boy?"

"He'll live. But they think he may have suffered some brain damage. It may be permanent. The doctors aren't sure yet. You still haven't told me why you're here."

"I felt the boy's spirit last night. It called for help. You felt him too, didn't you?"

"What are you, a medicine man or something?"

"Or something." He smiled, then sobered. "What are you feeling just now, Sara?"

"Loss. Failure. Water. Drowning."

"The failure is from your mind. The water and drowning from your gift. The loss," his voice softened, "is from the boy. His soul has been scattered. He is not damaged. He is lost."

"He was underwater too long, Mr. Hawk. He's brain-damaged."

"You don't believe me. Go see the boy. Judge for yourself." He half turned, glancing back toward the path. "Your husband is coming. Good day." With a quick nod, he stepped off the rocks to the water's edge. Following the shore, he turned, sliding gracefully into the trees.

A few minutes later, John stepped beside her. "Was that who I think it was?"

"Yes."

"What'd he want?"

"To see where the boy—" She stopped, caught her breath and continued. "He said he heard Joshua's cry last night and that Joshua's soul has been 'scattered.'"

"Yeah, right. Sam Hawk and I are going to have a little talk later on. Are you sure you're all right?"

"I'm fine."

"No you're not." He turned her to face him, then pulled her into his arms. "You're exhausted. You need to rest, you need to go home." He hesitated. "I just got a call from Tom. Joshua's woken up."

"I need to see them."

"I don't think that's a good idea, Sara."

"I do."

John gave in with a soft sigh. "All right. I'll drive. Ed can drop my car off at the station."

Sara now understood the meaning of "hollow footsteps." Hers

seemed to echo through the corridors of the Yale New Haven Children's Hospital.

Outside Joshua's room, doctors gathered, speaking in hushed tones. They fell silent as Sara and John approached.

John flashed his badge. "I'm Detective Allbrooke. I'm also Joshua's uncle. How is he doing?"

One of the physicians, an older man, shook his head. "He's sustained permanent damage, both motor and memory."

"Are you telling me he won't remember the kidnapper?"

The doctor shook his head. "He probably won't recognize his own parents."

"Countless children have been under water for longer than Joshua and survived without permanent injury. What happened?" Sara's harsh voice filled the hall.

The doctor's face flushed with sympathy. "You're right. Some children have been under water for an absurd amount of time and not sustained any permanent damage. Others . . . well, others seem more fragile. As for what's happened or why, we really don't have answers right now. There's still a lot of 'practice' in medicine, and there's a lot about the individual human brain and makeup that we still don't understand. We've scheduled further tests, but my gut as a physician tells me the damage is fairly extensive."

Sara pulled on John's arm. "I need to see Judy."

The doctors parted.

Joshua lay still under white blankets, staring blankly at nothing. A dozen monitors kept a steady beep.

Sara probed deeply and quickly. Joshua was gone.

Judy sat next to the bed, rocking methodically back and forth, her hands limp in her lap. Tom leaned across the bedrail, encouraging his son to return. He looked up as they entered. Sara caught her breath; in the space of one night, the man had aged a lifetime.

"Did you find the son of a bitch?"

John shook his head.

The man's gaze rested on Sara. He started to speak, then seemed to think better of it and returned to his vigil.

Judy stopped rocking. Like a badly jointed marionette, she rose. The wires snapped. Her hands came up like claws, her face distorted into a horrible mask of rage as she rushed toward Sara.

John moved faster. Stepping in front of his wife, he grabbed his sister's hands and forced them down. Tom reacted almost as quickly, grabbing his wife from behind, pinning her to his body.

"You bitch!" Judy's screech filled the room. "You saved all those other children. Why didn't you save Joshua?"

"Judy, I tried. The kidnapper never left. I didn't catch the clues soon enough."

"You're a goddamned psychic. You're supposed to know these things. Why didn't you at least warn us?"

"Just because I'm a psychic doesn't mean I know everything. If I had had the slightest idea something was going to happen, I'd have told you." Sara stopped. The room fell silent. Her mind swirled with unspoken truths. He'd warned her it was a good night to strike. Sara had known before Judy and Tom left that another child would be taken. And maybe, God help her, she'd known deep down that he was going to strike the family.

Judy saw the guilt. Glaring daggers at Sara, she shook her husband off. "You were jealous. That's why you did nothing. You envied me my children because you can't have any. You're evil. You killed my son's soul." Judy glared at John. "And you're just as bad. You married the bitch. As of this day, I have no brother."

Before John could reply, Judy turned away.

Sara stared at the woman she had once called a friend. Judy hadn't accused her of killing Joshua, but of killing his "soul." Maybe Samuel Hawk was right. Had Joshua's soul been scattered? Could such a thing happen?

Numbly, Sara turned and walked out the door. John followed her. There was nothing more she could do, nothing more she knew how to do. She glanced back as they turned down the corridor.

Neither Judy nor Tom had moved. Did Samuel Hawk know what to do? Was that why he'd gone to the site?

Sara stopped at the car as her husband opened the door. Looking up into his soft brown eyes, she shook her head. "No more. I quit. I helped this time because it was your nephew, and I failed. No more. I'm sorry, John, but you are on your own now. With the music, with . . . everything." Silently, she slipped into the seat.

John drove with one hand, holding Sara's hand with the other, his mind torn between the scene at the hospital, the conversation at the car, and something else—something he couldn't put his finger on, but it had been bothering him all night. He turned down Elm Street, releasing Sara's hand to wave at the next-door neighbor as she drove past in her green Jeep.

He hit the brakes just shy of the garage. Green. The night before, as he was heading back from the scene of the crime, his lights had hit a green Rover. It had passed as he'd turned onto the road from Joshua Point. In fact, he'd followed it all the way back to Milford. It had turned a block before John turned onto Elm Street.

He blinked, trying to recall the license plate, a habit that years of law enforcement had ingrained in him. The last three numbers came to mind, as did several other things. One, the conversation he'd had a month before with the captain about Caleb Remington, and two, Caleb drove a green Rover. In fact, he supposedly had a fleet of them.

John needed to call the office as soon as he had Sara settled in. Damn. What if it was Caleb's car?

CHAPTER 10

John was in deep shit and there was no way around it.

"You've got a call."

Nodding to the sergeant, he slipped into his office, shutting the door against the noise of the station. It had been a damned long day, and the only thing he had to show for it was a knee that hurt like hell.

"John Allbrooke here."

"It's Tom. You ever answer your cell phone?"

There was a brief, uncomfortable silence.

"You still there, John?"

"Yeah. Sorry, my damned knee's acting up again—it hurts like hell. And my cell phone keeps cutting out. How's everything going?"

"That's one of the reasons I called. Final test results came back today on Josh." Tom's voice broke. "It doesn't look good. We'll be able to potty train him, maybe, teach him some simple speech; not much beyond that."

"I'm so sorry, Tom. How's Judy?"

"She's gone somewhere in her mind. I can't reach her. She focuses on Josh twenty-four seven. I think she's forgotten she has two more children and a husband."

"I—" Both men spoke at the same time.

John stopped. "Go ahead."

"I need to give you a heads-up. Judy's talking about speaking with the press."

"Tom, you've got to stop her. The captain, Sara's boss, and you and Judy are the only ones who know she does more than just look at music. Are you going to use your clout to help my sister, or Sara? She can't take another New York."

Tom snorted. "I'm not stupid, John. And I don't have a vendetta against your wife. Judy wishes I did. I'll try to keep her quiet, but you know your sister once she makes up her mind about something. And she's convinced Sara purposely waited too long to help Joshua. Frankly, if you can keep Sara working with the police, I think she is your only hope of catching this maniac—and that's no reflection on your police work."

"Thanks for that, Tom. I agree. But after tonight, it may not be that easy."

"Why?"

"I'm calling her brother back in for further questioning."

Tom whistled softly. "Sara's not going to like that. She was pretty pissed the first time you brought him in."

"Yeah. Go figure. But they don't know each other. Hell, they weren't even raised together."

"But the bottom line is that he's her brother."

Sara shuffled the papers, studied them, and shuffled them again. It was a game, one she hated playing. But her actions and Rachael Duncan's own nerves kept the tall, slender woman perched on the edge of her chair. That appealed to Sara.

She stopped her hands, the notes in place, although there would be no real need to refer to them. "Billy's doing very well, despite the incident with the substitute," Sara began. "In fact, I think he's made a break-through of sorts. He's beginning to act, rather than react. And he's relating better to the other students in small ways. That's an exceptional step forward. Regarding homework, he has good days and days he goofs off, much like any other normal seven-year-old. Is there anything you'd like to say?" Not "ask," but "say." Sara had used the word purposely.

Rachael licked her lips, betraying her nervousness. Her dark brown eyes flitted around as if looking for a friend or savior. When she spoke, her voice was very soft. "No. No, I can't think of anything."

"Billy's a sensitive boy, Mrs. Duncan. Love and understanding will take him further than discipline and negligence."

"Are you saying . . .?"

Sara's green eyes pinned the woman's brown ones.

"Just because you had him for a few months as a baby, Mrs. Allbrooke, doesn't mean you know him or own him."

"I know him because I teach him. As for owning him, he's not a commodity, a desk or a chair, he's a human being."

Rachael rose. "And he's my son."

"Then treat him like a son."

Rachael's eyes flashed, her face reddening, matching the carrot-colored hair that now almost stood up straight. She half rose and leaned forward, slapping her hands on the desk.

"Why you . . ."

Never flinching, Sara leaned farther forward, her firm voice low and cold. "You better pray that I never have to make a choice between helping a child and holding on to my job."

"Are there any problems here?"

Rachael whirled around to face St. Mary's principal.

Anne Stockton stood straight, a quizzical yet knowing expression on her face. "Anything I can help you with, Mrs. Duncan?"

"No," Sara spoke up, "she was just leaving. Good evening, Rachael."

Sara watched Rachael stalk away, then leaned back in her chair, her voice barely a whisper, "Oh, shit. I think I just told Rachael, in a roundabout way, that I'm working with the police."

"It wasn't roundabout, Sara. You told her. I just hope she was mad enough to forget it." Anne suddenly smiled. "Don't worry. If it comes up anywhere, I'll just tell people you were angry and not paying attention to what you were saying."

"Thank you." Anything else Sara might have said was interrupted as the strains of "Rhapsody in Blue" filled the air. She reached for her phone, glanced at the caller ID, and felt her heart drop into her stomach. It wasn't like John to call her in the middle of something as important as the parent-teacher conferences.

Sara pushed the button to connect the call. "John. Are you all right?"

"I'm fine. I just wanted to give you a heads-up . . . Oh hell, Sara, there's no easy way to say this. We picked up Caleb a few hours ago. We're re-interviewing him."

For a few minutes, there was silence. When she finally spoke, her voice was cold enough to freeze the hinges of hell. "I'll be right there."

Before he could say anything, she cut the connection.

Caleb Remington was every inch a gentleman and a man in absolute control.

John and his young partner O'Brien had picked him up unannounced at the Remington summer home in Milford. Despite the secretary's comment that Mr. Remington was on vacation, the man had come to the door dressed for a business meeting. *Maybe there's a leak in the department*, John mused to himself, and decided to pursue that later.

Even more strange, Caleb forwent the presence of his attorney. The man was either stupid as hell, innocent as the angels, or just damned arrogant. John was betting on arrogance—and just maybe, this time, it was his weakness.

"Take him to the basement interview room," John ordered the younger detective when they reached the precinct. "I'll be there in a moment."

O'Brien nodded and led Caleb into a small room that boasted two chairs, a scarred desk, and four concrete walls. Caleb calmly sat down before the detective could order him to, then looked up at the man. It was as though he were waiting for the curtain to rise on the next act of a Broadway play.

John watched the scene through the one-way window, absently thumbing through the file he held. He was letting O'Brien handle this part of the interrogation, for the experience.

"Can you verify where you were on these dates?" the detective asked as he turned a piece of paper around for Caleb to see.

Caleb studied the paper, then hesitated, that kind of hesitation that had earned him a lethal reputation in the boardroom. When he finally spoke, his voice was decisive. "Regarding the first date, I was at the office. My secretary can verify that. The second date, I was visiting a friend."

"Can anyone confirm the second date?"

"My friend can. I'll give you his name and address. He is, however, out of the country for the next three weeks."

"That's convenient."

Caleb remained silent.

Frank O'Brien followed the methodology of how to conduct an interrogation to the letter. Thirty minutes later, he was nowhere. He glanced up at the window, the shake of his head barely discernable.

John rose. It was time to take over. Walking into the interview room, he signaled O'Brien to leave. As the door closed behind the young detective, John threw the file on the table.

Nonplussed, Caleb looked at it, then raised cold green eyes to John. "Good cop, bad cop. I take it you're the bad cop."

"Let's say I'm the cop with some knowledge you've not shared with us."

"I have actually been wondering when you were going to call me in."

"What do you mean?"

"From what I have read in the newspapers, you have nothing. The only thing left is to recall slighted boyfriends or family members and see if you can trip them up. I do fall into one of those categories."

"So you don't mind coming in again?"

"I didn't say that. I am surprised you didn't do the initial questioning."

"Sometimes I like to watch." John glanced purposely down at the file, his voice barely a whisper. "I know what you are. I know who you are. And what isn't written down in that file, I can imagine. I have a very good imagination. I spent four years in the army; never had much to do with black ops, but I know there isn't anything you guys can't or won't do. You're more than adequately trained to pull off these kidnappings and not get caught."

"Yes, I could, but I didn't. I am not the man you're looking for."

John leaned on the desk. "So what were you doing on the Thimble Islands on Thanksgiving?"

"Visiting a friend, as I told your partner."

"We're well aware of your paramours. You seem to have a different woman on your arm every time a camera clicks for the society page."

Caleb shrugged. "I like women. But the friend I visited is male."

"We'll check it out. But if I ever catch the slightest hint that you're even remotely involved in all of this, I'll kill you before anyone else can get to you."

At the threat, Caleb's eyes darkened, then cleared. For a moment, the two men simply stared at each other.

"I assume, then, that I'm free to go?"

John straightened. "Frank has a few more questions."

He left the room and nodded at the young detective who waited beside the door. "Re-ask some of your pertinent questions. See if we get the same answers. I'll close the interview when you're done."

"John." He heard the click of Sara's heels a split second before he heard her voice. He turned around, never realizing his name could sound like a curse.

Her face was set, her dark eyes flashing pure green fire. She was mad, damned mad.

"Anyone give you any trouble upstairs, hon?"

"One young cop decided to get in the way."

"Oh Lord, that would be Russ. Is he still alive?"

"More or less. Why did you bring Caleb in again?"

"We are not singling him out, Sara. We will be re-interviewing a lot of people."

"Caleb's not 'people.' He's my brother."

"Yes, and he's a perfect suspect. A loner, intelligent, family member. And because the two of you were raised apart, he could have some kind of an ax to grind, something you don't know anything about."

"You were wrong then and you're wrong now. Besides, what makes you think you'll get anything different this time?"

"It's been awhile. Things happen. People get confident, superior, and that's usually about the time they make a fatal mistake. Brother or not, you don't know Caleb that well."

"I know him well enough to know he's not a violent man."

"That's not what the army says."

She glared at him, lips tight in silence.

"He trained at Fort Benning, Georgia, and spent four years active duty. He's still a reservist. Where were you then?"

"Mother told me he was out of the country. I assumed he was going to school or running one of our foreign offices."

"Sara, he was on the Thimble Islands when Joshua was taken. I saw his car as we were driving back."

"And this is the first time you tell me. If he was there, he had a damned good reason."

"Then we need to find out what that reason was."

She turned away. "Tell my brother I'll be waiting upstairs. I'll see *you* later."

John listened to the repeated questions. Caleb never deviated from his original answers. Twenty minutes later, O'Brien walked out, shrugged, and shook his head.

"Go get a cup of coffee, Frank, you've earned it. I'll close."

John walked back into the interview room, shutting the door soundly behind him. Caleb still sat calmly, watching the man carefully as he entered.

"You know the routine, Remington. In your case, don't try to leave the country."

Silently, Caleb rose to his full six foot four inches and held out his hand, his moss-green eyes like his hand hard and steady.

Surprised, John took it. He was even more surprised at the man on the other side of the handshake.

"I hope we meet under better circumstances next time, John. Give my love to Sara."

"You can do that yourself. She's waiting upstairs."

John studied the man as he walked away. Good looks and a net worth of twenty million or so made Caleb a first-class lady killer. But did it make him a kidnapper? John shrugged and turned back to his office. Either way, the man was dangerous.

Four years, and a lifetime separated Sara from her younger brother. She watched as Caleb walked up the stairs, heading for the doors. Seeing her, he changed direction.

Where she was small, fair, with curly red hair and freckles splattered across her nose, Caleb favored the dark Celts. Dark mahogany hair framed hard-cut, yet distinguished features. His lean frame towered over her, moss-green eyes staring down with some indefinable emotion.

"Are you all right, Caleb?"

He nodded almost imperceptibly.

"I never suspected this would happen again, you being called in," Sara said softly.

"You mean John didn't tell you?"

"Not until about forty minutes ago. According to John, you were at the summer house. Can I give you a lift home?"

"Thanks."

They drove in silence, the twenty minutes to his residence seeming like an eternity of unspoken thoughts and feelings. It was hard, Sara mused to herself, to know where to start.

She edged the jeep past the ice ruts and pulled up in front of the large, rambling Cape Cod that had been the Remington's summer house for as long as she could remember. From what she could see in the porch lamp's soft light, little had changed.

"Would you like a cup of coffee?" Caleb leaned down from the half-open door.

She hesitated. Memories flooded back, some good, many not so good.

"There are no ghosts, Sara. You're safe."

"I'll need to call John."

"Call him from the house. It'll be warmer."

She followed in silence, her mind a whirl of thoughts. Beyond a few letters, forms, and the perfunctory cards during holidays, Sara had to admit that she knew little about her brother. Any closeness they had as children was shattered the day Sara was sent away to live with their grandmother.

It was, however, logical that Caleb should be the executor of their grandmother's will; after all, their father had trained him to run the family business. He'd continued as head of the company when their parents died.

Sara had decided early on that she wanted nothing to do with the Remington business or money, and to that end, she'd signed over her voting power to Caleb. Any monies her shares made were sent back to her brother.

He took her coat. "You can wait in the front room or join me in the kitchen." His soft voice brought her back to the present.

"I'm more of a kitchen girl."

He smiled. "Good. Irish coffee?"

"Light on the whiskey, heavy on the cream." She gave a half shrug. "Cop's wife. It may only be a couple of blocks, but I still have to drive home."

The kitchen took her breath away. Changes had been made. Gone were the old maple cabinets and cast-iron AGA cooker. A six-burner stove with double ovens sat in a sea of gray granite counters. Sleek white cabinets lined the walls. A built-in espresso machine sat in a niche next to two large refrigerators.

"Told you the ghosts were gone," Caleb said, a smile in his voice.

Sara perched on a stool and rested her elbows on the cool granite. "John would kill for this, especially the coffee machine."

"You've got the money for it."

"That's Remington money, you should know. I sent it all back to you."

"And I placed it in a savings account in your name. You're still a Remington, Sara, like it or not." He seemed to hesitate for a moment, then continued. "You shouldn't have worried about me tonight. I knew I'd be called back in. I purposely shifted my schedule so I could be here."

"One of your 'friends' give you a heads-up?"

"No. I knew. The same way you know things, or at least the way you used to know things."

It took Sara a full minute to take in what he had said, and another minute to find her voice. "I still have the gift—but you . . . you're gifted?"

Caleb nodded.

"Impossible. The Slane gift only passes to the female." She leaned forward. "You *are* male, aren't you?"

"Very. No problems at all in that department," he added drily, grinning. "And you're wrong. Several male ancestors possessed a gift. The men don't pass the talent down to their children like the women do. I am precognitive." He pushed the cup of Irish coffee to her.

Sara found it difficult to hide her shock. "How long have you had it?"

"As long as I can remember."

"But who? How?"

Caleb smiled. "Remember Maggie, our cook-cum-housekeeper -cum-nanny?"

Sara nodded. A ghostly scent of fresh-baked scones suddenly filled her nostrils. Maggie had made the best scones and frequently snuck the delicacies to Sara and Caleb.

"Maggie discovered it. And with her Irish forwardness, she had no trouble telling Mother the way it was. With Mom's help, Maggie taught me how to handle the gift and keep it quiet."

"In other words, Mom didn't want our father to know about it."

He nodded.

"That was more than she did for me."

His lips compressed into a hard, thin line. "I didn't go around with bleeding cuts and massive bruises."

"You were lucky." Sara took a sip of the hot coffee, tasting nothing.

"Maybe," Caleb agreed, "but I don't think Nana taught you under the constraints Mother was forced to follow."

Crystal clinked on the granite counter as Sara set the glass down. "Don't expect me to feel sorry for our mother. She tossed me away when I was eight."

"She sent you to her mother, to Nana, because she knew it was the only place you could be taught safely. It haunted her her whole life. It also left me with half a mother, a grandmother who couldn't see past you, and a father who—I know we will both agree—was a cold, heartless bastard."

The air was getting too thick. Sara started to push the chair back but Caleb's hand stopped her. "Don't run, Sara. We need to talk, and now. There's a lot I need to tell you, and I am the only one who can. We are the only family left."

"I am not running anywhere. And what do we have to talk about? I was the pariah. I was sent away because Mother didn't want me to upset our father, and he couldn't stand me. You were the chosen one, the good son. I was—"

"You were what you were supposed to be, a Slane female with a hereditary gift." He hesitated. "Do you just find the music for the police or are you using your gift?"

It was Sara's turn to hesitate. Her work with the police, with John, was supposed to be a secret. John's captain, her principal, and Tom and Judy Caine were the only ones to know what she actually did; although tonight at the conferences, she had almost given the secret away to Rachael. Sara shuddered. If Rachael put two and two together, it could be dangerous for her, for John, maybe even for the children she'd try to save if she continued to use the gift.

But Caleb was her brother, her only living relative. She remembered the sturdy little boy who followed her everywhere, the times she openly defied her father and protected Caleb, the way he cried when she left. Caleb was her family.

"I use the gift. To the kidnapper, it's a game; he even calls it that. He taps into my mind, gives me clues that explain the clues in the music. It's confusing to explain, I know, but I need what he says to find the children in time."

"Can you control him?"

"Not really. Sometimes I think I am, but I'm not certain. I want to stop playing. If I stop, maybe he will. But on Thanksgiving . . . it was John's nephew the maniac took." Her eyes fell to the swirls of cream over the dark coffee—foam on a stormy sea. "I was late. I was too slow, too tired to catch the clues . . ." Her voice trailed off.

"There was nothing you could have done. Pure evil is at work here. Pure, practiced evil."

"No. He's just a sick monster, a psycho, nothing else."

Caleb studied her for a few moments before speaking. "You don't have a clue as to what I'm talking about when I talk about evil, do you?" Frowning, he stepped back and leaned against the far counter. "Grandmother—Nana, never taught you about evil? She never trained you at all, did she? She just expected you to use the gift and cope with whatever you came across."

"What are you talking about?"

"There are ways. Ways you can use your gift but still protect yourself, still have control. Nana never taught you any of those things, did she?"

"No. For God's sake, I work with children. Children aren't evil."

"There are a lot of psychiatrists who would disagree with that today."

Sara slid off the seat. The thought that a child could be evil was upsetting. Bad, yes. Children could be bad, but evil? Never. "That's not important right now. I . . . I am handling this. But Caleb, you're precognitive. That means you see something before it happens."

He nodded.

"You could work with the police. You could warn them when a child is about to be taken."

"It doesn't work that way. And I can't work with the police."

"Why not? That's what this damned gift is all about—helping others."

"No one knows about my abilities, and I'd just as soon it remain that way."

"Abilities, plural?"

Caleb hesitated. "I'm also an empath, though not a strong one."

"You feel things?"

"I sometimes get images, impressions from touching someone or something. But no one can know about this."

"Not even John?"

"Especially not John."

"Then you're willing to let a child die?"

"No one's died yet. You've found them in time."

"And you're businessman enough to know the law of averages is against me."

"You'll—" he stopped.

The hair on the back of Sara's neck rose. *What has he seen? What does he know?* For minutes, they stared at each other.

"I need to get home." Sara was out of the chair before Caleb could move. He caught her at the closet and pulled her around. A stunned look flashed across his face.

"You're an empath as well."

She stepped back. "No. I don't get feelings or visions by touching people or things."

"Really? You don't feel what happens to those kids?"

"No, Caleb, I *become* the child. I see through their eyes, feel through their skin. If they're hurt or cold, so am I. If they're beaten, choked, molested . . ." She stopped. "That's why I get bruises and marks. You say I'm facing evil that I need to stop. Okay, you know what happens to me. Help me stop it. Help me help the police."

"No."

"Are you afraid the business world will find out how you really make your money?"

A wry smile crossed his face. "One of our ancestors tried that. He was burned at the stake as a witch. You can thank Harvard for my business acumen. But no, I'm not comfortable with the business world knowing of my peculiarities."

Grabbing her coat from Caleb's waiting hands, she shrugged into it. The conversation was over. He wasn't going to help.

Sara's hand was on the doorknob when she stopped. She had to try one more time. "For centuries, Slane women have used the gift to help others, often at the risk of their own life. I hate what I am. I loathe what I go through, but I save lives most of the time. That's what this so-called gift is about. If I could, I'd stop it, pass it on, destroy it, leave it behind."

She faced him. "John said you were in the army. Is that true?"

"Yes. I was black ops. I've done things even you can't imagine. But because I went in as a grunt, because I didn't ask Father to pull in any favors or rely on the Remington name, he stopped speaking to me. He held that silence until I left the military."

"He was never quiet with me. He once called me a freak, an abomination. He's the reason I got dumped on Nana. But then you already knew that. You would think it would have forged a bond between us."

She was down the steps and at the gate when she stopped again. "Your talents, your training, they would be an asset to the Milford police."

"Yes."

She waited. Nothing. He wasn't going to change his mind. "You really are a bastard."

"You're not the first person to call me that."

"What were you really doing at Joshua Point?"

"I was visiting a friend, a man Maggie introduced me to years ago. He's been a mentor, a teacher, ever since. Something did draw me to Joshua Point that evening on my way back to Milford. A soul was hurt. Joshua Caine isn't brain damaged; his soul has been scattered. Sara, answer me one question. How do you do it? How do you go through everything and keep your sanity?"

"I have John."

Sara pulled into her driveway, cut the engine, and leaned her head against the steering wheel. *His soul has been scattered.* Samuel had used those same words. What kind of people were they? It didn't sound strange coming from Samuel, but from her brother. Somehow, CEO and psychic just didn't seem to mesh.

John was right about one thing. Sara didn't know her brother. He was right about something else too. Caleb Remington was a violent man.

"Got a minute?"

Captain Lyle Parker looked up and beckoned. "Come on in, John. Grab a coffee."

The captain's coffee looked strong enough to float a horse, shoes and all. But John took a cup; it was what he needed this morning. Whatever had transpired between Caleb and Sara the night before had left his wife in a lousy mood and wanting to talk. In short, it had been a night of little sleep.

Gratefully, John sat and rubbed his knee, trying to loosen the ache brought on by the cold.

"Knee bothering you?"

John nodded. "Sometimes I have the feeling that I'm getting too old—" he looked hard at the captain, "—that *we're* getting too old for this shit."

"Today I'd agree with that. Heard it didn't go down well with Remington last night."

"No. I did take his drinking glass down to the lab for a DNA sample."

"What we need is the kidnapper's DNA."

"Yeah, I know. But I've got a feeling about this."

"Something else is bugging you. What is it?"

"I had Luke run a sketch through the computer a while back. It was a man I saw at Charles Island. It seems, though, that Sara's seen him at three of the crime scenes. I think there could be a connection—"

"There is."

John turned at the voice and found himself staring at the man he'd drawn.

"John," the captain gestured toward the man, "I'd like you to meet Samuel Hawk, retired detective from the Navajo reservation in Arizona. These days, I'm told, he sometimes works as a consultant for them. He's asked to work with us on the kidnapping cases."

"Have you been stalking my wife?"

"Let's say . . . I have been following her."

"Why?"

"The information that came back from your computers is about my son. He was arrested years ago for beating a man and served several years in prison."

"That's the information we got. Why do you want to work with us?"

Hawk pointed to the chairs. "May I sit?"

At Captain Parker's nod, Samuel pulled up a chair, sat down, and began to speak. "Four years ago, our reservation was hit by a kidnapper. He would take a child and leave clues—play a game, if you will. Five of the six children were found alive. The sixth, a young girl, was murdered. I think this same person is now taking children in Milford."

"What makes you think that?" the captain asked.

Samuel glanced at him. "He used songs, our songs, to give the clues, and he was a white man."

John looked at his captain, then turned back to Samuel. "How do you know he was white?"

"We found one set of footprints left behind—purposely, I think—at the last scene. They belonged to a white man. The similarities between the cases are too close not to consider the possibility that it's the same person. Has Sara ever been to Arizona?"

John shook his head. "No. But according to our research, Caleb Remington owns property in Tucson and flies down occasionally."

"Who is Caleb Remington?"

"Sara's brother. Were you following her because you thought she might be connected to the kidnapper?"

The old man hesitated. Would John and the captain understand his quest? He shrugged. "Anything is possible. I had to make sure."

CHAPTER 11

If the smells of cinnamon, pine, and sugar cookies floating through the halls or the gaily decorated doors and rooms couldn't convince Sara that Christmas was near, the students could. From the first bell of the morning to the last bell in the afternoon, they were whirling dervishes of activity and noise.

She raised a hand. "Settle down. We're not starting the game until everyone is quiet."

"Yes. Let's play a game."

Sara grabbed onto the corner of her desk and bent over, certain her eyes were going to pop out with the pain.

"Are you all right, Mrs. Allbrooke?"

Jesse's concerned face wavered inches from hers.

"Go, Jesse. Get Mrs. Stockton. Tell her . . . tell her I'm not well."

Vaguely, she heard the classroom door slam. Hand over hand, she felt her way around the desk and sat carefully in the chair. The class was quiet, too quiet. She didn't have to see them to know the children were scared. Licking her lips, she tried to form the words that would comfort them. Nothing got past her frozen jaw.

It was at that moment that Anne Stockton entered the classroom, and immediately took over.

"Children, everything will be fine. Mrs. Hamilton," she

beckoned to the woman following her, "will be your teacher this afternoon. Please behave as though Mrs. Allbrooke is still here."

Several minutes later, Sara leaned against the corridor wall gulping air.

"I take it he's struck again?" Anne's voice was terse.

"Yes."

Sara collapsed in a chair in Anne's office, fumbled for her cell phone, and hit speed dial. John answered at once. "What's up?"

"He's either got a child or he's going after one."

"Did he say anything?"

Before she could answer, the assistant principal Beth burst through the office door. She ignored Anne's attempts to wave her away, her voice shrill as she spoke. "One of Mrs. Pennington's preschoolers, Dillon Archer. He's missing. We can't find him anywhere."

"Sara, what's going on?" John asked. "Did you get anything?"

"Just a 'let's play a game.' I think we know who the missing child is. The teachers can't find Dillon Archer."

"Shit! Right under our fucking noses. Tell Anne to alert the cops at the school. I'm on my way."

"John, you have to get me home. Now. You are working this one solo."

"Are you sure?"

She nodded, then realized John couldn't see her. "We'll pull Kelly out of her second grade class and bring her to the office."

"Good. I'll pick up Kelly's husband on the way to the school. I'm assuming Jerry's at the restaurant. As soon as we get there, I'll have someone take you home."

Sara cut the connection and put the phone in her pocket.

"You've quit?" Anne's voice was quiet.

"Yes."

"Stay here, Sara." Anne looked over at Beth. "Come with me. You'll need to cover Kelly's class."

In the sudden silence, Sara leaned back, closing her eyes and mind to everything. The maniac was still there. She could feel him trying to push in. But there was no child. *Is Dillon Archer already dead?*

A white-faced, firmly in-control Kelly Archer stepped into the office and turned to Anne. "All right, talk. What is it? Is it Jerry? Was there an accident at the restaurant? I told him that old stove wasn't working properly."

"No, Kelly, it's not Jerry. It's Dillon. He may be missing, possibly kidnapped."

"Impossible. I just saw him at lunch. This kind of thing doesn't happen at St. Mary's . . ." Her voice trailed off, her eyes dulled. "Yes it does. It's always about St. Mary's students." Her glance fell on Sara. "Are you going to help with the music, the notes . . . whatever it is he leaves?"

Sara shook her head. "I'm not feeling well. I had to leave class."

Kelly gave a quick lopsided grin. "Are you sure you're not pregnant?"

Sara shrugged. "John's bringing Jerry with him. I know John can find your son."

Everything seemed to crash into Kelly at once. As her legs began to shake, Anne and Sara were already guiding her to a chair. Tears flowed down her cheeks. Anne placed a comforting hand on Kelly's shoulder. "Hang on. Until we know something for sure, we wait."

Three pairs of eyes swiveled up to the clock.

A sudden knock startled the women. Anne opened the door to a grim-faced policeman. His eyes found Kelly. "Mrs. Archer?" He held up a piece of paper. "We found this on the playground beside your son's jacket."

Kelly sobbed into a Kleenex as Anne and Sara attempted to calm her. It seemed like hours, but by Sara's watch, it was less than fifteen minutes later when John walked in with Jerry hard on his heels. Taking Kelly into his arms, Jerry tried to comfort his wife.

"He won't make it. His autism. He won't make it in this weather." Kelly repeated those words over and over.

John read the note the officer gave him, stuck it in his pocket, and ushered Sara quickly out of the office. At the car, he pulled out a blanket from the back, wrapped it around her shoulders, and ushered her into the front seat.

"John, I—"

"Hush. Go right to bed. I'll call you when I get a chance." He gave her a quick kiss, then looked over at Frank. "Get back as soon as you can." With that, he stepped back and shut the car door.

Sara pulled the blanket tight around her shoulders and tried to stop shivering. After a glance at her, Frank turned up the heat to high.

Twenty minutes later, he pulled into their driveway. Shakily, Sara climbed out.

"Are you sure you don't need any help?"

Mumbling words of thanks, she declined Frank's offer and stumbled up the porch stairs. It took her three tries to get the key in the lock and open the door.

Normally, Max launched himself at Sara or John as they came into the house. Today, though, the shepherd seemed to sense something wasn't right. Going straight to Sara, he moved beside her, then thrust his nose under her hand. It was his way of saying "hold onto me."

"Take me upstairs, boy." Slowly, the big dog angled for the stairs, making sure Sara held on to his scruff. At the top of the stairs he turned into the bedroom, then waited patiently while Sara took off her shoes and slipped into bed. She pulled the covers up and reached for the heavy blanket she kept at the foot of the bed. Her vision dimmed as she laid her head on the pillow. Despite her attempts to hold the child and kidnapper at bay, Dillon Archer slipped into her mind.

The wind sliced through her, cutting her skin. She jerked back, closed her mind, and fought the pull to become the boy. Still, she saw bare feet, snow with mud squelching up between the toes. She braced herself for his fear, his call for help. It never came. Instead, she felt an open curiosity, a calm acceptance of what was going to happen.

She saw the kidnapper grab the boy's hand, holding it so tightly it must have been painful. Her own hand felt momentarily crushed. He dragged the barefoot child through the slush. Her feet were cold. She could feel the slush and mud between her toes. She couldn't stop from becoming the boy. She could stop the kidnapper from entering her mind, sort of. Again, he tried, and again, she was able to shut him out. Suddenly she understood why. Dillon was not frightened. Everything was all right. At the bridge, she saw the kidnapper stop and drop a heavy length of chain with a clunk. Still, she felt no fear from the boy.

The kidnapper turned and bent his head to the child. Sara held her breath. Would she finally see him? She stared upward into a face devoid of features. In some way, the kidnapper protected himself. She would never see his face through the eyes of a victim.

At that instant she knew that Dillon Archer was calmly accepting his own death. He didn't need her, yet the instinct to comfort him was strong, and that she couldn't do. Guilt spread across her like a thick quilt.

Minutes after the K9 police dogs arrived, Samuel Hawk drove up in a battered pickup. He went directly to John.

"What do you want me to do?"

John looked into eyes that were still sharp, despite the face's age. "Walk the perimeter with the men. Scour both sides of the fence. See if you can find something, anything that will tell us something about this bastard, or at least tell us which way he went."

Samuel nodded and joined the ranks of police and volunteers.

They worked until the light failed, covering every inch of the grounds, every foot of the building. Nothing was found beyond the piece of paper that gave them the notes of the song.

Headquarters had the song in the first half hour. It was "Shall We Gather at the River." Unfortunately, Milford possessed four rivers within its borders: the Housatonic in the west, the Oyster in the east, and the Wepawaug and Indian rivers flowing through the center of town.

Other volunteers joined, combing the banks of the rivers. As they were thinly spread out and in most cases not properly trained, the chance that clues would be missed was high. But it was all Milford had, all they could do. Nothing else had fallen into place.

John stared at the cell phone in his hand. One call. That's all it would take. One call.

"She'll help, John. You know she will. All you have to do is ask."

He looked into Samuel's weathered face. The man had proven as diligent and competent as any Milford cop. And like the rest, he'd found nothing. "How did you know?"

"I guessed a long time ago. I read the articles about her and the New York fiasco. It made sense that she wouldn't want to work with the police again. But you are her husband. You, she could work with. You, she could trust."

"Yeah. She wants to quit, Samuel. And I can't blame her. You don't know what she goes through. Besides, we're not even close to fulfilling our end of the bargain."

"There's nothing to find. He is a hunter. A good hunter never leaves clues."

"He's a damned criminal. They always leave something. They always make mistakes."

Samuel said nothing.

Walking back to the car for a couple of flashlights, John glanced at the heavens, murmuring threats no God-fearing man would use. Time was running out. Time, as usual, was not on their side.

He pulled the collar of his coat up and flexed his fingers. Even with gloves on, his hands ached. Handing the spare flashlight to

Samuel, he and the Indian retraced their steps, moving carefully along the school fence perimeter. The flashlights moved slowly back and forth like an exotic lightshow.

Samuel grabbed John's arm. "Turn off your light."

John did as ordered. For minutes, the two stood in the darkness—listening, waiting.

Above the soft wind, a twig snapped.

"There," Samuel pointed. Figures stood at the edge of the trees on the other side of the fence, almost a hundred feet away. "You get the boy. I'll get the other one." As he spoke, Samuel grabbed the top of the five-foot chain link fence and vaulted it with ease.

One figure disappeared into the trees; the other remained still.

Despite his age, Samuel sprinted into the woods, following the shadowy figure. Branches slapped his face as he wound through saplings and evergreens. He slid when the terrain dipped down, barely able to keep his boots under him. Then he was standing on a concrete sidewalk. He looked up and down the street. Nothing moved. There was no sound of an engine, no lights. At the far end of the block, an old pickup suddenly growled to life. Tires screeched as the truck pulled out and sped down the road.

With a soft curse, John took off his coat and wrapped it around the shivering, dirty little boy. Dillon did not seem frightened. As John lifted him up, Dillon automatically wound his arms around John's neck. The detective couldn't help it. He squeezed and cuddled the child, laughing and speaking absolute nonsense.

Looking around, John realized that there was no way he could climb over the fence with the boy in his arms, and he wasn't about to put the child down. He followed the fence line until he came to the sidewalk, then turned, walking across the parking lot and into the school.

Everyone jumped as the office door swung open. In moments, Dillon was surrounded by his mom and dad.

John stepped aside. This was the good part of being a cop. This was what made it all worthwhile—the long hours, bad coffee, fast food, piles of paperwork. This was why he loved his job.

Carefully, keeping Max close beside her, Sara tottered down to the living room and flipped on the gas fire. Max's weight hadn't warmed her feet. In fact, they felt frozen. They ached. She draped an afghan over her shoulders and sat with her feet to the fire.

She saw the child lifted. Warmth enveloped her.

She pulled the afghan off. Was it over? Was it the warmth of death she was feeling? Was death even warm? Who lifted the child up? She lay back, suddenly feeling relaxed, and let sleep overtake her.

The roughness of an unshaved face and the softness of a pair of familiar lips woke her up. She opened her eyes to the love of her life. "Is Dillon all right?"

"He's fine. A little dirty, a little cold, but fine. You know, when we found him, I don't think that kid was afraid. I don't think he was ever afraid."

"He's autistic. They process, see things differently than we do. Kelly and Jerry okay?"

"They were ecstatic when I left. Move over." He gently pushed her over, took off his shoes, and cuddled beside her on the large chaise lounge. "How are you feeling?"

The shakes she had controlled for so long seized her body. John pulled her closer, enveloping her in his warmth. "I'm here," he said softly.

Between chattering teeth, she forced herself to talk. "I didn't . . .

think it would be so hard. I wanted to play. God, I wanted to play. I felt some of the things that maniac threatened Dillon with. I tried to stop his voice. Sometimes I could; other times it was almost as if he was yelling at me. Dillon never reached to me for comfort, and I never tried to give him comfort. What kind of a monster am I? Knowing what was happening to him, I never tried to reach him. How can someone not comfort a child?"

"Did the boy ever reach out to you for anything?"

"Not really. I knew he was there. I could feel him. I even saw him. I knew what I should do—but I didn't do anything. I couldn't."

John bent his head, his lips lost in her thick red hair. "You are trying to make yourself into a bad person. You are not bad. Don't even go down that path. The most important thing right now is that he's safe. He's all right."

"No child is safe until we find this monster. I saw Samuel pull up just before Frank drove me away. Was he helping you? I thought he was kind of a consultant, the way you talked."

"He was helping us. He may be old," John paused, "he may be older, but he is still one sharp ex-cop—or rather, ex-detective."

"Did he see anything?"

John chuckled. "You mean the sharp-eyed Indian tracker? No, Samuel didn't find anything. But he heard them by the fence. While I got Dillon, he chased the bastard almost a block, saw a truck pull out, even got a part of a license number. The vehicle was reported stolen this afternoon. We haven't found it yet. When we do, trust me, we'll go over it very carefully. Samuel did remark at one point this evening that all I had to do was ask, and you would help."

Sara pulled out of his arms. "He knew I was working with the police?"

"I think he guessed it. He spoke of reading a newspaper article about your work in New York City."

"He would have been wrong. I wouldn't help. I told you I was quitting and I am. Asking wouldn't have done any good."

He was quiet for a few minutes, his voice gentle when he spoke. "That's not like you, Sara."

"It's going to have to be 'like me' from now on. I . . ." she faltered, looking down. "I'm pregnant, and I'm not taking any chances with this child's life."

He pulled her closer, his grin growing wider by the minute. "Are you sure?"

"Positive. I saw the doctor this morning before school. I'm about six weeks along. I wasn't going to say anything until I was at least two months, but . . ." She took a deep breath. "I'm in textbook condition and I intend to stay that way."

"You were pregnant during Thanksgiving."

"Yes, but not far enough along to affect things. At least that's what I'm praying for."

"Was it like the other times today?"

She nodded. "Every time the kidnapper linked with me, the baby fluttered. And every time I thought of trying to reach Dillon, I had the same kind of pain I had when I miscarried."

"Then I'm glad you stayed out of it. I don't want you taking any chances with our child. We're going to have this one and she's going to be strong and healthy."

"So you are already planning on a daughter?"

John grinned. "The first child of a Slane, and I quote your grandmother, is always a girl." He looked deep into her eyes. "I love you Sara Erin Slane Remington Allbrooke."

The kiss was long and deep, and for several minutes, Sara forgot about everything else. She was happy, she was pregnant, and she was with the man she loved. The events of the night suddenly crashed into her mind. She pushed John back.

"You said you found him with someone? He wasn't tied up or in a cage or a box?"

"No. I almost think the man was trying to put Dillon back into the schoolyard. Your plan not to play the game just might have worked. He let the boy go."

"Did the police ever figure out the song?"

From his pocket, John pulled out a piece of paper on which he'd scribbled the notes.

Swinging her legs off the chaise lounge, Sara took the paper to the piano and plucked out the notes. "It's 'Shall We Gather at the River.'"

"That's what we came up with, though not as quickly as you did. We never got any further. Dillon could have been by any of the rivers. The sad thing is, with his autism, he will probably never be able to tell us anything about the kidnapper."

Opening the hymnal, Sara read through the verses several times, then shook her head. "I couldn't have found Dillon on this song alone. Without the links, the clues, I wouldn't have stood a chance in hell of finding him."

"I know."

She glanced at John. "So what am I missing? What else was different about this night?"

"Dillon was holding a scrap of paper in his hand when I picked him up. I also copied it." He handed her a second piece of paper.

Sara looked at her husband's scribbling. *"I let him go. You figure out why."*

"You did what?" Joe spoke quietly into the phone, his heart hammering. His father had never mentioned anything about taking another child. Joe said a quick, silent prayer that the child had been found and was all right.

"I let him go," the faceless voice repeated.

"Why?" Joe asked. He listened quietly to the explanation. He understood part of his father's thinking—Joe had let Joshua live and convinced his father he was playing mind games with Sara. His father was trying the same thing, but with a deeper thought process that was dark and sick.

Joe gave the expected comments at the appropriate time.

When Malachi grew quiet, Joe spoke honestly. "You really do know how to screw with their minds."

His father agreed and changed the subject.

"I've taken care of everything, just like you wanted." Joe answered the questions and hoped his voice sounded sincere. "I also sold another piece to a rancher in southern Mississippi. Told him I'd deliver it. Since I'm done here, I figured I'd leave tomorrow."

He cut off his father's dark protest. "I'll go straight there and back. Figure three days tops. I need to go slow, but I'll be back by the end of the week. I'll be back in time for the solstice. He's paying cash, five thousand dollars. We can use that right now."

As usual, the money placated the old man. Joe also knew his father wouldn't come straight home from Milford. He'd hole up somewhere for a day or two with a whore, or maybe several whores. Joe just hoped that one or more of them did not end up as one of Malachi's sick sacrifices.

Joe cut the connection. He couldn't stand to hear any more. The carving was already packed, allowing him to leave early the next morning. What the old man didn't know was that the piece had actually sold for eleven thousand. The extra money would be sent to Serafina—anonymously, of course.

Standing in the snow, he turned slowly in a circle, taking a last look at what he had been working on for the last couple months. His father had been right about one thing: They had had snow in the West Virginia mountains, but not enough to prevent the December 13th "solstice celebration."

The seven cabins—once part of an old hunting camp—were ready. They were primitive, rough, but would do until his father could lay his hands on some really big money. Windows had been fixed, roofs repaired, doors replaced. Joe had cleaned out the chimneys and even re-rocked some of them. They had been scrubbed and filled with roughly made bunks and coarse blankets. They weren't comfortable, but they were adequate.

Closing his eyes, Joe pictured each CEO, banker, and just plain rich man who would call this place home for three days. They would come in Fords, Chevys, Humvees, and SUVs, galled that they couldn't drive the BMWs and vintage Rolls Royce's they were used to navigating around in. They would participate in rituals the old man set forth. In drunken, drug-induced stupors, they would consummate acts they could only dream of, believing they were gaining power by their actions. In the end, they would believe everything the old man told them, and he would tell them plenty.

It was all a lie. In their minds, breaking every commandment written would allow them true freedom, but nothing could be further from the truth. Joe knew this personally. But they would ply his father with wealth. He would become their second god.

The only thing left was to find the village virgins. His father would have to do that, if there was such a thing. Joe knew the old man had his eye on a few girls. "Virgin," though, was a stretch.

Walking slowly back to his truck, he edged back up the mountain, wondering if his father had guessed Sara's secret. The old man hadn't mentioned anything.

For a second, Joe feared for Sara. Malachi had been pissed that she hadn't played his latest game. According to him, she had shut down, blocked him, ignored his taunts and threats. He half smiled to himself. Maybe Sara was actually playing the psychological game.

Joe turned his thoughts away from his father and the darkness. Taking the carving to Mississippi gave him three days of freedom, three days to think of Serafina and savor dreams of a life that could never be.

CHAPTER 12

"POLICE FIND MISSING CHILD," the headline screamed across the front page of the *Milford Herald*.

Caleb reread the article, noting that Sara was never mentioned

He stared out the window. Fresh snow-covered Boston, its white purity hiding the sins of the city. He shook his head. He'd never been a religious man—spiritual, but not religious. Why, then, did words like "sin" and "purity" pop into his mind?

"Mr. Remington. Mr. Duncan and his associates are here."

That was the "why." William Duncan was still pressing to take over Remington's, and there was something oily, dark, not quite right about the man and his business dealings.

"Take them into the boardroom, Irene. See to their needs. I'll be there directly." He cut the link. In the words of that great mythical detective, Sherlock Holmes, the game was afoot. He leaned back in his chair. They could wait—PsyOps 101.

Twenty minutes later, Caleb strode into the boardroom. His green eyes took in the men. Only William and Abigail met his stare head-on. She smiled, tentatively.

So the old man's throwing feminine power into the mix. As ordered, Duncan's counter proposal was in front of Caleb's chair, open. He sat, beginning without preamble. "What do you want, Duncan?"

The man's thin lips curled into a half smile. "Same thing I wanted the first time we met: a merger."

"That's not going to happen. You heard my offer at the first meeting. It still stands."

"Have you looked over the new proposal?"

"It wouldn't matter if I had."

"Based on this new proposal, Remington's has a lot to gain."

"And even more to lose. You either underestimate me or overestimate yourself. I don't know which and I don't particularly give a damn." With the back of his hand, Caleb sent the proposal flying down toward William. "My answer is the same as it was the first time we met. Take my initial counter or leave it."

"That's not good business, Remington."

"It's my business."

William Duncan leaned forward. The smile was gone. His blue eyes darkened and narrowed into slits. "You don't know who you're fooling with now."

Darkness was rising in the room. Caleb glanced down. The midnight-blue sapphire in his antique silver ring glowed. He moved his hand, hiding it, and smiled slowly. "I believe the answer to that comment is 'neither do you.' Since you aren't prepared to accept my offer, consider this meeting at an end. And Duncan, don't bother me again. I have no intention of becoming even remotely involved with you or anything you own or control."

He hit the intercom button. "Irene, please show Duncan and his people out."

The words were hardly out of his mouth when the door opened.

"Mr. Duncan, if you please." His secretary's voice was cool, in total control.

There was nothing the Scotsman could do. He nodded to his associates, who rose and filed out, and then he rose. "You've made a mistake, laddie, a bad mistake. This isn't over—not by a long shot. I need your company. No, not need; I want it. And by God, I'll get it."

"Is it God or the devil that you look to, Duncan? Whichever, you'll never have Remington's. Now stop bothering me."

"Aye, you don't know what the word 'bother' means. I've just begun, Caleb Remington. I'm going to become your worst nightmare."

"Get out."

The old man turned, and with a dignity Caleb hadn't believed he possessed, he walked out. Abigail remained. Only when the door closed did she rise, walking softly, confidently to Caleb, a smile in her eyes and on her lips.

"I don't believe my father meant any of what he said. He doesn't need Remington's, but he could use it to grow, and you're businessman enough to know that when any company stops growing, it's because it's dying. My father doesn't want that to happen to either company. He wants what you've both built to continue on—a legacy, if you will—long after we are all gone. Please, look over the new proposal. It benefits you and him. It's fair. I helped draw it up."

As she spoke, she reached out, touching Caleb's arm.

His first reaction was to jerk away. Instead he merely stepped back out of her reach. No matter how angelic Abigail Duncan looked, she was her father's daughter—completely.

"If you want to save your soul, you need to leave him. But I don't think you have the guts to do that."

"Why should I? I like it where I am."

"I'm sure you do. You're also a liar. The new proposal's nothing more than a thinly disguised takeover. It'll never happen. Go peddle your wares someplace else, Abigail. I'm not interested."

The smile froze. She turned, went to her seat, and picked up her briefcase. At the door, she stopped and faced him. "You'll be sorry."

He leaned forward, laying his hands carefully on the conference table, letting her see the ancient Masonic ring with its glowing sapphire. "So will you."

The color drained from her face. She stepped back, turned and fled.

He sat hard, barely controlling the tremors that ran through his body. When he was calm, he hit the intercom button. "Is everyone ready?"

Irene's voice came across competently as usual. "Everyone you requested is in the boardroom on the third floor. And the PI Richard Peterson is in your office. His words were, 'I have some interesting information.'"

Caleb hesitated. "Send refreshments down to the boardroom. Tell them I'll be there in half an hour. I'll meet with Richard now. Oh, and Irene, lock this room up; it needs to be cleaned again."

As he stepped into his office, his gut told him the dance wasn't over yet.

Joe watched the proceedings from the main cabin. Everything about the solstice had sickened him. He felt dirty and wondered for the thousandth time what someone as good as Serafina saw in him. He glanced at the sky. The darkness was receding; the solstice had been a success for his father. Rituals had been well participated in, and the village virgins had played their roles realistically and left with healthy bonuses.

Except one. Greed and the promise of even more money kept the third "virgin" behind. It was her death that sealed the final ceremony. Each man, his hand covered with blood, gave a killing blow. When she died exactly, no one knew. Who killed her exactly, no one knew.

This lack of knowledge, this guilt, was the strongest bond that could be forged. And if the men denied their deeds . . . cameras, cunningly hidden by Joe, had taped the whole thing. It was a strong piece of possible blackmail. Something his father could and would use.

Each man stood silent in the half circle, watching the dawn. Malachi swore he knew their thoughts; at least that was what he'd told Joe. The power of each man was puny, but their arrogance was strong. And it was this arrogance that would be their downfall. The men thought they were on the edge of controlling God himself. The old man knew it was he who would have the control.

Joe knew the rest of his father's plan, and it would be tricky. Malachi would have to take it slowly, but he was convinced he would show the men Satan's power. He was convinced he was the son of Satan. Once the men recognized this, they would be Malachi's minions forever; and he—a backwoods, West Virginia good old boy, Vietnam POW, and almost felon—would have gained admittance into some of the most powerful families in the States. He would finally have the money and power to pay back mankind and the Christian God for letting him be born—for forcing him to live a life of agony and poverty. And if challenged, he would grind into dust those who opposed him.

Joe knew his father would have liked to use a child for the final sacrifice, but Joe convinced him that the men weren't ready for that. According to Malachi, a late-born lamb didn't give the same power, but it gave enough to impress the new coven, to feed them, to bind them.

Joe's thoughts suddenly turned to Sara. Her silence at the last kidnapping concerned him. Why was she so quiet? Was her child somehow endangered by the links with him?

He had felt her fatigue when he took Joshua, but she was still strong—damned strong. Did she think if she stopped playing the game, the kidnappings would stop? Possible. He knew Malachi dreamed of the day when Sara finally realized the old man was stronger; that Malachi Campbell could force her to do anything he wanted her to and she would be powerless. Joe dreaded that day.

His father began to chant softly. One by one, the others took up the song, watching intently as the sky grew brighter. For some, the new sun meant warmth. For others, a new beginning, a promise that their new god would bequeath to them every physical thing, every warped and twisted desire they sought.

Raising the blood-filled chalice, Malachi dipped the flat oat bread into it, took a bite, and passed it on. Each man followed suit.

They stood side by side in the coldness of the morning, watching the cars leave the valley. Joe glanced at his father. The old man was staring at him. Did he guess the empathy Joe felt for Sara? Did he comprehend the love Joe held for Serafina and his son? Did he know how much Joe wanted to live another life? Sudden fear for Serafina and his son shot through Joe.

"It was a good solstice."

Joe nodded.

"We can almost trust them now. Once we have Sara's power, they will be ours. Nothing will stop us then. Nothing." Malachi turned to his son, his glare boring into Joe's moss-green eyes. "Just remember, accidents are simple. They can happen anywhere, even in New Orleans. Go home, JJ. I'll shut things up here."

The old man turned and headed for the nearest cabin.

Joe walked to his pickup. He hated being called JJ. It reminded him that he was named, in part, after his father. Loathing for what he'd witnessed and participated in filled Joe. But nothing matched his fear.

He had to warn Serafina. He would break his vow and see her, explain things to her. He didn't believe in the bullshit that had gone on the last few days, but his father did. Those beliefs not only mentally unhinged the man but also made him doubly dangerous.

Joe laughed to himself. Two women, his mother and grandmother Slane, had condemned him, and his father had taken his soul the rest of the way to hell. That was his sacred trinity.

Half an hour later Joe stepped out of his pickup and walked to his studio. He needed money, money to get to New Orleans and lots of money to give Serafina. He needed to sell another carving, and he knew which one he was going to part with.

The carving had graced his workshop for almost five years. Now it graced the eight-thousand-square-foot country home of a very wealthy couple in Aspen.

The almost life-sized woman seemed to erupt from the solid hunk of maple, her long locks flowing. Her right arm pulled a small boy close to her side, while the broken chain of a slave dangled from the outstretched left hand. Perched on her shoulder was a small owl. From the folds of her tattered skirt one shapely calf and foot emerged. The ankle was scarred.

It was Serafina as he saw her. The broken chain was his leaving. It had freed her. The scars, that was what a life with him would give her. The owl was her protection and her wisdom, and the boy, that was their son.

He had loved having it in his studio. It was as though Serafina could actually watch him work. But the $120,000 figure he had quoted the Aspen couple had been eagerly accepted.

Pocketing the cash, Joe left, turning his pickup toward Denver. There was enough for a roundtrip plane ticket, a rental car, a hotel room in New Orleans, and long-term parking in Denver. What was left, which was most of it, would allow Serafina to disappear for a while, a long while. It could buy a new life for her—if he could talk her into it. What he gave his father would please the old man.

Joe stepped off the chill of the plane. It was only nine in the morning but already the New Orleans air was heavy with moisture and warmth. He glanced at the hazy sky, noticing the build-up of clouds to the south, and he shivered. Hurricane season might be over, but he could feel it, the makings of a storm—a large storm—the last thing on earth the city needed.

Swinging the rental car off the highway, he meandered down into the French Quarter. At Jackson Square he turned, driving the narrow streets behind the church.

He slowed down. It was there—just as he remembered.

The small house was barely discernible behind the wrought-iron gate and brick wall. Beyond that gate, he knew, was a small courtyard in the manner of the French. There was a small fountain that still worked. Bougainvillea and hibiscus grew in profusion, adding to the privacy and seclusion. In the center was a large magnolia, its gnarled limbs professing its determination to stay alive in this land of brick and mortar. Beneath the tree sat an iron bench, big enough for two people and a child to relax on.

The place appeared empty. He checked his watch. Ten thirty. Serafina would be at the shop by now. It was only a few blocks away. Should he park and walk that way, or should he simply wait in the car until lunch, when she would close the shop and come swinging home?

He killed the engine, locked the car, and headed toward the shop. The sooner he got this over with, the sooner he could return to Denver, grab his truck, and drive back to West Virginia. The less time he was gone, the fewer questions the old man would ask. Besides, he needed to know if she was going to listen, if she was even going to let him speak.

Two blocks and several turns later, Joe was in the heart of the business area of the French Quarter. Small shops sold everything from mojo and magic to glistening white beignets and thick chicory coffee.

He stopped in front of the small shop and stared into the window.

She was there, tall, elegant, her dark hair turbaned with a swath of bright cotton. Her smooth coffee-colored skin glowed, her dark eyes bright as she spoke to a customer. She was exotic amongst her silks, threads, crystals, and perfumes.

He took a deep breath. Even before he opened the door, he smelled it, the deep, musky scent of rare flowers with a gardenia base. What other flowers she used, she would not tell. The combination was her secret, her scent and hers alone.

She looked up. He braced himself. Six years with no contact. How would she react?

Her eyes warmed, her lips curled faintly into a smile, her voice soft, thick with the south. "It's been a long time."

CHAPTER 13

"It's a good thing the cops didn't find this crime scene." Sara knelt on the floor, picking up broken ornaments and torn tinsel. Five steps away, Max lay in abject sorrow, his head down on crossed paws.

She looked into his mournful brown eyes. "It's not working, pal. You've had your eye on that angel since John put it on the tree."

Hearing no real censure in her voice, the dog jumped up, gave a sharp bark, and bounded to the door.

With a half sigh, Sara rose. She couldn't stay mad at the big lug for very long, and that bark was his way of saying, "I need to go out."

She glanced at the Christmas tree. At least it was still relatively intact. If Max left it alone, John could help her take it down on his next day off, if there ever was such a day.

Grabbing her hat and coat, Sara followed the dog out and into the side yard. Leaning against the porch, she vowed that this summer they would build a fence. Max never went far but he could get into trouble in a matter of minutes. Mrs. Hardin's cats, an old Maple tree, and a ladder truck were an example of that. Thankfully, most of the neighbors were indulgent.

It was quiet, as quiet as Christmas and New Year's had been.

Sara had never realized how much life Judy and Tom brought to the season. She'd never realized how much she liked having them around until they weren't there. Judy still wasn't speaking to them and Tom was caught somewhere in the middle.

According to John, he and Tom still spoke, but not as often as in the past—and Sara was fairly certain Judy didn't know about it.

Joshua was learning but it was pitifully slow and pitifully little. The doctor's diagnosis had proven sadly accurate.

I should have kept them in Milford that night. If only—Sara stopped the thought. The if-only game was as dangerous as the what-if game.

Her heart still believed that a large part of Joshua was somewhere out in the cold, dark waters of Long Island Sound. Her mind told her that was ludicrous.

She wanted to believe that he could be fixed, that someone would find the pieces and fit them back together, that one day Judy would have a whole son. That, too, was ludicrous.

Sara laid a hand on her stomach. Her gift was closed. Even the thought of linking with the kidnapper or a child trying to reach her caused agitated flutters from the baby. She couldn't take the chance. This child would be born—alive. Maybe someday she could do something for Joshua.

She glanced up. Max was frozen, staring at something behind her.

"Mrs. Allbrooke."

Whirling around, she caught sight of the interloper and stepped back. Hat in hand, Samuel Hawk dipped his head in apology.

"I'm sorry. I didn't mean to startle you. John isn't at the station. I took a chance he'd be home."

"He's not here, Mr. Hawk. But if it's important, you can reach him on his cell."

"I tried. No answer. It isn't that important. I just wanted to let him know that the videos yielded nothing unusual. Your kidnapper knows the city very well. He was shrewd enough to stay away from places where he might be captured on camera." The old man shrugged. "But then, he is a hunter."

"Why would you call him that?"

"If he's the same man who hit the reservation years ago, he's a hunter."

Sara stared into eyes that were dark with warmth, humor, sorrow, and a touch of anger. Her apprehension melted. How could she have ever been afraid of him?

"Would you like a cup of coffee? Maybe I can reach John."

"Coffee? Like what John sometimes brings in?"

"Yes."

His eyes lit up. "I'd like that very much, Mrs. Allbrooke. My friends say I'm a coffee addict."

"The name is Sara."

He nodded. "Please. Call me Samuel."

Smiling, she turned for the door. For once, it took no threats or coercion to get Max back inside.

Samuel warmed his hands on the hot cup, then looked up with a grin. "It gets cold on the mesas but not like this. I'm feeling my old bones these days."

"How long will you be here?"

"I don't know. I'd like to stay until this man is caught, but I have a bad feeling that that won't be anytime soon." He was silent a moment. "You did stop the gift, didn't you?"

"Yes. You knew I was thinking about doing that the first night we met."

"John told me about what you go through. I don't blame you. Add to that the risk of losing your daughter and—"

"So you think it's a girl too?"

"I know it is. So do you. You don't like the gift you've been given, do you?"

"I hate it. It passes from Slane woman to Slane woman. We don't ask for it, it's just there. I'm sure there were many who didn't want it. I'm tired, tired of being different, of seeing things, feeling things, of having no real control over my life."

"Control is an illusion, Sara. There is always a reason for what we are and the gifts we possess. We may not know what that reason is, but it's there. They will pass on to your daughter. Learn to handle them. Learn, so you may teach her."

He fell silent, his weathered skin a deep red. "Forgive me. I don't usually go on like that."

Sara stared, not really seeing him. She had thought only of having a child. Her grandmother's gift of healing had posed no problems; and strangely, the gift had completely bypassed her mother. Sara had never thought about how the gift might affect her child.

"What have I done?" The whispered words were out before she could stop them.

Samuel's large hand engulfed hers, grounding her with his strength. "You created a life out of love. There is nothing wrong with that. She will have a gift and you will teach her."

"How do you know?"

"I'm old enough to know and understand some things. For instance, I don't think your quitting will affect the kidnapper. He will continue to play the game."

"But he let Dillon go."

Samuel Hawk hesitated, dropping her hand. His eyes grew bleak. "Sometimes when we hunt a coyote or wolf that has been after our sheep, we sacrifice a lamb to draw out the hunter."

"You think Dillon was a 'sacrifice'?"

"I think it is a possibility—a mislead, if you will." His eyes traveled down. "That's an interesting cross you wear. I've never seen anything like it."

Sara fingered the cold, heavy silver. "It's Celtic. The first Slane woman of each generation to receive the gift receives the cross. According to stories, there's another one around, only it's gold."

Her hand warmed the metal. "I think this one must have been enameled red at one time. If you look closely, there are flecks of red in the carved grooves." She dropped it, the warmth against her skin suddenly annoying. It was another shackle, another reminder of who and what she was.

Samuel rose. "I'd best be going. My daughter worries when I'm home too late."

"I'll tell John you came by."

"There is no need to bother. I'll see him tomorrow."

At the door, he paused, glancing up at the murky sky. "There is a storm coming, a bad one. Take care, Sara, and be careful. I once told you that when a gift is stopped, there may be repercussions. A payment may be demanded."

"What kind of pay—" Before she could complete the question, he was down the stairs and halfway to his car.

She watched him drive away. He had never explained what kind of payment would be demanded.

Samuel pulled into the driveway of his daughter's New Haven home and killed the engine. He pushed back the excitement of having actually seen the cross, then looked up.

There was a storm coming, a storm of shadows. The darkness he'd seen over the reservation so many years before was descending on Milford, and the darkness would win again. They weren't going to catch the bastard. He would have his way here, then move on to some other unsuspecting town.

Samuel took a deep breath. He needed to go home. He needed to return to the reservation, to smell the sand and dust, feel the crispness of a morning.

He'd call Leon after supper and tell him what he'd seen. Only time would tell if Sara was the one they sought. But time was something he didn't have. He said a quick prayer for Sara, for John, for Milford, and went inside.

"Are you sure, Richard?" Caleb threw the report on his desk and stared at the nondescript wheat-haired man who lounged easily in the chair.

"Positive. Your brother-in-law had a run-in with William Duncan Jr., who is your Mr. Duncan's son. The police report and original trial transcript are there." The man nodded toward Caleb's desk. "It's an interesting read. Defense attorney claimed that John planted the gun on Junior, sorta forced him to shoot. It was never proven, but it did place some doubts in the jury's mind. Attempting to kill a cop is a bad offense anywhere. They could have put him behind bars forever. He got eight years with possibility for parole in five. Pretty sure John will shoot down those attempts."

"Does Sara know about this?"

"She knows about the child. When the little boy was released from the hospital, he spent the summer with her and John, until the system found him a permanent foster home. Unfortunately, it didn't work out. The boy's actually one of your sister's students now. His name is Billy, Billy Duncan."

"What else do you know?"

"Duncan Sr. has more hands in more pies than Sara Lee. And he's not too careful about his associates. But then, I assume you already knew that."

Caleb nodded. "Now tell me something I don't know."

"Well, from what you told me, his daughter nailed it. He needs to grow his business. I'm not much of a businessman, but some of your concerns would mesh, others wouldn't. Oh, and one other thing. John visited Junior in prison. Something to do with the kidnappings. I think your brother-in-law feels the kidnappings are a strike against him, not your sister."

Caleb studied the investigator. Richard was an excellent judge of situations and people, and it wasn't the first time he'd used his expertise in the civilian world.

"Do you think John is bad?"

"A bad cop?" Richard shrugged. "Not directly, no. He's too decent a person. But you gotta understand, Caleb, in his job, frustration is the biggest turner. You put the bad guys away and some fancy lawyer gets them out. They hurt someone else and the cycle is repeated. Would John do something to stop that? Yeah, I think he would step over the line for a child. Hell, he's worked with kids since he entered the police academy. He still coaches little leagues and is an active Big Brother. But is he a 'bad' cop? No."

"Has his job put Sara in danger?"

"No more than any other cop's wife. Well, maybe a little, in view of her . . . talents."

Caleb quirked an eyebrow. "How do you . . . oh, you found the New York article."

Richard nodded with a half-smile.

Caleb flipped the folder open, then closed it. Something was missing. He could feel it. "Is there anything else?"

Richard did something Caleb had never known him to do—he hesitated.

"There are a couple of things that are funny—strange funny. Your Mr. Duncan seems to have joined some kind of an organization, for want of a better word. I wasn't able to find out much, but something just isn't right—again, for want of a better word. I do know one thing. The few small businesses that sort of opposed his takeover plans are no longer in existence."

"You mean they're out of business?"

"No. I mean they're gone, caput, blown up—factory fire, explosion, something that wiped them off the face of the earth. Of course, they're all accidents. At least, that's how the insurance reports read. My gut says he's dangerous. Damned dangerous."

"Thanks for the warning, Richard. Consider yourself still on the payroll if you hear anything else, and enjoy the bonus."

"Of course I'll enjoy it." Richard smiled, then sobered. "I still have your back, bro. Always did like working with you." Richard rose. "I'll let you know if I hear something."

Caleb's voice stopped him at the door. "Richard."

The man turned.

"This organization, could you call it a cult?"

For several minutes, the man pondered the question, then slowly nodded. "Yeah. That's possible, Caleb, real possible."

"Be careful."

Richard nodded and left.

For several minutes, Caleb remained seated, deep in thought, his left hand drumming the desk. At last, he stood, a plan firmly in place. One of the key issues at the board meeting downstairs would be security.

Serafina was still beautiful. The candlelight, the warmth of the home, the small boy who dozed in her arms – it was all beautiful, peaceful, good. Everything Joe wasn't.

He pushed back slightly from the table; he needed breathing room. He'd forgotten the taste of truly good jambalaya, and Serafina was an excellent cook. The heavy, sweet red wine topped off a meal fit for a king.

"Want me to help you get him to bed?"

The woman smiled and shook her head. "It won't take but a minute. And I'm used to it. There's some fresh pecan pie if you have room. Help yourself."

With that, she gently shook the child and helped him stand. She swayed gracefully down the hall, her arm around the sleepy boy.

Joe tipped more wine into the glass. He needed that more than the pie. It was time to talk, time to tell her why he was really here. He could hear the thudding of his heart as he went over and over what he was going to say and how he was going to say it. It sounded good in his mind. He hoped it sounded good aloud. More than that, he hoped Serafina bought it.

"No pie?"

He looked up and shook his head, holding up the glass. "This is fine."

"Would you like to go outside? The courtyard is beautiful tonight. There's a full moon."

Sitting had stiffened his bad leg. He teetered for a moment before finding his balance, then followed her out, admiring the sway of her hips, feeling the lust building. He put the feelings aside. He was no longer good enough. Not that he had ever been.

"Why are you here?"

Serafina was never one to mince words.

"You're in danger," he blurted out before thinking. "So is the boy," he added.

Her face paled slightly. "Who puts me in danger?"

He dropped his eyes.

"Oh." She looked away for several minutes as though digesting the information. When she looked back, her face was composed. "He wants me dead, then?"

"Yes."

"And the boy?"

He nodded.

"Why?"

He wanted to squirm, but couldn't under the steady gaze of her liquid brown eyes. "He thinks you have too much power over me. I'm not giving him my all."

"Yet, you and I haven't seen each other for over six years."

He knew the look on his face said it all.

She placed her hand over his, her voice gentle, her touch soft. "I know it's you who's been sending the money. I also know you've been here, seen me, but not been seen by me—or so you thought. You do not know my powers, or my love. I felt you, knew when you were close. You are not giving him your all because you are not an evil man. You never were."

"I've done things—"

Her hand shushed his lips. "We've all done things we are not proud of. You showed the kind of man you were when you saved a life and almost lost a leg in the process."

She took her hand away, allowing the silence to flow over them. When she spoke, her voice was still soft. "I am not without friends. But what would you have me do?"

"He knows where you're at. What you are. Leave. Take Joseph with you. Go someplace where he will never find you. Southern California, Washington. I'll help. I'll give you money. You can start a new life." He wanted to say, "start a different life," but stopped. Some things, she would never agree to. She would not leave her beliefs, her manner of living behind. She would always help people.

She reached up again, her hand caressing his face. "Poor boy. He uses me to get back at you. It isn't fair, but it is the way of the world. I can't. I cannot leave. New Orleans is my home; beyond that, it is my heritage and the heritage of our son. I would have him stay here. Learn. And use that knowledge to help others."

Joe rose shakily, pacing the narrow space. "For God's sake, Serafina, I'm talking about your life, about our son's life. He's powerful, has powerful friends now. He can kill you. I've seen him do it. He wants you dead. That means he'll stop at nothing to get you out of the picture. You're just an obstacle in his way."

"And if I'm dead?"

"He thinks he'll have me completely."

"We both know better than that."

Once more, silence ruled the small garden. It was Serafina who broke it. "I will not leave my home, but I will be careful. I will take precautions. And I will see that Joseph is protected. As I said, I am not without friends."

He reached across to cup her face in his large hands. "If something happens to you . . ."

"If something happens, it was meant to be and there is nothing we can do about it. I am not a fool, Joseph. I know what he can do, but he doesn't know what I can do. It is an advantage—a small one, but still an advantage. Your warning has given me an even greater advantage. I will be ready."

"And I can't talk you into hiding someplace safe?"

She shook her head. "If he really wants me, there is no safe place. You know that."

He hung his head down, feeling the tears. Then she was beside him, touching her lips to his, lightly, like a lover who does not know if she will be accepted.

He wrapped his arms around her, drawing her close. He deepened the kiss, his hands moving down her back to her waist. Moments later, they were lying on the patio. He didn't notice the hard bricks, only the soft woman beneath him. It had been a long time, too long. He needed her. This one last time, he needed her. She pulled him closer.

With a soft chuckle, the figure moved from the shadows and turned a corner, moving silently away from the house. Malachi had seen enough. At least he knew his son was still a man. And now he not only knew where the bitch lived, he knew what she looked like.

His shoulders straightened. The farther away he got from the house, the lighter he felt. That was one powerful woman. He rubbed his hands together in glee. Her death would give him a helluva lot of power, perhaps even more than he had gotten from the death of Sara's grandmother. And it would take her death to cement Malachi's hold over his son.

He stopped at a crosswalk. Taking a deep breath, Malachi inhaled the fragrance and decay that was New Orleans. He liked this town. He liked the darkness of its power, its taste, its feel. Maybe he should stay for a few days, get his bearings, and have some fun. Then he needed to get back to Milford before Joe returned. He needed to do a job, and he didn't want his son shadowing him.

A couple of women stumbled past him, high on drugs or booze. He could also sample some of the wares.

"Excuse me, could you tell me where I could get a good meal and some good booze?" The women stopped and turned. He quickly flashed a hundred, then pocketed the bill. "I've never been to New Orleans. Where are the good parties?"

As he studied them, the women smiled. He returned the smile. It was going to be an interesting evening.

CHAPTER 14

The house was dark. John pulled into the drive, his heart thudding in his chest. Something was wrong. He knew Sara was home. He'd spoken to her less than an hour ago but there were no lights on, and Sara didn't like the dark.

He pushed the front door open carefully, ready for anything. She sat alone on the sofa. He reached for the light.

"Don't."

Her voice was husky, raspy, as though she'd been crying. Reaching for the switch, he flipped the fireplace on. At once, gentle flames bathed the room in a soft half-light.

"What's wrong?"

He knelt beside her, taking her cold hands in his. It wasn't just her hands that were cold, he realized, and he grabbed an afghan off the sofa, throwing it over her shoulders.

"Is the baby all right?"

"The baby's fine."

"For God's sake, what's wrong, Sara?"

"She'll be cursed. She'll have the same gift that I do. She'll go through what I go through. I don't want that for our child."

He stifled a sigh of relief. "Is that all?"

"Is that all?" Her voice rose several notches. It was her fighting voice. Sara was ready for battle.

He winced and rubbed his hands over her afghan-clad arms.

"I didn't mean it quite that way, honey. It's just, with everything that's happened, I thought maybe you were losing the baby. You don't know if this baby will have the gift. You're just guessing. And you don't know what that gift will be. It's always different in each person. At least, that's what you told me. Besides, you have a good chance of being wrong. The child's mine too. And there's not a psychic bone in my body."

She smiled through the tears and touched his cheek. "She will have the gift. It's because I am psychic that I know. It always passes from mother to daughter, and the first daughter has it the strongest."

"Then we'll deal with it. She won't go through what you did. There will be no condemnation, no name-calling, no separation from her family. She'll stay here. We'll learn to cope and we'll help her— help her adjust to and accept what she is. I'll help. I'll do all I can."

"But—"

"No buts. She's still half my child. She'll be logical as well as gifted."

"You don't really buy into the psychic thing, do you, John?"

"Honestly, I don't know if I do or don't. I've seen you find children, lost and kidnapped, when no one else could. How you do it, I don't know. It defies logic. But you succeed where others fail. That, I accept. If our daughter can do that or something like that, if she can help people like you do—well, that's a precious gift."

"I've hated what I do, what I am, for so long. I sometimes forget what the end result can be."

"Don't ever forget that. Maybe one of these days you'll even see the face of the kidnapper."

"I don't think that will happen. My link is with or through the child. I think the only reason I hear him is because he wants me to for some reason. He controls that, not me. That's why it's so hard to kick him out of my mind."

"But—"

"You really don't understand, do you?"

He shook his head.

"Trust me on this. The kidnapper is a peripheral entity, but a strong one. Speaking of which, Samuel Hawk was here today."

"What'd he want?"

"He took a chance you might be home since you weren't at the station. Nothing came through on the videos."

"I didn't think it would, but it was worth a try."

"Is Samuel a good cop?"

"Very. What makes you ask?"

"I don't know. Sometimes it seems like more than just the kidnapper brought him to Milford."

"Damn! Damn it to hell."

Caleb slammed down the lid of the laptop. He had only been gone a little while. The meeting had only lasted two hours. So when in the hell had RemTech become vulnerable? He'd checked Remington's financials the day before, gone over every holding, every division. Even in his world, things didn't change that fast or dramatically. Unless . . .

He hit the phone. "Irene. In my office. Now!"

Two seconds later his secretary was at the door, face sober.

"Tell Ken I want him in my office immediately. Get ahold of Steve; pull the stocks. And get Lou Jenkins on the phone."

She was gone almost before he finished. He stared at the closed door, then swiveled his chair to face the harbor. It looked cold, dirty, forlorn. Something wasn't right. He could feel it.

RemTech was his baby. Fresh out of business school and against his father's advice, he'd bought the floundering software company.

He'd also bought its founder Lou Jenkins, a mechanical field engineer who'd gotten tired of crawling through plants, jungles, deserts, and wives. Lou saw where things were heading. He went back to school, then started Tech, Inc.

Lou had a penchant for everything but business. His baby was dying almost before he taught her to walk.

Caleb's phone buzzed.

"Mr. Jenkins on line two, sir."

"Lou—"

"Caleb, what the hell is going on? Some ass-wipe from WD just sauntered into my office as though he owned it. Said there were going to be some changes."

"Did you say WD?"

"Yeah."

William Duncan. The name shot through Caleb's mind. "Lou, did you authorize any stock sales."

The man snorted. "You know I can't do that. All that business crap comes out of your office and your office alone. Look, I got the brass coming from Washington this afternoon. I need to know what's going on."

"I—" Caleb stopped. Ken walked in; slithered was a more accurate description. Caleb stared at his second-in-command. That not-right feeling punched him in the gut.

"Lou, I'll call you back in a few minutes. Everything's going to be fine. If the son of a bitch comes back, have him thrown out." He hung up, staring at the man sitting across the desk.

"How much did he offer you, Ken?"

The man licked his lips and twitched. "I, ah, don't know what you're talking about, Caleb."

"Mr. Remington." Irene's voice on the intercom cut through the tension. He picked up the phone.

"Caleb, I just spoke with Steve. He had orders to sell RemTech stock until he was told to stop. Things didn't feel right. When he tried to contact you, he was told you weren't to be disturbed. On his own authority, Steve pulled the stock off the market fifteen minutes ago."

"How many shares?"

"Thirty percent of RemTech. Duncan's on the board. You still maintain fifty-one percent. Sara has five; five is still with the public. Steve pulled the remaining nine percent. Caleb," fear or anger shook Irene's voice, "I didn't take that call."

"Were you away from your desk at all this morning?"

"Yes. I was nauseous earlier on. I went into the employee lounge and lay down for about half an hour while Resa manned the phones."

"I'm assuming you aren't pregnant?"

The sixty-year-old secretary gave a short laugh.

"Did you drink or eat anything before you fell ill?"

"Just my usual coffee. Resa brought it to me."

"Has she done that often?"

"A few times, but not many. I was unusually busy this morning."

"Where is she now?"

"On lunch break. Just a moment, Caleb."

Seconds later, Irene's dry voice came back. "Her desk is empty. I think we can assume she's not returning to work. And Richard Peterson just called. He said it's important. Under the circumstances, I told him you'd call back."

"Did he say what it was about?"

"No."

Caleb's thoughts returned to the situation. He still controlled RemTech and Irene was all right, although he'd insist she see a doctor. The downside: William Duncan was on the board.

"Send Steve a box of cigars and thank him for the pull. I'll talk to him later about a way to prevent this from happening again."

"Do you want a list of those still holding stock?"

"Buy-back letters to ensure control?"

"It might be a good idea. I know you control the company, but a little more weight won't hurt in a negotiation."

"Give me a few minutes on that one."

"Caleb," Irene hesitated, "do you think Duncan would go after Sara or Sara's stock?"

The question caught him by surprise. "I never thought of that. I will look into it, though. And Irene, thanks for the heads-up on that one."

He hung up the phone. "Why did you do it, Ken?"

The man licked his lips again. "What do you mean?"

"Don't play games. I'm not in the mood. Why did you authorize that much stock to be sold?"

The man leaned forward. His eyes told Caleb that he still thought he could pull out of this. "You don't realize what RemTech's R-and-D dream team is costing the company. We need fluid funds for that government contract you're trying to get. This was the best way to get them."

Caleb didn't buy it, any of it. "We're not trying to get the government contract, Ken. We've got it. How much did Duncan offer you?"

The thin-faced man sneered. "Two mill and CEO. You want to best the deal?"

Caleb leaned forward. "I don't deal with bastards, especially stupid bastards. You're a fool and you haven't done your homework. Duncan's headman has worked for him for almost twenty years. He's not about to replace him with someone he can buy. Get your stuff and clear out. If you're still in this building in fifteen minutes, I'll have security throw you out."

White-faced, the man rose. He was at the door when Caleb spoke again. "You just flushed the last six years of your life down the toilet."

Ken faced him, his eyes questioning.

"Don't ask for a recommendation, Ken. Now get the hell out of my sight."

He waited until the door closed, then buzzed Irene. "Get Lou back on the phone, please. And have security escort Ken Owens out of the building if he's still here in fifteen minutes."

He faced the windows, lacing his fingers together. Was Irene right? Would Duncan go after Sara? Had he somehow put his sister in danger?

He turned to the ringing phone. "Lou?"

"Yeah. You get everything straightened out?"

"Yes. Seems we had a traitor in our midst. Duncan got thirty percent of RemTech's stock."

"Son of a bitch!"

"My sentiments exactly. He's on the board now."

Lou gave a short laugh. "The old codger may be sharp, but my money's still on you, Caleb. Are we set on the contract?"

"We've got it. So go keep the Pentagon happy—and you're right, I'll handle Duncan."

Caleb clicked off, wanting nothing more than a hot cup of coffee and a few minutes to chill. His eyes strayed to the cabinet. A short bourbon would taste even better than coffee—he checked his watch—but not at ten in the morning.

He buzzed Irene. "Get me a coffee, please, and get Richard on the line."

Five minutes later, a hot coffee was at his fingertips and he was back on the phone. "What have you got, Richard?"

Fear strained through the investigator's voice. "Not over the phone. We need to meet."

"My office, fifteen minutes."

"Not a good idea. Four o'clock at the old Boston church. They're doing some renovations there. And Caleb, you need to do a thorough sweep. Everywhere."

The line went dead.

CHAPTER 15

She threw her books on the sofa, let a bouncing Max outside—praying he wouldn't get into too much trouble—plopped on the couch, and put her feet up on the ottoman. She'd spent the day cleaning messes, refereeing arguments, and guiltily hoping her class would catch laryngitis. The quiet would have been a very welcome break from all the noise.

She was thankful when the day was over, and she wasn't the only teacher to complain. If children were a barometer, Milford was in for yet another storm. January and February had been bad, and now it appeared as though March would be equally wet and snowy.

Sara turned to the picture window. The colored and gray Cape Cods looked dirty, barren, lonely. Milford hadn't seen the ground since late August. But things would look different in the spring. That knowledge kept her going.

Was it all worth saving? Sara knew the answer before she asked herself the question. Yes. It was. But how did she do it? How did she save the children? Did she play the game, or stop? If Dillon was a sacrifice, as Samuel had indicated he might have been, then why did the bastard let him go, especially as she hadn't played the game? Was the game changing? Was he going to let all the children go now? And if she did play, what would it do to her baby? Could she risk her own child to save another?

Fire flashed through her brain.

"Let's play. Name that song in seven notes."

"No!"

Silence. She waited in the quiet. The minutes ticked by. Nothing. She glanced at the clock. It was almost four o'clock. John had already told her he would be late for supper, but she felt the need to eat something now. After all, she was eating for two.

Going into the kitchen, she prepared a sandwich and sat down. Still nothing. Perhaps it had been her imagination. The voice hadn't really sounded right. Besides, the madman had never said, "name that song in seven notes." It sounded like something a gameshow host would say.

She placed a hand on her stomach. There had been a few gentle flutters, but the baby had definitely settled down. Yes. She was just imagining things.

A scratching at the door made her jump. Rising, she let Max in, then sat on the sofa. A quick nap was all she needed. She was just a little tired. That's what was wrong. She was tired.

A ringing phone woke Sara out of a sound sleep. She grabbed it, her "hello" sounding sleepy even to her ears.

"He's hit again." John's voice was tense.

"When?"

"About half an hour ago, near as we can make it."

"Who's the child?"

"Miriam Landry."

A chill crawled down Sara's spine. "Anne Stockton's granddaughter?"

"Yes."

"Does Anne know?"

"Anne and her husband were spending the evening with their daughter when the four-year-old disappeared."

"And I suppose no one saw anything?"

"No. Miriam was there one minute and gone the next. There was a note in her boot. Do you want the musical notes?"

She did. Oh, God, she did. Even as the thought crossed her mind, a cramp hit her. She couldn't.

"Give it to the police." Sara hit the off button and stared at the dimming light. It was going to be a long night.

It was a late, dirty afternoon in Boston. There was a storm brewing. In the stillness, Caleb sensed it.

He strode down the sidewalks filled with people leaving work, feeling for a moment like a salmon swimming upstream.

He'd put out all the fires for the day. RemTech was saved, even though Duncan was now a part of it—or so the Scotsman thought. Caleb had ordered a sweep of the offices and his penthouse apartment, unsurprised when bugs were found.

Several more heads had fallen that day, mainly in his personnel department. The woman who had hired Resa Garrett without checking credentials was now looking for a job, as were several office managers. Duncan had even used several contract companies that provided plant services and computer services to spy on the Remington's.

It had been a thorough shakeup for his company, and Caleb feared it wasn't over.

He pulled the collar of his coat up. It was cold, bitterly cold, and getting dark. Why Richard had chosen to meet at this time and location, Caleb couldn't fathom, but he intended to find out when he saw his friend.

The wail of a siren cut the cold air. Caleb stepped back with the rest of the people, ignoring the walk signal, watching as a fire truck and emergency vehicles careened around the corner, followed closely by two police cars. A few seconds later, the sirens stopped.

"Shit!" Caleb swore under his breath. The accident was close. Too close.

He turned the corner, then another. The old Boston church stood there, its walls illuminated by the red lights of police and rescue vehicles. He pushed forward only to find his way blocked by a policeman.

"Sorry, you'll have to go around. There's been an accident."

With grumbles, most of the people moved off. Caleb remained where he was.

"What happened?"

The cop shook his head. "Damnedest thing. Piece of sheet metal flew off the scaffolding. Damn near beheaded a man. Forensics and CSI will have fun with this one. No wind today."

Caleb looked beyond the cop. A body bag was being zipped up. Just before it closed, he saw a shock of wheat-colored hair and froze. He had a feeling there would be no meeting with Richard, ever.

Pivoting, he headed back to his car, anger a cold hard lump in his chest. He'd stop at the police station, tell them he thought he might know the victim, maybe even ID the body, then go home and have the bourbon he had contemplated earlier. At least there wasn't a wife or girlfriend to comfort. Richard Peterson had been a loner.

At the corner he stopped, looked back, and almost doubled over with the pain. He felt as though someone had sucker punched him. Straightening up, he stared at the old church. Shadows that shouldn't be there moved slowly over and away from the building. Only Caleb saw the residue of evil left behind.

He turned and broke into a jog. Home this evening wasn't a penthouse in Boston; it was a summer home in Milford. He pulled his cell phone out as he moved. Chopper would be the quickest way to get there. He glanced at the sky. He would have to check the weather. Hopefully the storm would hold off, or at least not be too bad. He'd call Irene from his car and talk to the police in the morning.

Sara flipped on the lamp. Darkness had fallen and still no word from John.

The kidnapper had probed several times—deep flashes of darkness and anger that had left her head feeling like a melon shattered on hot pavement. She laid a hand across her stomach. Each probe sent a spasm through her child.

Lights flashed through the dimly lit room. Someone pulled into her drive. A few moments later there was a knock. Sara went to the door, knowing full well who stood on the other side.

Anne's tall, spare frame filled the dark space. "You know why I'm here?"

"Yes."

"Things are different when it's your own flesh and blood."

Sara motioned her in, shut the door, and silently faced her friend.

"You've got to help the police, Sara. They've only guessed at the song, and they haven't come up with anything else—except that they don't have much time."

The older woman looked out the window into the night. "I know I'm asking a lot, but Miriam's the only child my Sally will ever have, the only grandchild I'll ever have. You were there. You know she almost died giving birth."

Sara walked to the couch and sat, her head zinging.

"Play, Sara. Remember Joshua."

She closed her eyes, shutting out Anne, struggling to block the dark words that sang in her mind, and the thin plea for help.

"Answer me. Play the fucking game or the child dies. I will kill her. You know I will."

"No!" Her eyes flew open. Anne was staring, her mouth open.

"You're in touch with him, aren't you? Find out where Miriam is. Please talk to him, Sara. Don't let my grandchild die."

The door flew open. John kicked it shut with his foot, his eyes traveling from Anne to Sara. He went to his wife, kneeling in front of her, taking her cold hands into his.

"Are you all right?"

She pressed her lips together and gave a small shake of her head, showing silently what she couldn't say out loud: *I'm not answering you, him, or anyone.*

"Don't answer him, Sara." John glanced over at Anne. "You need to leave. Now."

"Why are you here? Why aren't you out trying to find my granddaughter?" Anne demanded, her voice ragged.

"I saw you leave the scene. I had a pretty good idea where you were going."

"Do you have anything?"

John's eyes never left Sara. "We think we've got the song."

It began softly, then gained volume—the voice of a frightened child screaming for help, for safety. The edges of Sara's world dissolved into a gray mist.

She was cold, frightened. Rough hands bruised and scraped her tender flesh. One bootless foot left a trail of blood as the man dragged her over ice and snow. Tears froze on her face. She wanted to scream. In her mind, she did.

Sara crooned softly, promising help, safety.

"Sara!"

Her eyes focused. John's face was inches from hers. The little girl gave her no choice. She had to play.

"Give me the notes."

"No."

"Give me the notes, John. I have to play."

"But our baby—"

"I can't be that selfish."

He handed her a piece of paper. Stumbling to the piano, she played them once, then over and over using different keys, different

145

timing. The ragged edges of a tune popped into her mind. "'Lead, Kindly Light.' Is that what you came up with?"

"Not as quickly as you did."

Sara almost fell off the bench as she reached for her songbook. John grabbed her, steadying her as she leafed through the music. It was hymn 123. One hundred twenty-three minutes to live. How much time had already elapsed? She focused on the words.

"Light. Lighthouse."

"That's what we guessed. There are several in the area. We're working with the New Haven police, but no one's found anything yet."

She looked again at the lyrics. Verses randomly caught her eye.

> *Lead, kindly Light, amid th'encircling gloom*
> *Lead thou me on!*
> *The night is dark, and I am far from home . . .*

> *I loved to choose and see my path; but now*
> *Lead thou me on!*

"Sara. Speak to me, bitch!"

"He'll give you a clue, won't he?" Anne asked, her voice shrill and trembling. "You told me he always gives you a clue. Talk to him." Anne moved closer to Sara.

John stepped between them, facing down the woman. "He let Dillon go, Anne; he might let Miriam go too."

Sara's eyes fell on the final verse of the song.

> *The night is gone.*
> *And with the morn those angel faces smile,*
> *Which I have loved long since and lost awhile!*

"He's threatening to kill her. He's never used the word 'kill' as strongly." Sara's voice sounded dead, resigned, even to her ears.

"Talk to him."

She looked into Anne's frightened face. "It won't do any good." She turned to John. "The light falls on a path. The path goes to the water. I hear the waves."

A voice tore through her mind.

"I can do it right now. I can kill her."

Sara leaned forward, clutching her stomach. The flutters were becoming punches.

"Are you all right?" John asked frantically.

"I—"

"Talk to the fucking kidnapper!" Anne screeched.

Sara closed her eyes.

"That's better."

"I'm not here for you." She swung her thoughts to blond-haired Miriam. For just an instant, she saw through the child's bright blue eyes.

"Lighthouse Point, New Haven—in the water. The path—it's not used much, overgrown, a distance from the lighthouse. But it catches the edge of the light." She looked up. Tears flowed down her cheeks. "I don't know which direction."

John flipped out his cell, spoke tersely to the person on the other end, then cut the connection. "I've redirected the men. Are you all right?"

"I'm fine. Take Anne. You don't have much time."

Dimly, she heard the door close.

"Where are you?"

"You go to hell," she heard herself say to the madman.

"Sara . . ." the voice wheedled.

She laid a hand across her abdomen, closed her eyes, and reached for Miriam. Curse or not, this was her gift. It was time to use it to comfort the child she had tried to ignore.

"Miriam, it's Sara. Hold on, darling. Help is coming."

CHAPTER 16

John looked down at the child. He'd known, even before they recovered the small form from the Sound's cold waters, that Anne's granddaughter was dead. Standing back, he allowed the police photographer to do her work.

Pulling his hat down in the face of the stinging wind, he looked away. Fifteen years on the force told him the child didn't die of exposure or drowning. She was murdered, brutally, callously.

He walked back to Anne. Oblivious to everything, the woman stared at the still figure that had been her only granddaughter. She looked up as John approached. The hate from her eyes almost pushed him backwards. He stopped in front of her.

"We would never have reached her in time, Anne. He was killing her while he was speaking to Sara."

The woman said nothing. He stepped past her. There was no helping Anne Stockton. He glanced at his watch. It had taken the forensics team almost forty minutes to get to the scene and another twenty to photograph everything. Finally, the body was being bagged and put into a waiting ambulance. Something in his gut told him to get home.

He caught Samuel's eye. "I'm going to see how Sara is. If

everything's all right, I'll meet you at the precinct in about an hour."

Samuel shook his head. "Make it later. I know the weather is bad, but that might have made the kidnapper careless. I want to check things carefully."

John nodded and headed to his car. Slipping in, he turned the engine on, flipped on the heat, and slowly pulled away, ignoring the cold stares from the bystanders. It would hit the morning news. He could see the headlines now. "POLICE USING PSYCHIC IN KIDNAPPING CASES—PSYCHIC FAILS—CHILD DIES." If John knew Anne, and he was fairly certain he did, she was about to crucify Sara. He punched in the code for home.

"You okay, hon?" he asked when Sara picked up.

"Where are you now?" Her voice sounded strange.

"I'm leaving the scene. Miriam's dead."

"I know. I held her in my arms. I held her as he killed her."

"Then you know that even had you played the game from the first, you would have failed."

There was a moment of silence. "Get home as soon as you can."

"Is it the baby?"

"I'm not sure."

"Sara, do I need to call an ambulance?"

"Just get home."

He cut the connection, leaned over, and pulled the light from the floor. A minute later, he was heading down the highway, lights flashing.

"You bitch!"

The words crackled through her mind.

"You made me do it! You made me kill her!"

Sara tried to shut out the ravings. A cramp cut through her stomach. She pulled her knees together in a vain attempt to keep the warm blood from seeping out of her body.

Sara opened her eyes, smelling Lysol, Clorox, and something else she couldn't name. The steady beep of the fetal monitor filled her with hope and fear. It had been close; for the past few hours, the doctors had plied her with medicines to stop the spasms and calm her and the child. They had succeeded. She still carried their daughter.

"How are you feeling, honey?"

Sara turned to see John's concerned face and gave a crooked half smile. "I'm not up for a marathon right now, but I think we're going to be okay." She reached for John's hand. "I was right."

"About what?"

"If I play the game, I lose the baby. She can't take the probes."

"So now you think it's a girl?"

Sara smiled and shook her head. "I know it's a girl. The nurse told me."

John smiled back, then sobered. "I should have listened to you. I'm sorry. But you're definitely quitting now." His fingers gently touched the bruises around her throat. "When I brought you in, you kept mumbling that he was choking Miriam. Now I know how you knew."

Sara nodded silently, fighting back tears as John smoothed her hair.

"Don't think about anything right now except getting well and coming home. You're stopping the game. We're going to have this child, and both of you are going to survive. Understand?"

She nodded.

He leaned over and gave her a quick kiss. "Get some rest. I'll be back in the morning."

Sara felt the void when he closed the door.

"Murderer."

She caught her breath.

"Play or there'll be another dead child, and you'll be a murderer."

She rolled over, closing her eyes, blocking out everything.

John didn't even know if Caleb was in Milford or why, but the lights told him someone was in the rambling Cape Cod summer home. He cut the engine, wondering why in the hell he'd driven out of his way to come here.

For a moment he just sat. The night had finally gotten to him. His muscles screamed for sleep, his head pounded like a freight train running through a tunnel, his knee felt like someone had driven a red-hot poker into it. He pulled out a cigarette and lit it, then drew in deep as he stared at the porch light. He was scared, damned scared. A line had been crossed tonight. Now, he was dealing with a killer. And if the bastard could kill a child, he could kill Sara.

Was Caleb connected? In John's mind, Sara's brother was still the loose cannon; the man had the skill and training to kidnap, kill, and terrorize. But had he? John had no proof. Sara believed Caleb was innocent, and without the proof, John needed to accept that. His wife was right more than she was wrong, and she believed in her brother, truly believed in him.

John stepped out of the car and leaned against the still-warm vehicle. The night closed in on him, smelling suddenly of filth, blood, vomit. There had been another child, a boy, almost dead, not from a deranged psycho, but from a drug-high father.

William Duncan Jr. swayed in the light of the bathroom door, his rail-thin body arrogant, his eyes mean and high on drugs. He was laughing at the cops, and they knew why.

They could cuff him, take him to jail, but his father had good lawyers—and William Duncan Jr. wasn't stupid. They'd find nothing. And Rachael was too dumb, too high, and too scared to press charges.

They might get him for beating the kid, but his father's lawyers would cut deals. He might not even go to jail. If they got him that far, his father would make sure the jail was the right kind, the kind where inmates didn't take offense at child beaters.

John knelt on the floor, a blanket in his hand, and covered the child. Keeping his voice soft, gentle, he spoke until the boy's sobs turned into hiccups and finally stopped. He stayed beside the child until the paramedics arrived, letting the little boy know that someone actually cared.

Anger struck when the paramedics lifted the thin, broken body onto a gurney. John glanced up at the uniforms. Both men shook their heads. William Duncan would get away with it again, and there was nothing anyone could do.

He glanced at the cops. "Keep that bastard here. No one comes in or out while you're turning this place upside down."

Without a word, he left.

Half an hour later he returned, minus a watch and all the cash in his pockets. Nothing was said. The cops were old to the game. They knew something was up.

It was childishly easy. Tell William he looked sick, push him into the bathroom, pull out a bag of drugs, and slip the gun into his hand. Turn it, keeping your hand on the trigger, and take the bullet.

That night he had crossed a line. It was the first time. It wasn't the last. So what kind of a man was he to pre-judge Caleb? What if Sara was right? What if Caleb was innocent? He needed to talk, to tell someone what he had done that night. He didn't know why, but he had the strangest feeling that Caleb would understand.

John snubbed out the cigarette, noticing the faint shake in his hand, and walked up the wooden steps of the old Cape Cod. Caleb answered the door seconds after John rang the bell.

For a moment the two men stared at each other, each one looking as though they'd just come from the depths of hell.

"I don't know why I'm here," John stated simply.

Caleb nodded. "I do. So Sara was helping the police?"

John nodded.

"It's time we talk. Let's go into the kitchen. I'll put some coffee on. You look as though you could use a cup."

In the silence John swirled the cream floating in his coffee, then looked up into green eyes that reminded him of Sara. "Do you know what's going on?"

"Not really. I've surmised some things based on being called in and questioned. Sara alluded to a couple of things, so I'm pretty sure I know what you are thinking. Could I do what this kidnapper is doing? Physically, yes. I've the training to capture and contain. Would I? No. I couldn't and wouldn't do what he's done to any child, and I would never put my sister through what I know she's going through."

"Sara's in the hospital. She almost lost our baby tonight."

"I figured something like that was going on."

John's fist slammed down on the granite counter. The soft thud echoed through the room. "How did you know? How in the hell did you know I was going to pick you up and take you in for questioning that evening?"

"I'm precognitive."

John sat back, stunned. "You're gifted. I thought that only happened to the women of Sara's family."

"Several of our male ancestors have had some kind of gift. It's just not passed on to their children. It's the female line that insures the gift will continue. But I can tell you one thing. This man is not out to get St. Mary's or even Milford. This man is out to get Sara. She's in grave danger—but I think you figured that out tonight."

"No. My thoughts tonight led me to believe I was the ultimate target. I busted a man named William Duncan Jr. a few years ago. His old man's rich. I think father and son are coming after me through Sara."

Caleb froze. "My company's having to deal with Duncan Sr. Not good dealings, I might add. I lost a friend this afternoon, a close friend, and it wouldn't surprise me to find out Duncan was behind his death."

John held his cup out to Caleb. "I believe we could both do with a bit of the Irish. It's going to be a long night."

Caleb nodded as he reached for the whiskey bottle.

Through the murky fog, the edge of the lighthouse beam cast an almost obscene aura over the crime scene. Like a sickly yellow limelight, it pinpointed the spot where the child had died.

Samuel stared at the scene, then ducked under the yellow tape and walked down the path. At John's request, he'd worked with the forensic guys, his dark eyes searching every grain of sand, every rock for something, anything that would lead them to the killer. As usual, there was nothing.

At the water's edge, he stopped. The Sound was angry. Slate-gray waves fought each other, their peaks lathered in white foam.

He felt her. Miriam was still here. Her soul was not scattered, but confused, split.

The hum began in the back of his throat. He reached into his pocket, withdrew a pack of cigarettes, pulled out a handful, and skimmed them of paper. When he finished, his hand was full of loose tobacco. He had no sacred corn, but this would do.

The hum became a low chant. He faced the four directions, singing softly, willing the girl's spirit and soul to come together. He would send her home, whole.

A screech broke his song. He looked up. A lone hawk wheeled lazily in the night winds, dark shadow against dark sky. There was a sudden shimmer in the night sky; then the hawk caught the current and lifted from sight.

Hawk frowned. The shimmer—the same thing had happened on the Thimble Islands. What did it mean? He waited, feeling the night, then smiled to himself. Whatever the shimmer was, the girl's soul was at peace. The song had worked.

But nothing else had. It was the same man; he no longer doubted that. The monster who had started his spree on the reservation five years before was now hunting in Milford, and once again, the evil had eluded Samuel.

Or was he just too frightened to face it? Samuel turned away from the waters. He had tried many times in the past weeks to contact Leon. The Hopi wasn't answering any of his messages.

Samuel was being avoided. He knew it. Leon was scared Samuel wanted to go home, and that didn't fit in with Leon's needs.

Was Sara one of the three who would save the Hopi at the end times? He didn't know . . . and yet he did. Deep down, there was something that told him the truth. Did she know?

Now wasn't the time to ask. John had called from the hospital. She had almost lost the child. The man was frightened—Samuel heard it in his voice. And if Sara lost another baby, no one wanted to guess what might happen to her.

Samuel was back in the car when his cell phone rang. He checked the screen. Leon. "About time you got back to me."

"Sorry, Sam. I've been busy. Had to go out into the field."

"You mean you had to work." Samuel chuckled at one of their old jokes.

"Something like that."

There was a strained pause.

"What did you find, Leon?"

"Nothing. I thought I was really on the track. I thought we had something. This was the man who would save us. He seemed real, strong, honest. It was nothing. He was a smoke man. So how are things going with you?"

"As I told you in my messages, Sara has stopped using her gift. At least, almost. She used it tonight to help a friend and almost lost her baby. She will definitely stop now."

"The one we seek is a fighter. This woman isn't."

Anger flared through Samuel. "She is a fighter. She's fighting to keep her child."

"She takes the easy road."

"No. She takes the path she has to to survive."

"It is not ours."

"You don't know that. Leon, I've been working for you for several years now. I've interviewed lots of people. She is the closest I've found to being what we seek."

Leon's chortle broke the silence. "You believe in her. You don't want to admit it, but you believe she may be the one we seek, or maybe one of the three we seek."

Samuel took a deep breath. The old Hopi knew him—perhaps better than he knew himself. "You are right. Sara serves, helps, and is gifted. I think it is very possible she is the one we seek. And I think her brother just might be the second of the three we seek."

"So what do you want to do now?"

"I want to come home."

The line fell silent. "Are you ill?" Leon's voice was strained.

What could he say? Should he tell his old friend he was frightened? Should he tell him he had heard his own death chant? "No, I'm not ill."

"Stay awhile longer, Sam. I know you want to come home. I know why. But I need you there. *She* needs you there."

Samuel pulled the phone away and stared at it. What did Leon know? He wouldn't ask Samuel to stay unless there was something else, something he had missed. But Leon was right about one thing. Samuel had the strangest feeling that Sara would need him.

"I want to be home by summer."

"You will be."

Before Samuel could add anything, the line went dead.

He leaned back and stared at the misty snow-covered trees. In his mind he saw the town of Milford cloaked in a shadow of evil that would stay there until something or someone lifted it.

He gave another sigh. Summer seemed a long way off.

CHAPTER 17

"PSYCHIC REFUSES TO AID POLICE—CHILD DIES"

John glanced at the first line beneath the heading: "Milford PD has been using a psychic named Sara Allbrooke to help find children taken in a recent kidnapping spree. This time, however, Allbrooke refused to work with the police . . ."

John couldn't read any more. With a loud "shit," he tore the taped newspaper off the front door and tore it into shreds as he looked around, ready to run down anyone who looked remotely suspicious.

"It's all right." Sara placed a white hand on his arm. "We knew this could happen."

"Yeah, well, they never fucking mention the kids you saved, or doesn't that count?" He shoved the door open and stepped in front of Sara just in time to catch the full brunt of a charging German shepherd.

"For God's sake, Max, get down."

"I think he needs to go outside, darling."

John looked down at his wife. "How can you be so calm about all of this?"

"I don't have a choice." Her hand shifted to her slightly

protruding stomach. "Now take the monster out while I fix some coffee."

"I have a better idea. You sit. I'll fix the coffee when I get back."

The phone rang as Sara moved to the sofa. Grabbing it, she barely had time to speak before a voice screeched through the line.

"You killed that child! If the police hadn't listened to your evil, they would have had her in time. You're the spawn of Satan—"

Sara slammed the receiver down and stared at the blinking light. It appeared new numbers would be in order for their house and cell phones. She'd stopped listening to her cell phone messages hours ago and had finally turned the thing off.

Things were going to change. That was apparent. Could she handle it? She held her hand over her stomach. She had no choice.

"You okay?"

"It seems I'm the spawn of Satan now."

John pulled her to him. "Don't let them get to you. They're angry, frustrated. You're the only person they know to yell at."

She looked into his gentle brown eyes. "I love you."

"I love you too."

The ringing of the telephone interrupted the moment. Sara pulled away and picked up the receiver, ready for whoever was on the other end.

She listened quietly, then spoke. "Come on over." Hanging up, she turned to John. "That was Anne. She wants to talk. Any guesses as to what it's about?"

"I don't know, but don't go looking for trouble."

"I'm not. But we both know she's going to—"

He pulled her back into his arms, cutting off the rest of her sentence. She leaned against his chest, listening to the thud of his heart, his soft breathing. He was her safe harbor.

A doorbell broke them apart.

"That was quick," John kept his eyes on Sara as he spoke.

"I'll get it." She shoved him toward the kitchen. "You make the coffee."

A stern-faced Anne Stockton stood at the door. Sara stared at the older woman. She had aged in the last day—even beyond that, she had hardened. "Come in."

The woman strode in with brusque determination and a clipped "thank you."

Sara stood at the door, waiting patiently for Max to complete his duty. In minutes, the dog was on the porch and walking quietly inside, staring intently at the tall stranger.

Shutting the door behind the dog, Sara faced the woman she had called a friend for almost ten years. Much of the frigid air from outside remained in the room, surrounding Anne.

"Would you like some coffee?"

"No."

So that's how it's going to be. "Throw your coat on the sofa. John's in the kitchen. We were just getting ready to have a cup."

Silently, Anne followed her and took the offered chair. John whisked around and handed a cup to Sara, then grabbed one for himself and sat.

Sara rolled the hot cup between her cold hands while a silent Anne sat like a statue, devoid of warmth, friendship.

"I'm sorry about Miriam, Anne. I would have done anything to save her."

"That's a lie. I had to beg you to help."

Sara set the coffee down. "I was afraid I might lose my child if I helped—and something wasn't right. He was killing Miriam as we were speaking. He never had any intention of letting her live."

"I don't know about that. My gut tells me you're trying to salve your conscience. If you had acted earlier—"

"She still would have died. He would have seen to that. In the meantime, you went to the papers. You told them the police were using a psychic and that I was that psychic."

"Yes, I did. I wanted you to feel my pain."

Sara unwrapped the scarf from her neck. Dark blue bruises covered her throat. "I did feel it. I felt every bit of it." A long silence fell across the table. "When do you want me to quit?"

If Anne was surprised by the question, she didn't show it. "Your resignation will be effective immediately."

"On what grounds?"

"On the grounds that you are a danger to children."

Cold anger flared through Sara. "And what are you basing that on?"

Anne hesitated, clearing her throat before she spoke. "It's based on—"

Sara waved a hand. "Don't bother. If I fight this?"

"The board is prepared to fire you. If you leave quietly, there won't be a stink. The records will show that you left due to 'extenuating circumstances.' If you put up a fuss, we'll crucify you."

"And of course, you'll support this?"

"I'll lead the charge."

Sara stared at the woman. She'd often wondered what mistake would cost her her friends. What surprised her most was the lack of pain. "It sounds as though I might as well forget about any jobs in Connecticut."

"At least in Milford."

Sara rose and moved to her small desk in the alcove. It was done in one sentence and a signature. Turning, she handed the paper to Anne. "You've got it. Now get out."

"I'll give this to the board immediately."

"You do that, Anne."

The woman grabbed her coat, folding the piece of paper as though it were a prize and slipping it into her pocket. She stopped at the door, her back to Sara and John. "The funeral was yesterday. The least you could have done was come."

"John just brought me home from the hospital this morning."

"Oh." Anne glanced around.

"Connecting with the killer and Miriam almost made me lose the baby."

For an instant, the woman's features softened; then the mask of anger was back. "Well, if you had lost the child, you could have had another one. My daughter can't." The slam of the door reverberated through the small house.

John moved behind Sara, pulling her against him.

"I did all I could," she said. "I was with her at the end. I held her in my arms."

His arms tightened around her shoulders. "How? I thought you became the child."

Sara shrugged out of his warm embrace and turned to face him. "It's happened only once before, when I was working with another psychic and the New York State police. I told you about the boy kidnapped by his father, how I believed the man could be talked down. The other psychic didn't want to wait, and in the end the father snapped. He killed his son, then himself. Just before the child died, I was catapulted from his body. One moment I was the child, the next I was holding him in my arms as he passed over. The same thing happened with Anne's granddaughter."

"I'm glad your survival instinct is strong. I never thought until now about the possibility of you dying with a child." He caught her chin and lifted it up. "If you feel like crying, go ahead. You deserve it."

"I've already cried. My tears were for Miriam, for a promising life cut short by a man who never should have been born." She leaned into John, burying her face in his shirt. "I'm so damned mad I could . . . I know now what my grandmother meant when she said she could get so angry she spit nails. How dare this bastard force me to choose between my baby's life and another child's. How dare these people judge me." She stopped, catching her breath.

John chuckled as he hugged her tightly, breaking the tension in the room. "You'll make it, Sara Allbrooke. You'll make it just fine. Now let's go upstairs and get some rest."

"Are you there, Sara?"
A knife cut through her foggy brain.
"Bastard."
"How do you know my parents weren't married?"

"You mean they knowingly created a monster?"

There was silence. Had she been dreaming? She glanced over at John's still, snoring figure.

"You'll pay for that."

Placing a protective hand over her stomach, Sara closed her mind to his ravings. She shut the door, praying fervently that she could keep it shut.

Caleb grieved as he read the article. Sara and John's secret was out. There would be no rest for either one, and there wasn't a damned thing he could do to help.

Papers lay strewn across the office. From Boston to New Haven, from front page to third page, they all claimed the same thing. They were attacking his sister Sara, and he was helpless. He closed his eyes, remembering all the times she had protected him from their father.

At least he'd been there to talk to John.

He slammed the cup down. The coffee tasted like shit and it wasn't Irene's fault—it was everything else. Richard was dead. It was ruled an accident, although no one could explain how it had happened.

Caleb knew he was missing vital information and that fact didn't sit well. Richard had been scared. Caleb had heard that much in his voice. But scared of what? It took a lot to frighten the man who had gone into black ops with him. What had Richard needed to tell him? And why did it have to be away from the office?

"Mr. Remington."

Irene's official voice. Duncan must be in the reception area. The man owned thirty percent of RemTech and he was already trying to make waves. Beyond that, Caleb was certain he was still trying to maneuver a merger.

"Mr. Duncan's here."

"Show him into the . . ." Caleb almost said office. No. That wouldn't work. He didn't want the dark bastard anywhere near his office. "Show him to the fourth-floor meeting room—and Irene, no refreshments. Not even a bottle of water."

Caleb sat back, a small smile raising the corners of his mouth. The room was rarely used. It was small, windowless, and too dismal for his tastes. He had halfway decided to turn the area into a storage room; but for now, it would be perfect. It was easy to clean and just maybe it would make Duncan uncomfortable enough to stay away.

He waited twenty minutes before walking in.

William Duncan Sr. sat at the end of the table, his lawyer daughter on his right. Her briefcase was open, papers spread out on the scarred table.

The man was pissed. That was apparent to Caleb. Yet, Duncan kept his temper under control, meeting Caleb with an outstretched hand and a smile that didn't quite reach his eyes.

Caleb ignored the gesture and sat, a mug of steaming coffee in his left hand.

"What do you want, Duncan?"

"Not even the veneer of niceties, huh?"

Caleb remained silent.

"We have a government contract coming down. I think we could do better—a lot better—on the terms. After all, it is about making money. And I have a healthy sum invested in my thirty-five percent."

"Thirty."

"Thirty-five, Remington. You never got those buy-back letters out, did you? Now it's just a question of getting your sister's shares and those elusive nine percent your broker pulled."

"You still won't own the company."

"Ach! That's just terminology, boy. I'll run all of Remington's eventually." He nodded to his daughter, who opened a folder and spread out still more papers.

Caleb recognized the contract. He smiled, reached into his pocket, and threw a handful of bugs across the papers.

"The source of your information may be somewhat incomplete from now on. The government contracts have already been signed. RemTech's R&D department is already working on it. And stay away from my sister. Your son's already shown his stupidity for messing with my brother-in-law. Is it genetic? And your contract . . ." Caleb reached across the table, his hand bumping the coffee cup. In seconds, a dark liquid spread across the papers.

He leaned back, watching as Duncan's daughter jumped up and grabbed the papers, shaking them. Very little coffee flew out. The liquid soaked into the folder as though it were a sponge.

With a half-smile, Caleb rose, picked up his cup, and nodded at the soggy papers Abigail held.

"Contract negotiations ended a month ago."

At the door he stopped and turned, green eyes pinning Duncan's cold blue ones. "It was your renovation company working on the Boston church, wasn't it? A friend of mine was 'accidently' killed there. If I ever tie you to Richard's death, I'll make it my life-long duty to break you and the companies you own. Don't come back unless I call a board meeting."

He strode from the room, caught the elevator, and exited on the penthouse level. Seconds later, he was in his kitchen, carefully pouring the remaining contents of the coffee cup down the drain. He had an idea what Richard had glommed onto now. He had an idea of what he was facing.

The dance was becoming macabre.

"Why'd you do it?" Joe kept his voice low, respectful, his cell phone tight to his ear. He felt as though he had been punched in the gut as the newspaper headlines glared at him from the ancient sofa that occupied a corner of his studio. Again, his father had kidnapped a child when he wasn't around. How could he watch the children, help them, if he didn't know what was going to happen? Was it just hours, days, or months since he'd left New Orleans? It

"Positive." She slid a cup of coffee across the counter. "And it is a lot of work, but I love doing it. I just wish . . ." Her voice trailed off.

"You wish you could be in a classroom," John finished for her.

Sara nodded. "It's strange. I can't teach children, but they still value my assessments, and I think most of my recommendations for the special-needs children have been implemented."

"I still don't understand what you do."

"I analyze reports, tests, and assessments on special-needs children, then try to develop a curriculum that will allow them to learn or continue learning." She stopped. But it wasn't teaching, and her heart still ached to be in the classroom. She was allowed to go into schools and observe students, but nothing else. It was the teaching she missed so desperately. "Thank God for my master's in child development."

"Do you think Anne had something to do with all of this?" John waved an arm at the papers.

"I don't know. She commended me often for being a good teacher. But actually recommending me—I don't think so."

"You miss her?"

"I miss the children. I woke up thinking about Billy this morning, wondering how he's getting along. Did I tell you I got a call about him a few days ago?"

"No. Who called?"

"A school in Hartford called New Hope. They've been working with autistic children for the last ten years. Their premise is that autistic children frequently have highly developed extrasensory perception."

"ESP?"

"Yes. I checked the school out. They're legit. And their success rate for weaning these kids off drugs and returning them to a public school environment as productive, normal students is phenomenal."

"How did they get your name?"

"Rachael Duncan. She told them I had been Billy's teacher. They knew who I was, and it didn't bother them. In fact, they were very interested in my abilities. They seemed to feel my gift might have actually created a bond with Billy."

"You didn't happen to tell them that you fostered the child for almost four months?" John asked drily.

She stuck her tongue out at him. "Yes, I did. Rachael's trying to get him into the school, which leads me to think he's not doing very well at St. Mary's." She hesitated. "They've asked me to come up to New Hope to view some of the work they do."

John's hand closed tightly over hers. "I know where you're going with this—if you can be instrumental in turning Billy around, maybe St. Mary's will ask you back. It's not going to happen, honey."

She looked away, irritated that John could read her so easily.

"It won't always be like this," he continued. "Just give things some time." Letting go of her hand, he pushed his stool back and stood. "I need to get going. I have an appointment."

"Billy's father?"

"How'd you know?"

"Reading people is a two-way street. Besides, you've never once thought the kidnapper was after me. It's a logical assumption that you would go after people you thought might be a threat to you."

He gave a half smile. "You've been married to a cop too long."

"Duncan's in prison. He can't do anything."

"His daddy's got more than enough money to orchestrate something like this; besides, Junior asked for this meeting."

"But wouldn't it be wiser to go after the father since he has the money?"

"It's because he's got so much money that I can't go after him, not until I have something very concrete on the old buzzard. Caleb thinks there's a very slender chance of that happening."

"You two are becoming quite chummy."

John leaned over and gave her a quick peck. "We have a mutual interest: you. And I'm actually going to use Junior as bait. I've already cast out a few nets."

"How do you do that?"

"I scare and intimidate."

"Why couldn't you have been an insurance salesman?"

"You wouldn't have been as intrigued by me. I should be back in Milford by three or so. I'll stop by the house to make sure you're getting some rest before I go into the office. In the meantime, you'd better get dressed and get your reports done. I feel like a big steak at a cozy restaurant tonight."

"Sounds great, and I don't have to get dressed until we go out. I work at home, remember?"

With a chuckle, he turned.

Sara followed him to the door, watching out the window as he drove away. Maybe she would get dressed. She glanced at the mantle clock. The ticking was abnormally loud. Threads of restlessness set her teeth on edge.

William Duncan Jr. clunked in, his gait hampered by more than the chains. He moved like a man who'd lost a fight. John stared. One eye was black. A cut on the other side of his face had been butterflied. It looked like John might have "cast a net" in the right place.

He waited in silence as the chained man sat. For several minutes they stared at each other.

"Got a light?" Duncan Jr. finally asked.

"Not one I'd give you."

Duncan leaned forward. "Know this, you cop bastard. I don't know anything about your bi—wife. I've got nothing to do with any kidnappings. I wanted you to hear that from my lips. I'm not after you. I just want to do my time and get the hell out of here."

"Is this what you called me in to say?"

William leaned back. "You might want to check out my father."

"What do you know?"

"Nothing. I'm guessing. You can look up the records. The old man hasn't contacted me since the trial. I'm the prodigal son, except I can't go back."

"Don't expect me to feel sorry for you."

"I don't expect anything in this fucking world, especially not from dear old Daddy."

"Turning over evidence on anything illegal your father's involved in could get you freed early. I'd see to that."

"Yeah, well it could also get me killed." William rose. "You're barking up the wrong tree with me. I'm the sapling, not the oak."

He got up and tottered to the door, stopping when John spoke. "Why is it you never ask about your son?"

"I guess the same reason my father never sees me. If you think my father's a bastard . . . Well, evil begets evil. One day my son will try to screw me, just like I'd like to be able to screw my old man." He glanced back. "My father's the one you should be looking at." He clanked down the hall.

John sat in silence. That hadn't gone down like he'd thought it would. Caleb. He'd put in a call to Caleb. See if his brother-in-law might have something on the father that he could share.

John walked out of the prison and headed toward his car, a prickly feeling running up and down his spine.

Halfway down the corridor, William Duncan stopped and turned to the cop following him. "Hey, I need to make a phone call."

"You can—this afternoon in the rec hall."

"But it's to my father. I need to speak to my dad."

The guard ignored the plea and pushed him forward. "Move. No special privileges allowed."

A slow smile creased William's face. By the time they reached his cell, he was whistling. He had done what his father requested. He took a deep breath, inhaling the ghostly fragrance of a cigarette. His deed was good for at least a couple of packs and maybe even some of the really good stuff. Maybe the old man would surprise him with an early release or a better prison.

It was a clear day, roads dry, so why in the hell was he stuck in yet another traffic jam? John slapped the steering wheel, then noticed the state patrol along the side of the road. They looked harried and hassled. He leaned back. There was nothing he could do except be late getting back to Milford.

Half a block away from the station, John's cell phone chimed. He glanced down, silently cursing himself. He'd forgotten that he promised Sara he'd stop by the house first. He answered the call, prepared to give an abject apology. "Hi, hon—"

"He's going to strike again."

"Hold on, Sara."

John twisted the wheel, spinning into the police parking lot, then stopped and cut the engine.

"How's the baby?"

"Asleep so far. The killer just popped into my head."

"I'm at the station now. As soon as I know something, I'll call. And Sara, don't let him in."

"I won't."

Sara laid the phone on the coffee table. It would be all right. John was where he should be. She was home, safe—

"Sara, it's time to play!"

She fought to block the voice.

"Remember what happened last time you tried to keep me out?" The voice was smooth, like silken oil.

"Get out of my head." It felt like it took a physical shove, but Sara got the door to her mind closed. The baby kicked. Nausea

welled up in her throat. The pounding in her head was increasing; it was in sync with the mantle clock.

Gershwin's "Rhapsody in Blue" sent shockwaves along her nerves. She grabbed the phone.

"John?"

"He struck about thirty minutes ago." His voice sounded peculiar.

"Who is it?"

"It's Allen. I'm with Tom and Judy now."

"Oh, dear God. What happened?"

"The boy was playing hide 'n seek with his sister. Went to hide and didn't come back. Judy found his torn shirt in the back shed."

"Was there a note?"

There was scuffling in the background. A voice screeched, almost shattering Sara's eardrums.

"You bitch. We don't want your help. You've destroyed one of my sons; keep your filthy mind off Allen. Stay away. Do you hear me? Stay—"

Angry voices put an end to the tirade. John's voice came back on the line. "Sorry about that, honey."

"Give me the notes when you get them. I'll try to link with Allen."

"Sara, don't."

"I can't let Judy lose another child."

"What about ours? Look, I doubt the boy will even talk to you. According to Tom, Judy's been feeding him horror stories about you."

"I've got to try."

John's voice rose several notches. "Even if it costs us our child? We'll find him. Just let us do our job."

The phone went dead.

Sara leaned back, closed her eyes, and placed her hands over her stomach. Feeling her own child, she reached out. Blackness met her. She sent her mind out into the darkness. There was nothing, not even stars. What if she couldn't link with Allen? What if stopping the gift had . . . What if Samuel was right? *When a gift is refused, payment is demanded.* What if she was paying for shutting down the gift? What if she no longer possessed the ability? What if . . .

Opening her eyes, Sara jerked up and took a deep breath, calming the pounding of her heart. John was right. The what-if game was dangerous—too dangerous and destructive to play now. Helping children, linking with them, that was her special talent. She hadn't lost it. *Wouldn't* lose it.

Closing her eyes, she plunged deeper, calling Allen's name, seeking the child she'd known. She heard nothing but the echoes of her own thoughts and fears.

John put the phone back in his pocket. Red eyes and a face ravaged by hate stared at him. Judy's hand lashed out for the second time. He caught it inches from his face and held it.

"Are you crazy, John? Are you buying into her gibberish? She's evil. She kills children. She killed Anne's granddaughter. She almost killed Joshua. These kidnappings are part of her plan—but she's not going to win this time. She's not going to kill another child. She's not going to kill Allen."

"And what about the children she saved?"

John watched his sister as she feverishly sought to find an answer to his question.

"She planned it, John. It's all part of her plan."

"Stop it." Tom's voice lashed out.

Judy freed her hand and whirled to face her husband. "She killed—"

"She didn't kill anyone, Judy," Tom said wearily. "Joshua's not dead and they never had a chance with Miriam. As far as we know, Allen's still alive. John trusts her, and so do I." He looked past his wife to John. "What do you need us to do?"

"Stay by the phone. We need to find the notes." John pushed by his sister.

Gershwin. Sara grabbed the phone.

"John?"

"Are you sure you want them?"

"Yes."

"C, D, F, F, F, D."

She took the phone to the piano. One run was enough to recognize the melody. It's 'That Old-Time Religion.'"

"Are you sure?"

"Positive."

"I'll let headquarters know in case they haven't figured it out yet." He hesitated. "Did you try to link with Allen?"

"Yes."

His smile came through the phone. "I figured you weren't going to listen to what I said. Promise me that at the slightest twinge, discomfort, anything that doesn't feel right, you will stop, pull out—whatever you have to do to break the link. I won't risk losing you or our child."

"I promise, John, but—"

"No buts. I know you want to help. I know you don't want Judy to lose another child. She won't. I promise that. Now, were you able to link with Allen?"

"No."

"I was afraid of that. Just be careful, Sara. You and our daughter are my world and I don't want anything to happen to either of you. You just let me do what I do. Okay?"

"If I can reach the boy, I'll call. I won't take any chances."

"Okay. Gotta go." There was a click, then nothing.

Sara stared at the phone as a wet nose wormed its way under her hand. Max. She looked into his dark brown eyes. The dog had grounded her before. Digging her fingers gently into his fur, she surrounded herself with love and called Allen's name.

"Talk to me, Allen. It's Aunt Sara."

The faint essence of a soul brushed her.

"You're the bad lady."

"No. You used to come to my house and play with Max. I told you stories. Remember Thanksgiving?"

"Momma says you're bad."

"I help find lost children. Are you lost?"

There was a moment of confusion.

"I'm not sure."

"What do you see?"

Darkness and silence answered her question. For a brief second, she thought she'd lost the link.

"The bad man just left. He comes and looks, then goes."

"Are you wet or cold?"

"No."

"Do you recognize anything?"

There was no answer.

"Can you hear water? Are you near the Sound or a river?"

There was still no answer.

Sara opened her eyes. Why had she asked Allen if he recognized anything? Something was different. Thoughts whirled around her head. She straightened up suddenly.

She hadn't been the child. She wasn't seeing through Allen's eyes. She was seeing through her own. She was a watcher. But what had she seen?

Carefully she went back over each question and answer. She hadn't seen Allen at all. She had seen a maze of boxes and wires.

Panic rose in her throat, threatening to choke off all air. Had she lost the gift? Could she no longer link with children, see through their eyes? She took several deep breaths, calming her racing heart. No. It had happened before. When children were about to die, she was catapulted out of their body. It had happened with the little boy in New York and with Miriam. Was Allen about to die? Was the boy at death's door?

The music. She picked up the hymnal, locating the almost classic piece of music. There was no mention of anything tangible—no storms, rocks, lights. More importantly, there was no mention of water.

Nothing came—but the words chilled her. The last two choruses popped out: "It will do when I am dying" and "It will take us all to heaven."

It was an allusion she didn't like. Leaning back against the sofa, she opened her mind to all possibilities and waited.

Long moments passed with no change. Sara raised her eyes to the mantle clock. The ticking that had disturbed her earlier now seemed almost menacing. She swallowed, recognizing the taste of fear. Clock. Time. Old time. She grabbed her phone, punched in the code, and started to speak the minute he picked up. "John, it's got something to do with clocks, with time."

"There are no clocks close to water."

"He's not near water. Drowning or exposure aren't issues. I think—I'm guessing from the words of the song that he's in the middle of everything. Somewhere close. Someplace where the bastard can show his power, thumb his nose at everyone, particularly the police."

John's curse roared through the phone. "Damn. I'll bet he's at the courthouse. Right under our noses. There's construction going on there. It would be easy to get in and out without being noticed. Call you back later."

The muffled sound told her he hadn't hung up. They were still connected.

She glanced back down at the verses. Three times. Everything was repeated three times. "It will take us all to heaven." She looked up at the mantle clock. Two forty-five.

Pain cut through her. She doubled over, the phone still at her ear. Then there was nothing. Only a strange, dead silence. Even the clock seemed to have stopped ticking.

"You missed it. It was easy and you missed it. It will take us all to Heaven."

Had she heard right?

"John," she screamed into the phone. No answer. "I love you," she whispered. Frantically, she hit the disconnect button. It was several minutes before she got a dial tone. She tried John's number and got a busy signal. She tried again with no luck. That damned phone. He'd been having trouble with it for months.

A number popped into her head; she dialed the police station. Four rings later, the phone was answered. She didn't wait.

"This is Sara Allbrooke. My husband's on the way to the courthouse. I think it might be booby-trapped. I think there might be a bomb there." It was the only thing she could think of that would get everyone's attention; show the kidnapper's power over life and death. "You've got to get everyone out of the building."

"Just a moment, ma'am."

"Don't give me a moment—" The woman's voice was gone. Seconds later a male voice picked up.

"Sara, its Captain Parker. Are you sure?"

"Yes. I think I saw explosives in the clock tower. It's set to go off at three. When the clock strikes three."

She was speaking to a dial tone. She rose and grabbed her purse. She had to get to the courthouse and stop John. She glanced at the mantle clock. She had ten minutes.

Throwing the door open, she doubled up as another pain hit her. At once, Max was by her side. She struggled to stand. John couldn't die. Not John. She loved him. Had he heard her say it over the phone? He had to know. She could save him. She had saved others, saved children. She could save her husband.

With her hand in Max's fur, she staggered to the car and opened the door. Max jumped in before she could protest. Grabbing the wheel, she hauled herself into the seat. She tore into her purse, searching for the keys. They weren't there.

She yanked down the visor. Nothing. The keys must be in the house. Another pain hit her. She almost fell out of the car, thankful that Max had followed. Leaning on the big dog, she climbed the steps up to the porch and went back in.

Stopping in the living room, she looked around. She took a deep breath, trying to calm her beating heart and concentrate. There. On the piano. Her keys were on the piano. She had almost reached the instrument when another spasm tore through her. She stopped, then took a step forward and grabbed the keys.

She was at the door when the mantle clock struck three. She felt the voice at the first bong.

"Relish your last moments."

She clung onto the doorframe. At the second bong, she saw John. His arms reached up to hold onto a piece of scaffolding—strong arms she knew so well. "Get the bomb squad in here, and someone find that boy." Her husband's voice was strong and calm.

"I love you, John," she whispered. The third bong. A blinding flash ripped through her world. Everything evaporated. Particles of dust danced in the light and settled into rubble. Cries and screams mingled with the groans and crashes of timbers giving way.

Suddenly she was looking through the dust and smoke. John was gone. "I love you," she whispered again as she shut the door and staggered back to the sofa.

CHAPTER 19

It was dusk. Max growled at the sound of the doorbell. Sara didn't move.

"Open up, Sara. It's Captain Parker."

"Go away." Her voice was rough, throaty.

"Let us in. I brought Jane with me."

"No." If Lyle and his wife couldn't come in, it wasn't true. It hadn't happened. All she had to do was keep them out.

"Honey." She recognized Jane's voice. "Honey, your door's unlocked. Lyle and I are coming in."

Max made no fuss when the two entered. He remained beside Sara, his head in her lap. Vaguely, she was aware of Jane sitting beside her, of the woman putting her arm over Sara's shoulders. The captain pulled up a chair in front of Sara, taking her cold hands in his warm ones. No one said anything.

"We got everyone out, Sara, except for three policemen. They stayed with John, to help him. Most of the people had already gone home . . ." The captain's gentle voice trailed off. "We found Allen. He was curled up in some bushes near Tom and Judy's house, asleep. He's fine."

"He wasn't asleep. The kidnapper used chloroform. It was never about Allen. It was never Allen." She looked into the captain's dark eyes. "It was about me, about John."

"Honey, is there anyone we can call?" Jane asked quietly.

Sara shook her head. "I need—" she stopped.

"What do you need?" Jane prodded.

"I need to go to the hospital. He told me I was going to lose the baby. I think I am."

Sara stared at the white ceiling of her hospital room. The magic meds weren't working this time. There was no sleep she could take refuge in, no place she could hide and pretend that everything was all right.

Soft voices spoke outside the room. For one brief moment, hope flared. It sounded a little like John. She listened carefully. No. It was her brother. It was Caleb.

A few moments later the door opened. He entered quietly, pulled up a chair beside the bed, and sat down.

"You're supposed to be asleep," he said softly.

"What are you doing here?"

"I'm the next of kin. Captain Parker didn't know who else to call."

"You can go back home. I'll be fine."

Glancing up at the monitors, he ignored her words. "The baby's going to be all right. She's a helluva fighter. Did you know it's a little girl?"

"It's true, isn't it?"

Caleb remained silent.

"If you tell me it's true, Caleb, I'll believe it."

"John's dead. So are three policemen—men who went in with him to help. Allen Caine is fine, and you still have John's child. Right now, you need to get some rest for her and for you."

"Oh, God," she moaned as fresh tears gushed from her eyes. "It's my fault. He was angry with me."

"Who?"

"John. He didn't want me to speak to Allen. I did it anyway."

"I think he knew you would. You did what you had to, what the gift gives you the power to do."

"He's mad too."

"John?"

"No. The kidnapper. I wouldn't play the game. We knew it would endanger the baby. I just wanted to speak to Allen, to comfort him—see through his eyes, help him. I didn't know I was speaking to the kidnapper the whole time."

She looked at her brother, focusing on his moss-green eyes, taking in the similarities and the differences to hers.

"I sent John into that building. I told him Allen was there. It was so easy. It was all in the song, except . . ."

Caleb covered her hands with his. He could feel her hysteria rising.

She jerked away.

"I should have known. I'm the damned psychic. I sent John and three policemen to their deaths."

"You were tricked, played. He knew what you would do and what would happen. He knew John would be the first one there. He planned it that way, Sara. Allen Caine wasn't the victim. John was. You know that. Right now, you have a child to protect. She's probably the only life you can protect. Do it. Don't let her die too."

Sara flinched at the harshness of his voice.

He watched. The fire died in her eyes. She took a deep breath. He studied her closer. She was thinking, acting.

She took another deep breath. "Thank you, Caleb. You really can go now."

He scooted his chair closer to the bed, whipped out a tissue from the box on the bedside table, and handed it to her. "No. I had a part in all of this. I could have taught you how to block him and still play the game. I didn't. I didn't want to get involved." He hesitated. "You don't know this, but Mother . . . our mother put a lot of stock in family."

"Really? I'd never have guessed."

"There were reasons why she did what she did. Reasons I'll explain one day. I think you are next on the kidnapper's list. I think he's going to try to kill you." He raised a hand before she could speak. "I don't want to lose the only family I've got left. And I don't want to lose a niece before I even have a chance to know her. I'm staying."

"You'll teach me?"

"Yes."

"I'm afraid to go to sleep, afraid he'll jump into my—"

"—dreams. Don't be. I'm here. You're protected."

"How?"

"Never mind how, just sleep. I'll keep you safe, just like you kept me safe when Father was on the rampage."

"You remem . . ." Sara's tongue was too thick to finish.

"I never forgot," Caleb whispered.

Cold rain fell from a cement-gray sky. The heavens were crying. Caleb moved closer to Sara, his umbrella protecting her from the drizzle, but not from the misery that filled her soul. She touched the casket gently. Its raw chill penetrated her gloved hand.

Sobbing and tears surrounded her. Milford was struggling to cope. The town wasn't used to losing one policeman. Today they were burying four—three uniformed officers and one detective. It was too much.

Across the casket, Judy stood with one arm through Tom's, the other curved protectively around her children. Her eyes held the vacancy of a stone statue, until they glimpsed Sara; then hate and fury flared through them.

Sara looked away. John was gone. The casket held nothing but dust. He had literally evaporated in the explosion.

She stepped out from under the umbrella and raised her face to the rain, stifling the desire to scream. The gift had brought her to this.

A hand pulled her back. "Are you all right?" Caleb mouthed.

She nodded. She wouldn't cause any kind of scene. She just wanted it over. She wanted to curl up and hide somewhere, anywhere. Her safe harbor was gone. Touching the mound of her stomach, she cried silently; their daughter would never know the gentle, loving force that had been her father.

Sara's eyes scanned the crowd and stopped on Samuel Hawk. He stood apart, in the shelter of the trees. He nodded to her.

She was still staring when Caleb touched her arm. Her gaze turned to the priest. He was waiting for something. She looked down at the single ivory rose she clutched, knowing what the man of the cloth waited for. It was such a final gesture.

Caleb's hand curled over hers, giving her the strength she needed. Together, they placed the rose on the casket.

The priest had barely finished the final benediction when the air was rent by explosions. Seven guns fired three times. The sound was picked up by another squad, then another and another as Milford gave each of her newly dead the traditional twenty-one-gun salute. Each shot tore through her, shattering her nerves, her soul.

At the last volley, the wail of pipes cut through the heavy air. It was only when the last notes of "Amazing Grace" died away that people moved. They relaxed, shook hands, offered condolences, and greeted each other in subdued tones. Alone in the crush, Sara slipped away, stopping in front of Samuel.

"Why didn't you join us?"

"I do not know these people that well. I was afraid I would be intruding."

"You wouldn't have been. John spoke highly of you and of your work."

"He was a good man. Take comfort that he lived a good life and died a good death."

Caleb called to her from the graveside.

She ignored him, staring deeply into Samuel's dark eyes. "You once told me that if you shut down a gift there are repercussions. Is that why John died? Is that why the other men had to die?"

Caleb arrived at her shoulder. "Sara, what's—"

"Not now, Caleb. Samuel, please, I need to know."

Compassion flooded the old man's face. He glanced at Caleb, then focused on Sara. "John and the others died because there is evil here—not because you stopped using your gift. But, in my son's words, use it or lose it. If you have a gift you don't use, God, the Great Spirit, whatever you call the creator, eventually takes it away. That's the penalty I was speaking of."

Sara swayed. Unreality blanketed her. "I was slow. It was my fault. I stopped using the gift. I made him mad—" She was babbling. She knew it but she couldn't stop. "If I'd have kept playing, he wouldn't have killed . . . I killed my husb—"

"Enough, Sara." Caleb's command broke the dam.

Her knees gave way. The tears flowed freely.

Gently, Caleb and Samuel pulled Sara to her feet, supporting her through the crowd to the parked cars. At Caleb's wave, a uniformed chauffeur opened the door of the black BMW.

Caleb helped her in, then stepped back as Samuel leaned forward. He touched her shoulder. "You did not kill your husband or those men. The blame is not on you. It is on the evil that is here."

Samuel was shutting the door when Judy shoved past, stopping him. She bent down to look at Sara. "So a son wasn't enough? You had to kill my brother too?"

Caleb moved before anyone else could. Grabbing Judy's arm, he pulled her upright and dragged her from the car, then pushed her toward her husband. He glared into Tom's bleak face. "If you can't control this woman's venomous tongue any better than that, you can kiss your political career goodbye, Caine." He slammed the door and faced Samuel, his hand out.

"Thank you for your help, Mr. . . . ."

"Samuel." The old man took the offered hand. "Samuel Hawk. I worked briefly with John." He looked down at Sara through the car window. She sat like a carved figure, staring out into nothing. "Take care of her. She and the child she carries are precious."

Caleb nodded, his arm almost numb from the controlled power that had flowed through it at the handshake. Walking to the other side of the car, he slid in beside his sister.

"Do you need to go to the hospital, Sara?"

She shook her head. "No. I'll be all right."
He motioned for the driver to pull away.

Sara turned to the window, watching first the graves and then houses speed by. They were several miles down the road before she realized they were heading to the summerhouse.

"Caleb," she turned to her brother, "I need to get home. People will be dropping by."

"Your house is ready for guests. A woman I frequently employ as a planner and hostess has seen to everything. She'll give your apologies and let people know you're in no condition to carry on."

He took her hand, holding it tightly. "Maggie will take care of you. She brought me through some pretty turbulent times after you left."

"Does she still make Irish stew and apple tarts?"

"Yes, she does. You could use a bit of coddling, as Maggie would say."

"What about Max?"

"According to Maggie, he's already full of good Irish cooking."

"You're going somewhere, aren't you?"

"Boston, for just a few days. I don't have a choice. If it were something I could cancel, I would, but . . ."

"Caleb—"

"I know you want to go home. But the doctor wants bed rest." He glanced pointedly at her stomach. "You know it's for the best. And you know Maggie would love looking after you."

He was right. Sara turned back to the window. Maggie Fahey, the Irish housekeeper, had been the one bright spot in the Remington household. But, God help her, Sara had sworn never to return to that place and now she was going for the second time in just months.

She shifted uncomfortably. Life was taking strange twists, and she didn't like it. But the thought of Maggie almost made her smile; the woman had always been a safe port in a stormy sea. Today, Sara felt she would never be more in need of a safe harbor.

Maggie stood at the front of the summer home, the corner of her apron in her hands. To Sara, she had not changed at all. Maggie seemed timeless. The gray hair was still firmly in a bun, the blue eyes still sharp. Maggie had always been a breath and a twinkle away from laughter, but today she stood still and solemn.

The woman waited until Caleb helped Sara from the car, then took Sara firmly into her arms, patting her hair and crooning to her as though she were still a child.

"Ah, you wee Colleen, it's the worst you've been through. But things will get better. You've a child comin' and there is no greater joy. But for now . . ." She held Sara at arm's length. "For now, you need a warm bath and a good Irish Stew, chased by a wee bit of good Irish whiskey."

"But the baby," Sara objected.

"A wee nip will not be hurting either one of you, I'm thinkin'. And I've already talked to your doctor and he agrees."

Maggie was a formidable force when in full sail—and today all the sails were unfurled. Sara leaned her head on the woman's shoulder. Today, she could use Maggie's strength. She would use it tomorrow also, and every day until she was strong again. It wouldn't take long. Maggie never let anyone lean too long.

She was in the darkness of her soul. Would she find her way? Could she find peace?

Samuel rubbed his work-worn right hand. The brother had power. Power had been exchanged with power in the handshake. Two things he now knew for certain: Sara and the man were blood, and he was strong.

The old Navajo smiled to himself. She was in good hands. Would it help? He had no sense of her future and it bothered him. But he did know that if Sara wasn't who the Hopi sought, she at least held the key.

Should he ask Leon for more time? Perhaps he should study the brother? He shook his head. It all revolved around Sara, and now was not the time to talk to her. He would not interrupt the path she and the man were taking.

On impulse, he pulled out his cell phone and punched in Leon's number again. He had been trying to reach the Hopi for days; perhaps today, in this place of sorrow, he would be lucky.

Leon picked up on the first ring. "Sorry I haven't been able to answer your calls. I was—"

"Leon, I'm coming home."

"What?"

Before his friend could launch into any rhetoric, Samuel continued, "I'm coming home. I can't and won't speak with Sara right now. John is dead; my work with him is over."

"What happened?"

"A bomb exploded in the courthouse clock tower. It killed John and three other men."

"I am sorry, Samuel."

"I am no use here now. It's time I go home."

"Samuel—"

"No arguments, Leon. When we meet, I'll go over what I've learned and what I suspect. For now, I need and want a rest."

As the silence lengthened, Samuel knew he had won. Leon's voice was soft when he spoke. "I think you may be right. Are you coming straight in?"

"No. I'm stopping in to see Amelia Talks-a-lot about their pow wow. And I'm hoping to spend some time with Robert Stillwater. You owe me this break."

"I do. Keep your cell phone on." The line went dead.

Samuel slipped the phone into his pocket and headed down the slippery grass slope toward his ancient truck. He was sad; he had lost a friend. He was frustrated; he was no closer to finding the man who had struck the reservation years before. And a young woman he admired had endured one—almost two tragedies. But there was a small song in his heart; he was going home. It felt good. He just hoped Leon was wrong. He hoped they still had time.

Stepping into his truck, he ignored the sudden, quick shimmer in the gray skies.

Joe Campbell stood apart from the mourners. Water dripped through and darkened his red hair and streamed down his rough wool coat. Three things caught his eye: Sara's fall, Caleb's catch, and the stranger who helped.

She still carried the child. That was obvious. His father had failed with that one. Joe was glad about it. A part of him applauded her strength.

There was also a bond between Sara and her brother, though Joe had been led to believe they were estranged. But the stranger . . .

Joe shivered, and it wasn't from the cold. Something emanated from the Indian, something he recognized. Serafina had the same aura about her.

One thing was certain: His father had done it this time. The state of Connecticut—hell, maybe even the whole of the US would be looking for them. No hole would be deep enough, no place remote enough to hide.

In a way, he was glad. Maybe this meant it would all be over soon. His thoughts turned to New Orleans. Serafina might finally be free of him and his father. She could live her life without fear, raise their son with hope.

Turning, he limped down the sodden grass to the waiting pickup. He had been working on the cabins when a blurb on his cell phone had headlined the news. He'd left everything and driven back to Milford, hoping all he'd read was wrong. It wasn't.

He took off his wet jacket and slipped into the truck. He needed to get back to the valley and finish up the cabins, then return to Stroudsburg. He prayed silently that the solstice would come and go with no further trouble.

CHAPTER 20

Caleb's guts twisted with anger, his words snapping with fear. Clutching the phone, he realized it was taking a physical effort to keep from lashing out at his Milford housekeeper.

"When did she leave?"

"Around one-ish, Mr. Remington. She was just outside of Patterson when she called. Said she'd run into heavy traffic, and with the weather like it was, she was pullin' over to wait it out. I've not been able to reach her since. I'm assumin', based on what I've heard on the television, that she's still waitin' for the weather to clear."

"She may have a damned long wait. Why in the hell didn't you stop her, or at least contact me? And why in the hell is she going back to Slane's End?" The family farm was a good four- to five-hour drive from Milford. Sara wouldn't have made the decision to go there lightly.

"It's her home, boyo. Remember? She was raised there, and I've no doubt but that she had a strong connection with her grandmother. As for the first questions, I did try to stop her and she was having none of it. And I did try to reach you. Nothing was working, Caleb. I couldn't get through on your cell and there was no answer at the penthouse or the office."

The fact that Maggie Fahey used his first name alerted him to the fact that he was treading on thin ice.

Maggie's voice softened. "I thought she was getting along grandly, for all that she's been through. She's been eatin' well, restin', and most nights she sleeps well. She did not seem a bit restless, though she did seem a bit lonely. I know she misses John, and I think, with all that's gone on, she was missin' you. But—" Maggie hesitated. "She saw her house yesterday. It wasn't pretty."

"Damn! When?"

"Comin' back from her doctor's appointment. She made Jeffrey drive past it on her way back here."

"Is it bad?"

"Aye. There's trash about it and foul words have been sprayed across the little place. Signs sayin' all kinds of nasty things are littering the yard. She was upset when she got home. But this mornin', the way she acted, I thought she had come to terms with everything. I thought she would at least wait and talk to you. I was wrong. She ate a good breakfast, then upped and grabbed that lovable dog, got into her car, told me to tell you she would be all right, and drove away."

Caleb collapsed into the chair. Fear melted into worry, worry back into anger. He muttered half to himself, "I can't protect her there. She's too far away."

Maggie snorted. "You know better than that, Caleb Remington. She doesna have to be with you for you to protect her. What concerns me is her husband's not been dead quite a month. She needs more time to do the healin', especially with a baby comin'." The Irish was thick in her voice. Maggie was more mother to him than his own mother had been. She also knew him better than he knew himself. More than that, she had the "seeing." She had been and still was both mentor and teacher.

"You're right. And you've not heard any more from her?"

"It's these bloody storms. I can't get through—and I'm sure she can't either. She'll be fine. She's probably already at Slane's End."

"Thanks, Maggie. If you hear anything, call me immediately. I'll do the same."

He cut the connection and buzzed his butler. "Make a pot of coffee, Andrew. Please," he added quietly. His gut told him it was going to be a long night.

He swiveled the chair to face Boston Harbor, then reached for the phone. It was probably hopeless, but he had to start trying. The damnable thing was he needed to be in Boston another two or three days—thanks to William Duncan.

Your fault! Your fault! The swish-thump of the wipers whispered the phrase with each swipe across the glass.

Sara reached out a hand and rubbed the moisture from the inside of her windshield as Max whined softly.

It was stupid, she told herself for the hundredth time. She wasn't to blame for John's death—and yet the empty space in the bed, in her heart, told her something different.

If she could just hear his voice one more time, tell him she was sorry she tried to link with Allen. If she could . . . what? It was over. He was gone. And she—

Her stomach moved with the sudden soft kick. She laid a hand across it. She had to protect this baby, John's baby. But first, she needed to heal her body as well as her soul. She couldn't do that in Milford. Not the way the town felt. She needed to go home.

Home! The word kept pace with the "your fault!" message. Slane's End wasn't really home anymore. Milford was. Yet it was Slane's End that would heal her; she knew that beyond a shadow of a doubt.

Skirting Stroudsburg, Sara ignored the Garlic Festival signs and headed into the country. Trees cast gothic shadows against rolling hills bandaged with dark patches of tilled earth. She drove through a wet, humid, black world with only dim headlights to light the way.

Suddenly a large shadow vaulted across the road. Sara hit the brakes, twisting the wheel hard. Her head slammed into the side window as the car slid into the muddy ditch. One moment there was the screech of brakes, the grumble of tires churning through mud and brush, and the next instant there was absolute silence.

Sara leaned back, her hand across her stomach. The baby was quiet. Reaching across the seat, she ruffled the coarse fur of a whining Max. "You okay, fella?" He licked her hand.

Taking a couple of deep breaths, she waited for the shakes. They didn't come. The tears had dried up as well.

Grabbing a flashlight from the glove compartment, she opened the door and stepped into ankle-deep mud. Wading to the front of the car, she checked the bumper and both sides as well as she could. Nothing. She stopped, listening to the silence, then climbed out of the ditch. Flashing the light down and along the road, she checked for blood, anything dark. Again, nothing.

Her knees were beginning to shake as she stumbled back to the car, silently thanking God that she had missed the deer. Leaning against the cold metal, she looked up. Headlights were coming down the hill. Her hand tightened on the flashlight.

A hundred feet away, the vehicle slowed down; it hadn't been going that fast anyway. It finally stopped just across from her. She studied it. Somehow, the old truck looked familiar.

"Are you all right, ma'am?"

"Joe?"

A man stepped out, peering at her in the darkness. "Ms. Sara. Is that you? Are you all right?"

"Yes, it's me, and I'm fine. I missed the deer. Unfortunately, I found the ditch."

"Could've been worse if you'd hit the deer. A big buck's been jumping the roads hereabout, causing quite a stir. Most folks can't wait till hunting season opens."

"Do you still do odd jobs for Harold?"

"Some. Why?"

"Do you think you could get hold of him? Have him pull me out?"

"There's no need for that. That car of yours ain't that big. Just give me a minute to turn around and back up."

Five minutes later, Joe had his ancient truck where he wanted it. Pulling a heavy length of chain from the back, he hooked it to his bumper, then bent down and started clearing mud and grass from the front end of Sara's car.

"You visiting?" he grunted as he worked the chain around the car's front axle.

"Sort of. Actually, I'm going to stay at Slane's End for a while."

"Things all right at the farm?"

"They're fine." She hesitated. Joe probably didn't know anything about Milford. "My husband was killed three weeks ago."

Joe rose slowly, taking a few minutes to brush the mud off his clothes. He seemed to be looking for the right words to say. His voice was soft when he finally spoke, his usual mountain twang almost gone. "I'm sorry to hear that, Ms. Sara. Maybe it's a good thing you're here. I've always thought of Slane's End as a healing place."

He seemed to shake himself, then pointed to the car. "Get on in, put it in neutral, and try to steer as best you can. Should have you out in a jiffy."

A few minutes later, Sara's car was back on the road.

Unhooking the chains, Joe threw them in the back of his truck and limped back to her window. "You want me to follow you to the farm?" The twang was back.

"No, thank you. Are you sure you're all right" Sara nodded toward his leg.

"I'm fine, just pulled a few muscles in that bad leg of mine, getting in that ditch."

Sara opened her wallet and peeled off a fifty.

He shook his head. "There's no need for that, Ms. Sara."

"I know. What are you doing down here anyway? You don't usually come down to Stroudsburg until midsummer."

"It's been a harder winter than I expected. Didn't lay in enough goods. I've been picking up odd jobs, trying to make ends meet."

"Then this will help." She pressed the money into his hand. When he looked uncomfortable, she smiled. "Tell you what. Next time you're around the farm, bring me a woodcarving. In fact, if you're looking for some part-time work, I'm sure Henry could use your help."

With a quick grin, he stuffed the money in his pocket. "That, I could do. You sure you don't want me to follow?"

Sara looked out into the night and shook her head. "No. I'll be fine."

With a tip of his hat, the man crawled into his truck, turned it around, and left.

She watched the taillights disappear, feeling very much alone.

The porchlight was on when Sara pulled up in front of the old farmhouse. Silently, she blessed Caleb. It had been his idea after their grandmother's death to hire their neighbors, Cora and Henry, to manage the Slane farm.

Max exploded from the driver's door and ran for the bushes lining the front porch. He remained there for several minutes.

Sara laughed. "You've been holding out on me. I told you at the last stop that you'd better make it good." Relieved, the big dog jumped on the porch and lay beside the door as though he had lived there forever.

The ring of Sara's cell phone broke the silence.

She grabbed the phone and checked the screen. "Hello, Caleb. You're up either awfully late or awfully early."

"Late. Are you all right?"

"I'm fine. Just tired."

"And my niece?"

"She's sleeping, and I hope she stays that way for a while."

"I'm sorry you saw the house, Sara. I was told about the vandalism. I should have had it taken care of right away."

"It wasn't your fault. You didn't do it." She fell silent. How many times in the past weeks had people told her the same thing? "I just needed to come home."

"This is your home."

"No. The summerhouse never was home, and—"

"I'll see that your house is cleaned up. I've already hired security guards. Do you want me to sell the place?"

"No. Just try to keep it clean. I'll probably return once things settle down."

"I once promised myself I'd never set foot on Slane's End again."

Sara laughed softly. "I made the same declaration about the summer home. You'll have to explain someday why you feel as you do about the farm. We're a fine pair, aren't we?"

"We weren't exactly the Brady Bunch growing up. I still need to teach you how to protect yourself."

"Can you break your promise and do it here? I'd feel more comfortable here, safer, and I did go to the summer home."

He gave a short laugh. "Not for very long. Guess I'll have to come there. Sara—" He hesitated. "The vandalism—"

"I know. I know. It's just a few people. That's what John would have said. He gave his life for that town and I'll bet none of the homes of the other officers who died were vandalized."

"They didn't house a psychic who was secretly working with the police. John would have been right. Milford still has good people. Lots of them."

"Yeah."

"And you're still in danger."

"I'm sure the bastard needs time to plan the next event. After all, he needs to top blowing up a portion of the Milford courthouse and the clock tower, and that's going to take some doing. I'm sure I'm safe, at least for a little while." She caught her breath. "He accomplished what he set out to do, Caleb. He destroyed the one person I loved most in this world. He's out there somewhere, celebrating."

"If you're right, that makes you the ultimate target. Can you think of anyone who would want to do this to you? Anyone you've hurt, slighted—hell, I don't know, killed?"

"John and I went through all that. For God's sake, I'm a first grade teacher. I've never been in a position to make that kind of enemy—well, until I became the town pariah."

"I still wish you would have stayed in Milford. I need some more time in Boston."

"I'll be fine."

"As soon as everything's wrapped up, I'll come to Pennsylvania. If you need anything, anything at all, call me. I can be there in an hour or less if need be."

Sara laughed. "No, you can't. But I appreciate what you're saying."

"See you soon."

She pressed disconnect and looked around, listening to the silence. It was, she realized, very loud.

CHAPTER 21

Sara stopped at the front door of the old farmhouse, a bag of groceries in her arms. She had cloistered herself at the farm for almost a week before finally running out of the meager supplies Cora had provided. The shopping spree in Stroudsburg had been interesting. Everyone knew who she was, but few knew what had happened. She found herself relating events she did not particularly want to dredge up. After a while, she answered questions with, "I needed a vacation."

She took a deep breath, breathing in a heat that was just this side of hell. Something was wrong. The air was heavy, still, the day absolutely quiet; that kind of silence where no birds sang, no insects buzzed. Except for an occasional stomp, even the horses were still.

She glanced at Max. Against her command, he had shot out of the car the moment the door was open. He lay on the porch, tense, only his ears moving. Like radar antennas, they flicked back and forth.

"Let's go in, boy."

As soon as she opened the door, he shot inside the house and sprawled on the linoleum floor, ears still moving. Sara put the bags on the kitchen counter and flipped on the ancient radio. The steady drone of the announcer's voice added a touch of surrealism to the quiet. Her hand had just landed on the refrigerator handle when she realized what it all meant.

"Sara? Sara, are you home?"

"In the kitchen, Cora." She glanced up as the woman walked in. Tall and spare, Cora was the epitome of a horse breeder's wife. She and her husband owned the neighboring farm, and like Sara's own family, Cora's grandparents and parents had brought their place through depression, drought, flood, and a market that, today, did little beyond acknowledge the trotting horse. The funds they received from managing Sara's farm helped them a lot.

A fraught tightness around Cora's mouth confirmed what Sara had already guessed. "Tornado?"

Cora nodded. "We're under a watch and it doesn't feel good. Is my daughter here?"

"No. At least, I haven't seen Tammy, but I just got home."

"She sometimes walks over here in the afternoon. She loves to sit in your grandmother's room or putter around the garden. I kept her at the farm the last week, didn't want her to bother you. I figured you needed some time alone."

Sara glanced out the kitchen windows. Dark clouds were building. Lightning flashed. "We'd better go take a look." Minutes later, it was clear Tammy wasn't in the old house. They stepped onto the porch and into a gust of hot wind that died almost as quickly as it started.

"Check the garden, backyard, and sheds, Cora. I'll catch the barns."

She strode off, Max close on her heels, a rumbling whine coming from his throat. Cora's husband, Henry Welton, met her at the stable doors.

"Did I just hear my wife?"

"It seems Tammy's gone on a walkabout again."

"She won't be far. Despite everything, she's got a sixth sense about the weather and a strong instinct for survival." His eyes traveled from the darkening sky to the velvet muzzles that pushed their way over the tops of the box stalls.

When the crops failed in the 1930s and the depression slammed into the country, Sara's grandmother turned to trotters to save the farm. It was considered almost sacrilegious for a woman to breed and even occasionally drive the big Morgans in races. But her grandmother realized that, though people might not have enough money for food, they'd find the money for a bet or two. Several other farmers followed her lead. Today, the barn's tack room wall was proof of the champions that had kept the farm going.

"I'm going to turn them out into the pasture and open the back gates so they can get into the woods." Henry's soft, deep voice broke into her thoughts. "Then I'm going over to my place to do the same thing."

"Good move. I'll help," Sara added as another sudden gust of wind blew dirt and leaves into the barn. Henry shouted for one of his sons to open the back pasture gates, and then he and Sara turned to the stalls.

Making sure Max stayed out of the way, Sara opened the first stall and within minutes had the big Morgan mare haltered. Though the horses were growing nervous, between the two of them it took less than twenty minutes to halter and release them into the pasture. Only the stallion remained.

Henry led the haltered stud out with admonitions. "Now don't go fooling around. I don't want any late foals."

"Do you really think that's going to do any good?" Sara asked with a grin.

Henry smiled back. "No. But it makes me feel better." He sobered. "I know—for the breeding program, this isn't the smartest thing to do, but I don't like the way this storm is coming. I'd rather an unplanned foal than dead horses."

"I agree. You get going. Cora and I will find Tammy. We'll use the shelter here."

Walking back into the barn, she called Tammy's name several times again, her eyes searching the lofts. There was no rustling of hay, no sign of the awkward, shy woman who was once her closest friend. Max's growl stopped her search.

Stepping outside, Sara looked up. Her heart stopped. From the darkened, broiling sky, a funnel cloud was forming.

"Cora!" she screamed, her heart beating again only when she saw the woman run from the sheds, stop, turn, and freeze.

Sprinting as best she could across the yard, Sara grabbed Cora's hand and pulled her toward the far side of the house.

"Tammy. I have to find Tammy!" The woman tried to jerk away.

"It's too late. We need to get to the cellar, now." Though the wind swallowed Sara's words, Cora knew what to do. Both women turned for the side of the farmhouse. It took their combined strength to open the cellar door against the building wind. Once opened, Max bolted past them and down the steps.

"There should be a lantern and matches on the table just to your right," Sara shouted against the rising wind as she bolted the door. The noise dulled as the door slammed shut. Sara was catching her breath when she heard the match strike, then Cora gasp. Whirling, she saw the figure of a woman shadowed in the half-light.

Long white hair, laced with strands of gray and webbed with twigs and leaves, stood out like Medusa's snakes, dwarfing a pale, fragile, lined face. Tammy's pale blue eyes stared blankly at them.

Cora pulled her daughter into her arms. "Lord, child, I was scared to death. Why didn't you come when we called?"

"She probably couldn't hear us."

The cellar door gave an ominous shake. Sara took another step down. "Grab the lantern, Cora. We need to go to the back of the cellar."

The older woman did as asked, her hand never leaving her daughter's arm until they were beside the twin wooden cots. Placing the lantern on a crate, she sat, pulling Tammy down beside her and rubbing warmth into her daughter's cold hands.

Sara eased herself onto a cot. Max's heavy head dropped onto her lap. She studied the woman who had once been her closest friend. There was only a year between Tammy and her, yet the woman she stared at was old. "Hello, Tammy. How have you been?"

Tammy smiled tentatively. "He told me." Her voice sounded rusty, barely used; those three words had been her complete vocabulary for over twenty years.

Timbers creaked. The air grew heavy, thick. Sara swallowed hard, trying to clear her ears against the building pressure.

"Lord, I hope everyone's okay at home." Cora's voice was shaky. "Did you see the size of that twister?"

Sara nodded.

"Baby all right?" Cora asked gently.

"She's fine."

Cora stroked her daughter's wild hair. "I know some would think it a blessing if I lost Tammy or put her away, but just the thought puts me in an absolute panic."

Sara gave a quick laugh as her hand rested on her stomach. "I think I can understand that right now."

"Can you? I've lived with fear since the day you found her—fear that one day that bastard, whoever he is, would come back and finish what he started."

Sara could only stare back in silence and surprise.

"You heard right," Cora said roughly.

"I've never known you to be afraid of anything. I never thought . . ." Sara's voice trailed off.

"Children can do that to you."

The din of the storm grew louder, rolling the ground, making speech impossible. Max whined, pushing himself as close to Sara as he could.

Suddenly, there was absolute silence.

"He told me." Tammy looked around and started to stand. Cora pulled her back down, her eyes on Sara. "Things need to settle a bit before we go out. As close as that was, I sure hope it missed your grandmother's place."

"It did. God wouldn't want to argue with Nana."

"You're right about that." Cora laughed, then sobered. "I haven't had a chance to tell you how sorry we all were about John."

"Thank you."

"We also heard about what was done to your house. Are you here to stay?"

"I don't know. People here don't seem to mind who—or maybe what—I am."

"You are your grandmother's granddaughter; they wouldn't."

It took Sara and Cora several pushes to get the door open. Sara pushed the last of the debris away with her foot and stepped out into air that was crisp and clean, as though everything bad had been blown away.

The yard was littered with leaves, branches, twigs, and pine boughs. She ran sharp eyes over the house. A couple of windows were broken and a large square of tin had been pulled from the roof. Otherwise, everything looked okay. The barn also looked intact, aside from a door hanging somewhat askew. A couple of the fences were down; Henry would have to fix them before the horses were brought in.

Like a child, Tammy turned slowly around, looking more at the sky than at the boneyard of broken branches. Her pale eyes caught Sara's as she pointed a shaky finger toward the dark clouds. "He told me. He told me."

"Where are you, Sara?"

The unexpected pain drove her to the ground. Twisting her arm around the porch railing, she pulled herself up.

"Go away!" Quiet filled her mind. He was gone. But for how long?

Something wasn't right, and it wasn't just the documents in front of him.

Caleb stared past the men in the boardroom. The large glass

windows of the Foster building framed the Boston Harbor, but what he saw now was less than picturesque. A storm was building. Dark, broiling clouds filled the sky, sweeping over murky waters to the city. Something wasn't right here. Something wasn't right with Sara, either. The sudden thought was like a punch in the stomach.

"Mr. Remington, we need your signature."

His gaze fell on the men seated around the heavily carved mahogany table. Entrepreneurs, developers, builders, destroyers, sharks. For all their knowledge, money, and experience, they could not see what he saw, feel what he felt. They recognized only the pulse of money and profit.

He closed the folder. The deal was not for his company; despite the hours these men had spent telling him he was a perfect fit.

He rose. "Gentlemen, based on my analysis—and in some cases the lack of proper business analysis—I am reluctant to continue."

"You're not signing?" The red-faced Taft was close to shouting.

"No, I'm not."

"Would more time help you?"

Caleb turned to Alexander Evanston, the ever-present diplomat. "Sorry, Alex, no, it won't help. Remington's is withdrawing from the deal."

Ignoring the grumbles, Caleb grabbed his briefcase, stuffed the contract in, and strode out. He stopped at the window across from the secretary's desk and took a deep breath. The opulence and heaviness of the boardroom was uncomfortable to him. He preferred the clean, classic lines of his own offices.

Pulling out his cell phone, he entered the code for his secretary.

Irene answered on the second ring. "I was just getting ready to leave you a message."

"Has Sara called?"

"No." Irene's voice dropped. "Duncan and his daughter swept in about half an hour ago to see you. When I told them you weren't in, they were adamant about waiting. I put them in the fourth-floor dungeon for about fifteen minutes, then told them you would not be returning and had them escorted out."

Caleb chuckled. "You know I'd like to turn that area into storage, but as long as we're working with the likes of Duncan, maybe we should keep it. You did great, Irene. Thank you. Do you know what he wanted?"

"His daughter has found some areas where she believes she can save you a great deal of money," Irene said drily. Changing subjects, she added, "I take it the contracts are signed?"

"No. I walked away from the deal."

Irene heaved a sigh. "Thank God. That deal just didn't feel right. Caleb, I've been listening to the news. Pennsylvania has been hit by a series of strong storms, including three major tornados this afternoon. The Stroudsburg area was one of the hardest hit. I doubt I can reach Sara by phone, but I'll keep trying."

"Do you think the chopper could make it there?"

"No." Irene's voice was quick and firm. "There's another storm front moving in."

Caleb remained silent for a few moments, running scenarios through his mind. Could he wait until tomorrow? Something told him no. "Irene, have the Rover filled up and brought around. Get Andrew to pack clothes, enough for a couple of weeks, and tell him to throw the black bag in."

"I'm glad you're going. I have the strangest feeling that Sara needs you."

"I've got the same feeling. See you in about fifteen minutes." He cut the connection. Glancing down at the streets below, he watched the people milling about. He wasn't the least bit surprised to see Duncan and his daughter walk up and stop to speak with a group of men gathered by the door. He was even less surprised to recognize many of them as the men he had just had the business meeting with.

What the hell was going on? What were they all up to? Caleb didn't like the answers his mind gave him.

Henry drove up to the house, a cell phone connected to his ear. Stepping from the pickup, he hugged Cora and Tammy before surveying the damage.

"Nothing we can't fix." He turned to Sara. "That twister was a bad one. Main road to Stroudsburg is blocked from our direction, and I don't know how many neighbors and friends were in its path."

"Is Slane's End still a gathering point?"

"Yes." Distant movement caught Henry's eye. Two vehicles were making their way slowly past broken limbs and downed trees. "And it looks like our first victims are here. Can you handle it, Sara?"

She nodded. "Send them to the house. Cora, grab the first aid kits from the barn. I'll see what Nana's got around the kitchen."

"Ms. Sara, Mr. Welton asked me to see if there was anything you needed."

Sara looked up into Joe's gentle but sober face. Sometime in the early afternoon, he had turned up and offered his help.

"How's Henry doing?" she asked.

"Fine. Everyone's accounted for. Serious injuries are already at the hospital. Ms. Pence, here, is the last one."

Sara held a poultice to the old woman's torn scalp, nodded to Joe in relief, then looked down at the woman who had been her grandmother's best friend.

"Ms. Pence, I'm going to get Joe to drive you to the hospital. I think you're going to need a few stitches."

"Your grandmother keeps silk thread in the drawer by the door there. Just whip them in."

Sara smiled weakly as her stomach heaved, and patted the old woman's thin shoulder. "You know a woman in my condition shouldn't see too much blood. Besides, that was a pretty hefty blow. I think the doctors need to watch you for a while."

Rheumy, faded eyes stared up at her. "Sara Erin Slane Remington Allbrooke, I have a head as hard as granite. I'll be fine."

"I know you will. But I still want you to see the doctor." Sara glanced at Joe, pleading silently.

With a quick nod and smile, he took the old woman's arm. "Ms. Pence, I'm done here and I need to get back into town. Roads still aren't open so we're going cross-country. Can you show me the way?"

"Then what?"

"I'll drop you off at the hospital so they can sew up that scalp and check you out. You don't want to be upsetting Ms. Sara, now do you?"

The old woman glanced from Sara to Joe, then gave a "humph" and let him help her up.

"I know what you two are doing. At least they'll give me something for the headache."

Once the door had closed behind them, Sara collapsed on the sofa beside Cora. "I hope I remembered everything right."

"You did just fine." Cora patted her knee. "Your grandmother would be so proud."

Before Sara could comment, the front door opened and Henry stuck his head in. "Roads are open."

"Did we lose anyone?" Silently, Sara ran through a mental list of their neighbors.

"Nope. Couple of broken arms. Yancy Croft has a broken leg. Slater's house is gone. Olson's gonna need a new barn and Henson lost a milk cow. Otherwise, we're fine. The boys are bringing the horses in now."

Sara pushed away from the sofa and rose.

"Where do you think you're going?" Cora demanded.

Sara stared into the woman's thin face. "I need to check on the horses. I'm sure a poultice or two will be needed. I'm also certain there are some scrapes and cuts to look at."

"Henry is not going to let you near those horses in your condition. They'll still be skittish and flighty." Cora glanced at her husband for support.

"Wife's right," he shrugged.

"Henry, I've just spent four hours doing something I know very little about. Nana took care of the people. I took care of the animals. It will actually feel good to be doing something I know how to do."

He shrugged and turned to go, Sara trailing after him, ignoring Cora's protests.

She followed Henry into the stables, the feeling still with her. She had had it all day—the feeling that she no longer belonged, that Slane's End was no longer her home.

CHAPTER 22

Caleb leaned against the desk, speaking softly to his secretary. "Get hold of David and tell him to come up. He'll be in charge while I'm gone." Caleb hesitated a moment, his mind working with the speed of a racecar. "I'll expect updates from you, Irene."

"You'll have them, sir, daily." Irene spoke briefly into the phone, then glanced up. "David's on his way."

Caleb walked into his office, his mind still whirring. Sitting at the expansive mahogany desk, he opened the left-hand door and spun the dial. Within moments, the small safe was open. Pulling out four battered leather journals, he placed them carefully into his briefcase, then turned back to the window. He didn't like the weather. He didn't like the feel of it. He didn't like the feel of anything. As much as he hated to admit it, even to himself, he would be glad to see the farm—and he would be very glad to see his sister.

Caleb's hands tightened on the steering wheel of the Rover. Since leaving Boston, he had fought rain and wind and out-run two tornados. He glanced at the sky. Descending darkness made it look even more menacing. Was it natural or demonic?

He slowed down, pulling off the highway and into the town

of Stroudsburg. It had been years since he had seen the farm. He'd been overseas when Nana died, and he'd missed the funeral. Although the farm was left to Sara, the old woman's will stipulated that Caleb would be the executor over its financial side.

That was the first time he and Sara had had an in-depth, adult conversation. They'd agreed to keep Henry Welton on as trainer and offered him additional compensation to oversee the place. Thanks to Henry, Slane's End was a well-run operation. But there was still pain. His own grandmother hadn't thought him important. She had focused all her love and attention on Sara, never realizing her grandson was also gifted.

His father would have had a stroke had he ever guessed his son's real talent. Caleb sobered at the thought. The knowledge would have made his mother's life more of a living hell than it already was. As a child, he'd envied Sara. She'd laughed, played, and got dirty while he studied, wore suits, and stayed clean.

A neon sign caught his attention. He pulled into the gas mart. Something told him to keep his tank full, and when Caleb had that gut feeling, he listened to it. Stepping from the car, he flexed his hands. They were tired. He needed a break. A hot cup of coffee after he filled up wouldn't hurt.

Inside, Caleb endured the polite questions and stares from the young woman on the other side of the counter. He was a stranger driving an expensive car, and he wasn't that bad looking. It was a lethal combination for the girl. He felt her loneliness, her discontent. He was reaching for the coffee when it hit him—power; dark, black power. Power that blocked out all light.

"Don't worry about that. I'll clean it up and get you another cup."

He blinked. Coffee lay thick across the counter. Pulling a hundred from his wallet, he slapped it down.

"Keep the change."

Minutes later, he was in the car. Sara was in trouble. He needed to get to the farm.

Samuel Hawk held his hot coffee in both hands, savoring its fragrance and strength. Over the cup, he studied Amelia Talks-a-lot.

For once, the old woman wasn't living up to her name. She was as silent as her needle moved in and out of the fine, thin leather. The beading was exquisite. Even with the light of a single bulb flickering over the table, he could see the detail. How she did it in the dim light, with hands beginning to twist with age and arthritis, he did not know.

It was still, yet he heard the wind whistle and the trees talk. The night was as unusual as the day had been. He'd arrived in the quiet morning and was halfway through his first cup of coffee when Amelia looked up, a strange expression on her face. "Bring it with you. We are going to the cellar."

He followed her gaze. The sky looked like something from a kachina's nightmare.

They tromped into the dirt cellar, feeling the ground move as the storm raged overhead. It began softly, Amelia's chant. He added his own voice, the clicks of the Navajo interweaving with the soft vowels of the Chippewa.

Quiet.

"What were you praying for?"

Amelia's dark eyes glowed. "I asked for protection. Promised my firstborn."

Samuel grinned back. "Nathan is thirty-five years old. He may have a problem with that."

"Perhaps, but it worked. My house still stands above us. What were you praying for?"

"That I didn't die in a dirt cellar beside a Chippewa woman."

She laughed and slapped his arm as she rose. "You could do worse, Navajo, much worse. Come. I'll make you some fry bread— the old way, with plenty of grease."

Samuel followed, his mouth watering. The problem with the younger generation, particularly his daughters, was that they didn't know how good the things that were bad for you tasted.

"Was she the one?" Amelia looked up from her beadwork.

Samuel shook his head and set the coffee down. "I don't know. I need more time."

"Then why are you going home?"

He stared at the woman. Should he tell her that he had heard his death chant? That the man who had brought evil to the reservation now played a dangerous game with Sara, and somehow he, Samuel Hawk, was woven into the game? Or should he tell her that Sara, if not the one, would quite probably give birth to the one they sought?

"The girl has gone home to the family farm, or so I was told. Her husband was killed. She almost lost her baby. It's never been the right time to question her."

"Sounds like too much is happening in her life to throw the Hopi 'savior' bit in. What's her name?" Amelia asked softly.

He hesitated. But Leon had sent Amelia on similar quests. Why shouldn't she know? "Sara. Sara Allbrooke."

The woman's needle hesitated in its upward motion. "You were in Milford?"

"Yes."

"Sara's eight miles down the road. She's Nana Slane's granddaughter."

The old man was glad the coffee cup wasn't in his hand. He would have dropped it. "Are you sure?"

Amelia nodded.

He sat back, staring at her in wonder.

"There is no such thing as a coincidence," they both said at the same time.

Samuel turned to the darkness. He knew now what the trees were trying to say. "Where does she live?"

"Take the main road west out of town. At around eight or nine miles, cut south. You'll see the signs for Slane's End."

Samuel pushed his chair back and rose.

"What's wrong, old man?"

"Everything."

Sara gave the faucet another twist. Hot water streamed across her shoulders, steaming up the old bathroom. It didn't help. The knots were still there. The tension that filled her body with aches and stiffness refused to go away.

Treating the horse had felt natural. It brought back memories—good memories—but things were different. Neighbors still welcomed her warmly, despite the stressful situation of the day, but there was that nagging feeling that Slane's End was no longer home.

John had loved her grandmother, but Nana's country living was uncomfortable for the big man. He was city. He loved his towns. Sometime during their years together, Sara had found that same love. Her "bit of wild" in the backyard of their Milford home was all the country she needed. As the years passed, their trips to the farm had become fewer.

Toweling off, she slipped into a nightgown. Maybe she should call Caleb and tell him to meet her back in Milford.

Leaning against the bedroom's windowsill, she let the darkness of the night embrace her. She was lonely. No, not lonely—abandoned. They were all dead: Nana, her grandfather, her parents, and now John. It was only herself, her child, and Caleb; and Caleb had his own life to lead.

Her eyes fixed on the land. Clouds cleared. A new moon cast its feeble light across the farm. Shadows. They spread slowly across the fields, moving forward, encroaching on the old house.

A cold fear froze her bones as she stepped back and pulled the curtains shut. Nothing looked familiar. There was no comfort out there, no safety.

"There's no safety anywhere, Sara."

The spasm took her to her knees. *Close the door,* her mind screamed as she struggled up. *Control him.* But she couldn't. Her mind was a muddy quagmire, her body frozen in it.

"You control nothing, Sara. My son should have been the one."

Her limbs unfroze, but they weren't hers anymore. She moved to someone else's bidding, shuffling across the wooden floors.

Looking down, she saw the kitchen doorknob was in her hand. *No,* she screamed silently. *Do not go out there! Do not leave the house!*

Her feet stepped out onto the porch and down the stairs. Vaguely, she heard Max barking but knew he couldn't get to her. The door was closed.

Grays and blacks colored the cold, alien landscape that she stumbled through. Mentally, she fought to return to the safety of the house, but each time she tried to turn, a searing pain cut through her belly.

Her child was fighting, twisting, struggling to survive. Pain dropped her to her knees. Something lifted her up and drove her on. Hands that didn't feel as though they belonged to her opened the pasture gate. The pond. He was taking her to the pond. Why?

She knew the answer. Water was death, not life. A voice shot into her head: *"The preacher was wrong about my son, about me. You die in water. It is not life."*

Sara stepped into the mud at the pond's edge, her feet taking one step, then another. Cold slime squeezed up between her toes. It had felt good as a child; now it felt dirty, lethal. She sank to her ankles in silty sludge. A broken chorus of "Shall We Gather at the River" filled her head.

The water was at her knees.

She demanded, cursed, begged, yet inch by inch, her feet moved forward. At her thighs, the cold water hit her child. The contractions almost drove her to her knees. But that meant a watery death. He didn't want that. Then what the hell did he want? Her limbs took her farther into the dark waters until they reached her chin. Her hands flailed upward, her left brushing the Celtic cross between her breasts.

She grabbed it even as it burned her hand. A sudden cacophony of voices filled her mind, drowning out the madman's commands, drowning out the song.

Above the noise, she heard a new voice—a soft voice. *"Come back, Sara. Let us help."*

Her nostrils flared, bringing in a scent she knew she could

never forget. John. Strong arms wrapped around her, dragging her back. John wasn't dead. He was here, but his hands were so rough.

She struggled to help, knowing deep down she was fighting. She couldn't control her limbs.

"Sara."

A second, familiar voice cut through her.

"Sara," the voice repeated. "Give me your mind." Another pair of strong hands clasped her. "Shut the door, Sara. There's a safe place. Go there. Take the baby with you."

"I can't. Pain."

The rough hand touched the top of her head. White light exploded into nothingness.

CHAPTER 23

Sara opened her eyes. She was lying on the grass, covered in slime and mud. It was so quiet she could almost hear the trees growing. Her hands pressed against her abdomen. The cramps eased. The child rolled, then stilled.

She looked up. Samuel Hawk and her brother hovered over her. "What are you doing here, Samuel?"

He sat back on the grass, a thin smile etched into a face that now looked ancient. "It's a long story. One best told over hot coffee and in dry clothes."

"If we help, can you walk?" Caleb's voice was strained.

"Yes."

Both men stood, then reached down and grabbed an arm. With their combined strength, she rose, tottered, and started walking, leaning heavily against them.

The walk back to the farmhouse seemed to take forever. The cardboard world was still black, white, and shades of gray. Sara sighed with relief when Caleb closed the doors to the strange landscape.

"I'll make coffee. Sara, you get a shower."

She glanced at her brother. "You two need one as well. There are fresh towels in the cupboard by the hall bathroom. I'm assuming you've got a change of clothes with you, Caleb. Samuel, you'll find some of Grandpa's jeans and shirts in the bureau in the front bedroom. They should fit."

She was at the door when Caleb's voice stopped her. "You're safe. Don't worry."

Sara clutched the doorframe, not looking back. "How can you say that?"

"Because I know."

She scrubbed her body hard. When the mud and slime were gone, she scrubbed it again. At last, she leaned back against the shower wall, letting the hot water run over her, breathing in the steam as it fogged the bathroom once more.

The scent. She pushed back from the tiled wall. It was back again, thick. John's scent. She inhaled deeply. He was still with her. She closed her eyes, feeling his hands gently caress her back and shoulders. Then he was gone. Reluctantly, she opened the door, letting steam and the scent escape, feeling her back and shoulders finally relax. Turning the water off, she slipped into a robe and grabbed a towel to wrap around her head. Her reflection stopped her.

Slowly, she lifted the cross from her neck. There, between her beasts. The outline of the cross was branded into her skin. She turned her palm up. The same brand marked her hand. Dropping the heavy silver, she closed her robe and tightened the belt.

Caleb pushed a mug of coffee across the table and sat heavily on the old chair. "What brought you here tonight, Mr. Hawk?"

"You can call me Samuel. The same thing that brought you here. Sara was in danger."

"You were at Joshua Point, the Thimble Islands."

Samuel nodded. "As were you."

"Why?"

"For the same reason you were. Joshua Caine is not brain-damaged. His soul—"

"Is scattered," Caleb finished.

The old man nodded again.

"Why Sara?"

Samuel wrapped his gnarled hands around the mug, savoring its warmth. "I am not a threat to her. There are things I need to know."

"What things?" Both men turned to Sara, standing in the doorway. "What things, Samuel?" she repeated.

For the first time since they met, the old Indian seemed uncomfortable. "Things that will bring you no harm and give me answers."

Sara took the mug Caleb offered and sat beside him. "That really doesn't answer my question."

"I think it's the only answer Samuel's going to give for now," Caleb said quietly. "Am I right?"

Samuel nodded toward Caleb. "Yes. But only because the time is not right." Samuel looked pointedly at Sara's stomach. "You have much on your mind now. Too much for . . ." He didn't finish.

Sara turned to her brother. "I didn't expect you until Monday."

"Things weren't going . . . something just didn't feel right. Samuel, how did you know Sara was in Stroudsburg?"

"I didn't. I was heading home to Arizona."

"And you just happened to stop here?"

"Amelia Talks-a-lot lives in Stroudsburg." Samuel grinned. "She comes by her last name honestly. But she is a friend and a good woman, even if she is Chippewa. She's hosting the pow wow this year in Stroudsburg and needed some guidance." Samuel glanced at Sara. "I mentioned your name to Amelia. She not only knew you, your grandmother, and where the farm is, but she also knew you were here. Small town, I believe."

Sara nodded. "She was a friend of my grandmother's. I went to school with her son."

Pushing the chair back, Samuel rose. "I'd better be getting

back. I need to get an early start tomorrow. I will drop the clothes by on my way out."

"There's no need for that. Thank you, Samuel, for being here."

When Caleb would have stood, Samuel motioned him down. "You are tired, and you have much to talk over with your sister. I can see my way out."

At the kitchen door, he stopped and turned to Sara. "You have a gift. It is greater than you know. But listen to your brother. There is much he can teach you." His gaze swiveled to Caleb. "You are stronger than you realize. Explore all paths." He hesitated one more minute, his dark eyes pinning Caleb's green ones. "Have you ever heard of the Hopi prophecies?"

Caleb remained mute.

With a shrug the old man walked out.

"Did we do that?" Caleb asked.

Sara looked down at the bruises on her arms. "No. They're from whoever walked me into that damned pond." She tore her eyes away and looked up. "Something's wrong, Caleb. My psychic link has always been with children. That's my gift. I've never dealt with adults and have only dealt peripherally with the kidnapper."

"And tonight wasn't a peripheral link."

"No. Anything but. And there's more." She raised her hand, palm up. "Why would this happen?"

Caleb stared mutely at the imprint of the cross.

"I have the same marks on my chest," she continued. "Which one of you sent the pain away?"

"Samuel."

"How?"

"I think he's a shaman. Medicine man. I don't know what they call them today. The only thing I can tell you is that he's a very spiritual and powerful person."

"Who shut the door?"

"I did."

"Is that what you're going to teach me how to do?"

"Yes."

"Caleb." Her voice was almost a whisper. "What are you?"

He hesitated. "I'm an adept. Do you know what that is?"

"Beyond Webster's definition of the word? No."

"It simply means I've studied what some call witchcraft, spiritualism, the occult, and many forms of religion. I am aware of levels. I live by faith in a Christian God and believe in much more than most."

"That's a helluva answer, and it means nothing to me. Are you a warlock?"

He grinned. "No such thing. Witch is both male and female."

"You're a witch?"

He tilted his head, neither confirming nor denying her question.

"Have you ever heard of the Hopi prophecies?" she asked, deciding to take a different tack.

"Yes."

"Then why didn't you answer Samuel?"

"Because right now I don't know who the good guys are."

"But you said he was spiritual."

"That doesn't always mean 'good.' Instinctively, I trust him—at least, I want to. But—" he stopped, searching for the right word.

"You're not sure enough to put our lives on the line," Sara finished.

He nodded. "And until I'm certain, I'm being very careful."

"Caleb, I have a Presbyterian background—not strong, but good. If you're thinking of teaching me witchcraft or anything to do with witchcraft, forget it."

"Do you believe in Satan?"

The question took her by surprise. "I believe in evil."

"I didn't ask that question. Do you believe there is an entity known as Satan?"

"I don't know."

"Come on, Sara. It's a basic concept of Christianity, Islam, and Judaism."

"I guess I do."

"You have to do better than that."

"All right, there is a Satan. What does that have to do with anything?"

"It's got everything to do with what's going on. What you're fighting is evil in almost a pure form. Do you know what an exorcist is; what they do?"

"It's usually a priest who chases out demons from the possessed."

"Almost right. To be precise, it is a Catholic priest, a very highly trained and knowledgeable Catholic priest. There aren't many in the church today and they are strictly limited to performing only a small number of exorcisms. They drive out demons, Satan, Satan's minions. It is real. An adept strives to destroy those demons and help repair souls. Sometimes it works, sometimes it doesn't."

"Do you work with an exorcist?"

"I'm not going to answer that question. Know that I am a Christian with, let's say, extra training. For now, that's all you need to know. I'll be teaching you the first thing every novice psychic learns: protection. How to protect yourself, which leads to controlling your gift. Why Nana didn't teach you that, I'll never understand."

"Maybe because I've only ever worked with children. What harm can a child do?"

"Probably none, although some people today would argue that point."

"Just protection. That's all I need?"

"You know now, tonight, that this man can cause physical harm." He pointed to the marks on her arms. "Hell, you almost lost your daughter because of what he can do. Knowing you and your child can be free from that harm—knowing you can physically protect her—is liberating, Sara. It's strengthening. It may even result in you being able to thwart the kidnapper; see his face, physically stop him."

"You mean murder him?"

"Whatever's necessary. This man is playing for keeps. He proved that when he killed John. If he's not a demon in human form, he's shaking hands with the devil." Caleb rose. "For now, we both need to get some rest. Are you sure you're okay?"

"I'll be fine. Take the back bedroom. See you in the morning."

He squeezed her shoulder as he passed. "Don't stay up too late."

She watched him leave and took another sip of coffee. Murder. The idea was repugnant. And yet . . . the scent of John's aftershave drifted through the room . . . maybe.

Malachi Campbell leaned against a tree. His head felt like an overripe melon threatening to burst. He took deep breaths, fighting down the pain and acknowledging the rising anger.

It had all been so perfect. He had Sara in the water. One more step and the bitch would have drowned. Then the bastards had shown up—the Indian and that hoity-toity brother. And the fucking Indian threw him out of her mind.

He watched the lights go on in the old farmhouse. Only once before had he felt such power. It had come from Carl Light-horse, the man he owed his life to. He closed his eyes as a thick, fetid stench assailed his nostrils. It was the smell of the Vietnam jungle, hot, humid, decayed.

His first day out of camp, the squad was ambushed. When the gunfire finally stopped, Malachi, Carl, and two other men were prisoners. The lieutenant and the sergeant died within the first year. Forgotten by country and family, Malachi and Carl hung on to life.

Carl kept him alive. Taught him the secrets of a shaman, taught him evil and how to use it. Showed him power and how to gain it. Then one day, Carl did not wake up.

A few days later, Malachi was working in the rice paddies. He realized no one was watching him and slid silently into the jungle, never looking back. Three weeks later, emaciated, weak, and almost dead, he walked into a village, hoping it was friendly.

Not only was it friendly, but he was told the war had been over for almost four years. Once he gained his strength, several men took him over the border into Thailand, where he found a US embassy.

All POW camps were supposed to have been emptied at the end of the war. Quietly, embassy officials whisked him to a hospital in Germany, and the debriefings began. They didn't end until he was finally released from Walter Reed Army Medical Center. According to the government, his experience never occurred.

Malachi pushed back from the tree. He needed to get home. *Maybe the old Indian is a shaman*, he mused as he walked the path to the car. The Indian had caught him by surprise. It wouldn't happen again. He would match his power with anyone's. He had failed this time; he wouldn't fail again.

Slipping into the SUV, he started the engine and turned the heat up high. It wasn't that cold, but he could barely feel his hands or feet. He was thankful that his valley was just over the Maryland border into West Virginia, only about three and half hours away. He'd get home in time to have a good rest. He would be ready to greet the men, his coven.

Briefly, he thought of picking up Joe. That would ensure that his son attended the solstice. He nixed the idea. Getting home, resting, that was more important. Joe would get to the valley in time. He wouldn't dare disappoint his father.

In the meantime, he could use the drive to figure out another way to bring Sara and her brother down.

Amelia was still sitting at the kitchen table working her beads when Samuel walked in. Helping himself to a cup of coffee, he sat, elbows on the worn, yellow Formica tabletop.

"Girl all right?"

He nodded, then noticed the medicine bag on the table.

"You felt it too?"

She never missed a stitch. "It is not the first time."

"When did you begin to feel the darkness?"

Amelia stopped her sewing. "Almost four years ago, the day that Nana Slane died. She died the day she was supposed to come home from the hospital. Never made any sense to me."

"That happens sometimes."

"The darkness came that night."

"Do you have any idea who brings it?"

The old woman shook her head. "No. There are too many people going in and out of this town these days. What happened at the farm?"

"The one who haunts Sara Allbrooke walked her into a pond. Almost drowned her."

"She's not the one we seek, then. No strength."

"She's strong enough." The old woman looked up, eyebrows raised as Samuel continued. "She is like a child. She knows she can walk. She doesn't know she can run." He took a sip of coffee. "She is strong—far stronger than she knows. As is her brother. Together, they could be formidable."

"The Hopi prophecies speak of one, not two."

Samuel shrugged. "Some say three will come. Sara bears a child in late summer, early fall. A girl. She passes down a Celtic cross to that child. It is old, very old. Once, Sara said, it was red."

Amelia's needle lay still. "A cross. Prophecies of the three say that one will wear a red Celtic cross. Do you think . . .?"

Samuel shook his head. "I don't know."

"Is it the unborn child we seek?"

"I don't know. I don't know anything for sure right now."

They fell silent.

"You leave tomorrow?" Amelia resumed her needlework.

"Yes." He hesitated. "I have heard my death chant."

The old woman smiled. "I thought as much. At our age, old man, we've all heard the death chant. Do not put much stock in that." She looked up, her eyes darting around the room as though trying to see beyond its walls. "The way things are right now, do not put much stock at all in that."

"I need to speak with Remington." William Duncan held the phone tight. He could almost see the smug look plastered across the face of Remington's private secretary.

"He is not available at this time."

"Where in the hell is he? Is he even in the goddamned office?" Duncan's burr was getting thicker.

"Would you like to speak to Mr. Craig?"

"I don't want to speak to any damned hireling. I want to speak to Remington."

"He is unavailable."

Duncan slammed the phone down, the cradle cracking with the force, and grinned at the beautiful woman sitting across from him.

"He's with his sister. I'd wager my soul on it."

Abigail Duncan smiled back and nodded in agreement.

He pressed the speed dial, waiting patiently for the voice on the other end, then spoke without introduction. "I've lost Remington. I think he's at the farm, Slane's End, with his sister."

He listened to the voice for several minutes, scribbling down something that was being said. "Is everything still a go for the twenty-first?" Again, he listened quietly. "I look forward to it. My daughter and I will be there. Remember, she stays with me—no harm, no physical involvement. But I think, once you meet her, you'll find she's an asset."

He hung up the phone, gentler with the equipment this time, and smiled. "Malachi already knew where Remington was." He rubbed his hands together, delighted at the way things were going. "He is exactly where I said he was. Malachi gave me the number to the Slane farm. Remington's companies will be ours by the end of the summer."

CHAPTER 24

Sara wasn't anywhere in the house.

Caleb stepped onto the porch, heart pounding, telling himself there must be an explanation. He looked around. Nothing stirred. His phone vibrated in his pocket, making him jump. He pulled it out, pushed a button, and listened.

"Thanks for the heads-up, Irene. I take it he didn't want to talk to Craig?" Still listening, he started across the yard. "Good. Keep me informed." Stuffing the phone back into his pocket, voices from the barn caught his attention. He strode inside.

Sara knelt beside a stout bay, her hands working their way slowly down the mare's leg. Awkwardly, she leaned back, looking up at Henry Welton.

"It's still hot. If it were just a sprain, the poultice would have cooled it down by now."

"As skittish as they were last night, I don't imagine she kept off it much."

"I don't care. Call Anderson. I want this leg X-rayed."

Henry smiled. "I already have. Just wanted to see if you'd lost any of your sharpness."

Poised to say something smart, she caught sight of Caleb. "Care to help your sister up?"

"Sure. But in an argument with Henry, you're on your own."

He reached down, surprised by the strength of his sister's grasp. Once she was up, he stepped back. "You look at home here, with the horses."

A frown crossed her face. "I am. Or I was. Now I'm not so certain." She put her arm through Caleb's. "I feel the necessity for a very healthy breakfast this morning. Can you cook?"

"Well enough to satisfy you. Then we need to get to work."

At the porch, he held the door open for Sara, glancing out over the pastoral, peaceful setting of Slane's End. Marshmallow clouds filled the clear blue sky. Then it caught his eye—a line of darkness just at the horizon. It looked to be slowly but steadily gobbling up the light.

"Concentrate, Sara." Caleb's voice reverberated through the kitchen.

"I'm trying."

"You're not trying hard enough."

"I'm working."

"Not good enough," he shot back. "You're not concentrating hard enough on those books. Sara, you have to be able to function and block at the same time. What if he attacks your mind while you're driving over a bridge or on an icy road? Are you going to let go of everything to block him? You could kill yourself and your child. You have to control your mind."

Sara gritted her teeth and returned to the accounts. Caleb was right, but that didn't make it any easier. Her fingers squiggled on the ledger, producing something not in any way resembling the number eight.

"Sara!"

She glared up. Her brother looked composed, as though he were enjoying a social engagement. She wiped away the sweat that threatened to drip into her eyes. "What?"

The sudden zap went all the way down her shoulder to her hand. The pencil flew across the room.

"Dammit, Caleb, that's not fair."

"Wasn't meant to be." He leaned back, relaxed and grinning. "Shut the door. Protect yourself and your child, and function."

Wearily, Sara pushed the ledger back. "How long does it take to master this?"

"Some learn it in days, some in months, and some never."

"Why the push, Caleb? We've got time. He needs time to plan his next big move, unless . . ."

"Unless what?"

"Unless there's something you've foreseen?"

His silence unnerved her.

"What have you seen?"

"Nothing. I just want you prepared, able to control your mind, and protect yourself from this maniac. Let's try again." He rose, retrieved the pencil, and handed it back to her.

She looked down at the figures. The pencil dropped from her suddenly numb fingers.

"Damn it, Sara. What's wrong now?"

"I was thinking."

"Obviously, but not—"

"He told me."

Both Sara and Caleb jumped at the voice and the rattle of the screen door.

"Come on in, Tammy. I'm in the kitchen," Sara called. She took in her brother's dark expression. "I need a break."

A tallish, slender woman limped in, a carved figurine clutched in her hands. At the sight of Caleb, she stopped, her eyes widened with fear.

Sara rose and moved to her friend, putting an arm around the woman's thin shoulders. "This is Caleb, my brother. Remember Caleb? You saw him when he was little? Caleb, you remember my friend Tamar, Cora and Henry's daughter."

Hesitantly, Tammy held out her right hand. "He told me."

Standing, Caleb took the twisted fingers gently in his. "Good morning, Tamar. How are you?"

"He told me." She smiled up at Sara.

"Everyone calls her Tammy," Sara said. "Would you like some tea?"

Tammy nodded shyly and made herself at home at the big table.

"Looks like she's brought you a gift." Caleb nodded his head toward the carving Tammy still held.

Sara glanced at the figurine Tammy clutched. "Joe probably left it on the porch. Show it to Caleb, Tammy."

The woman pushed the piece carefully across the table.

"An admirer?" Caleb picked it up, feeling the warmth of the wood, the power of the artist.

"No. Joe lives in the mountains. He comes down during the summer to work odd jobs. He also sells his carvings in some of the shops. I ran off the road on the way up here and he pulled me out, so I gave him a fifty. That didn't sit well with him. He's a very proud man. I hinted that a carving would balance the books."

Caleb studied the piece. A young woman leaned against a horse, her hand caressing the neck. Both were pregnant, enjoying that brief moment of complete understanding and unity. He could almost feel the warmth of the mare's skin, the cool breeze that moved the woman's long curly hair. It throbbed with life, soul.

"He's brilliant. I'd like to see more of his work."

"I haven't seen him since the tornado."

"He told me," Tammy said.

Setting the filled cups down, Sara joined them at the table, carrying on the conversation as though Tammy were contributing. Forty-five minutes later, the thin woman rose. With a smile and a final "he told me," she shook Caleb's hand once more and left.

"Tammy was the one you found in the well, wasn't she?" Caleb asked. "Mother showed me some of the newspaper articles. She was proud of you."

"Really?"

He ignored the sarcasm. "Are those the only words she speaks?"

"Yes. As far as she's concerned, she's answering your questions and carrying on a conversation."

"Has she been like this since the incident?"

"Yes. Cora and Henry have taken her to doctors, hypnotists, therapists. 'He told me' are the only words they've ever gotten out of her."

"What did the newspaper articles leave out?"

Sara hesitated, her mind slipping back to painful memories. "She was the first child I linked with. She was kidnapped, held for almost five days. Yet she has never been able to describe her abductor, point him out in a mugshot. They found her in a well, hanging on for dear life. She'd been beaten, raped, tortured."

"Tamar." Caleb spoke the name softly. "Daughter of David and sister of Absalom, raped by her brother Amnon. She lived the rest of her life in the home of Absalom, a 'desolate' woman, at least according to Second Samuel, Chapter Thirteen."

"A student of the Bible?"

"I've studied many religious books. Did you ever try to connect Tammy's kidnapping with what was happening in Milford?"

"John went down that road for a while, but there weren't enough similarities to tie the cases together. Besides, that was almost twenty years ago."

"Joshua Caine isn't the only person with a scattered soul."

"What do you mean?" Sara straightened.

"I think if you were to go back to that well today, you'd find bits and pieces of Tammy." He seemed to give himself a mental shake. "We need to get back to work."

Sara grabbed the pencil, drumming it on the table. "Did you see the line of darkness at the horizon this morning?"

Caleb said nothing.

"It isn't natural. I've checked the weather. It's not showing on the radar. It's been there since you came, and it's spreading."

Caleb's hand moved to the Blackberry and clicked. His eyes

grew intense as he stared at what popped up on the screen. "No more for today."

"But you said—"

"I need you to go outside for a while."

Sara pushed back. "I need to check on the horses anyway."

"No. I don't want you anywhere near the horses. Sit on the porch, read a book, sketch a picture, knit an afghan—I don't care. Just don't leave the porch and don't go anywhere near the horses."

Sara could still smell whatever Caleb had concocted and sprayed throughout the old house. Sage, orange, lavender, even rose penetrated its deepest corners. The other scents he had used remained a mystery, but they calmed, enveloped, protected.

Rolling over, she sat up and looked down at her stomach. For the past hour, her daughter had been playing soccer. Sleep, evidently, was not on the program.

Grabbing her wrap, she slipped out onto the porch. The swing creaked as she sat, leaned back, and stared at the moon, which cast soft, real shadows.

"Can't sleep?"

"No."

The swing gave slightly as Caleb settled down beside her. "I was supposed to spend that summer with my friends. I was really pissed when they bundled me up and sent me off to camp."

"So that's why you weren't in Milford when I arrived. I never understood why Nana insisted I spend that summer with Mom and . . . Father. I was so happy at the farm. For the first time in my life, I felt as though I fit. I felt loved." She paused. "Two days after I arrived in Milford, I linked with Tammy, or rather, she linked with me.

"I thought I was losing my mind. I could hear, see, smell, and feel everything that was being done to her. When the link was broken, there were bruises and cuts on my arms and legs. I ran to Mother. She threw a blanket over me and hustled me back to my bedroom. She didn't listen to anything I said. Just told me to shut up and go back to sleep. God, I hated her."

Caleb closed his hand over hers, silently encouraging her to keep talking.

"The next morning I called Nana. Before I could say anything, Father jerked the phone from my hand and told me to get back to my room. For four nights, I went through hell. Finally, I couldn't stand it any longer. I ran away. He caught up with me a few miles outside of Milford and ordered me into the car. We drove straight back to the farm, where he literally dumped me out. It was the last time I ever saw him."

"Nana believed you," Caleb said softly.

"Tammy was found exactly where I said she'd be."

"Have you ever heard of the Slane journals?"

His question caught her by surprise. "Yes. Each generation described their gift in a journal and signed their name. Nana said they were lost in—"

"They weren't. I've got them."

"How?"

"The night the farmhouse caught fire, Mother saved them. She kept them hidden."

"Why?" Sara demanded. "And it wasn't the farmhouse that burned. It was Nana's bedroom, and Mother's. Nana and Grandfather were out checking on the horses when flames from their bedroom fireplace started the fire."

"I know all about the fire," Caleb said drily. "I've always suspected that our mother started it. She was convinced that something in those journals pointed to the downfall of the house of Slane. And she was convinced she was the one who would bring it about. At least, that's what she foresaw."

"Impossible. Mother had no gifts. It bothered Nana that she didn't, but when my abilities proved so strong, she figured there was a reason for the skip."

"Mother had the sight."

"No. Nana would have known. She would have seen it."

"Mom didn't want Nana to know. She kept silent, even tried to shut the gift down." He hesitated. "Sara, our mother didn't have an easy life. She lived daily with the fear that she had done or would do something to destroy the family. I think she chose to live as she did to protect us. That's why you went to Nana. That's why, when my abilities started manifesting, she hired Maggie Fahey as a nanny."

"What's Maggie got to do with anything?"

"She's fey. In other words, she has the sight. She taught me how to use my gift." He set four journals between them. "They're an interesting read."

Sara stared down at the ancient books. "When you saw me in the barn with the horses this morning, you said I looked at home."

He nodded.

"An hour after I arrived here, I almost called you. I wanted to go back to Milford, but I was just too tired to drive back. I don't belong here anymore. In fact, I don't know where I belong anymore. It's an unsettling feeling. It's frightening. When I came here as a child and Nana and Grandpa took me in, I was home. My world was this farm and the horses.

"In college I discovered teaching and loved it. A job brought me to Milford, and suddenly I had a job I loved and was good at, a man I adored, and a house that was a home. This became my world, and I was happy, content. Even the intrusions of the gift didn't seem as upsetting." Sara straightened up and twisted slightly to face Caleb. "Now I live in a town that hates me. I am not allowed to work at the job I love, and the man who was the center of my world is dead. All I have left now is this child and a gift that could kill her. I hate it. I wish sometimes that I had never been born."

"If you hadn't been born, a lot of children would have died. You keep forgetting the good you do. God, Sara, you save children. You find them when no one else can. That's something you need to remember, to hold on to. Things will, in time, fall into place, and I'll wager you will one day be teaching again." Caleb stopped. "I wish you had stayed in Milford. I would have felt better working with you there. Besides," he chuckled softly, "at least your madman couldn't have walked you into a pond."

"No, he probably would have walked me into the Sound with half of Milford cheering, 'drown the witch!'"

They both laughed softly as Caleb put an arm around her shoulders. "It will get better, Sara. I swear. You will find your way."

"All I keep thinking about is the ticking of that damned clock. If I could have just thought faster, acted quicker. I lost the only man I ever loved. Even at the funeral, John wasn't there. It was just a casket of dust . . ." Her voice trailed off.

"If someone is determined, at all costs, to kill you, your chances of living are slender. Your kidnapper was out to kill John. I don't believe you or anyone could have stopped him. That only happens in Hollywood."

Sara picked up the books, placing the worn volumes in her lap. "I'll read them. Do you honestly think I can control this madman?"

"Yes. I think you can control your mind and the kidnapper, and protect your daughter."

"Could he prevent me from linking with a child?"

"If he was strong enough, yes. But you keep forgetting just how strong you are. Don't. Soccer game over?"

"How'd you know?"

"I've been watching your stomach bounce for the last half hour."

He was at the door when Sara spoke, holding up the slim volumes. "What family prophecies do they speak of?"

"They talk about a red-haired woman and a son 'begat in violence and bearing no name,' to quote the passage. The son, 'being one with darkness'—again a quote—will bring about the end of the family. And no, I've never toyed with darkness."

Sara thought in silence for several minutes. When she spoke, her voice was subdued. "That passage is speaking of rape. You're not the result of rape, and you bear a name."

"That's the conclusion I came to. But something—and I never

found out what it was—convinced our mother that she was ending the line."

"What did you do while I was outside today?"

"It's the summer solstice," Caleb said simply.

"Which tells me nothing."

He smiled. "You need to get some rest. The coming days will be hard."

"Caleb." Her voice stopped him a second time. "Mother and Nana. They both died too soon, didn't they?"

"Yes." He closed the door softly behind him.

CHAPTER 25

A velvet darkness spilled over the road. In the stillness, only shadows within shadows disclosed that something lived.

Samuel drove carefully, his eyes roving the gently rolling hills of western Oklahoma. He was a few miles outside of Muskogee, the town made popular by the Willie Nelson song. Between Muskogee and Broken Arrow, there was a road, a very specific dirt road.

An ancient filling station came up on his right. Just beyond it, he saw the turn-off. It would take him up into the hills and rocks. It would take him to long-time friend and fellow shaman, Robert Stillwater.

Two miles up the dirt road, Samuel spotted the lights of the house. The long, chinked cabin sat just under a low bluff, blending into its surroundings. As he pulled up and cut the engine, the door swung open. The silhouette of a tall, thin man broke the light from a lamp. A sharp command cut off the barking of several dogs.

"Your timing, as usual, is perfect. We were just sitting down to eat."

Samuel stepped out of the truck, stretching his stiff back. "Whose cooking, yours or Millie's?"

"Millie's."

"Then my timing's right. What's for supper?"

"Fresh venison."

Samuel stepped onto the porch, eyeing his friend of more than forty years. "Good thing we Indians can hunt all year long."

"Not a problem. Besides, the poor thing dropped dead right on my front porch."

"With your help, no doubt."

Robert smiled, then embraced his friend. "It's good to see you. Come. We'll eat. Then we'll smoke some of the best tobacco I've had in over twenty years and we'll talk."

Samuel sat on the porch and stretched out his long legs, enjoying the stillness of the night. Beside him, Robert puffed on the ancient hand-carved pipe, then passed it to him. Samuel took a long draw, holding the sweet tobacco in until it flooded his soul, then exhaled slowly.

"There is a darkness over the east," he said. "My daughter has felt it in New Haven. Amelia Talks-a-lot feels it in Stroudsburg."

"What have you told the Hopi?" Robert asked.

"That I've seen a woman, a gifted woman who wears an ancient Celtic cross that was once red."

Robert took another drag off the pipe. "How are your daughters?"

"Rose is as well as can be expected, having married a white man. Helen presented me with a grandson early this spring."

"And your son?"

"Sam still guards the wild horses on the mesa by winter and works the ranches during the spring and summer. He no longer rodeos—and he still hasn't spoken to me. It's been four years. He still grieves, still blames me for his wife's death."

"It's not just you," Robert spoke softly. "He blames everyone for Joanna's death, especially himself. It's a poison. Have you had a singing?"

"He won't come. I've tried. He needs one, badly. I hope he will let me do it before I die."

Robert leaned forward and knocked the pipe against a railing, repacking it carefully and lighting it before speaking. "I've heard that young Jim Lightfoot is turning into quite a good singer."

Samuel remained quiet. Robert had just told him, in the gentlest way possible, that he would not be performing the ceremony for his son. Taking the pipe, he took another deep draw, blowing the smoke out carefully and waving it to the four sacred directions. His lips said a silent prayer for a good death.

The quiet stretched out between the two old friends.

"Is the white woman the one?" Robert asked at length.

"I don't know. She's powerful. So is her brother. They've touched souls, although the woman doesn't know it. She's with child—a girl. The child is also very powerful."

"When do you leave?"

"Tomorrow morning, early."

"Have you set a meeting time with Leon?"

Knowing Robert, Samuel smiled. "Why all the questions?"

"Stay. There's a gathering in Tulsa next week. A lot of old friends will be there."

It may be my last time to see them. Samuel shook his head at the thought. Why not stay and go to the pow wow? He would enjoy it. "Can you and Millie put up with me for a couple of weeks?"

Robert laughed. "I think so."

They both fell silent as the darkness deepened.

Working with the horses should have been calming. It wasn't.

Sara dragged herself up to the front porch and leaned against the rails. Beneath the sweet smell of hay and the scent of freshly mown grass, she caught the faint odor of decay, and though the sun was bright, the warmth didn't quite reach her.

She glanced up. There was a coldness to the blue of the skies. Even the horses stamped with irritation, restlessness. The madman was almost ready to strike again. She could feel it. Could she handle it?

"Shall we start?"

Thoughts broken, she turned to her brother.

"We need to get back to work, Sara."

"Is it worth it? I feel like I've only improved marginally."

Caleb smiled. "You're getting much better than you think."

"Yes, but we've been working for over a month. Sometimes I feel really stupid."

"You're anything but."

She hesitated as he held the door open for her. "He's going to strike again—soon."

"Possible. All the more reason to get to work now."

She slipped into the kitchen's coolness. The room cocooned her with the promise of sanctuary.

At the table, Sara picked up the book she was taking notes on. If they ever let her teach again, she would use more of these adventure stories of Lily the Lightning Bug. To her, they taught some of the more important concepts, like loyalty and trust.

Tightening her grip on the pencil, she focused on the words she wrote. The pressure in her mind changed, built. Caleb was, as usual, trying to get in. And she, as usual, was trying to keep him out and work. It was the same old thing that had gone on for almost too long, and she still couldn't get the hang of it.

Softly, Sara mumbled a few choice words as she looked down. She had pages of notes and accounting ledgers that were barely decipherable.

Closing the notebook, Sara tapped the end of the pencil against the table. She was tired, tired of the whole damned mess—of being pregnant, of making choices that sometimes meant life or death, of hearing voices, of being hurt. She had survived everything and everyone—the deaths of her grandparents, her parents, even her husband. Hell, she had even managed to survive her students.

Some learn it in days, some in months, and some never. Caleb's words rang through her mind. She was tired of not being in control; she was tired of being afraid. She had to survive. There was no other option. For her daughter, she had to survive.

She glanced over at Caleb. He was sweating. It beaded up on his forehead and ran in thin rivulets down his face to soak into his shirt collar. He was fighting to break through her defenses.

She reopened her journal, aware that Caleb's push was increasing. The pressure in her mind was building.

"Enough." Sara's voice rang across the room as she focused her anger and frustration. She slammed the door to her mind shut and pushed back hard.

Caleb's green eyes widened, flashed. His chair went over with a crash and skidded across the room. His head hit the far wall with a dull thud.

"Damn!"

She was at his side at once. Kneeling awkwardly, she took his hand, watching helplessly as he shook his head, trying to clear it. "Are you all right?"

"I'm going to have one helluva headache tomorrow. Otherwise, I'm fine."

"Did I cause this?"

Caleb looked up. "Yes, you did."

She leaned back in disbelief. "Oh my God, I'm sorry."

"No you're not."

"I didn't mean to."

"Like hell you didn't. It's been building up in you for the last month."

Their laughter began slowly as they helped each other up. By the time they were standing, Sara was laughing so hard tears streamed down her face.

"I—"

"You shut me out and never stopped what you were doing." Pride filled Caleb's voice.

"Are you sure it was me?"

"Yes." He hesitated. "Why?"

She sobered. "For the last few minutes, I've felt something beyond you hovering at the edges of what we were doing." Even as she spoke, darkness crashed into her mind. Falling, she twisted with her baby's pain. As her knees hit the cold linoleum floor, she slammed the door to her mind shut. The pain vanished.

She felt Caleb's arms around her and looked up into her brother's frozen face. "It's him."

It was even worse than the winter solstice.

The men had dropped their robes to dance naked around the fire. The day and night had been spent fornicating, drinking the blood of a sacrificed lamb, chanting—anything to gain more power. In the outside world, they were rich, powerful. Now they just looked pathetic.

The stink of sweat and sex permeated the wooden cabin. It was absurd to think this could give them anything except maybe a case of the clap.

Joe moved as far away as he could, practically hugging the door. He was the sentinel, the watcher. He couldn't—wouldn't participate. Not anymore. Serafina had seen to that. She had brought him back to reality, to sanity.

He dropped the thought. He must never think of her. He was dead to her, and she had to be dead to him. Her life depended on it.

A hand fell on his shoulder. "You've done nothing but watch."

Joe turned to his father and shrugged. "I've got what I need."

He felt the man's sharp scrutiny. "Is the boat ready?"

Joe nodded. "What are you going to do with it?"

"Take care of Sara and her brother, once and for all. And you're going to help, so don't ask why or give me any of your soft bullshit. They deserve to die. Look at you—kicked out of the family. And me—four years in a hellhole in Vietnam. That's what the great Slane family did to us."

"And when you've killed everyone, what do we have?" Joe asked.

Anger flashed across the old man's face. "Power. I've told you this before. Power. And you're going to be part of it. You're going to help."

Joe stared across the room.

Dawn found Samuel Hawk just outside of Oklahoma City. It had been a good month, filled with laughter, old friends, old stories shared as though new, and only a tinge of sadness.

From rolling hills, he entered the flat land of the Texas panhandle and wondered, not for the first time, why the Comanche had fought so hard to hold onto this country. Visions of sandstone cliffs and red sands danced through his head. He grinned. Indians sometimes fought hardest to keep the worst land.

He had just crossed into New Mexico when a sharp pain cut through him. Clutching his chest, he managed to get his pickup off the highway and kill the engine.

Heart attack ran through Samuel's mind until he realized the pain came from without, not within. Looking straight ahead, he saw darkness beyond the barren land. The pain finally lifted; the darkness did not.

He had to get back to Stroudsburg. Something was not right. Sara and Caleb needed him. He felt power shifting, swirling; some was dark, some was light.

Breathing easier, he reached for his cell phone, blessing the Hopi for insisting he have one. With shaking hands, he punched in the numbers. A few minutes later, a voice filled his ear with a gruff hello.

"Meet me in Santa Fe, Leon. I go no farther. The day after tomorrow, I start back for Stroudsburg."

He closed the phone, took a few deep breaths, and pulled back onto the highway. With any luck, he'd be in Santa Fe by early afternoon.

Samuel propped his feet up on the desk. From his hotel room at a Best Western, he could see the lights of Santa Fe, but it wasn't adobe storefronts and countless tourists he saw; it was the colored sands of Chinle. He was homesick, and he was too damned old to be homesick.

The thought of going back to Pennsylvania did not warm him, but he had to be there—with or without the help of the Hopi.

A knock brought him back to the present. He swung his feet to the floor, and a minute later, he was staring into the round, unlined face of Leon Many-trees. The Hopi didn't look particularly happy.

"I need to go back to Stroudsburg," Samuel stated softly.

Leon nodded in agreement.

Sara hunched over the steam from a cup of herbal tea Caleb had brewed. She clutched the cup tightly, her eyes half closed.

"Is there—" The shrill ring of the house phone silenced whatever else Caleb was going to say. He grabbed it. "Slane's End." Seconds later, he handed it to her.

She took the phone, a sinking sensation in her stomach. "Sara speaking."

"It's Anne Stockton."

The baby rolled, punching her hard. She placed a soothing hand over her stomach. "I take it this isn't a social call."

"Billy Duncan's been kidnapped."

She jerked up. "When?"

"Sometime this morning. I'm with Rachael now."

"Thanks, Anne."

Anything else Sara might have said was cut off as Anne continued, "We don't want you here, Sara. Even if the police call you in, Rachael will not let you in her house."

"I don't really give a damn." Sara slammed the phone down.

"What's going on?"

"Kidnapping in Milford. It's Billy Duncan."

"Do you think it's the same man?"

"I don't know." She punched in numbers, amazed at how readily they came to her fingertips. Vaguely, she was aware of Caleb speaking into his own cell phone.

A woman's voice answered on the fifth ring.

"Milford—"

"This is Sara Allbrooke. I need to speak with Captain Parker."

"I'm sorry, but he's very busy."

"You can put me through right now and save us a lot of valuable time, or I'll call his home, his private cell, whatever it takes to reach him, and let him know that you were less than cooperative."

"Just a moment." The woman's voice was ice.

"Sara, is that you? I was just getting ready to call—"

"Anne Stockton did that for you." She hesitated. "Is it the kidnapper?"

"Yes. We've got notes and a demand. You 'play' or he kills the child."

"He could do that anyway."

"The note says you can stop him."

"What happened?"

"Rachael went to wake up the boy this morning. He was gone. Letters were scribbled on the wall. His room's at the back of the house, so no one saw or heard anything. We don't even know how long he's been gone." The captain paused. "Thanks to Anne Stockton, Rachael is damned determined that you are not going to have anything to do with this. Hold on, Sara, I need to speak with someone."

Sara listened to the dreadfully familiar garble of words and background noise. How many times had John put her on hold like this? She closed her eyes. God, she missed him.

"Sara?" The captain was back.

"Where are you now?" she asked Lyle.

"Getting ready to head out to the Duncan house, at the top end of Henry Street. I wanted to call you in on this, but I didn't know . . . Rachael may not even let you in the house."

"That's what Anne just called to tell me."

"I wouldn't blame you if you kept out of this one, Sara."

"How will the police feel if I come back?"

"Relieved. You found things we couldn't. You saved those kids."

"Give me the notes."

"C, E, G, E, G. Thanks, Sara. I'm really glad you're going to be on this one. How long do you think it will take you to get to Milford."

She glanced at Caleb. "How long to get to Milford?"

"We'll be there in an hour and a half."

She relayed the message to the captain.

"I hope you aren't driving."

"I, ah," she glanced at her brother, "I don't think so."

"It could get nasty here."

"Maybe, but Billy is not going to die. I'm going to do everything

I can to save that boy, and no one—Anne and Rachael included—is going to stop me."

She slammed the receiver down for the second time and glanced up at her brother. "I have to go, regardless."

"It's what you do. The chopper will be here in about fifteen minutes. You need to get ready."

"Okay."

"He told me."

They both jumped and whirled around. Tammy stood at the door, her hair waving wildly about her pale face. It was the look in her eyes that made Sara step back. Madness had finally taken over the mind of Tamar Welton.

She came straight for Sara, her claw-like hands gripping Sara's shoulders, her voice shrill in its hysteria. "He told me. He told me." She repeated the words over and over again, shaking Sara.

"Tammy, stop! It's okay." Sara tried to free her arms.

The woman turned her head to Caleb. "He told me."

"Tammy." Caleb spoke soothing nonsense as he reached out, touched the side of her face, and ran his fingers down her neck and arm. She crumpled, eyes closed, as though she'd just fallen into a peaceful sleep.

Caleb caught her before she hit the ground, swinging the limp form into his arms.

"How did you do that?"

"Old trick. I'm going to put her in your bedroom. You'd better call her mother."

A few minutes later, Sara joined Caleb. He was patting the woman's face with a damp cloth, his voice still hypnotically soft. "Did you reach someone?" he asked.

"Yes. Cora's on her way over. Evidently, Tammy's been a handful the last few days. She slipped out when Cora wasn't looking."

Rising, Caleb tossed the cloth to Sara. "She should come to completely in a few minutes. Whatever you do, don't leave her alone until she's coherent—at least, as coherent as she ever is. I have a few more calls to make."

"What did you do?"

"I stopped her heart."

"You what?"

"Don't worry. It's beating fine now. Just stay with her."

Five minutes later, Sara heard Cora's voice at the front door.

"I'm in the front bedroom," she called.

Sweaty and breathless, the woman dropped beside her daughter. Tammy opened her eyes, staring beyond her mother.

"Sara, he told me. Sara." Tammy's voice raised a notch, her mouth stretching, working to pronounce a name she hadn't spoken in twenty years.

Sara froze, then managed to turn to Cora. "Has she ever said my name before?"

"No." Hope sprang into the older woman's eyes.

"He told me, Sara. He told me. He told me." The woman's agitation was building again.

Reaching down, Sara smoothed the wild hair from Tammy's face. "Shush. It's all right. I understand. You have to go home with your mother now. I need to go somewhere."

"He told me, Sara."

"I know and it's okay. Cora, can you watch Max for a few days? Caleb and I need to get to Milford. There's been another kidnapping."

"Of course. Is Max around?"

Sara shook her head.

"He's probably over at Bradley's," Cora said mater-of-factly. "I'll have one of the boys bring him back to the farm."

"What makes you think he's over there?"

"Because old man Bradley's been burning up my phone lines the last few days, complaining. It seems his retriever bitch is in heat and Max is 'keeping company.'"

"I'm surprised he hasn't shot him."

"He tried. Missed."

As Cora spoke, both women helped Tammy rise. With one arm

around her shoulders, Cora guided her daughter out the front door. On the porch, she stopped and turned to Sara.

"Do you think she's coming back?"

"Maybe," Sara said gently. "But let's not get our hopes up yet."

Cora reached out and squeezed Sara's arm. "I don't know if anyone's ever told you, but your grandmother was so proud of you."

As they walked away, Sara felt Caleb step up behind her.

"What did you do to Tammy?" she asked again.

"I told you."

She faced him. "She spoke my name, not once, but several times."

"That, I can't explain. Do you have the notes?"

She took the paper to the piano, plucking out what she'd written down.

"That's 'Michael Row Your Boat to Shore,' isn't it?"

Sara nodded. "And it's too easy. Something's not right." Closing the piano lid, she headed to her bedroom to pack, accompanied by a strange feeling of déjà vu. Ten minutes later, she joined Caleb in the kitchen, purse and a small duffle in hand.

"Think you can handle a chopper ride?" he asked.

"Think the seatbelt will go around me?"

Caleb grinned. "We added an extra link. Bridgeport's Sikorsky Memorial Airport can't take the company jet, but it will take a helicopter. I have one flying in from a private strip just outside of Patterson. He should be here in about," he checked his watch, "five minutes. It's the quickest way I know to get to Milford."

"You know Rachael doesn't want me there."

"I gathered that from your end of the conversation. Did you pack your hymnal?"

She patted her large purse. "It's right here."

The chopper set down in the front pasture, sending twigs flying and horses running. The pilot stepped out, shook hands with Caleb, and after a brief conversation, walked away.

"Come on," Caleb shouted over the roar of the motor.

"Where's he going?" She pointed to the pilot's departing back.

"He's driving the Rover back to Milford."

"Who's flying?"

"I am. I've had a private pilot's license for years, fixed-wing and helicopter. Compliments, in part, of Uncle Sam. Besides, this is my baby. I've logged most of the hours on her." He glanced at the sky. Clouds were thickening. "We've got to go."

Helping Sara in, he handed her a pair of earphones, then slipped into the pilot's seat. Minutes later, they were in the air. Sara grabbed onto the strap as the chopper bucked and ploughed through low clouds. The winds whirled widdershins around them, coming first from one direction and then from another.

"Are we going to make it?" Sara tried to keep her voice calm.

"Piece of cake. You ought to try coming in hot; that means under enemy fire."

"I've seen enough war movies to know that, and no thanks."

"It's just a couple of fronts colliding. We're still okay to fly and I'm skillful enough to keep us safe."

"Why did I ever think humility was part of your character?"

"Haven't a clue." He smiled, then fell silent, absorbed in his fight with the elements and the craft.

An hour and a bit later, Sara stepped out of the chopper, struggling to keep her shaky legs under her. Walking away, she fought the urge to lose her breakfast and possibly the previous night's dinner.

"You okay?" Caleb asked.

She swallowed hard and glanced at her brother. The rough ride had had no effect on him. In fact, it seemed to have heightened his senses, particularly his sense of humor. At that moment, she almost hated him. "I'm fine. How do we get to Milford?"

He pointed as a dark green Rover drove up.

Her mouth fell open and she turned on him angrily. "You mean, we could have driven here in the same amount of time I spent on that rollercoaster?"

Caleb laughed. "No. I've got several Rovers. I just happen to like green."

What am I going to say? How can I convince them? The questions went around Sara's mind as Caleb's chauffeur fought traffic. They were close to Rachael's house and she didn't have a clue.

"Just handle it, kid."

"Are you reading my mind?"

"No, but it's obvious what would concern you right now. It's also obvious you haven't arrived at a solution." He glanced up at a street sign. "We're there."

Sara caught sight of the Sound at the bottom of the road. Small white caps edged the colorless waves. The wind was dying down but the feeling of an approaching storm was still strong.

The front porch of Billy's home was filled with police coming and going. Strips of yellow crime-scene tape waved at the side of the gray and white bungalow and kept the pack of reporters at bay.

It was so familiar. Sara craned her neck, hoping for a second to see John come around the corner.

Caleb's warm hand rested heavily on her shoulder. He always seemed to know exactly what she was thinking.

She sighed. "I guess a part of me will always be looking for him." She wiped her eyes, brushed her hair back, and moved to open the car door. Caleb squeezed her shoulder, stopping her.

He nodded toward the two men in the front seat. "Dave and Chuck are going to run interference."

Chuck, the larger of the two men, stepped from the passenger side of the Rover and waited beside Sara's door. Dave stepped from the driver's seat and opened Caleb's door. Only when both men were at Sara's side of the vehicle did Chuck open her door.

Chuck remained on her right, Caleb on her left. Dave floated in the front near Caleb.

An arm flashed between the men and a microphone was shoved in Sara's face. "Are you here to help the police? You have already been partially blamed for the deaths of four policemen."

Sara could only stare at the hardened face of the strident female reporter.

Before she could react, Caleb grabbed the microphone and, none too gently, pushed the woman back. "If you remember, one of those policemen was her husband." His voice lashed out. A look from him sent the woman and a few other reporters stumbling back. Many of the more seasoned reporters gave way once they realized the two men escorting Sara and her brother were armed.

Two women stood on the porch in front of the door. Seeing Sara, they froze.

Straightening her spine, Sara threw her shoulders back and walked purposefully forward. It was time to go to work. After all, this was who she was and what she did.

CHAPTER 26

Captain Parker broke from the group and came forward, a welcoming smile of relief plastered across his craggy face. "How are you doing, Sara?" He gave her a quick hug.

"I'm fine."

"Don't expect a warm welcome."

Sara glanced at the crowd of reporters. "I don't."

He handed her a piece of paper. "One of the officers just found this in the mailbox. I have no idea when it was put there, but a preliminary check identified the writing as belonging to our kidnapper."

She looked down at the letters. "It's not like him to leave two songs."

"Yeah, and we can't figure out why. I hope you can."

"Has anyone worked on this one?"

"Yes. But I want to see what you come up with. I always feel better when everyone agrees."

"The first song is 'Michael Row Your Boat Ashore.'"

"That's what our men got."

They were at the bottom of the stairs. The captain stepped aside and Sara looked up into the icy eyes of Anne Stockton.

"So you're here to kill another child?" Her voice was as cold as her eyes.

"No. To save one." Sara climbed the stairs, her eyes never leaving Anne's.

"You think you can?"

"I know I can."

"What about that." Anne pointed to Sara's stomach. "Won't your baby die if you link with the kidnapper? That was your excuse for not helping Miriam. Isn't it enough you've already killed two children?"

"When did Joshua die?"

"He might as well be dead."

Caleb's and Samuel's words came to mind. "His soul is scattered, Anne. And he is very much alive."

"You're evil," the woman spat out. She glanced at Caleb. "Are you like her?"

"I hope so. I'm her brother and let's just say I'm here for support."

Reaching the top of the stairs, Sara stopped, her face inches from Anne's. "You can help me save Billy, or you can help the kidnapper kill him. I don't give a damn. But for now, get the hell out of my way."

She pushed the woman aside, vaguely aware that Caleb followed her. At the front door, she stopped again, her way blocked by Rachael Duncan.

"Rachael, move."

The woman glanced at Anne, her once harsh features slack with pain.

"Let her through. She can help," someone said from behind them.

Sara turned. Tom Caine was coming through the crowd and up the steps. Caleb reached out a hand. "Senator Caine."

"Mr. Remington. We never seem to meet under particularly good circumstances." He took Caleb's hand, his eyes on Sara. "Thank you for coming. I was prepared to coerce the captain into calling you. It seems someone beat me to it." His eyes fell on Rachael. "Let her help. She can, you know."

The woman trembled but didn't move.

Sara stared at the shaking woman, only vaguely aware that Caleb stood beside her.

Rachael's eyes darted from Anne's to Caleb's. Her shaking intensified. Lowering her gaze, she stepped aside and went into Anne's arms, clinging to the older woman as though she were a lifeline.

"There's a piano in the front room if you need it," Captain Parker volunteered, breaking the silence.

A moment later, all obstacles removed, Sara sat at the piano, picking out the new set of notes slowly. C, E, E, G, G, A, A. She played them again, increasing the tempo.

As the last note faded, Caleb reached down and hit the G again, then followed with several chords. "It's 'Eternal Father, Strong to Save.'"

"Are you sure?"

"Very." His voice was dry. "It's popular at military funerals."

Lyle nodded. "That's what our crime people came up with, though not as quickly as you did."

Hefting her bag up, Sara took out the hymnal, thumbing through the index. Hands shaking slightly, she found the hymns, dog-eared the pages, then flipped back to the first hymn Lyle had given her. "Damn, both have a slew of verses."

"Is that a problem?" Caleb asked.

"Yes and no. There are clues in the words, something that can tell me where he might be. More verses, more words to go through."

"I think it's time you tried to link with Billy," Caleb said. "But maybe you should see his bedroom first."

It was plain to see how the kidnapper got in. A simple slice of the screen, a quick jump. Any man in fairly good physical condition could do it. The kidnapper, despite a limp, was in excellent condition. He was, after all, a hunter.

"Caleb, what if—"

"See if you can pick something up."

"I'm not an empath."

"No, but feeling the scene may trigger things."

Sara glanced back at Captain Parker, who nodded. Pulling the tape aside, she stepped inside. It was cold. Sitting in the only chair, she took a deep breath and closed her eyes.

"Where are you, you bastard? Where are you taking Billy?" She sent out the thought, then sat back, waiting. Nothing.

She looked up at Caleb and shook her head.

"Your strength is your link with the child. Forget about the kidnapper. Try to reach Billy."

"How did you know I tried the kidnapper?"

Caleb smiled. "You're angry. You want to go straight to the source. Try the child."

Closing her eyes, she plunged into the void. Why hadn't the boy tried to reach her? *"Billy, it's Mrs. Allbrooke."*

"You're behind, Sara. I don't think I'll let this one live." The kidnapper's voice sent ice into her bones. A hand touched her shoulder; Caleb's calm voice broke the connection. "Don't let him frighten you. Billy is an old soul, a fighter. Go back to the child."

She took a deep breath, shutting the door to the kidnapper and going deep into her mind to find the child. *"Billy. It's Mrs. Allbrooke. I told you I'd be there if you were in trouble. Are you?"*

Nothing.

She opened her eyes. "Something's not right."

"If Rachael or Anne has spoken much to the boy, he may be afraid or angry with you."

"He's angry." All eyes turned to Rachael. "When you left, I told him you were a bad person. I told him that you let Miriam die and were afraid to come back to school. He got angry—very angry."

Sara shook her head. "I know Billy. If he won't talk, there's not much I can do."

"You can try." Caleb's voice was still calm. "He can't be the first angry child you've dealt with."

"You're their only hope." Tom Caine stood beside the captain, desperation in his voice. "You got through to Allen, even after Judy poisoned him against you."

"No, I didn't. It was all a lie. I never spoke to Allen. It was the kidnapper I was speaking to."

"Regardless, Sara, you are the only one who can stop him, the only one who can find Billy. Try. For Joshua and Miriam. For John."

Sara glanced down at the hymns, rereading the words. "He's in a boat . . . on the water. Could be a lake, a river, the ocean, the Sound. My gut tells me he's in a harbor."

"That's worthless information," Anne snapped. "Connecticut has how many miles of coastline and how many harbors?"

"Maybe not," Captain Parker spoke up. "We know it won't be private. He's going to take the child someplace public. Someplace where he can—"

"—flaunt the fact that he's right under our noses," Sara finished. "That should narrow things down a bit."

"Not enough," Caleb interjected. "You need to reach Billy. You told me you see through their eyes. Maybe you'll recognize something."

"The kidnapper's been very good at blindfolding the children; that's why I've had to use the hymns so often."

"Then you can't stop trying to reach Billy. He is your best choice."

She nodded at her brother and closed her eyes once more. Going down as deep as she dared, she called Billy's name. Power surged. She felt it. The gift was still there. She was rusty, but the gift was still there. She felt the silent, sullen child.

In one breath, she came up. "He's not trying to reach me."

"Try again. You have no choice," Caleb stated firmly.

Sweat dripped down her face as she stared at the photograph in her lap. A little red-haired, freckle-faced boy stared accusingly back. She had been trying for the better part of an hour to get the child to talk to her. Numerous times, she'd shut the kidnapper down, but all she felt was Billy's anger hovering at the fringes of her consciousness.

"Anything?" Caleb leaned against the door he'd shut to give her privacy.

"Nothing. He's not answering."

"Could he be unconscious?"

"I don't think so. Besides, even in the unconscious state, the mind is still working. Sometimes it's even easier for me to link with a child when they are out."

"Give me a minute, then—let's try something different."

Taking a stone from his pocket, Caleb turned to the door. "I can't rid this room of the hate and anger—it's too much a part of Billy's life now—but I can soften it and make sure nothing else gets in." Murmuring softly, he moved his hand across the door. After several minutes, he bowed his head and turned back to Sara.

"Are you ready?" He placed a hand on her shoulder. Energy flowed into her. Closing her eyes, she plunged down again, traveling deeper than she'd ever gone before. *"Billy. It's Mrs. Allbrooke. I'm here for you."* She sent strong thoughts out.

The faint essence of his soul touched her. It was just a quick brush.

"Talk to me, Billy."

"No!"

"Why not?"

"You left. You said you would never leave."

"I didn't want to go." She felt his confusion.

"You're bad. Momma said so. You killed Mrs. Stockton's . . ." His voice trailed off. Vaguely, Sara felt Caleb squeeze her shoulder.

"I couldn't save Mrs. Stockton's granddaughter. I tried. I almost lost my baby, trying to help Miriam. I didn't want to leave you, Billy."

"You don't have a baby."

She hesitated. How much would the boy understand? *"I'm going to have a baby, Billy. That's why I quit teaching. Talk to me. Are you okay?"*

"I'm . . . scrunched?"

Sara frowned. *"Scrunched? Are you lost? Do you know where you are?"*

"I'm not sure."

Air whooshed from Sara's lungs in relief. He might be frightened, but he was thinking. *"Is the bad man still around?"*

"No. He comes and looks, then goes."

"What do you see?"

For a moment, there was darkness. She feared she'd lost him. Warmth enveloped her. Caleb.

"I'm in a metal room."

"Can you walk around? Can you see out?"

"No. I'm scrunched. There's holes above me, but I'm not tall enough to see out. Besides, the lights aren't very good."

"Can you tell me anything else?"

There was a moment of silence. *"The floor's moving."*

"Billy, are you hot, cold?"

"No."

"Will you be all right if I leave for a moment?"

"Yeah, but I'm still mad at you."

"You will talk to me again, won't you?"

"Maybe."

It was time to feel, time to see through his eyes. She prayed he'd let her do it. Taking a deep breath, she merged with Billy's soul. Her shoulders touched metal, but even naked, the metal wasn't terribly cold. She rested her chin on her knees. She had no more room than that. No colors met her eyes, only a world of darkness.

"Come up, Sara."

She jolted upward, drawn by Caleb's voice. With a gasp, her

eyes flew open. "He's in a locker, a metal locker. On a boat, I think. He can't really see anything that's going to help us."

"Did he see anything when he was brought aboard?"

She thought for a moment; the connection was faint, but still there. "No. He was blindfolded, stuffed in a duffle bag, probably unconscious. He's seen nothing since the man entered his room."

She reached for the printed hymn verses and bent her head in concentration. "All the clues we've got are here. We just have to find them."

"Ms. Allbrooke, I'm getting wet. I'm scared." Billy's thoughts slammed into her mind. The paper fell from her hands. She felt the sting of salt water as it touched her feet, her bottom. Fear welled.

"It's all right, Billy. We'll find you soon. Is the man there?"

"No, but I heard him."

"What's going on?" Hands shook her gently as the question was repeated. "What's going on, Sara?"

"There's salt water coming in. The bastard's sinking the boat."

"Well, at least we know he's in a harbor and not in a lake," Caleb said.

"Naughty, naughty Sara. Still using that ugly word."

Instinctively, Sara placed her hand over her abdomen, shutting the door to her child but keeping the connection with the kidnapper. *"Where is he?"*

"You thought this one was going to be easy, didn't you, Sara? It's not."

"I know he's on a boat. I know you're sinking it."

"And it's happening so slowly that by the time anyone notices, your Billy will be dead."

"You have to give me something else."

"I don't have to give you a damned thing."

"If you want to keep me playing the game, you do." Sara held her breath, feeling the madman ponder the bait she'd thrown out.

"Let me see . . . E, E, E, F, E, or maybe C, C, C, E, E, D, C."

"Pen." Sara held out her hand. *"What else?"* She prayed there would be more. There had to be more.

"Figure it out."

She scribbled the notes as a sharp pain hit her eyes. He'd left too quickly. Rubbing her head, she looked up at Caleb. "We've got two more songs."

Sara sat at the piano, ignoring the startled faces of those around them. She played the notes several times. Silence was loud in the small room.

She repeated the notes, then swung into the opening cords of a song. "It's 'The Church's One Foundation.'"

"Are you sure?" Captain Parker asked.

"Yes. He seems to like that one. He's used it before. And like the other songs, it has a ton of verses."

She glanced at the second set of notes and picked them out. Nothing came. She played them again, changing the timing and the key. Still nothing. Sara grew steadily desperate as she repeated the notes again and again. It was a strange song. It didn't even sound like a hymn, but she picked up her hymnal anyway.

"You won't find it there."

Sara looked up into Judy's closed face. She hadn't even heard the woman enter.

Time hadn't been gentle to Judy Caine. Harsh lines edged a face that had once been soft and giving. She stood beside Tom, her hand tight in his.

"It's the only way I can find the song, Judy."

"It's not there."

"How do you know?"

"Because it's a Catholic song. It's called 'The Rosary.'"

The book dropped from Sara's hands. "That's not a hymn."

"No, it was a popular religious song in the forties and fifties. Our mother used to sing it to John and me." There was a catch in her voice.

"Do you know the words?"

She shook her head.

Caleb lifted his briefcase to the piano and opened it, taking out a laptop. Within minutes, he had the music.

Sara looked at the computer screen, reading the words. "Something's wrong, Caleb. He doesn't give four songs, and he's never left the Protestant hymnal."

"I have a feeling he has a reason for changing things."

"What would that be?" the captain asked.

Caleb turned to Lyle. "This is his final game. Billy won't be his only victim. I think he's after Sara. The only way he loses this time is if he dies. I may make sure that happens."

"I hope it doesn't come to that, Mr. Remington. I'd hate to have to arrest someone like you for killing the kind of scum we're hunting. But I would."

Caleb smiled without warmth. "If it comes to that, Captain, I'll either be 'innocent' or never caught."

There was something in his voice that told Sara he could do just that.

"Judy, what's a 'mystery'?" Sara asked as she reread the words.

"Each decade, or ten beads of the Rosary—and there are five decades—represents a mystery. For instance, the announcement to Mary that she would bear the Christ child is one. It's called the Annunciation."

"This doesn't fit," Sara said, her voice heavy with frustration.

"He's changing the game," Caleb replied. "He can do that. What better way to throw you off, yet keep you determined? He knows you."

She studied the words. "Mysteries, mystery, mystic, mysticism, mystic . . ." Her eyes fell to her open hymnal. The words of "The Church's One Foundation" filled her eyes.

It was there. The word literally popped out of the fourth verse. "Mystic. Mystic." She rolled the word off her tongue, a long-gone memory tickling the back of her mind. "Mystic. Mysticism. Water. Harbor. Seaport. Public. Popular. Under our noses. Everything he looks for." She stopped. "Billy's at Mystic—Mystic Seaport. He's in a boat in the harbor." She glanced at Caleb.

"Then we've got problems," Captain Parker stated. "There's a regatta there this weekend, the Antique and Classic Boat Rendezvous, I think it's called. We could be looking at a hundred boats or more in port right now, plus all the visitors. If he's sinking one slowly, we may not see it in time."

Caleb reached for his cell phone. "Just tell your people to start looking for boats that look to be sitting a little low." He turned and left the room, speaking softly to someone on the phone. Minutes later, he returned. "There's an open field just outside of Mystic. I'll take the chopper."

"What are you up to?"

Caleb faced the captain. "We're going there."

"The police will handle this."

"The police have handled it for over two years, and no offense, but they've never even come close to catching this man."

"Let us handle it, Caleb. I want the bastard alive."

"It's our lives on the line as well, Lyle. Because if he can only kill Billy this time, I guarantee you that Sara and I will be next."

"You have no proof of that."

"I don't need proof. I know."

The captain hesitated, staring deep into Caleb's eyes, then shrugged. "Okay. It might be a good idea for you both to be there. I'll sanction it—if you take me with you. Got room in that chopper?"

Caleb nodded.

CHAPTER 27

It was a perfect Connecticut summer's day, one made for families, picnics, and sailing. It was hard to believe that somewhere below the perfection, a child fought for his life.

Caleb skimmed the trees, sending leaves and blossoms scattering in the man-made wind. He was aiming for a small clearing. Beyond that lay Mystic Seaport, snug, quaint, its blue waters filled with a colorful array of sails and boats.

"What are you thinking?" Caleb asked.

Sara glanced at her brother. "A jumble of things. This is a helluva long way from Milford. Am I in the right place? Is it Mystic? Why did he let Dillon go and kill Miriam?"

Caleb shook his head. "That's something you'll have to remember to ask the bastard when we catch him."

"I will. Don't worry, I will."

There was a gentle thud as Caleb set the chopper down. Unsurprised, Sara noticed a green Rover parked beside the police car at the edge of the clearing.

Caleb shut the engine down and motioned everyone to wait. "I know it always looks good in the movies, but it's safest to wait until everything stops." He glanced back at the police captain. "It appears our rides are already here."

"Yep. And I need you two to remember that you are not involved in this—unless Sara gets more information. The feds and police out of New London are handling this. We're here by invitation, so I expect you to act as such. They have set up a headquarters at the Seamen's Inne Restaurant and Pub. You two will remain there until everything's over."

Caleb nodded as he stepped out. "My driver will follow your car in." Grabbing Sara's arm, he helped her out.

By the time she reached the car, sweat trickled down her shirt. "Ah, Connecticut and humidity." She stepped into the air-conditioned vehicle, enjoying the blast of cool air.

The baby gave a petulant kick as though she too felt the discomfort. "Easy, little one," Sara crooned.

"Baby all right?"

"She's fine. Changing positions sometimes annoys her."

"Follow the police," Caleb instructed his driver.

Sara settled back, closed her eyes, and reached out for Billy. *"Billy. It's Mrs. Allbrooke. Are you okay?"*

She waited. Nothing. *"Billy, talk to me."*

It was several moments before she felt his essence. His voice was weak in her head.

"Mrs. Allbrooke?"

"How are you doing, Billy?"

"I'm wet. It's getting cold."

In the cool of the car, Sara shivered as cold salt water bathed her feet.

"Are you still sitting?"

"Yeah. My shorts are wet."

"Hang on, Billy. We're close. Can you hear anything?"

"Noise. People talking, banging things."

"Do you remember anything else from this morning?"

"No."

"Do you want me to stay with you?"

"I'm kind of sleepy right now."
"We'll be there soon."
"Okay."

She felt the child slip away and opened her eyes to Caleb's worried expression. "You reached him again?"

"Yes. He may not be as strong as you think."

She glanced out the window, then turned to her brother. "All right, how in the hell did you get a car here before the copter?"

Caleb grinned. "Friends."

Mystic was bustling. Caleb instructed the driver to park wherever he could find a place and remain alert.

Helping Sara out, he pointed to a building surrounded by police and people. "I think that's where we need to be."

The inside of the restaurant looked like something from a movie set. Agents sat at tables interviewing locals and boat owners. Noise filled the small place. Everyone wanted to help, and everyone, Sara realized, had seen something or someone strange.

Papers were spread across tables as the harbormaster worked to plot the names and owners of each vessel in the port. Policemen were coming and going as they got new instructions on where to search next.

Caleb guided Sara to the back of the restaurant.

"Want something to drink?"

"Just water."

He was back in five minutes, a glass in each hand, and sat across from her.

"So, are we just going to wait?"

Caleb grinned at his sister. "No. I need you to check this out." As he spoke, he pulled a folded bar menu out of his pocket and flattened it on the table. The hastily drawn diagram listed most of the boats in the harbor and their location.

"How—"

"You don't think it took me five minutes to get drinks, do you?"

He pushed the paper across. "Use your intuition. Where are we most likely to find Billy?"

Caleb had drawn circles indicating where boats were docked. Each circle had a name or some scribbles that Sara supposed represented a name. She studied the paper. "The Rose—at least I think that says Rose—that's similar to 'rosary,' from the Catholic song."

Caleb flipped the paper around. "That's Rose. Can't you read my writing?"

"My first graders have better penmanship. Here's a boat called the Alleluia and one called the Magdala—religious connotations again."

"Is he close in or out?"

"Out gives him space to flee, but if he's sinking the boat, he won't need that. Close in—well, we already know he blends with crowds. It's harder to spot someone in the midst of people than it is alone on the edge." She looked up. "It could go either way."

Sara bent her head back to the paper, savoring the names, studying where each boat sat. After a few minutes, she leaned back. "Nothing. There're several that may fit name-wise." She pointed to the list. "There's the Abracadabra, the Hocus Pocus—magic names. There's also the Billy D." She looked up at Caleb's puzzled expression. "Billy Duncan."

"That's too simple."

"Maybe. Maybe not. I'm going outside. See if you can find out anything about this boat." Sara rose and headed out; she needed someplace quiet to think and concentrate.

Stepping into the soft afternoon sunlight, Sara crossed to the harbor. Caleb joined her a few minutes later.

"The guy I talked to is a thirty-year local. He said the Billy D. showed up about four months ago. He figured someone bought the old fishing trawler to restore her but realized how much it would cost and just putters around with her now. Sometimes she just sits and sometimes the guy takes her out—no rhyme, no reason, no schedule."

"Does he know the owner?"

"No. The guy pretty much sticks to himself. The only thing he could tell me about the man is that he walks with a slight limp."

Sara stared at her brother. "Old boats sometimes ride low in the water and no one thinks anything of it."

"Yeah. They also sometimes have metal lockers below," Caleb added.

"Billy could be on that boat. Let's go."

"Whoa." Caleb grabbed her arm. "You're seven—eight months pregnant and you're going to take on a kidnapper? I don't think so."

"I need to get closer."

"Okay." He held her arm for a companionable walk along the water.

The Billy D. was anchored at the outside edge of the harbor. *Deeper water*, thought Sara. Easier and quicker to escape if he decided to go that route.

She studied the old boat, feeling it wallow in the still sea. Peeling paint and weathered wood made it impossible to see any kind of a watermark. Was it floundering?

"Okay, now what, Sherlock?" She glanced at her brother.

Caleb arched an eyebrow to her. "You first, madam. Can you get any kind of a reading?" He took her arm to steady her.

Sara closed her eyes. *"Billy. Talk to me, Billy."*

"It's cold, Mrs. Allbrooke. I don't feel so good. Are you coming soon?"

"Very soon, honey. Is the water getting deeper?"

"Yes. I'm standing now. My feet are so cold."

"Hang on, sweetheart."

She felt her brother's grip tighten and opened her eyes. "He's close. Very close." She studied the old boat. "I'm not certain. But he's not doing well."

"Are you sure you were talking to him?"

"It felt like it. Are you going for the police?"

"There's something we don't know, something . . ."

"Another trap?"

"I don't know. But the sooner I see if Billy's out there, the better."

Sara stared at the small boats buzzing around the harbor. Many were only using one oar to move around. "So, how are you at sculling?"

"I've done it, can do it. I won't win any prizes for form. For now, I want you off the pier. If I'm not back in ten minutes, get to Captain Parker."

"But—"

"No buts. I need you safe. Go."

Before she could comment, he was gone, striding down the boards as though he belonged to the harbor. His body language told Sara he was ready. She ambled away, checking her watch, trying to appear touristy.

The scene was an artist's composition. Every pattern and color magnified the glassy blue water and cerulean skies.

A shadow passed over. Sara glanced up. Clouds were forming on the horizon, quietly bunching up, quietly preparing to change everything. Something was coming in, and it was coming in quickly.

"You all right?"

She whirled to a grim-faced Caleb. "Nothing?"

He shook his head. "The local was only partly right. The man who bought the Billy D. will be fixing her up to live on. She was the first fishing boat he worked on some fifty years ago. It's a homecoming for him."

"Are you sure?"

"Yes. I saw him just as I got to the dinghy, introduced myself, and shook his hand. That told me all I needed to know."

"So we're nowhere."

"We know he's close." Caleb's green eyes rose to the sky. "A squall's coming up, and fast. Let's get back to the Seamen's Inne."

"We can't. We haven't got the time. We've got to find that boy, now."

"Sara, we need to go back over that list. And there are some questions I need to ask the captain."

The bustle on the docks picked up noticeably as they made their way back. Everywhere, people were preparing the boats for rough weather. By the time they reached the Seaman's Inne, the brisk breeze had become a full-fledged wind.

Caleb guided Sara to the back. Snatches of conversation all seemed to reach the same conclusion: The squall wouldn't last long, but it was going to be rough.

As soon as she sat down, Caleb handed her the menu with his list on it. "Go back over this. See if anything catches your eye." Then he was gone.

Sara rubbed her chilled hands together, studying the names and positions of each ship. A pounding broke her concentration. Looking up, she shivered. Rain lashed the front windows. The temperature had taken a quick dive.

"Anything?" Caleb asked when he came back.

"Nothing. You?"

"*Sara, have you forgotten how to play? Talk. Question. Revile me.*" His voice set her brain on fire.

She leaned forward, her head in her hand. All right. He wanted to talk. She'd talk. "*You know we're here?*"

"*You caught on, but maybe not fast enough. Billy may be another Joshua with this storm.*"

"*I need another clue.*"

"*A song?*"

Sara stifled a frustrated scream. "*I don't give a damn whether it's a friggin' song or name. Give me something and stop fucking around.*"

"*Such language—and from a first grade teacher. No songs. Eternal lost friends.*"

"You bastard!" The pain was growing intense. Sara slipped a hand down to her stomach. *"Enough!"* She broke the connection.

Strong fingers bit into her arm, jerking her all the way back to the present. "What happened?"

"Another clue."

"Another song?" Caleb asked.

"No. Words. 'Eternal friends.' No, he said 'eternal lost friends.'" She looked back down at the paper, running her finger along the names. Nothing popped. She tried it again. Her hand stopped. A chill froze her blood and time seemed to stand still. What's this name?" she asked softly.

Caleb jerked the paper around, peering at his writing. "It's the JoWAll."

"John William Allbrooke—lost friends."

"That seems like a stretch."

"It's what his perverted mind would concoct. I'd stake my life that Billy's on that boat."

"I'll be right back."

Two minutes later, he returned, Captain Parker in tow. "We haven't gotten aboard that boat yet," the captain explained tersely. "It's locked up. A note says that the owner is at the Steamboat Inn. No one's had a chance to follow up on it."

"Anything from the locals?" Caleb asked.

"Nothing beyond the fact that it docked here about two months ago and hasn't left the harbor."

"He's on that boat." Sara stared at Caleb. "I know he is. You've got to get out there now."

"I'll get some men," Lyle said.

Caleb raised his eyes to Sara as the captain left.

"What do you want me to do, brother?"

"Link with me. See what I can't. Guide me in."

"What?"

He leaned over the table. "You can do it. Get into the kidnapper's mind. Give me the layout of that damned boat. Watch my back."

"I—we've never tried that."

"We don't have to try. We're tied by blood—that's the strongest bond there is—and we're both gifted psychics. You've read my mind at times and I've read yours. If you can link with lost children, you can damn well link with me."

"But—"

"Just do it." He rose and strode into the storm.

Get into the kidnapper's mind, keep him from knowing what you're doing, link with Caleb, and watch his back. Piece of cake. Sara groaned, placed both hands on the table, and slipped into the darkness.

Billy came to her at once. *"I'm scared. The boat's moving. The water . . ."*

"You're going to be all right. Hang on, Billy, my brother's coming," she crooned. Then she cleared her mind and turned her thoughts to Caleb, surprised at the anger and language she met.

"Caleb!"

"It's bad out here. If I ever get my hands on this son of a bitch, I'll kill him."

"Do you see the boat?"

"Hell, I can't see my hand in front of my face."

Sara looked down at the paper. *"It's almost at the end of the docks. It's the second one in. There's a boat in front of it. How are you going to get to it?"*

"Don't worry about that. I'm almost there. Have you spoken to Billy?"

Even as the words entered her mind, Sara choked, her mouth filling with water. She spit and continued spitting and struggling to breathe. Vaguely, she realized someone was coming toward her. She waved them away.

"Caleb, hurry. He's almost under." Minutes of darkness filled her mind. *"Caleb!"* she screamed silently.

"I'm on the deck. Christ. It's an old PT boat. The hold could be full of water and she'd still ride high. No one would notice if she was sinking."

A sudden blast lashed through Sara's mind. *"Watch out!"* Pain sliced through her arm. She closed her eyes tighter, strengthening the link, giving Caleb all the power she could as he fought.

A wrenching tore through her. For an instant, she feared the connection had been broken; then she realized that Caleb had thrown the assailant across the boat. She felt something else.

"Billy can't breathe."

"Which way?"

"Five feet in front of you—stairs. The ax. By your feet. Grab it. Use it on the locker door."

At the edge of her mind, she saw a shadowy figure, something in his hand.

"Caleb!" Sara's mind screamed. *"There's someone else. Move. Caleb, move."*

Cold, briny, oily water rose over her. She gasped for breath. Beneath her hands, the baby trembled, kicking out viciously. Sara had no option. She cut the link; her last image was of something raised high, coming down hard.

CHAPTER 28

"Come on, honey. Come back."

Sara heard a snap. Her nostrils filled with the pungent odor of ammonia. Pushing the hand away, she struggled to sit up—only to find herself firmly pinned back to the earth. She opened her eyes to a pair of kindly gray eyes almost lost in a sea of wrinkles and framed by frizzy salt-and-pepper hair.

"Don't move too fast, hon. You went out like a light."

Sara suddenly realized she was lying on the floor. "Did I fall?"

"Slither's a better word." The old woman caught Sara's train of thought instantly. "I'm sure the baby's fine. Not havin' any pains, are you?"

"No. Billy. Did they find Billy?"

"The little boy who's been kidnapped? No."

"What do you mean, no? Where's my brother? Where's Caleb?"

The woman looked confused for a moment. "Oh, you mean the man helping the police? He's sitting on the back end of the ambulance right now, getting put back together."

"What?"

Sara struggled up, grabbing onto the woman's hands for help.

"Be careful, now. Where are you . . .?"

Sara didn't hear any more. Staggering past tables, she made for the door.

A light rain still fell, the last remnants of what had been a bad squall. Caleb sat in the back of the ambulance, a paramedic bandaging his arm, his chauffeur and bodyguard nearby.

"Where's Billy?" Sara halted in front of her bother, her shaky knees threatening to buckle.

"Sit." He pulled her down. "You look as though you're going to pass out."

"I've already done that."

"You fell?"

She glanced at the paramedic who had looked up from what he was doing. "'Slither' was how the waitress described it. Where's Billy?"

"You can probably answer that better than I can. But I'm loath to ask you to try right now. There was a second man. He took the boy."

Closing her eyes, she sought out Billy. Warmth enveloped her.

"Sara."

She looked up at Captain Parker. "He's okay. In a car, truck—I can't tell which—I think a truck. They're going—" she stopped, replaying what she'd seen through Billy's eyes. "They're heading west. He's sitting in the front seat."

The captain ran his hand over his face and shook his head. "Christ, what do I do? Put out an APB for anyone with a redheaded boy sitting in the front seat of something?"

"It's all I've got, Lyle."

Thanking the paramedic, Caleb rose and grabbed Sara's arm. She was at the end of her strength. He could feel it. "We're going back to Milford, Captain, to the summerhouse. If she gets anything, I'll be in touch."

"Damn! Damn the man! Damn him!" Curses whirled through Malachi's mind.

He forced himself to stop. It was his fault. He should have paid closer attention to the warnings. Duncan and even Joe had told him that Remington might be a force to be reckoned with.

Joseph, his own son, his blood—he should have seen that coming. It was that witch in New Orleans who had turned his Joe. Hell would be heaven to what he now had in mind for his son.

So much for seeing the face of Satan. Malachi had seen Satan the night of the solstice. The king had made his presence known to him. That told him he couldn't fail. Sara and Caleb were marked for death. Yet, he had failed, thanks to his own son.

He pulled the hat lower over his eyes, drifting with the crowd, blending. No one noticed he was dripping wet. Everyone who'd been unable to reach shelter in time was drenched. Only he dripped salt water.

Moving past the crowd, he headed toward his car. His arm was killing him. Damn! The ax should have cut Remington's arm off. Actually, it should have cut his fucking head off. Whatever—it should have stopped the man. It hadn't. He had gotten the wrong angle, made a mistake. No. Something had stopped it.

Malachi glanced around at the conglomeration of cops, cars, and people. Remington would live. So would he. He had a plan. He always had another plan. But it wasn't supposed to work this way. Sara was supposed to be at the bottom of the boat with the boy. And Remington was supposed to be fish food. The thought that he had missed, missed badly, tightened his gut until red spilled out of his eyes.

Stopping at the SUV, Malachi slipped in. Like a good, abiding citizen, he pulled out of the parking lot, watching, obeying rules, alternative plans running through his mind. He slapped the steering wheel. Of course! That was it! He needed to get to Stroudsburg fast. He would go back to the beginning, back to what Joe started and never finished so many years ago. Tammy. Tammy was the bait that would lure Sara back to Stroudsburg. Tammy was the bait that would lead Sara back to the Slane cabin, to the place where it all started.

Sara deserved a little more time of suffering. Then he would wipe the Slane seed from the face of the earth. He would be victorious. He could feel it. This time he would win. Sara and Caleb would die!

A policeman motioned him to stop. His heart slithered to his belly—until he realized it was to clear a bit of traffic. Leaning back, he sent his mind out. He found Tammy. It was easy. He would be there by night. The rest would be simple. She was waiting. He would finish what his son started. A bit of pride swept through him. Joe had had a good imagination; had done some good work, at least in the beginning. It all changed when he met that New Orleans witch.

Malachi leaned back. Joe was right about one thing. He was finally tired of the fucking game. He was a prince now, a son of the dark king. It was time to end things—everything. He grinned. *Sara, say goodbye.* She would be first, the brother next. He would be ready this time.

His thoughts turned to Joe. His son was a traitor. He had turned against his father and his king. But what could Malachi expect? Joe bore Slane blood. For that, he had to die, and Malachi would relish killing his son with his own hands.

He settled deeper into the car seat. There were places to go and things to do.

Tammy lay in the darkness, her eyes wide open. Something was wrong with her world. She could feel it, but her attempts to explain it got her nowhere. No one understood her.

Sara was leaving. She wasn't supposed to. They were supposed to spend the summer together. And why Milford? Sara lived with Nana, not her parents. Tammy's best friend would leave and Tammy would be alone.

Movement out the window drew her attention. Something was out there. Something she feared. Something she needed to face.

Rising, she walked into the bathroom. Her mouth tasted like dirty water. Her mother had forgotten to leave a glass beside the bed. Clumsily, she filled a glass and drank deeply. Her eyes caught her reflection in the mirror. She was only vaguely aware of the glass slipping from her grasp, shattering in the sink.

She studied herself. When had she gotten so old? Raising a hand to her wild hair, she smoothed it down. It was white, wiry—and her hands, veined, stiff.

Back in the bedroom, she dressed awkwardly and with difficulty. When had she gotten so helpless? She glanced at the clock. It was late, a deep night of heavy clouds and a heavy mist.

In the hall, she grabbed a coat and scarf from the closet. She could still hear him. He had come to her in the late afternoon. She'd gone to bed early, feeling him. He was calling now, but this time it would be different. It would be so different.

She glimpsed her reflection in the hall mirror as she walked past. Where had the time gone? Why couldn't she remember?

Samuel leaned against the already dusty side of Robert Stillwater's new pickup and stared at the skies. Even the brightest stars gave feeble light in the unusual darkness of the early morning. Dawn was still several hours away. Feeling a hand on his shoulder, he turned to Robert. The Cherokee held out a bag of food. "For your trip."

"From Millie?"

Robert nodded. "Venison on good fry bread and a jar of the sweet pickles you like so much. Plus two thermoses of hot coffee." His voice dropped. "There is also medicine, good tobacco, and my pipe." Robert smiled. "I want the truck and the pipe back in good condition."

"I could drive my own truck."

"Ha! Your truck should have been put out to pasture years ago. It is old, and your heater and air conditioner work only occasionally. This one will get you to Stroudsburg quicker and safer."

Samuel pulled himself up into the cab and slammed the door. "My old truck will be running long after this shiny thing has quit."

Robert smiled. "That is true." He placed his hand on Samuel's arm. "You got here so late last night, I hate to see you leave this early." He looked away for a moment, hesitating, then turned soft eyes to his old friend. "I know what you are feeling, but it is not age that slows you down. Whatever's out there is draining your strength. It is happening to all of us. Hurry, but take care. You must be strong for the battle, and you have at least twenty hours of driving ahead of you."

"I'll call David Eastman when I get around Danville. I can rest a few hours at his place. That should still put me back at Amelia's sometime tomorrow afternoon. You felt it this morning, didn't you, Robert?"

"Yes, there is a storm building, a storm of pure evil. Fight well and hard, my friend. Our prayers are with you. Both Millie and I have alerted others as to what is going on. Many prayers will go up in the next days."

Samuel nodded in thanks as he slipped the big truck into gear. He glanced in his rearview mirror in time to see the darkness engulf his friend.

"Why aren't you in bed?" Caleb asked as he strode into the den.

Sara looked up. "I could ask you the same thing."

"Go back to bed, Sara. You need the rest. You need it badly."

"So do you. How's the arm?"

"I'll be fine."

Both turned to the television as the weatherman tracked yet another storm.

"What is it with all these fucking storms," Sara mumbled.

"Storms cause chaos. Esoterically, evil is at its strongest during chaos."

"Do you think he's responsible for these storms?" She waved a hand at the weather map splashed across the television screen.

"Would you believe me if I said it was possible?"

Her answer was slow in coming. "Three months ago, I would have called you crazy. Now I'm not so sure. Are you sure you didn't recognize him?"

"No. The only thing I know is he's damned strong."

"Mad people often are. Where did the second man come from? Did you get a look at him?"

"As I told you earlier, no. But he was younger and faster."

"Have I been fighting two people all this time?" Her brother shrugged. "You think there's more to all of this, don't you Caleb?"

He hesitated. "I think there's a lot more to all of this, more than either of us know."

What in the hell have I done? More than that, what in the hell was he going to do?

Joe glanced across the cab at the redheaded boy who sat wrapped in his jacket, staring out the window. Safety. First, he needed to make sure they were safe. Then clothes and food. The boy had to be starving.

The battered truck zoomed along the backroad, the headlights showing little traffic. When lights from a car came close, the boy automatically lay down on the bench seat. Joe had made it a game for the child, and he played it well.

Where was his father now? What was he going to do? The questions swirled around Joe's mind. Malachi had to be up to something. He always had an alternative plan.

He sighed with relief when he saw the lights. The little place was still open. It was a little mom-and-pop store with everything from macaroni and cheese to jeans and jackets. The beautiful thing was that there were four small cabins in the back that the old couple rented out to travelers. Even better, they never asked any questions and they knew him.

"Lights." He glanced over at the boy, who immediately lay down, and rubbed the child's back affectionately, keeping the boy quiet, calm. At least the child had stopped flinching when touched.

Joe pulled into the store, stopped, and eased out of the truck. "I'm going to get some stuff. You stay here and don't let anyone see you. I'll be back in a few minutes."

The boy nodded, still lying on the truck seat.

Fifteen minutes later, cabin keys chained to a carved wooden spoon in his hand, Joe threw a couple of paper sacks into the back of the pickup. The boy was exactly where he'd left him.

Slipping in, he straightened his leg, rubbing it hard. It hurt like hell. The stairs, the fight, the run, the child's weight, the drive, it had all put a strain on it. Grabbing a bottle of aspirin from the glove compartment, he downed his usual six, then pushed the old truck into gear and drove behind the store.

They'd spend the night in a cabin, and as much as he hated to, he'd try to reach the old man. Joe had to know what was going on, where to be. Maybe he could . . . could what? No matter what he did, he'd never be able to redeem himself. Yet . . .

He stared down at the child. Lives were at stake. Many lives.

The small fire in the ancient fireplace chased away some of the night's chill. Dressed in jeans and a plaid shirt a few sizes too big, Billy Duncan silently downed the warmed Spaghetti and meatballs.

Joe watched and sipped hot instant coffee as Billy methodically ate. One plastic forkful of spaghetti, one sip of coke. *Does my son eat the same way?* The boy would definitely need a bath by the time he was through.

At the boy's last bite, Joe filled up the old tub and herded the spaghetti-covered child into the bathroom, making sure the door was left partially open. Lying down on one of the twin beds, Joe listened as he stared at the phone. The last thing he wanted to do was talk to his father. He punched in the number.

Malachi picked up on the first ring. The dark, graveled voice was harsh. "Why'd you do it?"

Joe remained quiet.

"Have you gone soft or over to the other side?"

So many lives depended on what Joe said next. A familiar scent wafted through the room—a heavy, exotic scent. "I'm tired of all the bullshit. I'm tired of watching naked men dance around, screw, and make asses of themselves all in the name of power. It's crap. You can't gain power from death. You don't gain it from screwing or from sacrifices or from dancing around the moon. It's bullshit—it's all bullshit."

"Shut up. You don't know what you're talking about. You are as evil as I am. Have you forgotten Joshua Caine? Remember what you did to that boy?" His voice lowered dangerously. "Remember what you felt? You can't tell me that wasn't Satan in your heart and your hands that night. Our faith is no joke. Sacrifices are necessary, and rituals are powerful."

"It's not my faith." Joe's voice was as soft as his father's.

"I've got the woman."

Joe's throat closed. Images of Serafina filled his mind. Was that why he'd smelled her perfume?

"The crazy one," his father continued, oblivious to his son's panicked thoughts. "The one called Tammy. The one you practiced on so many years ago."

Suddenly, Joe could breathe again. "I was fifteen, angry, and confused. I didn't know what I was doing or why I was doing it."

"Yes you did. You're feeling guilty thanks to that New Orleans bitch. She's made you weak."

"No. She gave me strength."

"You're bad, Joe, as bad as I am. Evil can only beget evil, and you are my son. Where's the boy?"

"He got away."

"You're lying."

"What did you do with the woman?"

"For now, she's chained to that well you put her in all those years ago. I figure Sara will be back in Stroudsburg tomorrow night. That is, if I allow her through the storms."

"You don't control the fucking weather. Then what?"

"It ends on the Sabbath night. It ends where it began. I need you at the Slane cabin. I can't take both of them on alone."

"And then?"

"Unless you've got the guts to kill the brat, I will kill him. Blood is power. Innocent blood is even greater power, and we both need all the power we can get to bring down the Slanes. I want you to share it all, be my son. But know this. If you don't do what I say, I will kill you, then I will kill your woman, and I will raise your son as I should have raised you."

Joe cut the connection. Heart pounding, he stared at the phone. Because of him, Serafina was in greater danger than ever before. So was his son. And Malachi would know whether or not he killed the Duncan boy. Joe had to do something. He had to change things. He had to get to the Slane cabin before the old man did.

Joe glanced up. Clad in Superman pajamas, Billy Duncan shuffled out of the bathroom. Joe pulled his knife from its sheath and ran a thumb down the very sharp blade. He had never really had a choice. Serafina had to live. So did his son. He had to protect them both, and there was only one way he could. He motioned the boy to come closer.

CHAPTER 29

Groggily, Sara stared at the plate of eggs and cup of tea that Maggie had placed before her. She couldn't remember when she had been this tired. She was reaching for the tea when Caleb walked in.

He sat down silently, grabbed the coffee, and almost emptied the cup before he set it down. His eyes fell on her. "You look like shit."

"How's the arm this morning?"

Caleb winced. "Things always hurt more the day after. I take it you didn't get much sleep."

"You would be right. When are we leaving?"

"Based on the way you look, sister, not until tomorrow, if then."

"Excuse me," Maggie interrupted from the doorway. "There's a call for Ms. Sara." Maggie's guarded expression as she handed the phone to Sara alerted Caleb. He straightened up.

With shaking hands, Sara grabbed the phone, recognizing the voice at once. "Cora, what's wrong?" She listened several minutes, trying to understand the garble. Finally, she interrupted, "Cora, put Henry on the line."

Henry's voice sounded old. "Tammy's gone. She walked out, or maybe was taken. I don't know which. I do know we didn't hear a damned thing. Cora got up to check on her this morning and she was gone."

"Have you called the police?"

"Yes, they're on their way. There's blood on the porch. Your name and Tammy's are written across the door. Do you think it's him?"

Sara hesitated. "I don't know. It's possible. Caleb and I will be there as soon as we can. You've got our cells. Keep in touch." She frowned as she gave the phone back to Maggie.

Was it her kidnapper or someone totally different? She looked up at Caleb. "We need to leave now."

"You're not goin' anywhere." They both faced Maggie, who stood like St. Michael at the gates of heaven, holding the phone as though it were a flaming sword. She'd said the words as only an Irish woman could—with the gentleness of a mother and the strength of an army commander.

"Maggie . . ." Sara's voice faded off.

White-faced and clear-eyed, the old cook turned to Caleb. "You can't take the lass now. There're more storms comin' and she's weary. It's not good for her or the babe to be this tired. She needs more rest, as do you. You'll be needin' all your strength for what you face."

Her clear eyes darkened, returning to their normal shade of blue. Color flooded her cheeks. She took a deep, shuddering breath, her voice softer, more natural as she continued. "Look at your sister, Caleb. She's banjaxed."

Caleb turned to Sara. A pale face of dark circles and dull green eyes stared back.

"Maggie's right. You're exhausted."

Sara rose and turned on him, anger, exhaustion, and her round belly robbing her of any grace she might have once had. "We don't have Billy. Tammy's missing. We can't wait because I'm a little tired. We leave. Now! He won't get away this time. He won't win. I will stop—"

"Sara," Caleb's calm voice interrupted, "it's not good for the baby."

At his quiet words, air and anger whooshed out of her. She collapsed back in the chair.

"Caleb—"

"We'll leave this afternoon, weather permitting, after you've had a chance to get some more sleep. Maggie can fix us a good lunch and a supper for the road."

She raised a tear-streaked face. They were right. She was so tired, even breathing seemed a chore.

"I'll fix you a wee glass of warm milk, and you can go back to bed for now." Maggie was gone before Sara could protest.

"What's 'banjaxed'?"

Caleb gave a soft laugh. "It's the Irish equivalent of being at the end of your rope, knackered, exhausted. You can't go any further."

Maggie reentered with the phone once more in her hand. "It's Mr. Welton again."

Henry's voice was ragged. "She took her coat and boots."

"Has she ever done anything like this before?"

"No. She's afraid of the night. It took Cora years to get her to stop locking her door." He took a breath. "There's blood and broken glass in the bathroom sink and a message on the vanity mirror in blood. Cora's pretty sure Tammy wrote it."

"What's it say?"

"'Help me, Sara.'" His voice dropped to a painful whisper.

"We'll be there this evening. Keep in touch."

Sara sat in the big recliner, wincing as lightning flashed and fireplace flames danced to the rhythm of the storm. It might be early afternoon, but it was as dark as evening.

"You should still be in bed."

She turned to her brother. "I caused this; it wasn't Mother. I think it's me who will bring down the Slanes."

"What makes you think that?"

"In some way, Caleb, I've attracted evil." Her voice dropped.

"The probes, the ones that caused me to almost lose the baby . . . could they have affected her? Could my child be evil, damaged in some way?"

"How long has this been floating through your mind?"

"Since John's death. If we hadn't gotten married, if he hadn't followed my gift, he'd still be alive."

"Stop making John a cardboard saint. He was a cop. He did what he had to. And he wasn't always a 'good' cop. He crossed the line—more than once."

"What's that supposed to mean?" Sara flared, sitting straight up.

"He planted evidence to get Billy's father jailed. He engineered the situation that got him shot. He took that bullet purposely."

"I don't believe you."

"Would you believe him?"

Her voice was dangerously soft. "What do you mean?"

"He came to me the night you almost lost the baby. He told me everything."

She rose to face her brother. "You're a liar."

"No."

He never saw her move until the palm of her hand hit his face. He grabbed it, holding the long fingers firmly. "He did what he had to do to get scum off the street, Sara. Our system rarely gives justice these days. But technically, he crossed the line."

She jerked her hand free, staring into eyes so like her own. "He had a reason. He wasn't a bad man or a bad cop."

"No, he wasn't. He was a good man trying to make a good difference in a bad system."

"What about his child, Caleb? What about our baby?"

"It's not a problem. Your child will be born normal. Now go get ready. Hopefully you'll sleep in the car. I'd like to take the chopper but the storms are too bad. It's going to be a long drive."

With a silent nod, she left the room.

Caleb strode into the kitchen and poured himself a fresh cup of coffee. Leaning against the granite countertop, he watched the lightning play across the Sound.

Was his niece evil? Had his mother been the innocent? Was it Sara who would bring down the family?

He headed to the library. The situation would bear his close attention, perhaps a lifetime worth of attention. Opening the library desk drawer, he withdrew a pistol, a Baby Desert Eagle. He would give it to Sara and show her how to use it, if she didn't already know how.

Feeling the cold metal, he said a quick prayer. *God, don't ever make me have to turn a weapon on someone in my family.*

The truck wove slowly along the litter-strewn road. Samuel raised tired eyes to the house. It was early afternoon. Amelia Talks-a-lot sat on the porch, wrapped in a blanket.

He killed the motor and stepped stiffly from the truck. "How did you know, Chippewa?"

She held up a cell phone. "David called me when you left. Storms slow you down?"

Samuel nodded.

"Come, Navajo. Coffee's strong and hot."

Moments later, he sat, aching hands wrapped tight around the hot cup. "You are a good woman, Amelia."

"Even for a Chippewa?"

He grinned. "Even for a Chippewa."

"Something's not right."

"I know. I followed the darkness from New Mexico and Oklahoma to here."

"These storms. There's something on the w—"

He held a hand up, reached into his pocket, and fished out a piece of turquoise. It still glowed.

She stared at it for a few moments, then raised her eyes. "Why?"

"I think the hunter is close but still needs time. These storms, they buy him that and they wear down the hunted."

"But who is the hunter and who is the hunted?"

Samuel shrugged. "I need to go see Sara."

"She may not be here yet. She went to Milford. Another boy was taken."

"Did she find the child?"

Amelia shook her head.

"Then she may not be home any time soon," Samuel stated. "I cannot see Sara giving up."

"She'll be here this evening."

He looked up, eyes questioning.

"Cora Welton's daughter went missing last night. My son Nathan was tracking her this morning at first light."

"If Nathan can't find someone, no one can. Who's Cora Welton's daughter?"

"Tammy Welton. Sara's best friend. The girl was kidnapped when she was thirteen. Twelve-year-old Sara found her. According to Nana Slane, it was the first time Sara used the gift. I'm taking fry bread to Cora tomorrow. That's what whites do when there is something wrong. They feed their bellies rather than their souls. In the meantime, you need rest. The bed is ready."

Rising, she walked toward her bedroom, stopping at the door. "If you grow cold, old man, I know a way to warm your bones."

"Right now you would only get cold bones, woman. But when this is over I would like very much to warm you." He smiled, remembering how taken he had been with the young, beautiful Amelia. If his heart had not belonged to another, well, his path would have been with this Chippewa woman.

Amelia smiled, sensing his memories and nodded, her eyes bright with laughter, her voice soft. "It's been over twenty years since we comforted each other, Samuel. I'll consider what you said a promise. Goodnight."

Samuel chuckled to himself. He might need more rest than

he'd counted on. If memory served him right, Amelia was an active lover.

Cora and Henry Welton stood on the porch of their farmhouse, watching as the SUV came to a stop.

"Have you heard anything, Cora?" Caleb asked as he stepped out and walked to the passenger side to help Sara out.

The woman shook a face lined with exhaustion and age, then walked down the porch stairs and took Sara into her arms. "But just knowing you're here eases my mind."

Henry came forward to shake Caleb's hand and give Sara a quick hug. "You all need to see the bathroom." He turned, leading the way.

Sara stared at the words written on the vanity mirror.

"Anything?" Caleb asked.

She shook her head. "I couldn't pick up anything in the bedroom either."

"Have you tried to link with Tammy?"

"Yes. Something or someone is blocking me."

Caleb reached over her shoulder, his fingers stopping inches from the blood. Light and warmth radiated up his arm. "The pieces are coming together."

"You're not an empath." Sara spoke more sharply than she'd intended, but the drive to Stroudsburg had been tense, with Caleb dodging tree limbs or trash blowing across the road. It seemed that as soon as they drove out of one storm, they drove into another.

He dropped his hand. "I'm not a strong empath. But sometimes I get images, insight."

"What's it mean?" Henry asked.

"It could mean she's waking up, remembering. It could also mean the game is almost over."

"She's coming back to us, isn't she?" a voice behind them said.

They all turned. Cora swayed dangerously in the doorway.

Grabbing the woman's arms, Henry and Caleb guided her back into the living room.

"Why Tammy?" Sara asked once they made it back to Slane's End. She hadn't wanted to ask the question in front of Cora.

Caleb looked at her across the kitchen table. "To lure you back here."

"He's never taken an adult."

"No, but Tammy's more child than adult right now. I have the feeling he's not playing a game anymore. He wants you dead—but he needs to make a point first, to make sure you know something. He knew you would come for Tammy, just like he knew you'd come for Billy."

"Then he knows my past. Do you think the police have checked the well where they found Tammy the first time?"

"Hard to say. Most of these cops probably weren't even out of high school when Tammy was kidnapped the first time. But I'd have made it the first place on my list."

Sara rose.

"Where're you going?"

"To where it all started."

"Are you sure you feel up to that?"

"I'm fine. I'll call Nathan and give him directions to the well."

"Nathan Talks-a-lot?"

Sara nodded. "Beyond being a Stroudsburg policeman now, he's a damned fine tracker."

Nathan Talks-a-lot was already waiting, leaning against his squad car, when Sara and Caleb drove up.

"Been a long time, Caleb." The big man pushed up off the car and extended his hand. "What, four, five years?"

Caleb shook the man's hand, smiling back. "Five years. Figured you were getting tired of seeing me."

"I was beginning to think you might be moving up here."

Sara glanced at her brother in surprise. "You? Up here? That often?"

"I had to make sure that Nana's will was carried out. Do you know where the well is, Nathan?"

"I should. I've been out there three times in the last ten hours." He grinned down at Sara. "That well and how you found Tammy is practically a legend around here. Everybody knows about it."

"Did you find anything?" Caleb asked.

"The first time, no. It was too dark and there was a drizzle. I got a better look at things later this morning, but in all honesty, there wasn't much there—what the rain didn't wash away, someone else did. After you called, I went back for a third check. In fact, I almost called Samuel Hawk in to look at the scene."

"Samuel's here?" Sara asked.

"Arrived at my mom's this afternoon. He's one of the best trackers there is."

"I take it you didn't call him." Caleb's voice was strangely soft.

"No. There just wasn't anything to see."

"But you felt something?"

Nathan nodded slowly. "Yeah. I think Tammy was here and I think she got away."

"Can we see the well?" Sara asked.

Silently, Nathan turned and headed into the woods. Caleb and Sara followed.

Five minutes later, they all stopped, staring beyond the yellow crime-scene tape.

"We cordoned it off this morning, just in case we missed something in the dim light," Nathan explained. He squatted and waved an arm toward the well area. "The kidnapper was shrewd. I found brush marks my second time here. Faint. But deep enough to tell me he came back after the rain to make sure we found nothing. I did find a partial print down the path beyond the well. It's small enough to be a woman's."

"What's your take on all of this?"

Nathan rose. "The bastard's playing a game."

"He's been playing a game for years," Caleb said drily.

"I mean, he's been here and gone and come back again several times. I have a feeling he's waiting. I heard something in the brush last time I was here. Couldn't find anything, though." The big man hesitated, then seemed to make up his mind. "I need to get back to the station. You're free to look around. If you find anything, give me a call. It's good to see you again, Sara. You too, Caleb." Then he was gone.

Sara faced her brother. "Does Nathan know what you are or what you do?"

Caleb shrugged and turned to study the area. "Maybe."

Twenty minutes later, Caleb and Sara headed back to the SUV. They'd found nothing.

It was a long night filled with dreams she could not even remember. She had tried to sleep late but couldn't. In the end, she rose, dressed, and fixed breakfast for Caleb. For the rest of the day, she paced the floor, waiting for word on Tammy. She heard the kitchen clock chime two. God, the day was dragging. She should be doing something, but nothing came to mind.

Echoes of thunder yanked her back to the present. Lightning lit up the sky. Rain pinged against the tin roof.

"Everything okay?" Caleb asked as he walked into the kitchen and grabbed a cup of coffee.

"Yes. You?" She glanced at the cell phone he'd spent the better part of the last several hours talking on.

"William Duncan's trying to take over various parts of Remington's."

"Billy's father?"

"Grandfather." Caleb's head jerked away. Red, flashing lights were pulsing in the dim living room.

Sara rose as his voice whipped out. "Stay here."

The policeman looked wet, miserable, uncertain, and frayed. "We tried to take her home but she pulled a fit in the squad car. The only thing we understood was 'Slane' and 'Sara.'"

Caleb looked past the officer. The second one was helping a drenched and filthy Tammy Welton out of the car. An equally sodden Max slipped out, following the girl. "Where . . ."

"She was walking down the highway holding onto that dog, heading this direction. I radioed Henry and Cora. They should be here any minute." He shrugged helplessly. "We didn't know what else to do."

Caleb's hand calmed the young man. "You did right."

"We really need to ask her some questions, but . . ."

"She couldn't answer them right now, even if she wanted to. I'll see that Henry and Cora get her to the station tomorrow, after she's calmed down."

The police seemed to feel they were off the hook. Minutes later, they were driving down the lane back toward the road.

"Tammy." Caleb's voice, like his hand, was gentle, soothing. Putting an arm around her shoulders, he helped her up the stairs. Sara held the door open.

Wrenching free from Caleb's grip, the woman flung herself into Sara's arms. The sounds were unintelligible, but it was clear that Tammy was trying new words.

Caleb reached out to the hysterical woman.

"No heart-stopping, Caleb Remington."

He smiled at his sister.

Sara rubbed the damp cloth gently over Tammy's dirty face. The gibberish had stopped but something was different. Sara looked into the woman's eyes. The vacant stare was gone. Pieces were fitting together. Tammy was coming home.

The screen door banged open. Cora ran across the room, pulled her daughter to her feet, and hugged her tightly. "My God, child. What happened? Where've you been? Why'd you run away? Are you okay?" She held the girl out at arm's length.

Tammy's mouth moved like a fish gulping for air.

"Honey—"

Tammy put a hand over her mother's mouth and tried again. Mouth moving, sounds shot forth. "Ah . . . ha . . . d . . . to . . . go."

Turning from Cora, Tammy limped to Sara and thrust a dirty, wet piece of paper into her hand.

Opening it, Sara frowned and looked up. "Cabin?"

Tammy nodded.

"The cabin? Our cabin?"

Tammy nodded more vigorously.

"What's it mean?" Caleb asked.

Sara turned to Caleb. "The Slane cabin. The family summer home in the hills near the quarries. It's about two hours from here. I can't even remember if you've ever been there. I don't remember going with our parents."

"Bo . . . th. He . . . wa . . . nts . . . you . . . both."

"He wants us to go to the cabin?"

"Yes. Sab . . . Sab . . . th."

"Sabbath—Sunday, today?" Caleb finished.

Tammy nodded. "He . . . says . . . it's . . . whe . . . re . . . it all . . . be . . . gan." She took a deep breath.

"Who is he?" Sara asked quietly.

For a moment, Tammy was strangely quiet. "My, you . . . r . . . kid . . . napper."

Joe left the mom-and-pop cabin at dawn, in the middle of yet another storm. He wasn't worried. He had plenty of time to reach the Slane summer home in the hills before the old man did. If Sara was there—and he knew the old man would do something to get her there—he had to convince her to leave. Convince both of them, if her brother was with her. They needed to go and let him do what needed to be done. He swallowed hard. What kind of a hell did God have for a man who killed his own father?

He was rounding the curve when the old truck coughed and died. He drifted to the side of the road. This might change things. Grimly, he climbed out of the vehicle.

Thirty minutes later, Joe slammed his hand hard against the side of the ancient truck, squelching the desire to kick the bloody thing into perdition. He couldn't find anything. Mechanic that he was, he couldn't find any reason for the damned thing to have just stopped.

Flipping open his cell phone, he tried again. No signal. That was strange. He'd been all over these mountains. There were very few places that technology hadn't reached by now.

The afternoon sun caught his attention. He'd been on the side of the road for hours. There had been no cars, no signs of life. If help didn't arrive soon, all of his plans would be down the drain.

A sound caught his attention. Finally, a car was coming down the road. If it was a local, they would stop. If it was a tourist, they'd drive past.

The car slowed down.

He let out a thankful breath. Maybe his luck was changing. Maybe he still had a chance to make things right.

CHAPTER 30

"I'm going with you."

"No, you're not."

"Yes I am, Caleb. You don't even know where the damned summer home is. I don't think you've ever even been there."

"GPS, Sara—just give me the address."

"No."

He opened the long, black nylon bag he'd thrown into the Rover before they left Milford. "The last thing I need with me right now is an eight-months-pregnant woman."

"No. But you do need bait."

"Well, it sure as hell isn't going to be you. We already know he's going to be there. I don't need bait."

"When he sees your Rover and that you're alone, he'll know I'm still here. I'll be as good as dead. Being with you may be the only thing that saves my life."

"I'll drive you to the police station or take you to Amelia's or Henry's."

"Caleb, I'm going. If I'm not in the car with you, I'll follow you in the farm truck."

He placed both hands on the bed and leaned over the ancient patterned quilt. God, how he wished Richard were still alive.

Richard would've had his back. They could have planned the op together, because that's what this was. Taken apart, it was nothing more than an operation. The kind he and Richard had planned hundreds of times, executed successfully, and most important of all, lived through. Why did a man who felt like a brother to him have to be killed in such a senseless accident? If it was an accident? If Caleb ever found out that Duncan had had something to do with that sheet metal flying off the roof of the Boston church, he would hound the man to hell. He straightened up and turned to the defiant pregnant woman still standing by the door.

"When was the last time you were up there?"

"Ten years ago." Sara's voice caught as she continued, "John and I honeymooned in the summer cabin. He didn't like it much. He wasn't much of a rougher."

"Can you describe the lay of the land?"

"I've been all over that property. I can tell you where every rock and hiding place is."

"Dress warmly, comfortably, and in something in which you can conceal a gun."

With a nod, she was gone.

Caleb set the bags back into the Rover. Everything had been checked, double-checked, and triple-checked. Nothing was being left to chance.

He glanced up as Sara threw a backpack into the car. She lacked training, know-how, but he knew she'd try. Would that be good enough? He shrugged. It would have to be.

As Sara moved to shut the back door, a hundred forty pounds of German shepherd edged past her and jumped. Anchoring himself in the backseat behind the driver, Max stared straight ahead.

"You—out," Sara commanded.

The dog's ears flickered, but he didn't move.

"Max."

"You've lost that one," Caleb stated.

She glanced over at him. "He can't go."

"Why not?"

"He's not an attack dog or watchdog or anything like that." She turned to the animal. "You were drummed out of the force. You're a wuss."

Max remained frozen.

With a grin, Caleb shut the door. "He'll warn us if someone's coming. That'll have to do." He walked to the driver's side, slipped into the SUV, and waited patiently as Sara hefted her bulk inside. For a moment, he stared at the old farmhouse, his mind working quickly and methodically.

"What are you waiting for?" Sara asked.

He started the engine. "I want you to tell me everything about the place. What does it look like? Where does it sit? Paths. Vegetation. Caves. Anything and everything you can think of. I need an accurate and detailed description of the area, at least as much as you can remember."

She nodded.

"The knowledge may save both of our lives," he added as he slipped the Rover in gear.

It was quiet, eerily quiet. The moon was still trying to come out from the clouds, but the storm wasn't over. Electricity still tingled down Sara's arms and danced in the distance.

Caleb drove slowly and stopped frequently, wanting to arrive in the evening. Now he traversed a dirt road that was nothing more than a sea of mud strewn with broken branches.

"Pull over. The fork is about a quarter mile ahead. You wanted cover. This is the best place not to be seen."

He slid the big vehicle close to the trees, flicked the light so it wouldn't come on when the door opened, and stepped out, moving quietly to the back of the vehicle.

Sara joined him.

Within minutes, he'd slipped into camouflaged rain gear,

painted his face, hefted weapons and ammunition, and secured the night-vision goggles with ease and expertise.

"Hunter's moon," Caleb thumbed toward the sky, "when it comes up."

"Is that good or bad?"

"It gives us both an advantage and a disadvantage. Don't worry. I'll find him."

"Caleb." Sara laid a hand on his arm. "Remember, you can't reach this man without me. It's me he links with. I'll be all right. The most dangerous animal is a female with her young."

A grin flashed across his face. "Just don't forget to link with me."

She was opening the driver's door to climb in when his voice stopped her. "Drive slow. I don't want to be trying to catch my breath and a killer. And Sara, if it becomes a matter of your survival or mine—no heroics. Save yourself. Save your child."

Before she could answer, he'd slipped into the night.

Hefting her bulk into the driver's seat, Sara moved the seat forward as far as she could, relieved when her feet actually touched the pedals. A low whistle and Max joined her up front.

She took the right fork, driving slowly, looking for the cut-off up the mountain . . . and sliding right past it. Backing up, she slammed the Rover into four-low and turned up the narrow dirt— now mud—road.

Driving the twists and turns up the hill, she tried to forget about the drop into the water. By the time the cabin came into view, she was sweating, her hands frozen to the steering wheel. Killing the engine, she waited in the darkness. Nothing moved. An unnatural, discordant silence reigned.

Despite her feelings, the cabin looked safe, cozy, even inviting. Her hand dipped into her coat pocket, feeling the cold metal of the Baby Desert Eagle. *Could I use a gun? Would I use the gun?* She eased out of the Rover, stretching out the kinks, and took a deep breath. John had forced her to hone her shooting skills. *Yes.* To save herself, her child, her brother, she could and would use it.

Walking around the car with Max at her heels, she stopped in front of the structure. *Is it empty?* She'd have to open the door to find out. Sara's fingers touched the key hidden above the door. Thrusting it into the lock, she turned it and slowly pushed the door open.

Caleb moved through the dense darkness of the forest, his mind replaying Sara's descriptions. Years before, the first quarry had been dug, robbing the land of granite and stone. When it filled with water, they dropped down, mining a lower spot, and when that filled, they moved to the last quarry, the lowest spot on the mountain. When it too filled with water, they left.

Time and erosion had broken some of the rocks down to the water level. Animals drank, and due to an enterprising ranger in the 1930s, eagles and bears enjoyed fish.

The cabin, built from the surrounding forest, perched on the edge of the highest quarry and melted into the landscape. According to Sara, the view of the three man-made lakes was spectacular.

One path and a road ran beside the quarries. Caleb slid into the forest, almost immediately finding the hunter's path that Sara had described. It paralleled the road for a while, then climbed up the mountain. He came out behind and below the cabin, moving like a ghost up and down the hills.

Something wasn't right. Samuel could feel it. He glanced at the clock. Amelia was still at the Weltons'. She had taken some more fry bread and beans over. According to early rumors, Cora Welton was in a bad way.

Stepping outside, he watched as a car barreled down the road.

With a screech of brakes, it stopped in front of the house. Amelia was out and on the porch in an instant, speed belying her bulk.

"Sara and Caleb have left."

"What do you mean, left?"

"Tammy came home this morning. Well, the police brought her back. The kidnapper must have let her go, or she escaped. I don't know which, but I've actually been talking to her. She said the bastard wanted to meet Sara and her brother at the Slane summer home—the cabin. Well, not exactly in those words. I drove past the Slane farm and they're already gone. According to Cora's husband, they left an hour or so ago."

"What took you so long?" Samuel fought a rising anger.

"It took me a long time to get it all out of Tammy. She did not want to speak of it, and her speech is difficult to understand. Samuel, the girl's not spoken for almost twenty years. Nathan will be here in a minute."

"Why Nathan?"

"He knows the way to the Blue Lakes, the Slane summer home. He will drive you there. Open yourself, Samuel. You must follow the power."

He felt the blood drain from his face. Amelia was right—but to open himself meant weakening his power against the darkness.

"I will help keep you safe and I'll alert others." As she spoke, she pushed past him. A few seconds later, she returned from the house, a 30-30 Winchester in one hand, a bandolier of shells in the other. "Take this. It belonged to my second husband. When I kicked him out, I kept the rifle. It worked."

With a half-smile, Samuel took the weapon, feeling it become an extension of his arm. That was good. It was his.

A truck roared into the drive. Nathan waved.

Amelia's hand stopped him. "You are not as old as you think, Samuel. And you have the experience of a hunter. Use it."

"You are a good woman."

"For a Chippewa." She grinned. "Go. We are with you."

Samuel climbed into the truck and nodded to Nathan. When

they reached the mountains, he would open himself. Until then, his spirit guides would guard him. Silently, he called the cougar and the eagle. The cougar was waking up, ready to hunt; the eagle was waiting.

The velvet blackness of a home that just needed light welcomed Sara. For a moment, she could have sworn she felt her grandmother. Stepping onto wooden floors, she turned left to the kitchen, a flashlight lighting her way.

On the drain board next to the cast-iron sink were lanterns. She shook one. It was full. Somewhat surprised, she reached beside the old stove, opened a drawer, and pulled out matches. In seconds, a soft glow illuminated the room.

Holding the lantern high, Sara turned slowly around, shining the light into all the corners; then she slipped into the bedrooms, repeating the same thing.

She returned to the living room, the illusion of safety shattered. Someone had been there—recently and often. The full oil lamp, the fresh linens; it all spoke of recent occupancy.

Max padded to the fireplace and lay down. There was no warning growl, no excitement. It told her that, for now, the place was empty. At least, she hoped that's what it meant. Fresh-cut logs lay in the woodbin, another sign that someone had been there recently. Within minutes, Sara had a small fire going. She threw on another couple of logs. Might as well be warm and comfortable.

Hanging up her coat, she stopped. What should she do now? Hide? Set a trap? No. That was Caleb's gig. Settling into the rocker, she grabbed an ancient afghan, throwing it over her lap. The light from the fire would be seen for miles. The bastard would know she was home. She wasn't hiding any longer. Leaning her head back, she closed her eyes, feeling the comfort of the gun resting in her lap. Now, all she could do was wait.

John stood in the light, raising their daughter to its brightness.

Sara opened her eyes to reality, shaking off the dream. A low, steady growl was coming from Max.

She looked up, confused, concerned, then rose, slipping the pistol into her pocket.

"Joe, what are you—"

"I thought you were dead." The man leaned weakly against the wall. "I thought I was too late."

He moved forward and Sara noticed two things—the rifle and the limp.

In the cover of the woods, with no moon yet, the night-vision goggles worked well. Caleb moved slowly, carefully—listening to everything around him, watching.

He heard it before he saw anything—someone, something, moving as quietly as he was. He stopped, ducking into the undergrowth, then saw him—a figure moving stealthily. Caleb shrunk back. The man had goggles also. He watched.

"You've got to get out of here. Now." Joe grabbed her arm, pulling her toward the cabin door. "You've got to go, Sara. I was late. The truck—the damned truck, then the storm. Maybe the bastard can control the weather. I don't know where he is. I don't know what his plans are, outside of killing you and your brother. But I know he's close, damned close. I can feel him."

Sara jerked away, facing the man she'd known, at least peripherally, for years. "What the devil are you babbling about, Joe? Why are you here?"

"Sara, where is Caleb? You have to go. You have to leave. My father means to kill you this time."

"Your father?"

303

"Yes. Your kidnapper." The man stopped, suddenly looking guilty. "At least, most of the time. The kidnappings, your husband's death . . . they were all part of his plan to destroy you, your family. He's mad. Worse than that, he's evil. You've got to leave now. Get out of here. I'll try to stop him."

"How? Why?"

"Sara, I'm your half-brother. My father raped your mother, and I was the product of that rape."

Sara felt her mouth drop open. "You're lying."

"No. Your grandmother threatened my father with jail or the military. He chose the army. Last group into Vietnam. He was captured on the first foray. He spent almost five years as a POW. Four of those years were after the war declared over." He grabbed her arm again, dragging her toward the door. "There's no time to explain everything. He means to kill you and Caleb and your child. You've got to leave, now."

Sara pulled away and stared at the man, memories flooding her mind. "You. You killed those animals, tortured them. I was so upset. I couldn't stop crying. That's why Nana sent me away that summer, back to Milford, so she could get rid of you." Her mind was working furiously. Scenes flew by. But she hadn't stayed in Milford; she'd come back home to the farm because . . . She looked up into Joe's moss-green eyes, eyes very much like Caleb's. Suddenly, her stomach fell. "I came back. You were gone and so was Tammy."

Time stopped. Joe was still, his eyes dropped down.

"You took Tammy. You—"

"I was angry, hurt. Nana threw me out like so much garbage. She called my grandmother, my father's mother, and told her what I had done, told her to come and get me. I ran away before my grandmother got there. I couldn't face her. I saw Tammy. She was your friend. I wanted to hurt you, so I took her, treated her like I'd treated the animals; then I scattered her soul. I didn't know I could do that. My grandma said I had the gift, but your grandmother never believed it. I showed her. I showed everyone."

His face froze. "Go." He shoved her hard through the open door. "Do what I say, Sara. Get in the fucking car now." He shoved her again.

Outside, Sara staggered, slipped to her knees, her hands in the mud. Joe moved forward, grabbing her arm and hauling her to her feet.

She came up with a handful of mud and threw it in his eyes.

Malachi stood in the shadow of the trees, rifle leveled. Sara was pulled up before he could aim. Damn it! His stupid son was in the way. He would take care of Joe later. He wanted that death to be slow. No one turned against him and lived to tell about it. He took a breath, ready for the split second that Sara would be in his sights. This bullet was for Sara, but not to kill her—no, he would tell her everything as the blood drained out of her body. And like her grandmother, there would be nothing she could do except die.

Joe reached blindly. His hand closed on Sara's arm, jerking her to him with one hand. "Son of a bitch!" He shook her hard. "Don't fucking do that again. I'm trying to save your life."

"I don't believe you," Sara screamed over the rising wind. "You're him. You're the kidnapper."

"Yes. No. You don't under—"

"I do." Caleb stepped out from the back of the house, rifle aimed. "Drop the gun. Sara, move out of the way." He moved forward, hard green eyes never leaving the figure, ignoring the driving wind and cold rain that was beginning to pelt him.

Joe pushed Sara away, his breath ragged. "Remington, you've got to get the hell out of here. He means to kill you both. You can't fucking stop him. No one can."

Caleb stopped a rifle's length away, his voice soft. "You mean 'you,' don't you?"

Joe was gibbering, he knew it, but he couldn't stop himself. "No. I—I helped my father sometimes, but when he did take those kids, I always waited. If Sara hadn't found them, I'd have released them. I always tried to be close until they were safe, even the ones I took."

"And Tammy?"

Joe stopped. "I did Tammy. I was fifteen. Sara's grandmother was going to help me. Teach me how to use the gift. But when Sara saw me torturing that squirrel, Nana kicked me out. I'll pay for that, and for Joshua. But I changed. I can link with Sara. So can my father. I didn't know how to . . . I tried. I couldn't fight him. No one can. He's pure evil. He has a fucking coven or something like that. I can't let him kill Sara or you."

"Why?"

Joe looked from Caleb to Sara, who stood apart, braced against the storm. His green eyes turned back to Caleb. "You're my half-brother. We're—"

Joe saw it then, movement by the side of the cabin, just beyond Caleb's shoulder.

"No!" Fear gave him strength and speed. He plowed into Caleb's midsection, driving the big man to the ground. The bullet caught Joe in the side, spinning him in a full circle and dropping him like a sack of potatoes.

Like a choreographed slow dance, Caleb rolled to his knee and raised the rifle in one fluid motion, aiming for the man who stood in the trees.

Keeping low, Sara staggered to the far side of the Rover.

Two shots fired simultaneously. Both men missed.

Joe rolled over, ignoring the white-hot pain in his side and pulled himself through the mud away from his father and brother. He'd given Caleb a chance. If anyone could stop Malachi Campbell, it was Joe's half-brother. If not . . . He tightened a hand against his side, staunching the flow of blood.

He needed to get back to the truck. He needed to get away. He needed to survive, for Serafina and his son.

Caleb fired a second time and missed. Taking a deep breath, he squeezed the trigger a third time, hearing the echo of another shot.

It caught him high on the shoulder, knocking the rifle from his hands. He fell and staggered to his feet, screaming for Sara to run.

It was too late.

Malachi stepped into the open, moving slowly forward, rifle aimed.

"Thought you were better than me, didn't you, punk? You don't stand a fucking chance against me. Your grandmother sentenced me to Nam. I spent five there as a POW. And I swore with every fiber of my being that I would get even. She owed me, owed me big, and wouldn't lift a finger to help when I finally got home. She kicked me off the farm. I swore then that I would wipe the Slane seed from this earth. It was my son who would inherit everything." He spit on the ground and wiped his mouth with the back of his free hand. "I'm going to kill you and your bitch of a sister, just like I killed your mama and grandmother, and the rest of your family." His voice was rising. "And it was all because I screwed your mother. Placed a bastard in her belly. She was asking for it," he screamed. He jerked the rifle to his shoulder and squeezed the trigger.

Nothing.

Malachi couldn't believe it. He tried again. It had jammed. The fucking gun had jammed. This wasn't supposed to happen. He pulled the knife. Shrieking as he ran, he slammed into Caleb.

The force drove Caleb backwards and down. They rolled around the yard, moving closer to the edge, to the drop that would plunge them into the first lake. Caleb was fighting with only one hand. Malachi still had two good arms; he had the advantage and he used it, feeling Caleb weaken as they grappled. Dropping the knife, Malachi slammed a fist into Caleb's face. Once, twice, three times. The third time, he felt Remington go limp.

He pulled the figure halfway up and raised the knife.

The shadow came out of nowhere. One moment, Malachi held a knife and a man. The next instant, his scream ripped through the valley as his flailing hands grasped air.

"Max!" The name tore from Sara's throat as the big dog's momentum carried both men over the edge.

Sara lurched to her feet and staggered to the edge, then dropped to her belly, clawing at the mud, screaming Caleb's name.

Soft flesh filled her hand. Grabbing it, she looked down into the pain-filled eyes of her brother, clinging onto the edge of the cliff.

"Caleb." Holding onto his hand, she twisted to get the weight off the baby and dug her toes in, pulling back.

"Help me. Try."

"Sara." Caleb's voice was calm. "Sara, let go. I can't hold on. All I'm going to do is pull you down with me, and I won't do that. Let me go."

"No," she screamed.

"Sara." A dark hand closed over hers, a soft voice filled her ears. "I've got him, Sara. Let go. I've got him."

She twisted, looking up into the dark eyes of Samuel Hawk.

"Let go, child."

Clawing out of the way, she watched as Samuel pulled her brother up inch by inch. When Caleb's shoulders cleared the edge, Samuel reached down and grabbed his belt, pulling him the rest of the way up.

Caleb lay in the back of the Rover while Sara struggled to stop the bleeding.

"Press harder."

"I'll hurt you."

"Yeah," he agreed. "You'll also save my life."

She put all her weight on the dressing, ignoring the groans emanating from Caleb's white lips.

Minutes passed. She waited, counting slowly to herself. At one hundred, she cautiously raised the pad. The bleeding was slowing. She pressed harder.

"Samuel," Caleb raised pain-filled eyes to the old Indian, "it's not done yet."

Samuel nodded, then picked up the rifle he'd leaned against the SUV.

"Where are you going?"

Sara's question caught the Indian by surprise. He looked at her brother while he spoke. "Caleb did not kill the man. I don't know if the fall did either. I need to make sure."

"What about the other one—Joe?"

Samuel looked confused.

"Joe Campbell." Sara put her weight on Caleb's shoulder. "The man who went over the edge is his father, Malachi. They were in it together."

"I didn't see anyone else," Samuel admitted.

Sara leaned back. The bleeding had almost stopped. She slapped on a pressure bandage, then unsnapped Caleb's holster and withdrew the Desert Eagle, placing it in her brother's good hand. "If the bastard comes back—kill him."

Sliding out of the back of the Rover, she turned to Samuel, pulling the Baby Desert Eagle out of her pocket. "I'm going with you. I need to know it's over. I need," her voice caught, "to find Max."

Sara pointed ahead of them as they left the Rover behind. She held out a small flashlight she'd slipped in her pocket before leaving Milford. "There's a path that leads down to the bottom of this lake."

Samuel shook his head at the flashlight, then slipped in front of her. "If he lives the light would only warn him. There is enough light by the moon to see what we need to see. Wait a moment before following me. If he is alive, it's better I meet him first." The old man melted into the trees.

Sara glanced up. The rain had stopped. The wind was silent. In the distance, she caught the echoes of thunder coming closer. The storm was circling. Taking a deep breath, she counted to a hundred, then walked into the forest.

CHAPTER 31

Keen eyes pierced the darkness. Ears caught sounds only animals could hear. Veering off the trail, Samuel made no sound, his movements quick and light as the air. He stopped, hearing Sara, then nodded to himself. She was a distance behind. That was good.

Sliding down the muddy trail, Sara's feet found level ground. She held the pistol ready and silenced her ragged breathing, moving forward as carefully as she could. Angling through the trees, she headed towards the water's edge, stopping beneath a pine. She froze, watching for any signs of movement.

Nothing. It was quiet. Only the water made sounds. She strained, trying to see beyond the darkness. She wanted to see a body floating face down. A low-pitched whine broke the silence. Turning in the direction of the sound, Sara slipped over rocks and pushed through the bushes that grew close to the water's edge.

She almost stepped on the animal. Half-submerged in the cold waters, almost hidden by undergrowth, Max lay panting. Slipping the gun into her pocket, she sat and tugged the animal onto her lap. He whimpered in pain.

Now what? Should I shout for Samuel?

Sara studied the man-made lake. Nothing moved. She didn't like it.

A low growl gurgled in Max's throat. She pulled the pistol and raised it, her eyes straining to see beyond the darkness. Something moved, rising from the waters.

"Don't Sara. You are not a murderer."

Samuel stood behind her. She hadn't even heard him.

"He killed John. And Miriam. He threatened children. I'm not a murderer. It's justice."

"He killed on my reservation, also. This is not just your justice. It is mine too."

He raised his rifle at the figure struggling toward the rocks. Aiming carefully, he took a deep breath, ignoring Sara, ignoring everything except the target. His finger caressed the trigger. He tightened it, then did something he had not done since he first learned how to shoot. He jerked the trigger.

The body slid off the rocks and slipped beneath the black waters.

Cursing, Samuel knelt beside Sara and watched the point where the body had disappeared.

"What's wrong, Samuel."

"I jerked at the last moment, like a child just learning to shoot. It might not have been a killing shot."

Samuel rose, rifle in hand, ready to take another shot if need be. His keen eyes combed the rocks and bushes around the lake's edge. They both watched, waited.

A whine from Max broke the lengthy silence.

"We've got to get him to a vet, Samuel. I'm afraid he's badly hurt. And we need to get Caleb to a doctor."

Samuel nodded and with one last look at the waters, turned to Sara. "Get the truck and bring it down. I will get Max to the road."

"Do you think Malachi's dead?" Sara's voice quavered.

"I believe so, but then, I want to believe I did not miss." He glanced at the lake. "This man has died as mysteriously as he lived. Go. Go quickly. We have wasted enough time here."

Samuel stretched the body of the German shepherd beside Caleb, chuckling as the big dog licked the wounded man's face.

"Here." Caleb handed Samuel his Eagle. "Put it under the front seat in case we run into some more trouble. Make sure the rifles are hidden. Some aren't exactly legal."

"How are you doing?" Sara studied Caleb's white face, made whiter by the absence of camouflage paint.

"Great. I hurt like hell and I'm beside a wet, smelly dog. How in the hell do you think I'm doing?"

"Do you want me to drive, Sara?" Samuel asked, pulling a blanket over the guns.

"No. I know the way. Hang on, Brother." She slammed the door shut. Minutes later, they were heading down the mountain. Sara gripped the wheel, negotiating twists and turns with confidence and memory.

"Stop!"

She slammed the brakes at Samuel's cry, sliding in the mud, stopping inches from the figure in the middle of the road. With shaking knees, Sara stepped from the cab and ran to the front of the SUV.

"Billy." She gathered the child into her arms.

"He told me to wait here for you," Billy sobbed. "Joe was hurt, but he let me go."

Sara leaned against the cold sterile wall of the hospital waiting room, thankful for the shower the hospital had let her take and the clean scrubs they'd given her to wear. A cup of coffee sat next to her.

Soft steps made her look up. Samuel came down the corridor, looking tired but successful.

"How's Max?" She handed him the coffee, knowing he'd like it even lukewarm.

"The vet says he will be fine. X-rays showed no problems, but they'd like to keep him a day or two. He's pretty badly bruised. How's Caleb?"

"Still in surgery. They're just doing some stitching, or so the nurse said. According to the doctor, the bullet didn't do any major damage or hit anything important. I think they're going to keep him here a day or two, also. Seems he lost a bit more blood than we thought."

"How are you?"

She smiled at the old man. "I don't think I've ever been this tired."

"And the baby?"

"She's finally settled down." As she spoke, Sara felt her child kick hard, then settle low. She looked up at Samuel, her lips curving in a half smile. "Could you do me one more favor, Samuel?"

"Of course."

"Get a doctor? My water just broke."

Laura Erin Slane Allbrooke came into the world with very little fuss—and, Sara thought thankfully, with only a few pains. The child's cry rocked the delivery room before she was completely out of the womb.

Sara settled the baby into her arms, glancing from the old man, who refused to be intimidated by hospital policy, to the child she held.

Vivid emerald-green eyes—old, yet new—stared back. Thick reddish-brown hair, soft and fine, covered her head and framed an almost heart-shaped face.

Sara swallowed tears, smelling the newness of her child—and something else. Bay Rum.

"Samuel, do you use aftershave?"

He grinned. "Indians don't shave. Someone protects the child."

Sara looked down at her child. She knew who it was. She wasn't alone. John was with them.

Samuel studied the child and mother. Behind them, the window showed a sky almost ready to greet the dawn.

"Sara, among my people, a newly born child is offered to the four sacred directions. Prayers of blessing and thanksgiving are sung. Would you be offended if I . . . could I . . .?" His voice trailed off.

"I would be honored." Sara handed the firmly swaddled baby to the Indian.

Holding the child and ignoring the startled looks of the staff, Samuel headed out through the hospital doors and into the clear, crisp morning. The first rays of the sun caught the infant as he held her high, chanting the ancient songs. He turned slowly, offering her to the four sacred directions. When a cloud came over, he lowered the baby, looking into bright green eyes gone dark and flat.

They cleared almost instantly, studying him with their ancient wisdom. Then the child smiled, and Samuel felt her power, innocence, and knowledge.

He turned and walked solemnly back into the hospital. The darkness in the eyes bothered him. It would be a secret, his secret. Softly, he chanted a song of protection and thankfulness. There was still much in this child, much he had to share with Leon. The Hopi would be pleased.

In the hospital room he gave the child back to Sara. For now, all was well. Caleb would recover with a new scar, one of many that Samuel had noted when they bound his wound. Sara and her child would thrive. For now, all was right in this world, and just maybe, an evil had been destroyed. He walked back outside. It was time to go home. He stared at the clouds and shivered as one momentarily blocked the early morning sun. For now, things were where they should be, but would it last?

Samuel turned away from the dark thoughts. Closing his eyes, he concentrated on the red mesas of his land.

"Was it true?" Sara turned to Caleb. "Was Mother raped? Did she have a son? Do we have a half-brother?"

Her brother shrugged and took her arm as they walked slowly from the farm's private cemetery. "I don't know. I've got an investigator looking into it. They did find a Malachi Campbell. He's listed as MIA. According to military records, he never returned from Vietnam."

"Surely if he was found or came back or whatever, there would be some kind of record—wouldn't there?"

"Depends."

"On what?"

"On what mood the government was in." Caleb stated firmly. "It wouldn't be the first time we didn't know all the truth about something."

"Did you find out where Malachi came from?"

"He was born in a small town not far from the summer cabin. Why do you ask?"

"That makes him close, physically. Do you think it all really happened?"

"It's possible. But we still don't have proof, and I still don't know how much of the story we can or should believe."

He stopped, glancing back at the fresh grave. "I'm glad you let me bring Mother home. I think, in spite of everything, she'd rather be here."

Sara followed her brother's gaze. "Somehow I think its best we're together right now—all of us, in whatever plane we're in. Isn't that what you call the other side—a plane?"

Caleb chuckled. "Sometimes."

"Judy called a few days ago. I won't say she was friendly, but she did want me to know about the work you're doing with Joshua. As if I didn't already know. He will get better, won't he?"

"It's a lengthy process. But I think the pieces of his soul will come together. And don't be too hard on Judy. You and Laura are the only living links she has with John, but there is still a lot of pain."

"There's pain for everyone, Caleb. I miss John daily, especially when I look at Laura. He would have been so proud." Her throat tightened at the thought of her husband. "What about Tammy?"

"Tammy's bringing herself back together on her own. Cora and Henry know I'm close if she needs help."

"And what do you think Wall Street and Washington would say about what you're doing?" Sara teased.

"Tom and I aren't even going to think about that. As far as the rest of the world is concerned, I'm backing his second-term election and we're good friends. Bottom line, though—one day Tom Caine will have a healthy son. That alone is worth the risk."

"I envy your talent. I couldn't do what you do."

"I can't find lost children. I think we're both well gifted. By the way, Samuel told me a woman had some words with you while I was in the hospital. His description matches Anne Stockton."

"It was Anne. She came with Rachael to pick up Billy."

"I take it she still wasn't friendly."

"I don't know whether she was pleased or disappointed that I showed up with the boy, but no, she wasn't friendly. When she saw Laura, she reiterated that I would not find a teaching job in Milford."

"Some people are like that, Sara. Some people are just like that."

Samuel stared ahead at the red-gold mesas, his heart singing. He was almost home.

The days spent in Stroudsburg had been pleasurable. Amelia, despite her penchant for talking, was a very comfortable woman. For a brief moment, he thought of his wife, dead now for many years. She would have liked the Chippewa woman.

He had said goodbye, knowing he and Amelia would see each other sooner rather than later; then he drove Robert's truck back to Oklahoma, enjoyed a smoke with his friend and reminisced about old times. In Santa Fe, he had fry bread and called the Hopi, knowing his information and knowledge would please Leon.

Their people had a chance now. They would survive despite Hopi and Mayan predictions.

Opening his window, Samuel inhaled the fragrance of the desert. Suddenly he slammed on the brakes and pulled to the side of the road, his eyes riveted on the dark, broiling clouds at the base of his mesa. The darkness was back.

Caleb strapped down the carrier while Sara held the baby. She looked around. She loved the farm, but it was no longer her home—and it was time to go home. Milford, the house she and John had lived and loved in, that was home.

"You're deep in thought," Caleb commented as he took the baby and strapped her into the car seat.

"I've enjoyed the last couple of weeks with you, Caleb. And I've learned a lot. But this isn't my home anymore. I used to think of the farm as a place of healing. Now I know that the healing takes place inside a person, not outside. It's being close to family—at least the family that we have left—that gives me the strength."

Caleb brushed a light kiss across her forehead. "You are going to be all right. John is a hard man to get over, but you will, and you will go on. And I'm glad you've changed your mind about family. We were separated so long; it's time we forgive and forget. Mom and Nana would feel the same way. You sure you won't wait until I can drive back with you?"

"I want to get home." She looked across the front seat to where Max sat, firmly belted in. "Besides, I've got Max for protection."

"Yeah, just try to teach him to tell the good guys from the bad. I don't relish being rolled over a cliff again."

Sara pulled Caleb's head down and gave him a quick kiss on the cheek. "Thanks for the Rover. But green . . . isn't there another color?"

"I like green. Besides, it matches my niece's eyes." He sobered. "Drive carefully and keep the cell phone on. I've got to be in Boston tomorrow, so I won't be able to make it back to Milford until next week."

"Duncan still giving you problems?"

"Sometimes I think the wrong man went into that quarry." He glanced at the sky. "It's getting late; you'd better get started."

She gave her daughter a final glance. Bright green eyes stared back, then suddenly went dark and flat. Before Sara could comment, they lit up again. Uneasily, she closed the door and slid into the driver's seat.

"Do you think Tammy will make it all the way, Caleb?"

"Each day that takes her further away from the last twenty years lets her heal a bit more."

Sara started the engine, dropped the SUV into gear, then slid it back into park. "One other thing. What are the Hopi prophecies?"

"You've heard about the Mayan calendar?"

"The calendar that stopped on December 12, 2012; therefore, the world was going to end on that date. Yes, I think everyone's heard about that."

"And obviously, nothing happened on December 12, 2012. Some say the world actually ends in 2018 or 2025 or 2032. There are several interpretations of the Hopi prophecies. They seem to see the end of the world more as an end to a way of thinking. People will become more spiritual, more cognizant of their brother in the new age. The Hopi also see a savior—and in some instances, three saviors—leading them into this new world. It's all open to interpretation, but alludes to the Mayan. You see, the Mayan people didn't predict that the world would end, only that a way of thinking would cease."

"What did Samuel have to do with all of that?"

"I'm not sure, but I think he's looking for the Hopi saviors. I wouldn't worry about any of it. See you next Friday—dinner's on you."

Caleb watched the SUV pull out of sight. For a moment, he was four years old and his warm, fun-loving sister was being ripped from him once again.

He straightened, feeling it—a darkness settling over the land. It didn't frighten or even worry him. He was ready. Now he had something to fight for. Something he had never really had before—a family—and no one was going to take that from him.

Turning away, he stepped onto the porch and grabbed his cases, then staggered, blindly reaching out for the porch rail.

Pain and a voice shot through his head.

"Let's play a game."

THE END

I hope you have enjoyed VISIONS. VOODO, coming out soon, continues the story of Sara and her brother, Caleb. Taking place in the beautiful and mysterious city of New Orleans, we meet Serafina. When her life and that of her son are threatened, Serafina asks for Caleb's help. Strange circumstances force Sara and Samuel Hawks to join Caleb. Together the four face the evil that has fled Milford and now threatens New Orleans. But it is not just the city in danger. Caleb, Serafina, Sara and Samuel will each find themselves fighting for their very lives.

S.T. McCrea holds a bachelor's degree in history. A retired world traveler, she lives on a small Colorado ranch. She shares her love of writing with her retired Navy Veteran daughter, five horses, two dogs, three cats and one burro. This is her first book.

S. T. McCrea